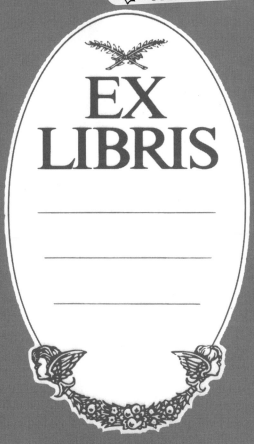

EX LIBRIS

Dear Reader,

Welcome to this very special collection of stories, brought to you as a celebration of the fortieth anniversary of Harlequin Romance!

Forty fabulous years and we're still bringing you the best in romantic fiction, and continuing our tradition of warm and wonderful love stories—with heroines you'd want as your best friend, and heroes to pine over!

This is an anthology to treasure, featuring three highly talented authors we know you enjoy. Bestselling author Betty Neels offers *Paradise for Two*—a classic story with all the ingredients you've come to love from this exceptional writer. From Australia, Margaret Way brings us *Fallen Idol,* a charming story written with all of this popular author's distinctive charm. Last, but not least, award-winning Rebecca Winters tugs at your heartstrings with the deeply emotional *Both of Them*.

We're delighted to bring you this perfect combination of talent, in this beautiful collector's edition. It's our way of saying thank-you to all our loyal readers—and we hope you'll continue to enjoy Harlequin Romance books for many years to come!

Happy reading,

The Editors
Harlequin Romance

About the Authors

Betty Neels spent her childhood and youth in Devonshire, England, before training as a nurse and midwife. She was an army nursing sister during the war, married a Dutchman, and subsequently lived in Holland for fourteen years. She lives with her husband in Dorset, and has a daughter and grandson. Her hobbies are reading, animals, old buildings and writing. Betty started to write on retirement from nursing, incited by a lady in a library bemoaning the lack of romantic novels.

Margaret Way takes great pleasure in her work and works hard at her pleasure. She enjoys tearing off to the beach with her family on weekends, loves haunting galleries and auctions and is completely given over to French champagne "for every possible joyous occasion." Her home, perched high on a hill overlooking Brisbane, Australia, is her haven. She started writing when her son was a baby, and now she finds there is no better way to spend her time.

Rebecca Winters, an American writer and mother of four, is a graduate of the University of Utah. She has also studied at schools in Switzerland and France, including the Sorbonne. Rebecca is currently teaching French and Spanish to junior high school students. Despite her busy schedule, Rebecca always finds time to write.

Harlequin Romance

40th
Anniversary

Betty Neels
Margaret Way
Rebecca Winters

Harlequin Books

TORONTO • NEW YORK • LONDON
AMSTERDAM • PARIS • SYDNEY • HAMBURG
STOCKHOLM • ATHENS • TOKYO • MILAN
MADRID • WARSAW • BUDAPEST • AUCKLAND

HARLEQUIN BOOKS
225 Duncan Mill Road, Don Mills,
Ontario, Canada M3B 3K9

ISBN 0-373-15319-8

Harlequin Romance Fortieth Anniversary Collection

Copyright © 1997 by Harlequin Books S.A.

The publisher acknowledges the copyright holders
of the individual works as follows:

PARADISE FOR TWO
Copyright © 1988 by Betty Neels
FALLEN IDOL
Copyright © 1984 by Margaret Way
BOTH OF THEM
Copyright © 1992 by Rebecca Winters

Printed in U.S.A.

CONTENTS

PARADISE FOR TWO

Betty Neels

Dear Reader,

Writing a letter to someone whom I have never met is a bit of a challenge. But I believe that we have one thing in common; you read romances and I write them. This makes a strong link between us, doesn't it?

I am always so pleased to have letters from readers who have enjoyed my books—I enjoy writing them and have never lost the thrill of typing "Chapter One" and wondering what the story will be about this time. The first book I wrote—a long time ago now—was in longhand, typed out (very badly) on a borrowed child's typewriter and sent to Harlequin Mills & Boon with not the least expectancy of having it accepted, let alone read. Many years and many books later, I still have the same thrill when I see the book in print.

Readers ask me where I get my ideas. Well, mostly from a glimpse of someone or something. A girl or a man in the street or a shop and I think, ah, there's my heroine or hero. Then passing through a village or the parklands of a country house—and there are plenty of both in this rural part of England where we live—I find myself thinking, "I wonder who lives there?" and that starts me off with the first few lines. I don't plan a story, it unfolds itself without much help from me.

Of course, it would be lovely to sit down and write and write while someone else does the chores, feeds the cats, answers the phone, does the shopping and makes pots and pots of Assam tea. So I write in odd moments during the day, and each evening go to my little study and work for two hours, sometimes longer, pausing to look out of the window at the trees around us. We live in a little house, a Toll House of ancient beginnings but added to from time to time. It has a garden the size of a handkerchief and flower beds that I have stuffed with bulbs ready for spring. I potter in it for a short time every day, raking up the leaves before nipping back to the typewriter.

Well, it's time I came to an end of my letter. I hope you enjoy *Paradise for Two*—it is one of my favorites, and I hope that it will be one of yours.

And a pleasant thought with which to end: however much the world changes, romance still means a great deal to everyone, even those who pretend it doesn't exist. Nonsense—we know better, don't we? It makes the world a better place.

My best wishes to you and yours,

Betty Neels

Betty Neels

CHAPTER ONE

THERE were two people in the room, facing each other across the breakfast-table—a small, elderly lady with iron-grey hair and very blue eyes in a pleasantly wrinkled face, and opposite her a girl with a charming face framed by curling russet hair and large hazel eyes, fringed by long, curling lashes.

'It's a splendid opportunity,' observed the elderly lady in a coaxing voice, 'and you would be doing a kindness—after all, Mrs Wesley is your godmother.'

Her companion frowned, her dark brows drawn together quite fiercely. She said in a no-nonsense way, 'Aunt Maud, I've only just left one job, and that was because I wanted a change—I've set my heart on that Ward Sister's post in Scotland,' she added as an after-thought. 'Besides, there's Walter...'

'Has he proposed again?' asked her aunt with interest.

'Well, yes...'

'You've accepted him?'

The girl smiled at the eagerness in her companion's voice. 'It's a funny thing, Aunt Maud, but I can't... perhaps it's because we've known each other for a long time and the gilt's worn off the gingerbread, or perhaps it's because Walter thinks I'm extravagant.'

'Well, you are, dear,' her aunt spoke mildly.

11

'I like clothes,' said her niece simply. 'Besides, it's difficult to find things to fit me. Everyone except me is size eight or ten.'

She stood up, and indeed she was nowhere near either of those sizes. She was a big girl, tall and splendidly built, her long legs clothed in elderly slacks topped by an outsize jersey.

Her aunt studied her thoughtfully. 'You won't marry Walter?' She sighed. 'Prudence, he would make a good husband...'

The girl frowned again. 'I don't want a good husband, I want to be swept off my feet, plied with champagne and roses and jewels—I'd quite like to be serenaded, too.' She glanced down at her magnificent person. 'But you can see for yourself, dear Aunt, that it would need a giant of a man with muscles of iron to get me off the ground. Shall I tell Ellen to come in and clear the table? I'm going for that job, I shall apply for it and post the letter this morning.'

Her aunt got up, too. 'Very well, dear. At your age I would have been delighted at the chance to travel abroad and see something of the world, but I dare say you know your own mind best. Your godmother will be disappointed.'

Her niece crossed the room and gave her a hug. 'Dearest Aunt, I have travelled a bit, you know, when Father and Mother were alive——' She paused a moment, and then went on steadily, 'They always took me with them. True, I've not been to Holland, but I don't suppose it's much different from England. Mrs Wesley will be able to find someone only too eager to go with her.'

Her aunt agreed meekly. It was barely half an hour later, as she sat in the sitting-room making out a shopping list, that Ellen announced a visitor.

Miss Rendell put down her pen and got up with every sign of pleasure. 'My dear Beatrix, how providential! I've been sitting here wondering if I should telephone you. Dear Prudence is even now applying for a post in Scotland, but perhaps you might dissuade her? She has no real reason for refusing to go with you to Holland, you know—indeed, she's very fond of you, and a complete change might check her restlessness.' She added vaguely, 'She wants to be swept off her feet.'

'And I know the very man to do it,' declared Mrs Wesley. She sat down. 'Let me have a try.'

Prudence, nibbling her pen and frowning over her application form, listened to Ellen's request that she should join her aunt downstairs with some impatience. The Vicar, she supposed, wanting someone to take a stall at the church bazaar, or old Mrs Vine from the Manor bent on getting Prudence to fill a gap at her dinner-table. Prudence, who had made her home with her aunt in the small Somerset village ever since her parents had died in a car crash, knew everyone who lived there, just as they knew her, and when she went to London to train as a nurse she still returned whenever she had leave. She loved the place and liked the people living there, from crusty old Colonel Quist living in solitary state in one wing of the vast house at the end of the village to Mrs Legg, who owned the village stores and ran the Post Office besides. She loved her aunt too, and the nice old house which had

become her home, but she loved her work as well;
she had spent the last six years in London, first training as a nurse and then taking over a surgical ward
at the hospital where she had trained. It was on her
twenty-fifth birthday, a month or so previously, that
she had decided she needed a move right away from
London before she got into a rut from which so many
of her older colleagues either could not or would not
escape. Scotland would do nicely; she would be really
on her own there and it would be a challenge, finding
her feet in a strange hospital and making new friends.
She let her thoughts wander as she went downstairs.
Perhaps she would meet the man of her dreams—a
vague image, but she was sure she would know him
if they met.

She hadn't expected to see her delightful godmother sitting with her aunt. She crossed the room
and kissed the proffered cheek. Mrs Wesley was a
formidable lady, not very tall but possessed of a well-
corseted stoutness, a handsome face and a slightly
overbearing manner. Prudence was very fond of her
and said warmly, 'How nice to see you, Aunt Beatrix.
I thought you were in London.'

'I'm staying there, my dear, but I've been the guest
of Mrs Vine for a day or so, and I thought I'd call
and see you both before I go back.'

'Oh—you mean to Holland? But you aren't going
to return there to live, are you?'

'Certainly not, but my sister is ill—did your aunt
not tell you? She has had a heart attack and needs
great care, so I shall go to her and do what I can. I
had hoped...' Mrs Wesley paused and heaved a shud-

dering sigh. 'But I expect we shall manage. In a few
weeks I dare say she'll be stronger. It's a pity I've
been told by my own doctor that I must take things
quietly for a few months, but at such a time one
doesn't think of oneself.'

'Why, Aunt Beatrix, what's wrong?' Prudence felt
quite shaken; she couldn't remember her godmother
being anything but in the best of health.

'Diabetes, of all silly things, my dear. I spent a few
days at a nursing home while they decided what I
couldn't eat and explained that tiresome insulin to me.
I'm not yet stabilised, they tell me, but when that's
corrected I need only take tablets.'

'You're having injections?'

'At the moment, yes. So tiresome, as I have to arrange for someone to come and give them to me—
the district nurse here has been most kind...' She gave
Prudence a quick look. 'That was why I'd suggested
that you might like to accompany me to Holland, but
of course, you young people must lead your own
lives...'

Prudence shifted uneasily in her chair. She was being got at, and since she was a kind-hearted girl she
could see nothing for it but to accept her godmother's
invitation; the idea of Aunt Beatrix wandering around
suffering from a condition she didn't fully understand,
even in her own native country, wasn't to be entertained for one moment. She mentally tore up the letter
she had just written to the hospital in Scotland, reflecting ruefully that here was one young person who
was being thwarted from doing as she wished...

'When do you go?' she asked, and saw the pleased

smiles on her companions' faces. 'I had intended to apply for a job in Edinburgh, but I'll see if they might have a vacancy at a later date.'

'Dear child!' Aunt Maud addressed her magnificently proportioned niece with no awareness of inappropriateness. 'Your dear godmother will be safe with you, and I dare say this hospital will be only too glad to offer you a job later on.'

Prudence smiled at her kindly; Aunt Maud, having lived her life in sheltered security, had no idea of the harsh world outside it and there was no point in disillusioning her. No hospital was going to wait while an applicant for a job waltzed off to Europe before taking up her job.

'How long do you intend to stay in Holland?' she asked.

'Oh, well—a month, no longer, by that time my sister should be well again, should she not?' Mrs Wesley added, 'She's in hospital, but if all is well she should be going home very shortly. I thought I might go next week.'

Prudence remembered without much regret that Walter had invited her to an exhibition of paintings on either Tuesday or Wednesday of the following week. He had told her rather importantly that it depended on whether he could get away from his desk; he was a junior executive in a firm of stockbrokers and took his work seriously; he also fancied himself as something of an expert on modern art. Prudence, who liked paintings to look like something she could recognise, had done her best to go along with his views, without much success.

'We shall fly,' observed her godmother, 'and naturally we shall be met at Schiphol and driven to Dornwier. Whether we shall remain there or accompany my sister on a holiday in order that she may recuperate from her illness, I don't as yet know.'

'You're sure your own doctor has no objections to you travelling, Aunt Beatrix?'

'Oh, yes, he quite saw my point of view.' Which was Aunt Beatrix's way of saying she had browbeaten the poor man into agreeing with her.

'Do you want me to meet you in London,' asked Prudence, 'or at the airport?'

'Perhaps you would come to my flat the day before we leave? Then we can travel to Heathrow together. Shall we say Tuesday of next week—provided I can get a flight then. I dare say you may have one or two things to see to before you leave.'

Clothes, thought Prudence and then, as a guilty afterthought, Walter. He would be annoyed, he didn't believe in young women being too independent. A woman's place, he had told Prudence on many occasions, was in the home.

Which was all very well, she had pointed out, but whereabouts in the home? Lying at ease on a chaise longue in the drawing-room, covered in jewels and pure silk, would be nice... Walter had no sense of humour; he had told her, in his measured tones, not to be foolish. It struck her suddenly that she didn't love him, never had, and that this invitation from her godmother presented her with an opportunity to make Walter understand that once and for all she really did not want to marry him. They had known each other for years now, and she wasn't sure when they had drifted into the idea of marriage. Certainly he had shown no overwhelming desire to make her his wife; on the other hand, she had been expected to tag along with him whenever she was at home, and in the village at least they were considered to be engaged.

She said now, 'If you'll let me know when you want me to come, Aunt Beatrix, I'll be there. There's nothing of importance to keep me here.'

She thought guiltily that Walter would be very annoyed to be designated as nothing of importance.

Ellen came in with coffee and the next half-hour was pleasantly taken up by Aunt Beatrix's plans; she had obviously got everything organised to suit herself, and Prudence wondered just how she would have reacted if she hadn't got her way. Aunt Maud was looking pleased with herself, too; Prudence looked at her two elderly companions with real affection, and when her godmother got up to go, bade her a warm goodbye.

'Tot ziens,' said Aunt Beatrix, who occasionally broke into her native tongue.

Prudence replied cheerfully, 'And *tot ziens* to you, Aunt Beatrix, though I'm not quite sure what that means! I must try and learn some Dutch while I'm staying with you.'

Walter called in that evening on his way home from his office in Taunton. His greeting of, 'Hello, old girl,' did nothing to make her change her mind about going away.

He sat down in the chair he always used and began at once to go into details about an argument he had

had with one of the partners that day. Prudence sat opposite him, listening with half an ear while she took the chance to study him carefully. He was an inch or two shorter than she was and already showing a tendency to put on weight, but he was good-looking and, when he chose, could be an entertaining companion with charming manners. Only, over the years, the charm and the manners weren't much in evidence—not with her at any rate. She said suddenly, cutting through his monologue, 'Walter, when did you last look at me—I mean, really look?'

He gave her stare of astonishment. 'Look at you? Well, I see you several times a week when you're here, don't I? Why should I look at you? Have you changed your hair-style or lost weight or something?'

'I don't need to lose weight,' she said coldly. 'I sometimes feel, Walter, like your daily newspaper or the old coat you keep behind the back door in case it rains…'

He gave an uneasy laugh. 'My dear girl, what's got into you? You're talking nonsense. It's a good thing you're going to this new job, you've been too long at that hospital of yours in London.'

'You've asked me to marry you several times.'

'Yes, well—there's time enough for you to make up your mind about that, in the meantime you need to be occupied.'

'You don't want to sweep me off my feet? Rush off with me and get married?'

She felt sorry for him, because he was quite out of his depth; stockbrokers didn't like to be rushed.

'Certainly not; marriage is a serious undertaking.'

Prudence nodded. 'Yes, it is. Walter, I don't want to marry you. I'm sorry if it puts you out—I mean, you expected me to marry you when it was convenient, didn't you?'

'I say, old girl, that's a funny way of putting it!'

'But it's true.' She got up and wandered over to the window. 'I'm going to Holland for some weeks to stay with an aunt who's ill.'

'You haven't any aunts in Holland.' She heard the tolerant amusement in his voice.

'Courtesy aunts, one of them is my godmother and I'm fond of her. I think it would be a good idea if we parted, Walter—we can stay good friends if you want that, but don't expect me to change my mind. I really will not marry you.'

He had got to his feet, too. 'Suits me. You're a nice girl, Prudence, but you like your own way too much—men like a degree of meekness in a woman, especially in their wives.'

'I'll remember that.' Her eyes, large, brown-flecked with tawny spots, thickly fringed, flashed sudden anger. 'I hope you find a suitably meek girl willing to marry you, Walter.'

He said seriously, 'Oh, I have no doubts that I shall.'

He looked so smug that she itched to throw something at him, especially when he added prosily, 'But I doubt if you'll—what did you say?—find a man to sweep you off your feet. No hard feelings, Prudence?'

'None at all, Walter.' She watched him go without a pang, but deep inside her she was conscious of panic; she was, after all, twenty-five years old and, although she had never lacked for men friends, she had never wanted to marry any of them. Perhaps she would never meet a man she could love and marry…

Aunt Maud bustling in to ask if Walter was staying to supper dispelled her thoughts. Prudence wandered across the room and shook up a number of cushions which were perfectly all right as they were. 'What would you say if I told you that I'm not going to marry Walter? We've parted quite definitely.'

Aunt Maud said: 'Well, dear, since you ask me, I feel bound to say I feel profound relief. Walter is an estimable young man, but in ten years' time he'll be pompous and bossy. None the less, he would be a good husband if one considers the material things of life—he would never allow his wife to be shabby, and the children would go to the right schools.' Aunt Maud sighed deeply. 'But no romance, that's something I think you might not be able to do without.'

Prudence flung her arms wide. 'Oh, you're so right, Aunt Maud, but where am I to find romance? And for the next few weeks there'll be no chance to find it at all—Aunt Beatrix is a darling, but she hasn't any family other than her sister, has she? And I feel in my bones that any doctors I may meet will be elderly and bald.'

Her aunt agreed placidly and kept her thoughts to herself.

There was a good deal to do during the next few days; according to Aunt Maud, Prudence's godmother came from a well-to-do family and her sister lived in some style.

'Somewhere in Friesland, isn't it?' asked Prudence,

her pretty head on one side, critically examining a dress she wasn't sure she wanted to take with her. And, before her aunt could reply, 'Do you suppose it will be good weather there? I know it's May, but it's a good deal farther north actually than it is here.'

'A knitted suit?' suggested her aunt. 'And tops and skirts—you could take a couple of thinner dresses in case it should really warm up.' She added casually, 'I should put in a pretty dress for the evening, dear— your Aunt Beatrix knows a number of people there, and you might get asked out to dinner.'

Prudence thought it unlikely, but her aunt looked wistful, so she packed a slim sheath of corn-coloured silk, deceptively simple and very elegant, and a silk jersey dress with long sleeves, a sweeping skirt and a square neckline cut rather low. It was of indigo blue, an excellent foil for her hair. It would give the balding elderlies a nice change from thermometers and stethoscopes.

Prudence drove herself up to London in her down-at-heel little Fiat. She had friends at the hospital where she had been working, and one of them, the junior in the team of theatre Sisters, had agreed to garage the car at her flat provided she might have the use of it, a plan which suited Prudence very well. She left the car, took out her luggage from its boot and hailed a taxi to take her to her godmother's flat. It was in an Edwardian building along the Embankment, very ornate outwardly, but a haven of quiet luxury once past its well-guarded entrance. Prudence left her luggage with the hall porter and took herself up to the first floor, to be admitted by her godmother's elderly maid, a dour, middle-aged spinster with the unlikely name of Miss Pretty.

Prudence greeted her cheerfully, knowing that beneath the gloomy face there lurked a loyal, kind heart. 'The porter's bringing up the luggage, Pretty. Is Aunt Beatrix in?'

'Waiting for you, Miss Prudence, and tea on the table.'

'Good, I could do with a cup. You are coming with us, Pretty?'

'Madam couldn't manage without me,' said Pretty austerely. 'Not that I care for foreign parts myself, although it's quite nice where we're going. Her stern features relaxed slightly. 'Madam's that pleased that you'll be coming with her.'

'I'm looking forward to it,' declared Prudence, and added, 'Shall I go in? The drawing-room?'

Mrs Wesley offered a cheek to be kissed. 'Dear child, how nice you look! Sit down and let's have tea. I thought a quiet evening? We shall be leaving after breakfast. That good man Best will drive us to Heathrow.' Best carried on a hired car business from the mews behind the flats, and Aunt Beatrix would have no other.

'And at Schiphol?' prompted Prudence, sinking her splendid teeth into a scone.

'My sister is sending her car to meet us.' Mrs Wesley sipped her milkless tea and watched her goddaughter make a splendid meal. She said with a trace of envy, 'You can eat anything you like? You don't put on weight?'

'Not an ounce, and that's a blessing, since I'm what

our Vicar calls a fine figure of a woman, which is a polite way of saying that I'm a big girl.'

Her godmother glanced down at her own ample proportions. 'You're tall enough to carry it,' she observed, 'and I flatter myself that I'm able to do the same.'

Prudence nodded a cheerful agreement and began on a cucumber sandwich.

They left the next morning, and Prudence, in the habit of throwing a few things into the back of the Fiat and driving away, was taken aback by her godmother's elaborate preparations for a journey which would take less than half a day. For a start, the amount of luggage was sufficient for a stay of several months, and comprised a number of old-fashioned and very bulky hatboxes, an awkwardly shaped leather case which Pretty clung to as though her very life depended on doing so, a large trunk which required two men to lift it, and a variety of suitcases. Prudence, with one case and an overnight bag, began to wonder if she had packed enough clothes to compete with such a vast wardrobe. It took some considerable time to hoist everything into the boot, and even then poor Pretty, sitting in front with Best, had a conglomeration of umbrellas, travelling rugs and the awkward box, as well as her own modest luggage. The sum of money to pay on excess baggage would be considerable—something which of course Aunt Beatrix, with a more than adequate supply of the world's riches, could ignore.

Prudence admired her almost regal indifference to the hustle and bustle of Heathrow when they reached it; it was left to herself, Pretty and Best to organise porters, find the right desk and settle the question of excess baggage, although to give Aunt Beatrix her due, she paid up without a murmur when asked to do so before making her stately progress towards the departure gate. Prudence, a law-abiding girl, had always thought one should arrive, as asked, one hour before the plane departed, but this was something her godmother had either overlooked or considered unnecessary. They bade Best goodbye and made their way through the security check and into the area set aside for outgoing passengers. It was almost empty and they were among the last on board. First class, of course, and Aunt Beatrix, in the nicest possible way, wanting her seat changed, a cushion for her head and the promise of a glass of brandy as soon as they were airborne. She disliked air travel, she informed the stewardess in a ringing voice, and expressed the hope that the Captain was an experienced man. Having been reassured about this and having had her seat-belt fastened, she gave Prudence, sitting beside her, her handbag to hold, arranged herself comfortably and went to sleep. The stewardess, coming presently with the brandy, gave it to Prudence instead. She drank it, since it was a pity to waste it, and ordered one for Pretty, who sipped it delicately, making it last for almost the whole of their flight.

Mrs Wesley woke as the plane started its descent to Schiphol, observed that the flight had been a pleasant one, and warned Prudence, who had the tickets, to be sure she didn't lose them.

The rather slow business of getting from the plane

to the airport exit went without a hitch; with the luggage piled high on three trolleys, they arrived in the open air to find a uniformed chauffeur waiting for them.

He greeted Mrs Wesley with great politeness, acknowledged Prudence's polite good morning with a bowed head and grinned at Pretty. The car waiting for them was a very large Mercedes into which Aunt Beatrix stepped and settled herself comfortably, leaving everyone else to load in the luggage, with Prudence giving advice which only Pretty understood and the porters taking no notice of anyone at all. But at length everything was stowed away to the chauffeur's satisfaction; he held the door politely for Prudence to get in beside her godmother, saw Pretty into the seat beside him, and drove off.

'We go around Amsterdam,' explained Aunt Beatrix, 'and join the motorway going north. We shall cross the Afsluitdijk into Friesland, and from there we drive across Friesland very nearly to Groningen Province. I think you'll find the country pleasant enough; there should be a map in the pocket beside you, dear, so you can see exactly where you are. I shall compose myself and take a nap—I find travelling very fatiguing.'

Prudence somehow choked back a giggle, and presently opened the map.

She hadn't realised quite how small Holland was. They were on the Afsluitdijk within two hours, speeding towards the distant coastline of Friesland; they must be almost there. Aunt Maud had warned her that she might expect to find her hostess's home somewhat larger than her own. 'I visited there once, a long time ago,' Aunt Maud had said, 'and I remember I was rather impressed.'

The car swept on, skirting Franeker and Leeuwarden, racing along the main road towards Groningen. What was more, Prudence had seen very few country houses, but numerous villages, each with its church, offering useful landmarks in the rolling countryside, and any number of large prosperous farms. She was wondering just where they would end up when the chauffeur turned the car on to a narrow brick road, and within minutes they had left the modern world behind them. There were trees ahead of them and a glimpse of red roofs, and, as though Mrs Wesley had secreted an alarm clock about her person, she opened her eyes, sat up straight, and said in a satisfied voice, 'Ah, we're arriving at last,' just as though she had been awake all the time. She said something to the chauffeur in Dutch and he replied at some length as they slowed through a small village; a pretty place surrounded by trees and overseen by a red brick church in its centre. The road was cobbled now and the car slowed to a walking pace as it rounded the centre of the village and took a narrow road on the other side.

'A lake?' asked Prudence. 'How delightful!' She was still craning her neck to get a better view when the car was driven between stone pillars and along a curved drive, thickly bordered by shrubs and trees. It was quite short and ended in a wide sweep before a large, square house with a gabled roof, a very large front door reached by double steps and orderly rows of large windows. There was a formal flower garden facing it beyond the sweep, and an assortment of trees in a semicircle around it. Prudence, getting out of the car, decided that it was rather nice in a massive, simple way. It might lack the mellow red brick beauty of Aunt Maud's home, but it had charm of its own, standing solidly in all the splendour of its white walls in the May sunshine.

The procession, led by Mrs Wesley with Prudence behind her and tailed by Pretty and the chauffeur, carrying the first of the baggage, mounted the steps, to be welcomed by a stout man with cropped white hair and bright blue eyes. He made what Prudence supposed to be a speech of welcome, and stood aside to allow them into a vestibule which in turn opened into an oval entrance hall. Very grand, reflected Prudence, with pillars supporting an elaborate plaster ceiling and some truly hideous large vases arranged in the broad niches around the walls. The floor was black and white marble and cold to the feet.

There were numerous doors, and the stout man opened one and ushered them into a large room furnished in the style of the Second Empire, with heavy brocade curtains at its windows and a vast carpet on its polished floor. Aunt Beatrix took off her gloves, asked Pretty to see that the luggage was brought in and taken to their rooms, and sat down in a massive armchair. 'Wim will let my sister's maid know that we have arrived,' she observed, 'but first we'll have coffee. I suggest that while I'm seeing my sister you might like to stroll through the gardens for half an hour.'

Prudence agreed cheerfully. 'And when do you take your insulin?' she wanted to know.

'Ah, yes, I mustn't forget that, must I, my dear? And my diet...'

'You have it with you? Shall I go and see someone about it? It's very important.'

Her godmother was searching through her handbag. 'I have it here, but I shall need to translate it. How many grammes are there in an ounce?'

They worked out a lunch diet while they drank their coffee, and gave the result to Wim, and Mrs Wesley said comfortably, 'I shall leave you to arrange dinner for me, dear; if you'll write it out I can translate it... I dare say you're clever enough to ring the changes.'

Prudence agreed placidly, concealing the fact that she was a surgical nurse and had always loathed diabetics anyway. 'You'd like me to see to your insulin, too?' she asked.

Her godmother nodded. 'But of course, Prudence.'

A small, stout, apple-cheeked woman came presently to take Mrs Wesley to her sister. Before she went, she suggested once again that Prudence should go into the garden around the house. 'My sister will want to meet you,' she concluded, 'but first we must have a chat.'

When she had gone, Prudence wandered over to the doors opening on to the terrace behind the house and went outside. The gardens were a picture of neatness and orderliness. Tulips stood in rows, masses of them, with clumps of wallflowers and forget-me-nots between them. All very formal and Dutch, she reflected, and made her way past the side of the house, down a narrow path and through a small wooden gate. The path meandered here, between shrubs she couldn't name, and there were clumps of wild flowers, ground ivy and the last of a splendid carpet of bluebells. She turned a corner and ran full tilt into a man digging. He straightened up, and said something in Dutch and turned to look at her. He was tall and heavily built, so that she felt quite dwarfed beside him. She had read somewhere that the people of Friesland and Groningen were massively built, and this man was certainly proof of that; he was handsome, too, with lint-fair hair, cut unfashionably short, bright blue eyes, a disdainful nose and a firm mouth. The gardener, she assumed, and murmured a polite good day.

He stood leaning on his spade, inspecting her so that after a moment she frowned at him. And when he grinned and spoke to her in Dutch she said sharply, 'Don't stare like that! What a pity I can't speak Dutch.' And at his slow smile she flushed pinkly and turned on her heel. So silly to get riled, she told herself, walking away with great dignity. He hadn't said a word—or at least, none that she could understand.

She went back into the house and presently she was taken upstairs to a vast bedroom and introduced to Aunt Beatrix's sister—Mevrouw ter Brons Huizinga, a rather more stately version of Aunt Beatrix, if that were possible, sitting up in bed against a pile of very large linen-covered pillows. Despite her stateliness, she looked ill, and Prudence eyed her with some uneasiness. She enquired tentatively after her hostess's health, and was reassured to hear that her doctor visited her daily and was quite satisfied with her progress. 'He should be here any minute,' declared Mevrouw ter Brons Huizinga, and, exactly on cue, there was a tap on the door and he came into the room. The gardener, no less.

CHAPTER TWO

AUNT BEATRIX swam forward and enveloped him in her vast embrace. 'My dear boy, how delightful to see you again and to know that you are taking such good care of your aunt! We've only just arrived…' She had spoken in English and turned to glance at Prudence, standing with her mouth deplorably half-open and with a heightened colour. 'Prudence, this is my nephew—at least, he's my sister's nephew; Haso ter Brons Huizinga. Haso, this is Prudence Makepeace who has kindly come with me so that there's someone to look after me. She's a nurse.'

Prudence offered a hand and nodded coldly. He didn't look like a gardener any more; he had rolled down his shirt sleeves and put on a beautifully tailored jacket, and his hands looked as though he had never done a day's work, let alone dig a garden. He held her hand firmly and didn't let it go. 'Ah, yes, Prudence, I've heard a good deal about you.'

A remark which annoyed her. She said sharply, 'You could have said who you were!'

He raised his eyebrows. 'Why?'

She was stumped for an answer.

He said thoughtfully, 'You aren't my idea of a Prudence.'

'Indeed?' She had managed to get her hand back at last.

He put his handsome head on one side, contemplating her. 'Small and pink and white and clinging.'

He shook his head and she said tartly, 'What a disappointment I must be, Doctor—er—ter Brons Huizinga, not that your opinion interests me...'

'Oh, dear, we've started off on the wrong foot, haven't we?'

Aunt Beatrix had gone over to her sister's bed, but now she paused in what she was saying and turned to look at them. She said in her rather loud voice, 'Getting to know each other? That's right, you young people will have a lot in common.'

'Young?' murmured Prudence unforgivably, and looked pointedly at his hair—there was quite a lot of grey in it. She was annoyed when he laughed. 'Well, I dare say you must seem young to my aunt,' she added kindly.

He didn't answer, but strolled over to the bed. 'Aunt Emma, I should like to take a look at you as I'm here. Would you like your maid here? Or better still, could Prudence help you?'

Aunt Beatrix got up. 'Why, of course she will. I shall go to my room until luncheon. Before you go, Haso, will you arrange a diet for me? I have a letter from Dr Lockett in London. Insulin, you know,' she added vaguely.

He opened the door for her. 'Of course, Aunt Beatrix.' He added something in Dutch to make her laugh and then returned to the bedside.

He was very much the doctor now. For Prudence's benefit he spoke English, although from time to time he lapsed into his own language while he talked to his aunt. When he had finished his examination he sat down on the side of her bed. 'You're doing very nicely, and now you're in your own house you'll do even better. You may get up tomorrow for a short time; I'm sure you're in capable hands.' He glanced at Prudence, who looked rather taken aback; she had been prepared to keep an eye on Aunt Beatrix, but now here was a second elderly lady to worry about.

'Aunt Emma has a splendid maid, quite able to cope if you would prefer that.' His eyes were on her face, but she refused to look at him. Instead she turned a smiling look towards the bed's occupant.

'I shall enjoy looking after you,' she said firmly.

'That's settled, then—we'd better deal with this diet, had we not?' He glanced at his watch. 'I have ten minutes to spare. Perhaps you could get the diet sheets and instructions about the insulin and bring them down to the small sitting-room.'

Prudence hadn't the least idea where the small sitting-room might be—indeed, she reflected, neither did she know where her room was. Presumably someone would tell her in their own good time. She wished Mevrouw ter Brons Huizinga a temporary goodbye and went through the door he was holding open. She had swept past him rather grandly, only to stop short in the corridor outside. She had not the least idea where to go.

'Aunt Beatrix will be in her usual room—go to the end of this corridor and turn left, it's the first door on your right.' He caught her arm. 'It will be quicker if I show you. Do you know where your room is?'

'No, but I hope someone will tell me before bed-time.'

He stopped, and she perforce stopped with him. 'Not much of a welcome. You should have been warned that the Aunts take it for granted that their minds are read and their wishes carried out without the necessity of them needing to put them into words.' He walked on again, turned a corner and nodded towards a door. 'There's Aunt Beatrix's room. The sitting-room is on the left at the bottom of the staircase.'

Aunt Beatrix was resting on her bed watching Pretty unpack. 'There you are, dear child. Luncheon will be in twenty minutes—in the family dining-room. Do you want something?'

Prudence collected the diet sheets, the insulin and the doctor's letter and went downstairs. Dr ter Brons Huizinga came to the door as she reached the last stair. 'In here, Prudence—you don't mind if I call you Prudence?'

He didn't wait for her to answer but started reading the letter, having first invited her to sit down. The room was rather pleasant, although she found the furniture rather heavy. But it was beautifully cared for, and the ornaments and silver scattered around were museum pieces. She glanced up and found the doctor's eyes upon her. He smiled suddenly, and just for a moment she liked him, but the smile went as quickly as it had come, and he turned away to a chair opposite hers.

'There couldn't be a worse diabetic than Aunt Beatrix,' he observed in his faintly accented English. 'Keeping her to a diet won't be too bad, but once she's stabilised and off injections, the chances of her remembering to take her pills are slight. However, we'll do our best.'

He got out his pen and spread the diet sheet on his knee and began to write it out in Dutch. Prudence sat and looked at him; he really was very good-looking, and far too sure of himself, almost arrogant. She wondered where he lived, and as he put his pen away she asked, 'Do you live here, too?'

'No. Now, the insulin...'

Prudence blushed at the snub, although she supposed she had deserved it. She listened to his instructions, received back the diet sheet and his own written instructions as well as the doctor's letter and the insulin, and got up to go.

'Presumably you're on the telephone if I should need you?'

'Indeed I am.' He opened the door and then shut it again before she could reach it. 'Tell me, did you expect there to be a nurse here to look after Aunt Emma?'

She raised her eyes to his. 'Well, yes, I did—I mean, Aunt Beatrix asked me to come along too because she was a little uncertain about the diabetes.'

'The naughty old thing,' he observed softly. 'I'll get a nurse from Leeuwarden; she can be here by this evening.'

'No, please don't do that, Doctor. I wouldn't know what to do with myself all day, and there'll be very little to do for your aunt.'

'Coals of fire, Prudence?'

'Pooh,' said Prudence roundly, 'such rubbish! Perhaps you'll be good enough to tell me what you want done.' She went on loftily, 'I've been in charge of a twenty-bedded ward for some years, so I'm quite capable of looking after both your aunts.'

'I have no doubt of it. I'll stay to lunch, and afterwards we can decide what's best for the pair of them.'

He opened the door and she went past him into the hall, not knowing where to go next. 'In here,' he said, and opened another door. 'Time for a drink before we lunch.'

'I should like to go to my room.'

He glanced at his watch. 'I'll get someone to take you up; come back here and I'll have some sherry poured for you.' He added carelessly, 'Don't be too long.'

A remark calculated to convince Prudence that it would take her at least fifteen minutes to see to her face and do her hair to her liking. And who did he think he was, giving orders in his aunt's house? She followed a cheerful young girl up the staircase and down a corridor at the end of which was the pleasant room she was shown into, with windows overlooking the grounds at the back of the house. Her clothes were already unpacked, she noticed, and there were towels and soap arranged in the adjoining bathroom. She sat down before the dressing-table mirror and peered at her reflection. Her face needed very little done to it; she dabbed on some powder, applied lipstick and took down her hair and did it up again, not because it needed it, but because the doctor had told her not to be long. Really, she admonished her reflection, it wouldn't do at all; she would have to see quite a lot

of him at least for the next few days, and she must
at least pretend to like him. Which reminded her that
it would be a step in the right direction if she didn't
keep him waiting too long.

If he had noticed that Prudence had been at least
twice as long as he had expected, he gave no sign,
and presently Aunt Beatrix joined them and they
crossed the hall to the dining-room, a forbidding
apartment with a massive sideboard weighed down
with quantities of silver and a table large enough to
seat a dozen people. The meal was simple but elegantly served, and her companions carried on a conversation about nothing much, taking care to include
her in it. They must be longing to lapse into their own
tongue, she reflected, but neither of them gave a hint
of wanting to do so, and when they had had their
coffee the doctor invited her into a small room leading off the dining-room and asked her to sit down.

The next half-hour was spent in a résumé of Mevrouw ter Brons Huizinga's state of health, with a polite request for Prudence to keep an eye on her and
call him if she was worried, and a somewhat detailed
discussion about Aunt Beatrix. At the end of it he
thanked her with cool politeness, begged her to say
immediately if she found her responsibilities too
heavy for her, observed that he would be in on the
following day and wished her goodbye.

Prudence sat where she was for a little while, contemplating the next week or so. It was obvious to her
that this was to be no ordinary visit. Aunt Beatrix,
much as she loved her, had behaved quite ruthlessly,
no doubt pleased with herself for having found some-

one to look after both herself and her sister. On the
other hand, in all fairness, she was going to live in
the lap of luxury, and possibly when she had found
her feet there would be the chance to do some sightseeing. She allowed her thoughts to dwell on the delicious cheese soufflé which had been served at lunch,
and decided that the pros more than outweighed the
cons.

Both ladies snoozed in the afternoons; Prudence
took herself into the gardens and explored. They were
too formal for her liking, but since it was a warm
afternoon she found them pleasant enough, and presently found a nice sheltered corner in the sun and
curled up on the grass and went off to sleep.

'Sleeping Beauty?' asked a gently mocking voice
which brought her wide awake, just for the moment
quite scattered in her wits so that she blinked up at
the doctor leaning over her.

'Oh, it's you again!' she declared crossly. 'I might
have known!'

'Not Sleeping Beauty,' he observed blandly, 'just
a cross girl. I came in on my way back from hospital
to tell you that I shall be in Amsterdam tomorrow and
probably for the next few days as well. I've left a
telephone number on the hall table; my partner will
come at once if you need anyone. He speaks English.'
He turned on his heel. 'You hair's coming down,' he
told her, and walked away towards the house.

She watched him go; never in her whole life had
she met a man she disliked so much!

She went back to the house presently, but only
when she had heard a car driving away. Aunt Beatrix

was in the drawing-room, the tea-tray in front of her. 'Go and tidy yourself, my dear, and we'll have tea together. My sister is still sleeping. Haso has been here again—I expect you saw him.'

Prudence said that yes, she had, and she would only be two ticks tidying herself for tea, and sped away to her room. She got back to the drawing-room just in time to remove a large chocolate cake from Aunt Beatrix's vicinity.

'You're on a diet,' she reminded her. 'You must keep fit so that you can help Mevrouw ter Brons Huizinga...'

'You're quite right, dear. I think you might address my sister as Aunt Emma. We're to be together for some time, and I have always thought of you as my niece.'

Prudence thanked her nicely and eyed the chocolate cake; it seemed mean to have some when her companion was nibbling at a dry-looking biscuit. She would probably lose a lot of weight, she reflected gloomily, and gave herself another cup of tea with plenty of milk and sugar.

She spent an hour or so with Aunt Beatrix after tea, then went to see Aunt Emma. Aunt Emma's maid, Sieke, seemed pleased enough to have help in getting her mistress settled for the night, a by no means simple task, since Aunt Emma was a law unto herself, knowing better than anyone else and determined to have her own way at all costs. Sieke cast her a grateful look when at last they had the lady with her incongruous wishes nicely settled against her pillows with the promise of a light supper to buoy her up.

They had not, of course, been able to talk together, Sieke had no English and Prudence had no Dutch, but they had had no need of words; it was apparent that Sieke was quite willing for Prudence to take over any nursing care necessary and felt no animosity about it.

Prudence went along to her own room, showered and changed into one of the pretty dresses Aunt Maud had advised her to pack. 'And a good thing too,' she muttered as she poked at her hair, 'if I'm to live up to the splendour of the dining-room.'

It was indeed splendid—white damask, shining silver and polished glass and a massive centrepiece which effectively blocked her view of Aunt Beatrix, resplendent in black velvet. Conversation, carried on in raised voice the length of the table, was concerned wholly with Aunt Beatrix's diet and her sister's health. Prudence managed to make a splendid meal before joining her godmother in the drawing-room for coffee, and then she sat listening to a somewhat rambling history of the family. 'Of course, your Aunt Emma married very well; her husband was a younger brother of Haso's father and they're a wealthy family. One wonders why the dear boy works so hard at being a doctor when he might be living quietly at his home.'

'Perhaps he likes being a doctor?' suggested Prudence mildly.

'Possibly. But his mother would like to see him married—there are several suitable young women…'

Not very interested, Prudence observed, 'Perhaps he's a confirmed bachelor. He's not young.'

Her godmother sighed and said reprovingly, 'A

mere three and thirty, a splendid age at which to marry.'

Prudence longed to ask why, but decided not to.

Her godmother proceeded, 'There's no lack of young women who would be only too glad to marry him.'

'Oh, really?' said Prudence politely. 'Then why doesn't he? Marry, I mean?'

'You don't like him,' observed her godmother suddenly.

'I don't know him, Aunt Beatrix. How could I possibly dislike or like him after only a few minutes' conversation with him?'

'That is, of course, true,' conceded her godmother. 'You'll naturally get to know each other during the next week or so.'

An unnecessary exercise as far as Prudence was concerned.

The following day gave her a very good idea of what was to come. She awoke refreshed from a sound night's sleep to find her aunt's maid standing by her bed with early morning tea.

Her, 'Good morning, Pretty', was answered a little sourly.

'Well, good morning it may be for some,' declared Pretty, 'but I'm sure I don't know.'

'What's wrong?' asked Prudence; it couldn't be too dire, the house's inmates were barely awake.

'There's Madam, wanting rolls and butter and croissants with more butter and marmalade, with scrambled eggs and bacon, and sugar in her coffee...'

Prudence scrambled up higher against her pillows.

'That won't do. I'll come and see my aunt, Pretty—it's no good her having a diet if she's not going to keep to it. Don't you worry now, go and have your breakfast, if you like. I'll let you know what's happening.'

She got out of bed and flung on her gown, a gossamer affair of crêpe-de-Chine and lace which matched her nightie.

'That cost a pretty penny,' declared Pretty severely.

Prudence agreed readily. 'I like pretty things.' She smiled at Pretty and stuck her feet into satin slippers trimmed extravagantly with satin bows, then took herself out of the room to visit her aunt.

Mrs Wesley was sitting up in her bed sipping milkless tea in a discontented fashion, and it took all of ten minutes to coax her to have the breakfast she was allowed and not the one she wanted, but Prudence was used to dealing with recalcitrant patients, and presently she went away to dress and go downstairs for her own breakfast—the last peaceful minutes she was to have until lunch time, as it happened. Between them, Mrs Wesley and her sister kept her busy for the entire morning; their demands for this and that and the other were numerous, uttered with charm and a stately determination to have their own way. It was a relief to everyone when they consented to rest on their beds after lunch. Prudence tucked them up with soothing murmurs, waited until she heard their gentle snores, and escaped into the gardens. It was a splendid day, warm for the time of year. She found a pleasant seat in a quiet corner and opened her book.

It was obvious that each meal was going to be a

battle of wills between herself and her godmother. Prudence reflected that it was a good thing that Mevrouw ter Brons Huizinga had a well-staffed household, devoted to her. There was to be no lack of help when Prudence was summoned to get that lady from her bed, an undertaking which took a great deal of time and almost all her patience. All in all, she thought as she got ready for bed that night, a busy day, and as far as she could see, all the other days would be the same.

They were, at least for the next three days, but by now she had a routine, frequently disrupted by the vagaries of the two elderly ladies, but none the less workable. Not speaking Dutch was a disadvantage, of course, but it was amazing what could be done with arm-waving and pointing.

The fourth day came and went and there was no sign of Haso, and although Prudence reminded herself that she disliked the man intensely, none the less, she wished he would come. It had been rather unfair, she reflected, giving way to a self-pity she seldom indulged in, that she had been left with the responsibility of the aunts. Of course, she could get his partner at any time, but that wasn't the same thing... She got into bed with something of a bounce and declared to the empty room, 'Well, I suppose he'll turn up sooner or later.'

Sooner, as it turned out.

She wakened to the sound of Pretty's urgent voice hissing at her.

'Miss Prudence, for heaven's sake, wake up—

there's something wrong with Madam, and there you are snoring your head off!'

Prudence opened one eye. 'I never snore.'

Pretty gave her shoulder a little shake. 'Oh, do listen—you must listen! I know there's something wrong, Madam's lying there and I can't rouse her! I can't think why I went to see if she was all right, but she's not...'

Prudence was out of her bed, feeling around for her slippers with her feet.

'Hyperglycaemic coma,' she said, although she still wasn't quite awake.

Pretty said sharply, 'Call it anything you like, my Madam's ill.'

She was quite right; Mrs Wesley, as far as Prudence could judge, was in a diabetic coma, although they couldn't think of a reason for it. She had eaten her diet, every morsel, at dinner—Prudence herself had seen to that—and her insulin had been the correct dosage. She took a brief look at her godmother and went swiftly to the telephone.

It was Dr ter Brons Huizinga who answered her, and she didn't waste time with so much as a hello. 'Mrs Wesley—she's in a hyperglycaemic coma— deep, sighing breaths. I'm unable to rouse her at all...'

He cut her short. 'I'll be with you in fifteen minutes.'

Prudence went back to her godmother and then got out the insulin and syringe. 'And if you'd go down to the front door and let the doctor in, Pretty?'

He was as good as his word; she was bending over Mrs Wesley when he came into the room.

He didn't bother to greet her, his, 'Well, what has she been eating?' was uttered in a voice which, while not accusing, certainly held no warmth.

'Her normal diet. I had all my meals with her and I'm certain of that.'

He was examining the unconscious figure on the bed. 'Aunt Emma—dined in her bed?'

'Yes, of course. She only gets up for an hour or two in the afternoon.'

'She had a normal meal this evening?'

Prudence's eyes opened wide. 'Oh, my goodness! Aunt Beatrix went to sit with her...but that was after Pretty had taken the tray away. She had coffee...' She gave a small gasp. 'Some friends called to see her today and left a large box of chocolates.' She stared as his expression changed. 'You think...?'

'Let us assume that it's the chocolates.'

He had nothing more to say, but set about the business of dealing with his patient, an intravenous saline drip, soluble insulin given intravenously, following this with an even larger dose by injection, a blood sugar test and specimens taken for testing. He worked quietly, quickly and calmly, talking only when it was necessary, taking it for granted that Prudence knew what she was doing, too.

It was early morning, two hours later, before Mrs Wesley showed signs of coming out of her coma. An hour later, after a small injection of insulin and glucose to counterbalance its effect, she was completely conscious. Prudence heaved a relieved sigh and longed for a cup of tea, just as Pretty poked her head round the door in a cautious manner and hissed, 'Tea?'

It was Dr ter Brons Huizinga who answered her in a normal voice.

'A splendid idea, Pretty—and while you are getting it perhaps you, Prudence, would go and get a fruit drink for my aunt.

There was a beautiful dawn breaking as she went down to the kitchen; she fetched the drink, gave it to a remarkably subdued patient and then accepted a cup of tea from the tray Pretty had fetched.

'I'm going back home,' observed the doctor. 'I want two-hourly testing, and for the time being around thirty grams of carbohydrate four-hourly. I'll be back after morning surgery, but please phone if you're worried.'

Prudence looked at him with cold dislike, but said with deceptive meekness, 'Very well, Doctor. Presumably you'll arrange for someone to take over while I dress, eat breakfast and cast an eye over your other aunt?'

He said cordially, 'Most certainly, since you feel you can't cope.'

She said tartly, 'Don't be so unreasonable—of course I can cope, and you know it, but I doubt if you intend to take your surgery dressed as you are and with a bristly chin, too. So why should I spend the morning in a dressing-gown until you choose to do something about it?'

'It's a charming garment; for my part, you have no need to dress.'

Her dark eyes flashed with temper; she said with chilling civility, 'I suppose you can't help being rude!'

He looked as if he was going to laugh, but all he said was, 'If you could dress yourself and eat breakfast in half an hour, I'll stay—but not a moment longer.'

Prudence sniffed, 'How kind!' She cast a glance at Aunt Beatrix, lying with her eyes shut, looking more or less normal again, and whisked herself away.

Pretty, encountered on her way to her room, promised breakfast in ten minutes, and Prudence, with years of practice at dressing at speed in hospital, showered, donned a cotton top and a wide, flower-patterned skirt, tied her hair with a ribbon, and, since the ten minutes was up, left her face unmade-up before going down to the kitchen where the faithful Pretty was waiting with coffee and toast.

'Mevrouw's cook may be out of the top drawer, but she hasn't an idea how to cook a decent breakfast. All this bread and bits and pieces to put on it—give me bacon and eggs and a mushroom or two...'

Prudence, her teeth buried in her first slice of toast, agreed indistinctly. 'When in Rome, do as Rome does,' she added, and helped herself to a slice of cheese.

'Madam will be all right now?' asked Pretty anxiously.

'I believe so—we caught her in time. I do hope she won't do it again.'

She munched steadily for a few minutes, swallowed her coffee and got up. 'I'll take a quick peep at Aunt Emma. Will someone see to her breakfast?'

'Don't you worry, miss, there's help enough in this place. Has the doctor gone yet?'

'No, but he will the moment I get back to Aunt Beatrix.'

'Such a nice young man!' Pretty allowed her stern features to relax into a sentimental smile.

Prudence didn't think this remark worth answering. She thanked her companion for her breakfast and flew upstairs, two minutes in hand.

Aunt Emma was still snoring peacefully; she skimmed along the corridor and went into Aunt Beatrix's room.

'Ah, there you are.' Dr ter Brons Huizinga glanced at his watch, an observation which did nothing to improve her opinion of him, uttered as it was in a tone of pained patience.

'Half an hour exactly,' she pointed out. 'If you'd give me your instructions…?'

He did so, watched by his patient, lying back on her pillows now, with the drip taken down, looking almost normal again. 'Perhaps you would be good enough to fetch the notes I left by my aunt's bed when I last visited her?'

He watched her with a slightly sardonic expression while she bit back the desire to tell him he could fetch them for himself on his way downstairs. With a slightly heightened colour, she went out of the room and Aunt Beatrix remarked from her bed, 'You don't like each other?' She sounded so disappointed.

Haso was strolling about the room, his hands in his

pockets. 'My dear Aunt—given the fact that we've both been out of our beds since about one o'clock this morning, and are in consequence a trifle edgy, I hardly think your observation applies.'

'Well, I do hope not. She's a sweet girl, and so sensible.' She studied his face. 'She's extremely pretty, Haso.'

'Indeed she is. Also not very biddable and a little too sharp in the tongue. Probably due, as I've already said, to having to get out of her bed so very early in the morning.'

'I'm very sorry…but the chocolates were most tempting.'

He smiled very kindly at her. 'I'm sure they were, only don't be tempted again. Be a good soul and keep to your diet, and in no time at all you'll be able to have all sorts of little extras. They make special chocolate for diabetics, you know.'

Mrs Wesley brightened. 'Oh, do they? Good. How is your Aunt Emma, my dear?'

'Doing very nicely. I'll go and see her now.' He kissed his aunt's cheek, nodded casually to Prudence, who had just returned, took his notes from her and went away, whistling cheerfully.

The day passed uneventfully; it was amazing how quickly Mrs Wesley recovered. By teatime she was sitting in her sister's room, exchanging somewhat exaggerated accounts of their illnesses. The doctor had been back again, pronounced himself satisfied as to their conditions, and gone again after a brief talk with Prudence. Very professional and standoffish he was too, she thought, watching his vast back disappearing down the staircase.

She wondered where he lived, but she hadn't liked to ask anyone, and certainly not him; she could imagine how he would look down his arrogant nose at her and tell her, in the most polite way possible, to mind her own business.

Mrs Wesley appeared to have learnt her lesson, and her sister was making steady progress; Prudence felt free to spend a little time on her own, exploring. The lake she had glimpsed on her arrival was close by; she found her way to it without much difficulty, circled it, poking her pretty nose into a boathouse on its near shore and then on the following afternoon wandering down to the village, where she bought postcards and stamps at the one shop; easily done by pointing to whatever she wanted and offering a handful of coins she had borrowed from her aunt. It had been foolish of her not to have thought of getting some Dutch money before she had left England; traveller's cheques were of no use at all.

The doctor called briefly on the following days. It was at the end of one of these visits that he surprised Prudence very much by suggesting that she might like to go to Leeuwarden. 'My aunts are well enough to leave to Pretty and Aunt Emma's maid for a few hours; you must wish to see a little of the country while you're here.'

She said baldly, 'I want to go to a bank and change my cheques. I had no idea that Aunt Emma lived so far away from a town...'

'Not far at all,' he corrected her. 'I'm going to

Leeuwarden after lunch tomorrow. I'll give you a lift.'

'How kind. How do I get back?'

'I'll show you where to wait until I pick you up.' He was refusing to be nettled by her faintly cross voice.

She thanked him with cool politeness, and since he just stood there, looking at her and saying nothing, she felt compelled to make some sort of conversation.

'The lake is charming,' she commented, 'and I walked to the village—are there other villages close by?' She gave him an innocently questioning look in the hope that he might say where he lived.

His laconic 'several' was annoyingly unhelpful.

Her two patients behaved in an exemplary fashion. She helped get Aunt Emma out of her bed before lunch, had her own meal with Aunt Beatrix, an eagle eye on that diet, and then hurried away to change.

She was not dressing to impress the doctor, she assured her reflection as she got into a jersey three-piece in a flattering shade of pale green, thrust her feet into high-heeled, expensive shoes, found their matching handbag and, with a last look at her pleasing appearance, went downstairs.

Haso was in the hall, sitting on the edge of a console table, reading a newspaper and whistling cheerfully. He got up when he saw her, wished her good day and added blandly, 'Oh, charming—for my benefit, I hope?'

'Certainly not, pray disabuse yourself of any such idea.'

'Not an idea, just a faint hope. I thought it would be nice if we could cry truce for a couple of hours.'

Prudence said calmly, 'I'm quite prepared to be friendly, Dr ter Brons Huizinga...'

'Call me Haso, it's quicker. Good, let's go then.'

There was a dark grey Daimler outside on the sweep before the house. He opened her door and she settled herself comfortably, prepared to enjoy the drive.

She certainly did. Haso took a small country road to begin with, joined a quiet main road after a few miles and then went across country until they traversed the outskirts of Leeuwarden. The scenery was green and calm, with cows in the wide fields and every so often a canal cutting through the quiet landscape. The doctor was on his best behaviour; he discoursed at length about their surroundings in a serious voice which none the less gave Prudence the uneasy feeling that he was secretly amused. But he had cried truce for the afternoon, and she for her part was prepared to keep to that. She answered him when called upon to do so, and felt vague relief when they reached the outskirts of the town—a relief which turned to indignation when he observed silkily, 'Boring, isn't it, being on our best behaviour? Shall we agree to disagree when we feel like it?'

She swallowed her astonishment, but before she could decide what to say he had stopped the car in a quiet street.

'Out you get,' he told her. 'Turn left at the corner and you'll find you're within yards of the centre of the town. You'll see the Weigh House across the street—I'll be there two hours from now. You can't get lost, the shops are all close by and there are several banks where you can change your cheques. *Tot ziens.*'

He had driven off before Prudence could frame a reply. She hadn't known quite what to expect, but certainly she hadn't imagined she would be dumped off with so little ceremony. She wasn't going to waste time over him; she went to the corner, and sure enough it was exactly as he had said.

She cashed her cheques, took a closer look at the Weigh House and then strolled around the shops; there were several small things she needed; it was rather fun to pick them out for herself and compare the prices. She spent quite a considerable time at a silversmiths, choosing beautifully made coffee-spoons for Aunt Maud, and then browsing around its counters. Indeed, it was pure chance that she glanced at the clock and saw that it was five minutes past the two hours she had been allowed.

The Weigh House wasn't far way; she could see the Daimler parked nearby and approached it with some trepidation; the doctor might be someone she didn't like, but he was also a man to be reckoned with.

She braced herself for whatever he was going to say.

Nothing. He got out of the car, opened her door for her and got back in only then, saying mildly, 'We'll have tea, shall we? I telephoned the aunts—everything is quite all right, so Pretty tells me. We'll go home—my mother would like to meet you.' He spoilt it all by adding silkily, 'And I'm sure you're dying to know where I live.'

CHAPTER THREE

As far as Prudence could judge, they were going back the same way as they had come, but presently she realised that the narrow brick road they were on was turning north. She looked in vain for landmarks, but the fields all looked alike, with distant clumps of trees, all looking the same as each other.

'Confusing, isn't it?' commented the doctor. 'We're only a few kilometres from my aunt's house—there's a narrow lane a little farther ahead which leads to it. Those trees ahead of us hide Kollumwoude, where I live.'

The village proved to be pretty: red-roofed cottages, one or two villa-type houses, a shop or two and, brooding over the lot, a red-brick house of some size, encircled by a cobbled street. There were high wrought-iron gates half-way round it, standing open, and the doctor drove through them. 'Home,' he observed laconically.

Very nice, too, decided Prudence, taking in the house before them at the end of the short, straight drive. It was three storeys high, its windows set in three rows of three, with a round tower at each end, both of which had a pointed roof like a gnome's cap, as had the central building, and added to one side was another smaller wing with yet another tower. The windows were shuttered and the walls here and there were covered by a green creeper of some sort. The whole gave a pleasing appearance reminiscent of a fairytale castle. Only, it wasn't quite a castle, it looked too lived-in for that: there were curtains at its windows and orange window blinds over them. She said rather foolishly, 'Oh, is this where you live?'

'Yes.' He leaned over and undid her seat-belt, got out and opened the door for her and ushered her towards the door before them. Of solid wood, it had a fanlight above which was a small balcony, supported by two pillars. The door was opened by an elderly man just as they reached it, and when he stood aside for them to enter, the doctor spoke to him and he replied in a creaky voice. The doctor announced, 'This is Wigge—and that's a good old Friesian name—he looks after us all.'

Prudence shook hands and Wigge smiled at her and waved her into the hall beyond: square and lofty, with white walls, a beamed ceiling and any number of rather dark paintings hung upon the walls. There was a wide staircase to one side, rising to a gallery above, and several doors on either side of her, while beside the staircase she could see steps leading down to a door with leaded panes and, beyond that, a garden.

Rather to her disappointment, the doctor led her through the hall and out of the door on to a paved walk, bordered thickly by late spring flowers; it extended along the back of the house, ending at a small, arched doorway set in the high red-brick wall which enclosed the garden.

Prudence would have lingered here too if she had been given the chance, but she was urged towards the

door which the doctor opened and invited her to go
through. Here was another garden, enclosed in the
same manner, its orderly beds filled with rows of vegetables, fruit bushes and the first shoots of a splendid
potato crop. There was a greenhouse running the
length of one wall and the sound of music coming
from it.

It was warm inside. Prudence, urged on by the doctor, began to walk along its length between pots of
tomatoes which yielded a fine array of begonias and
primulas and finally roses, not yet in flower.

The lady bending over a rosebush was undoubtedly
the doctor's mother; as she straightened up, Prudence
could see that she was tall, strongly built and good-
looking still. Her hair was silver-gilt, pinned back in
an old-fashioned bun, and her eyes were as blue as
his. She smiled when she saw them, turned off the
radio on the bench beside her and wiped her hands
on the gardener's apron she was wearing.

'Haso—how nice! And you've brought Prudence
with you.' She offered a hand. 'Of course, I've heard
all about you from your godmother, and I'm so glad
to meet you at last. We will go into the house and
have tea—Haso, will you find Domus and tell him to
finish these roses.'

She led the way out of the greenhouse, and Haso
disappeared into a small path completely hedged in
by shrubs.

'How do you like Friesland?' asked Mevrouw ter
Brons Huizinga. 'Not that you will have had much
chance to see anything of it, I dare say. Let us hope
that Emma and Beatrix will recover their good health

as speedily as possible.' She glanced at Prudence, walking serenely beside her. 'They are charming and I am very fond of them, but they have an independence of spirit—my husband had it also...'

Prudence couldn't think of anything to say other than a polite, 'Indeed?'

Her companion added drily, 'Haso is exactly like his father.'

Prudence wondered just what independence of spirit meant. Personally she thought it another way of saying that he was arrogant, sometimes rude. It wouldn't do to say so, of course; she murmured politely and followed her hostess into the house.

The hall looked just as grand from the garden door. They crossed its polished wood floor and entered a room opposite the staircase. It was large, high-ceilinged and lit by square windows with leaded glass and draped by heavy plum-coloured curtains. There was a magnificent carpet covering most of the floor, worn in places with constant wear over many years, and the William and Mary winged settee echoed the colour of the curtains as well as the muted blues and greens of the carpet in its tapestry cover. There were winged armchairs too, a vast display cabinet along one wall and still more paintings, mostly precious portraits. Prudence gazed about her frankly and her hostess asked, 'You like old furniture?'

'Very much. Aunt Maud has some nice Georgian pieces, but this is earlier. It reminds me of Mompesson House—that's in the Close at Salisbury...'

'Ah, yes—I have been there, and you are quite right, only I believe this house is older and somewhat larger. You must come soon and spend a day with me, and I will show you round.'

She motioned Prudence to sit in one of the armchairs and took one close by, turning to say to her son as he came into the room, 'You could bring Prudence over one day, couldn't you, Haso? In a few days' time, perhaps, once your aunts are recovered sufficiently.'

'Certainly, Mama, providing Prudence doesn't mind fitting in with my timetable.'

He looked across at her, smiling a little, waiting for her answer.

'Not in the least,' she said sedately, 'provided I'm free to do so.'

Wigge came in with the tea-tray then and the talk became general and then settled down to a mild discussion on gardening, Mevrouw ter Brons Huizinga's lifelong hobby.

'Haso has inherited my green fingers,' she observed happily. 'He usually finds time to potter for an hour or so at the weekend if he is free. He has done a great deal to improve Emma's garden—her gardener has no imagination at all.'

They had finished their tea when the doctor looked at his watch.

'I'll take you back on my way to Leeuwarden. I'll be back to change, Mama—I won't be in to dinner.' His mother looked a question and he went on smoothly, 'I'm taking Christabel out.'

So he had a girlfriend—even a fiancée?—and what a silly name the girl had, thought Prudence, saying her polite goodbyes, busy with a mental picture of the

young lady in question: tall and blonde, if the Frie-
sians she had met were anything to go by, cold blue
eyes and regular features, and self-assured. Prudence,
a good-natured girl, felt an unwonted dislike of her.

She was driven back to Aunt Emma's house briskly
and with a scant attention to polite conversation. As
she got out of the car, she said in a kindly voice which
she guessed might annoy Haso, 'So kind of you to
bring me back—was it your good deed for the day?
I do hope you have a pleasant evening with your
Christabel. She must be quite exceptional.'

She didn't wait for him to answer that, but raced
into the house, where she encountered Pretty in the
hall.

'What's the hurry, miss?' that lady enquired severely. 'Doctor brought you back, did he? All the
more reason to linger, I'd have thought.'

'Linger? With him?' Prudence gave a strong shudder. 'Besides, he's in a hurry to spend the evening
with his girl.'

'Got a girl, has he?' Pretty said, 'Hm,' and took
herself off; here was a titbit of news which Madam
wasn't going to relish. Pretty, a recipient of her mistress's confidences, knew quite well that she had been
nurturing sentimental ideas about her goddaughter
and her nephew.

Prudence, happily unaware of this, took herself off
to her room as well, where she went to the window,
to hang out of it and enjoy the gardens below while
she allowed her irritation to evaporate. She wasn't a
conceited girl, but people liked her, and several men
of her acquaintance had wanted to marry her, Walter

having been the most persistent. Although her heart
hadn't been touched she had liked them all, even been
a little fond of them, but none of them, she felt, were
capable of sweeping her off her feet, regardless of
whether she wanted to be swept or not.

She sighed heavily. In a week or two she would go
back to Aunt Maud and start looking for a job, and
if she didn't find one to her liking quite quickly she
might even give up her romantic ideas and say yes to
Walter. At least he appeared fond of her; Dr ter Brons
Huizinga didn't even like her, and, what was more,
he made no attempt to hide his dislike.

She went to peer into the looking-glass on the
dressing-table and poked at her bright hair. Perhaps
he didn't like its colour. She studied the rest of her
person; probably he liked slim-looking, delicate girls,
and she was neither. It struck her suddenly that she
was allowing him to occupy her thoughts far too
much. She pulled a face at her reflection and went
downstairs to find Aunt Beatrix.

That lady eyed her thoughtfully. 'You had a pleasant afternoon, dear? And you enjoyed tea at Haso's
home? Dear Cordelia—his mother, you know—is the
sweetest person. Wrapped up in her garden, of course,
but it keeps her busy. I believe she still misses my
brother-in-law, they were very close.'

Prudence sat down. 'I liked her. Has she other sons
and daughters?'

'Three daughters, married and living—let me
think—two of them in the Hague and the youngest in
Groningen.' Mrs Wesley peered at Prudence over her

glasses. 'All very happy, I believe. A pity Haso can't settle down too.'

'Perhaps he will—he's taking out someone called Christabel this evening.'

Mrs Wesley pursed her lips. 'The eldest van Bijl girl, good background—from *adel*, that's our aristocracy, you know—and very aware of it, too. By no means the partner for Haso.'

'Well, I suppose he'll decide that for himself.' Prudence sniffed. 'She sounds just right for him.'

'You speak as though you dislike him, dear.'

'Me? I don't care either way, Aunt Beatrix.' Being a fair-minded girl she added, 'He's a very good doctor.' She got up. 'I'll just run upstairs and take a look at Aunt Emma—temperature and so forth.'

Haso wasn't mentioned again that evening; they dined presently, Prudence feeling mean as she ate her sole, which was bathed in a delicious sauce and accompanied by croquette potatoes, courgettes in a cream sauce, and tomatoes with a forcemeat stuffing, while her aunt ate boiled fish, one potato and the courgettes without a sauce. She had prudently arranged for a larger flower arrangement to be placed between them, so that her godmother's eyes would be shielded somewhat from her companion's plate, which happily enough prevented her from doing more than glimpsing the trifle richly decorated with whipped cream which Wim, Aunt Emma's butler, offered her.

Aunt Beatrix, spooning up a tastefully arranged grapefruit, paused to say, 'I shall call on Cordelia—you shall drive me over, Prudence. We'll enjoy a pleasant chat. The grounds are delightful and I'm sure she will have no objection to you exploring them. Your Aunt Emma is very much better—I'm considering the idea of taking her on a short holiday as soon as Haso allows it. I should like to have you with us, of course...'

'Where to?' asked Prudence.

'I've always wished to visit the Channel Islands, and I believe Emma would like that. Not Jersey, it's too much of a holiday centre. Guernsey would be better.'

Prudence ate the rest of her trifle. 'Aunt Beatrix, I should really return home once Aunt Emma is better; I have to get a job.'

'I know, dear, of course you do.' Her godmother spoke with all the assurance of someone who had never lifted a finger to earn her own living all her life. 'But another week or so won't make much difference, will it?'

That it might actually make a difference to the contents of Prudence's pocket hadn't occurred to her. Prudence said non-committally, 'Well, let's see what the doctor says,' and Mrs Wesley, quite sure she would get her own way, agreed.

It was some days before they saw Haso again. His partner called, examined the two ladies, pronounced himself satisfied with the pair of them, cautioned Mrs Wesley not to eat anything she shouldn't, agreed with Prudence that since she appeared to be stabilised there was every chance of her having tablets instead of injections of insulin, warned her that Mevrouw ter Brons Huizinga shouldn't exert herself in any way, and took himself off with the remark that Haso was away and should she need any help she was to telephone him.

Prudence, having seen him off at the front door, went thoughtfully into the house. For a GP, Haso seemed to lead a very free life; she wondered about that and then told herself, rather reluctantly, that it was none of her business anyway. She didn't like him, she reminded herself.

All the same, when he arrived a couple of mornings later, she had to admit to herself that he wasn't a man to be ignored. It wasn't just his good looks and his size; it was ridiculous to suppose any such thing, but each time she saw him she had the feeling that they had known each other all their lives. Quite stupid, she reflected, greeting him with chilly politeness.

He didn't appear to notice that, his 'Hello' was casual and he wasted no time in small talk. 'Aunt Beatrix is ready for tablets?' He didn't wait for her to answer. 'I've brought them with me; start her off in the morning, will you? Keep an eye on her and do the usual testing—let me know at once if she backslides. I'll take a look at Aunt Emma. She should be well enough to be up and about for most of the day.'

He pronounced Aunt Emma remarkably fit and listened patiently to her plans to go on holiday. 'In a week or two, dear Haso, and I shall be quite safe, for Prudence is coming with us and she is such a good nurse. Beatrix thought Guernsey… It should be fairly quiet at this time of year—she knows of a good hotel.'

He said, 'I see no reason why you shouldn't go,

my dear, since Prudence has kindly offered to go with you as your nurse.' He shot a quick look at her, standing on the other side of her aunt's chair. She returned it calmly, aware that he had, in some way she couldn't guess at, realised that she had offered no such thing.

As he prepared to go, he paused as they went down the staircase together. 'My mother would like to see you again. I understand from Aunt Beatrix that she wants you to drive her over one day.'

He gave her a quick glance and she said snappily, 'I can drive.'

He looked surprised. 'Well, so I had imagined. Will you come to lunch tomorrow? My mother and aunt will want to gossip, I dare say, so please feel free to roam around the gardens or explore the house. I doubt if I can get back until the late afternoon.'

Prudence thanked him pleasantly; he might not much like her, but he had been thoughtful...

They left the next morning in the small Fiat Wim had for his and the staff's use, Prudence having flatly refused to drive the Mercedes or the slightly smaller BMW in the garage. Aunt Beatrix, mindful of her dignity, wasn't too pleased, but since Prudence assured her that it was the Fiat or nothing she allowed herself to be settled in the back of the car. Prudence, as pretty as a picture in a flowered skirt and deceptively simple blouse, drove off.

Haso's home looked even more beautiful as she drove up the drive for her second visit. 'Far too big,' observed her godmother. 'It should be full of children.'

'Well, I suppose it will be in due course once his Christabel gets started on a family.'

'Don't be vulgar, dear. Anyone would think you didn't like her.'

'I don't know her and I don't suppose I ever shall.' Prudence drew up before the door and Wigge had it open before she could get Aunt Beatrix out of the car. 'Shall I leave the car here?' she wanted to know.

Mrs Wesley addressed Wigge. 'He says yes, dear; we shall be gone before Haso gets back.'

A piece of news which for some reason she found disappointing. Perhaps she enjoyed crossing swords with him? She wasn't sure.

They had coffee on the wide veranda behind the house, overlooking wide lawns and lavish flowerbeds, and Prudence found Mevrouw ter Brons Huizinga even nicer than last time. She had a way with Aunt Beatrix too; her quiet voice, in contrast to Beatrix's ringing tones, soothing that lady's disgruntled comments about her diabetes. Lunch, when they sat down to it, was composed largely of dishes which Mrs Wesley was able to enjoy. As for Prudence, she barely noticed what she ate; her surroundings had caught her attention, and while she made polite conversation she contrived to look around her. The room was beautiful, with a plaster ceiling, its central oval panel moulded into motifs of fruit and flowers, its plain white walls hung with paintings. The chimneypiece was of a rococo design with candle holders, gilded woodwork and a vast mirrored wall, and the table they sat at was of walnut with a marquetry border and capable of accommodating a dozen people. She was hazy about dates, but she was almost sure that the chairs were ribband-backed. She longed to know, but it would hardly do to ask.

They had their coffee at the table when Mevrouw ter Brons Huizinga said kindly, 'Do go into the gardens, Prudence. You must be longing to—there is plenty to see.' She looked wistful, and Prudence wondered if she would have like to have gone with her instead of staying in the drawing-room listening to Aunt Beatrix, who, kind though she was, was a remorseless talker.

The afternoon was splendid. Prudence roamed right round the outside of the house, stopping every few yards to admire it. I could live here, she reflected, staring up at the large windows with their gleaming paintwork, and round the back, where the windows were quite different, smaller and narrow and latticed. The brickwork was older too, the house must have been added to from time to time.

She came back to where she had started and took a wide path under a pergola which would be a picture in a week or two. The path was brick, bordered by lavender hedges not yet in flower, and led eventually to a small pavilion with a pointed roof and a stone seat running all round it. The door opened when she tried it, to discover that it was furnished in a simple fashion with a chair or two and a small table. It was chilly there; she went out again, shutting the door behind her, and took a small path to one side, turning and twisting between thick shrubs and trees and which ended unexpectedly at a swimming pool, nicely screened by trees and with a small dressing-room on its further side. She sat down on a rustic wooden seat close to the pool, and it took some time to take it all in.

'Paradise,' she said out loud. 'Well, not quite—there ought to be two people in love. Paradise for two,' she sighed, 'that sounds like a popular song! I'll have to make do with just me.'

But there was no need for that; she got to her feet as she heard voices, although she wasn't sure from which direction they came. It was several seconds before Haso and his companion appeared on the other side of the pool. He stopped when he saw her and called across it. 'Oh, hello. All on your own?'

That's a silly remark, thought Prudence crossly, smiling brilliantly at the same time. The smile was for his benefit but, more than that, for the girl with him. Exactly as I'd thought, decided Prudence with satisfaction, taking a good look: a tall girl, so slim that she was thin, her dress hanging from her shoulders with no curves to fill it out. Her hair was fair, cut in a straight fringe and hanging almost to her shoulders, and her features were regular in a pale face. Her eyes would be blue, decided Prudence, although she was too far away to be sure of that, but she wasn't so far that she could see the instant antipathy towards herself. Probably Haso had told her all about the uneasy relationship between herself and him.

Haso was strolling round the pool to join her and the girl was coming with him. 'Why did you drive Wim's car?' he asked idly.

'Because I'm too scared to drive your Aunt's

Mercedes,' said Prudence coolly, and looked pointedly at the girl.

'This is Christabel van Bijl—Christabel, this is
Prudence Makepeace.'

'Ah, the English nurse,' Christabel smiled, her eyes
like blue flints. 'Haso has told me all about you.' She
offered a limp hand and Prudence gave it a good
hearty shake, and she made a show of rubbing it
gently. 'How strong you are—I'm sure my hand will
be bruised! However, I dare say you need to be sturdy
in your particular job.'

'Well, yes, but that's a good thing, isn't it? We can
look after the weaklings.'

Haso said something which sounded like 'Fifteen
all' and went on smoothly, 'Shall we go back to the
house for tea?' And he led the way back along the
narrow path with Prudence behind him and Christabel
at the back.

'You have explored the gardens?' he wanted to
know.

'Not quite. What I've seen is charming. The back
of the house is older than the rest of it, isn't it?'

'Seventeenth-century—the front is a hundred and
fifty years later...'

They had reached the house and went in through
the side door, across the hall and into the drawing-
room, to find his mother and aunt sitting by the windows opening on to the veranda, the tea-table between
them.

Christabel gushed over the two elderly ladies with
a charm which made Prudence grit her splendid teeth.
The girl finally sat down between them, declaring that

a cup of tea was just what she wanted most—no sugar
or milk—so fattening, she said with a sly glance at
Prudence. 'And I'd adore one of those little cakes,
but I simply don't dare.' She picked up the plate of
sugary tarts and handed them to Aunt Beatrix, who
foolishly took one.

Prudence darted out of her chair and whisked it
away just as her aunt was about to take a bite. She
said in a calm, reproving voice, 'That was a near
thing. So sorry to jump on you like that, Aunt, but I
dare say Christabel didn't know about your diet.'

There was a plate of bread and butter on the table—
very unusual in a Dutch house, but put there specially
for Mrs Wesley. Cordelia offered it now, saying in
her quiet voice, 'How very fortunate that Prudence
was so quick. It must be so tiresome to get used to
these changes all at once, but I'm sure you will find
it less irksome in time.'

She smiled around, pouring oil on troubled waters,
for Mrs Wesley was poking peevishly at her bread
and butter and Christabel was uttering an angry laugh.
'My nerves really won't stand it,' she complained
prettily, 'and how was I to know?' She raised blue
eyes to Haso, standing a little to one side, and gave
him a quivering smile.

He said blandly, 'I told you, but there is no need
to fuss, there is no harm done.'

He strolled over to Prudence and sat down beside
her. 'Very efficient,' he observed softly, 'and despite
your size, very swift on the feet.'

'You were nearer,' she told him.

'I was so sure you would deal with the situation, and after all, I've already done a hard day's work.'

Prudence bit into a cucumber sandwich.

'Have you really? A short day, surely—you were home at half-past three.'

'Ah, yes, but I began at five o'clock this morning.'

She refused to feel sympathy. 'Doctors must expect to work irregular hours.'

'I thought you would say that...' He was interrupted by Christabel, who called across the room to ask what they were talking about, but she didn't wait for a reply but added with a light laugh, 'Boring old hospital talk, I suppose. What a good thing that you have me to see you have some sort of social life!'

Haso had got up to hand round second cups of tea and didn't reply. There was nothing in his face to show any annoyance, but Prudence thought that under all that massive calm he was seething.

'We're going to the theatre in Leeuwarden this evening,' remarked Christabel chattily, 'a rather special ballet. Do you enjoy ballet, Prudence?'

'Yes, very much...'

She wasn't given the chance to say any more, for Christabel went on, 'When I was younger I took ballet lessons—I was considered quite good, but I grew too tall.'

'One needs plenty of stamina,' observed Prudence sweetly.

Aunt Beatrix got up to go home presently, and everyone went on to the steps to see them drive away. 'You must come again,' said Mevrouw ter Brons

Huizinga. 'On your own—I'm longing to take you round the garden myself.'

She leaned forward and kissed Prudence's cheek and stood waving as they drove away. 'Such a nice girl,' she observed as they went back into the house, 'and so sensible, too.'

Christabel gave a tinkling laugh. 'And so very big!' She turned to Haso. 'Drive me back now, will you, Haso, and come and fetch me at eight o'clock?'

'I'll drive you back, but I have to go to the hospital again—I shan't be free this evening. I did warn you that I can never be sure of my evenings—or my days, for that matter.'

'It's too bad! It's ridiculous that you can't take time off when you want.'

A silly remark that he didn't think was worth answering. He waited patiently while she bade his mother goodbye, kissed his parent and drove Christabel away.

Mevrouw ter Brons Huizinga went and sat down again and picked up her knitting, and Wigge came in to close the veranda doors and clear the tea-things.

'That's a nice young lady, mevrouw,' he observed with the dignified familiarity of an old family servant. He spoke in Fries and she replied in the same tongue.

'Yes, Wigge, and very pretty too.'

'That she is, and a good head on her shoulders, as they say.'

He went away at a stately pace, and Mevrouw ter Brons Huizinga laid her knitting aside. 'Such a pity,' she addressed the empty room. 'They're made for each other and neither of them knows it. And one dare not interfere.'

She went to the telephone and sat down beside it and had a lengthy talk with each of her three daughters.

Back at Aunt Emma's house her sister gave her a résumé of the day.

'Delightful. Cordelia is such a sweet person, and lunch was delicious—I was able to eat almost everything on the table, so very thoughtful of her! That Christabel girl came in at tea time with Haso—far too thin and quite shrewish. I do hope dear Haso doesn't allow himself to get caught—she's very possessive, I noticed.'

'Haso, to the best of my knowledge, has never done anything he hasn't wanted to do. Did Prudence enjoy herself?'

'I believe so—she went into the gardens after lunch and returned with Haso and that girl. They must have met somewhere there. I don't think the two girls liked each other.'

'Probably not. What is more to the point, is Haso interested in Prudence?'

Aunt Beatrix shook her head regretfully. 'If he is, he's concealing it most admirably.'

But Prudence was interested in Haso, not perhaps in the way her aunts would wish. She was sorry for him; she thought Christabel a dreadful girl, quite unsuitable to be his wife. She didn't know exactly what his status was, but she presumed he was a partner in a firm of doctors in Leeuwarden, and if he wanted to make his way in the medical world, then Christabel was going to be of no use to him, bleating on about the ballet and expecting him to be at her beck and call. Of course, she reminded herself, he deserved every inch of the girl, not that that would amount to much, she resembled nothing so much as a telegraph pole...

It was a waste of time thinking about the wretched man. She showered and changed and went down to join the aunts for the evening.

Two days later Mevrouw ter Brons Huizinga telephoned and invited her to spend the day. 'Just me,' she was told, 'and perhaps my youngest daughter—she has been on her own for a short time and Haso let her have Prince, his dog, to keep her company, but her husband is home again and she will be bringing him back. You can drive yourself over? Haso is in Leiden for a few days.'

When, wondered Prudence thoughtfully, did that man ever do any work? 'I'd love to come,' she said warmly. 'I must just see to the aunts after breakfast, but that won't take long as they are expecting old friends for lunch.'

She went to tell the aunts, and then to Wim to see if he would let her have his car again. She had picked up a few words of Dutch by now. 'Tomorrow morning?' she asked, and added in English, 'I'll be very careful.'

Wim smiled benevolently and said, *'Ja, ja'* several times, waving his arms to make sure that she understood, and she skipped up to her room, intent on deciding what she would wear. The weather was turning warmer, although there was always a cool breeze; she settled on a cotton top and matching cardigan and her flowered skirt. A pity Haso wouldn't be there…

The aunts were unexpectedly undemanding in the morning, and it was half-past ten as Prudence got into Wim's car and drove carefully out of the gates. The day was as fine as she had hoped it would be, and the country around her was green and lush under the wide blue sky. She didn't hurry, anticipating the delight she would feel when she reached the drive to the house and would get her first glimpse of it.

It was even better than she remembered. She slowed the car so that she could study it at leisure and presently stopped outside its door, where Wigge was already waiting.

There was another car parked on the sweep—a racy sports model. Just for a moment Prudence wondered if Haso had returned, and then she remembered that his sister would have driven over from Groningen.

Mother and daughter were sitting on the veranda, a tray of coffee on the table. With them was a large, fierce-looking dog with a shaggy black coat and yellow eyes. As Prudence joined them, Mevrouw ter Brons Huizinga spoke quietly to him and he got up and pranced to meet her. Prudence offered a balled fist, then rubbed the great woolly head, and her hostess said, 'Oh, good—you like each other. He's Haso's dog, but he's been taught to be civil to our friends. This is Sebeltsje, my youngest daughter.'

The girls shook hands, liking each other at once. Sebeltsje was almost as tall as Prudence, with pale hair and blue eyes and a pretty face, and nicely plump too. 'I knew Prince would like you,' she exclaimed.

'He looks fierce, doesn't he? And he can be, too. You like dogs?'

Prudence sat down and accepted the coffee offered to her. 'Yes, very much—I don't think we've got his kind at home, though. He's a bouvier, isn't he?'

'Aert—my husband—has promised me a puppy for my birthday.'

They talked idly for an hour before lunch, and after that meal Prudence was borne off by the pair of them, with Prince tramping at their heels, to enjoy a protracted tour of the gardens. It took quite a time and Mevrouw ter Brons Huizinga suggested that they went to the drawing-room and had tea. 'Sebeltsje will have to go soon, as Aert will be home.'

'He's a doctor,' explained Sebeltsje. 'Not in the same street as Haso, of course, but he is much younger. Besides, I tell him that one learned professor in the family is quite enough.'

'A professor?' Prudence did her best to sound casual.

'Oh, yes. He's senior partner in a practice too, but he does a lot of consulting work as well…' She broke off and got up to look out of the window. 'And there he is—look at Prince!'

The dog had gone to the door, his nose pressed against it, his stump of a tail wagging furiously, rumbling happily to himself. Sebeltsje opened the door and he pranced through and could be heard barking happily in the hall. Haso was talking to him, and Prudence was glad she had a few moments in which to regain the calm she had lost at the sound of his arrival. A calm she immediately lost again as he came into the room, kissed his mother and sister, looked at her with raised eyebrows and then walked across to where she was sitting and kissed her too.

'An unexpected pleasure,' he said smoothly, so that she didn't know if he was pleased or annoyed to find her there. She ignored the kiss—she could think about that later—and gave him a genial smile.

'Glad to see me?' he wanted to know, and accepted tea from his mother and came to sit next her.

'Well, I...that is, I thought you were away from home.'

'And now I'm here. If you have any questions about the aunts I shall be happy to answer them.'

Prudence was saved from answering him by his sister, who got to her feet, declaring that she would have to go. 'You must come and see me, Prudence,' she said. 'Could you drive over? Or better still, Haso could give you a lift next time he comes to Groningen.'

'I could drive,' said Prudence, so quickly that Haso gave a crack of laughter, and to her great annoyance she blushed.

She left soon after that, seen off by her hostess and Haso, who evinced no wish to see her again, and certainly a trip to Groningen wasn't mentioned. Which, considering her forceful reply that she would drive herself, was hardly surprising.

CHAPTER FOUR

Two days later Prudence was sitting in the drawing-room with her aunts, who were entertaining two friends to coffee—an old lady, tall and thin and beaky-nosed, who, she felt sure, disapproved of her on sight, and a slightly younger lady, very self-effacing and speaking only when spoken to. The conversation was terribly stilted and carried on mostly by the old lady in Dutch, although from time to time she addressed herself to Prudence, but as her remarks were for the most part searching questions about her work, home life and family, which Prudence answered politely but briefly, she gave up and began a lengthy conversation with Aunt Emma and Aunt Beatrix, which left Prudence stranded with the self-effacing lady, who spoke rather less English than Prudence did Dutch.

Which perhaps accounted for the look of pleasure on her face when Haso walked into the room. He greeted his aunts, shook the old lady's hand and that of her companion and nodded to Prudence. The old lady smiled graciously at him and the younger one simpered. Prudence gave him a wooden look and said nothing.

He didn't sit down, but stood with a hand of the back of Aunt Emma's chair, listening to the old lady holding forth. Prudence, not understanding a word, did her best to look interested, aware that her face bore all the animation of a cod's on a fishmonger's slab. Suddenly she wanted to be at home with Aunt Maud, going to the village shop, exchanging good-days with people she had known for years; their soft country voices music to her ears after the old lady's strident, high-pitched voice.

The doctor, watching her under his lids, smiled to himself, brought the conversation to a gentle close and said, 'I'm on my way to Groningen. I wondered if you would like to see Sebeltsje, Prudence? She phoned just now and invited you to lunch.' He turned to look at his aunts. 'No one has any plans?'

The aunts were instantly enthusiastic. 'How delightful! Prudence, you will like to see Groningen, won't you? I'm sure Haso will willingly wait a few minutes while you tidy yourself.'

They were all looking at her, the ladies with satisfaction because she was to have an unexpected treat, and the doctor with no expression on his face at all.

'I'm not sure...' she began, to be interrupted by his bland,

'Sebeltsje told me she wouldn't speak to me again if I didn't bring you.'

She got to her feet. 'I'll get my handbag.'

She contrived to do her face, run a comb through her hair and spray on a dash of Lumière before she went back to the drawing-room, where she wished her aunts goodbye, then shook hands with the disapproving old lady and her timid companion before being ushered out of the house and into the Daimler.

Prince was sitting in the back; he grinned at her as

she got into the car and they drove off, and he pushed his great head between them, breathing hotly down her neck and rolling his eyes with pleasure.

'Does he go everywhere with you?' she asked. There was something about the doctor's silence which made her anxious to break it.

'Almost always.'

'You've had him for a long time?'

'Two years. I found him tied to a lamppost in several inches of snow. He must have been all of four months old.'

Prudence put up a hand to stroke the shaggy head. 'Oh, the poor scrap! He's quite beautiful, too...'

'A fierce fighter and a splendid bodyguard. When I'm away and have to leave him at home, he guards my mother so closely, she can go nowhere without him.'

He drove for a little while in silence again and she looked out the window, trying to think of a topic of conversation. They were on a quiet country road, and when they reached a crossroads and went across instead of turning on to what was obviously the main road, she asked, 'Is this another way to Groningen?'

'Indeed it is, and much more interesting than the main road.'

As indeed it was, with a canal running beside it until they had almost reached the city, when he turned off on to the motorway which led to its heart.

Prudence looked around her with interest. Groningen was a good deal larger than Leeuwarden, with some splendid houses and numerous canals. The doctor threaded his way through the busy streets and presently turned into a narrow street, drove over a high-backed bridge above a canal and turned carefully into a cobbled square. Halfway along one side he stopped.

'Sebeltsje's husband is a doctor at the University—it's close by, although you can't see the building from here.' He got out and opened her door, and then let Prince out too.

The house was rather tall and narrow, with a mirror-back gable and leaded windows and worn stone steps leading up to its door. Haso pulled the old-fashioned bell and his sister came to the door. She flung her arms around him and smiled widely at Prudence. 'Oh, good—I did so hope you'd come. Haso, can you stay for lunch?'

She tweaked Prince's ears and he leant lovingly against her.

'No, sorry. Shall I leave Prince with you?' Haso spoke to Prudence. 'I'll collect you about five o'clock.'

He said a casual goodbye and took himself off, and Sebeltsje took Prudence's arm. 'Come into the sitting-room, we'll have coffee.' She led the way into a high-ceilinged room overlooking the street, furnished comfortably. It had panelled walls and there was a door in the wall facing the window. A stout woman came through it as they sat down.

'This is Joke—she looks after us.' Prudence smiled at her, and the woman smiled back and spoke to Sebeltsje and went away again, while Prince sat down between them, his eyes on two kittens curled up on one of the chairs. His yellow stare must have roused them, for they woke up, stretched, gave him a cursory glance and went back to sleep again.

'He's very fond of them,' explained Sebeltsje. 'Most bouviers are pretty fierce, but he's sweet with anything which belongs to the family, and of course he adores Haso.'

It was obvious that his sister adored her brother, too. She had a great deal to say about him as they drank their coffee. 'And now this awful van Bijl girl's after him. None of us can stand her, although she's very suitable for a wife. I suppose that's why he'll probably marry her. He's not in love with her—I asked him, and he said that since he hadn't fallen in love with any girl enough to want to marry her he'd settle for someone who would fit in with his life. Only, of course, she's trying to alter that; always fussing him to go here and there and all over the place with her.'

Prudence listened to these artless remarks with a good deal of interest. It was a pity that since Haso didn't love anyone he should have picked on Christabel for his future wife; couldn't he see that within a few years they would either not be on speaking terms or he would have given in to her wishes for a social life? For a clever man, high in his profession, he was singularly stupid. But then, clever men seldom had much interest in anything but what they happened to be clever at.

She didn't voice her thoughts, but murmured in an understanding way and fed Prince a biscuit which he swallowed at one gulp, his eyes blissfully closed.

'You are bored at the aunts' house?' Sebeltsje's question took Prudence by surprise.

'Well, no—it's a lovely lazy life and I have to keep an eye on them both. Besides, it's foreign.'

'Have you got a boyfriend?'

'No—no one in particular. But that's not quite true. There's Walter—I've known him for years and he rather took it for granted that I'd marry him...'

'So why don't you?'

'I don't love him.'

'Oh, well, of course you can't, can you? I was almost engaged to someone when I met Aert, and I knew at once that I wanted to marry Aert.' Sebeltsje added with certainty, 'You always know.' She got up and poured sherry into two glasses. 'Mama told me that the aunts were planning a holiday in Guernsey. You'll go with them?'

'They've asked me if I would go with them, and I suppose I shall. Though I ought to be looking out for a job...'

'Why don't you get one here, in Holland? There are several English nurses in the hospital here and in Leeuwarden—they get Dutch lessons to start with, but many of the medical terms are the same in both languages. Haso would find you a job—he's on the hospital committee and people listen to him.'

Just for a moment Prudence toyed with the idea—what a chance to prove to him that she was a good nurse! She said mendaciously, 'I've already applied for a job in Scotland—the vacancy isn't until August and I told them I would go for an interview when I got back.'

'Scotland? We spent our honeymoon there—I liked it. Perhaps you'll marry a Scotsman.'

'But you were married here?' A question which led naturally enough to a detailed account of the wedding, which lasted until they had had their lunch. They didn't hurry over the meal; they liked each other and there was plenty to talk about. By the time Prudence had been shown round the house and the long, narrow garden behind it, the afternoon was well advanced, and Aert arrived home just as Joke brought in the tea-tray. He was tall and thick-set, fair-haired and blue-eyed and nice-looking in a blunt-featured fashion. He kissed his wife, shook hands with Prudence and observed, 'Haso's coming for tea; the last two cases on his list weren't fit enough for surgery.'

'Oh, is he a surgeon?' asked Prudence.

They both looked at her in surprise. 'Didn't you know? Of course, he wouldn't tell you himself—he's a professor of surgery and operates here and in Leeuwarden, besides being a consultant at Leeuwarden and Amsterdam. Does quite a bit of travelling too, here, there and everywhere.'

Prudence felt her face flame. 'I thought he was a GP.'

She went even pinker when she looked up and saw Haso standing in the open doorway. He gave her a mocking smile as he crossed the room and sat down, but although he must have heard her he made no comment, only accepted a cup of tea with a casual greeting to his sister and Aert and immediately started on a gentle conversation about nothing much which lasted until he observed, 'I hate to break up this pleasant half-hour, but I've got a date this evening and I must deliver Prudence back safely.'

She bade her adieux unfussily, thanked Sebeltsje and was ushered into the Daimler, where she sat quietly while Prince, delighted to be with his master again, scrambled into the back of the car and, when Haso got in, rested his great head on her shoulder.

'Push him off if you don't want him panting down your neck,' said Haso.

'I don't mind.' Seeking a safe topic of conversation, she said, 'Have you had a busy day?'

'Yes. I shall be in tomorrow morning to give Aunt Emma a thorough overhaul. If she's fit, there's no reason why she and Aunt Beatrix shouldn't go on holiday whenever they want to. Aunt Beatrix seems stabilised.'

There had been no warmth in his voice; he might have been giving directions to a ward Sister. Prudence swallowed the words she longed to utter. 'Very well, Doctor,' matched his cool tones.

She sat silent, reflecting that he was the most disagreeable man she had ever met. She disliked Christabel too, but she found it in her heart to be sorry for the girl. Upon reflection, she felt sorry for Haso too.

Rather to her surprise, he went indoors with her when they arrived at Emma's house. The two ladies were seated one each side of a small rent table, each knitting some intricately patterned garment.

'There you are, my dears,' observed Aunt Emma. 'I'm sure you have had a delightful day together. Haso, touch the bell if you will—you will join us in a glass of sherry?'

'Regretfully, no. I'm already a little late, but I shall be here tomorrow morning to make sure that you're both fit to go on holiday.'

He kissed them in turn and went to the door. 'Prudence, I thought we might have dinner together tomorrow. I'll come for you around seven o'clock.'

The last thing she had expected to hear; her pretty mouth hung open in surprise, and by the time she had shut it, preparatory to making a cool refusal, he had gone.

'How delightful!' declared Aunt Beatrix. 'Haso can be such an amusing companion. So kind of him to take you out—you will enjoy every minute of it.'

Prudence said nothing, already planning a really awful headache which would start round about six o'clock in the evening of the next day and get worse.

When the telephone rang the next morning she went to answer it since there was no one else around. 'I should have warned you,' said Haso's voice in her ear. 'It won't be in the least use having a headache, I shall come and haul you out of bed and take you to dine in your nightie. A charming one, if I remember aright.'

Prudence took a swelling breath. 'Well, of all the nerve! I won't...'

She need not have bothered to speak. 'Wear a pretty dress.' He had hung up before she could say a word more.

She spent the day telling herself she wasn't going out with him, but somehow she found herself getting into the dark blue dress after spending a good deal longer than usual over her face and hair. Going re-

luctantly downstairs a few minutes after half-past
seven, she found Haso sitting with his aunts, listening
gravely to them. A purely social visit; he had been as
he had promised that morning, but his manner then,
that of a consultant visiting his ward, had hardly been
conducive to personal remarks of any kind—indeed,
beyond a few questions and directions as to his re-
lations' treatment, he had had nothing to say.

He got to his feet as she went into the room, and
greeted her just as though they hadn't seen each other
already that day. 'If there's one thing which teaches
a girl to be punctual,' he observed bluntly, 'it's a
nurse's training.'

A remark which Prudence found extremely vexing.
All the same, she wasn't going to let him have the
satisfaction of needling her. She smiled distantly at
him, bade her aunts goodbye and accompanied him
out to the car, glad she had taken so much trouble
with her appearance, matching his elegance.

She wasn't going to ask where they were going;
she had been dragooned into the evening, and good
manners, she hoped, would see that she behaved politely towards him, but she wasn't going to show any
interest. She would, she resolved silently, be the dull-
est companion he had ever had the misfortune to entertain.

All the same, she was surprised when he took a
small side road once they had left the village, instead
of the main road which would have taken them either
to Leeuwarden or Groningen. With a tremendous effort she refrained from asking where they were going.
Instead she remarked upon the pleasant evening, the

charm of the landscape and a variety of remarks about
the forthcoming holiday in Guernsey, to all of which
Haso replied in monosyllables, so that presently she
gave up.

After another mile or so of silence she remarked
tartly, 'I can't think why you've asked me out, because we have no pleasure in each other's company,
have we?'

'For that very reason—perhaps if we get to know
each other we might enjoy each other's company
more.'

'Yes, that's all very well, but I'm leaving shortly.'

'So you are at pains to remind me. Do you want
to know where we're going?'

'Yes.'

'Roodkerk—quite close by but difficult to reach,
it's off the main road. There's a restaurant there—De
Trochreed. Perhaps you don't know that in Europe
there's a chain of hotels and restaurants under the
name Romantic—I must add that the title implies
atmosphere, good service and food and private own-
ership—one does not have to be romantically inclined
to patronise them.'

He slowed the car. 'Here we are.'

Probably Haso was right and one didn't need to
feel romantically inclined to dine there, but certainly
the restaurant was conducive to romance with its soft
lighting, candlelit tables, beautifully appointed, and
the welcome as they went in.

The doctor was known; they were ushered to the
small bar where they had their drinks and chose their
meal before going to their table. The place was nearly

full and Prudence, glancing around her, was glad she was wearing the blue dress, for the women there were very well turned out.

She had allowed Haso to advise her as to what she should eat, and since the menu was wildly expensive she made no demur. New herrings, served in slivers on toast, because that was a favourite of the Dutch during the early summer; lobster served with a mouth-watering salad and tiny new potatoes, and an elabo-rate ice-cream dish smothered in whipped cream. She had a splendid appetite, and, although she hadn't wanted to come in the first place, the good food and her companion's casual talk were turning the evening into an unexpectedly enjoyable outing. By the time she was embarking on the ice-cream she had quite forgotten that she didn't like him, and was laughing and talking as though they were the best of friends.

It was as they were drinking their coffee that she said suddenly, 'Do you bring Christabel here?'

'Oh, yes, on numerous occasions.' His smile mocked her. 'She likes only the best restaurants. Women like to dress up and go to elegant places, don't they?'

She gave him a fiercely defiant look. 'Actually, I like fish and chips wrapped in a newspaper parcel and those coffee stalls where you can buy a mug of tea so strong that a mouse can trot on it, and cheese and pickle sandwiches.' Haso was staring at her with raised eyebrows and she hurried to add, 'I don't mean to be rude; this is super and I love dressing up...' She frowned a little, intent on explaining. 'What I mean is, it's the company which is important, isn't it?' She caught his eye and went pink. 'I haven't... I've made a mess of it.'

He said silkily, 'On the contrary, you have made yourself very clear. I can only hope that dinner compensates for my company!'

Prudence felt her cheeks burn. 'I'm so sorry—that isn't what I meant at all. At least...that is, I didn't want you to think I was the kind of girl who took umbrage if she didn't get the best of everything.'

'And what kind of a girl do you suppose I think you are?' He was leaning back in his chair, looking amused, which annoyed her, but she owed him an apology.

'Well, you don't like me—you never have, but that's my fault; I was annoyed because the first time we met you pretended to be the gardener.'

'My dear girl, I did nothing of the sort. It was hardly my fault if you chose to draw erroneous conclusions.'

It became suddenly important that he should tell her whether he liked her or not. 'Why don't you like me?' she repeated.

'And if I ask you the same question, do I get a truthful answer? I think not. I suspect that neither of us is quite ready to answer that.'

He smiled at her, and this time it wasn't even faintly mocking, but gentle and kind, so that she smiled back. After a moment she said, 'I expect you're right. It's called agreeing to differ.' In case he didn't quite understand, she explained, 'It means that we don't see eye to eye, but respect one another's opinions.'

'Armed neutrality—it sounds a splendid solution.' He lifted a finger to a hovering waiter. 'Let's drink to it.'

Champagne—on top of the sherry and the two glasses of hock. Prudence sipped cautiously. She had been brought up never to mix her drinks, and she wondered if she should refuse. But that wouldn't do at all; Haso had offered an olive branch of sorts, and she must accept it gratefully. She enjoyed the first glass so much that she accepted another.

'May you drink and drive in Holland?' she wanted to know.

'Certainly not. We'll have some more coffee presently if you're nervous at the idea of me driving while under the influence.'

He appeared as calm and casual as usual. She said, 'I'm not nervous; I don't suppose you would be so foolish.'

The restaurant was half-empty now and Prudence glanced at her watch. She gave the doctor an astonished look. 'Do you know what the time is? It's after eleven o'clock!'

He raised his eyebrows. 'My dear Prudence, you sound like the kitchenmaid on her evening out!'

She forgot about the armed neutrality. 'Well, of all the nasty things to say! You're the rudest man... I'm so sorry for your Christabel.'

She hadn't meant to say that, but the champagne, backed up by sherry and hock, had the hold of her tongue.

He smiled, not the gentle smile which had so delighted her, but a nasty curl of the lip. 'Shall we leave Christabel out of it?'

Prudence went red and took a last drink of champagne. 'I'm sorry. But your remark was beastly and I forgot that we'd agreed to differ. I've enjoyed my evening very much, thank you, and dinner was heavenly, only now I think I'd better go home.' She added, 'Before we quarrel.'

He laughed. 'Living up to your most unsuitable name?' He signalled for the bill and she said thoughtfully, 'Well, at least we've tried—to be friends, I mean.'

'Indeed, yes. But I feel that we should persevere— what is it you say? "If at first you don't succeed, try, try try again"? A remarkably sensible injunction. We might even manage to say goodbye with some semblance of regret.'

For some reason the idea didn't appeal to her. Haso annoyed her excessively, but all the same she was going to miss him. She sighed at the thought, and he watched her with a gleam in his eyes and a glimmer of a smile.

He drove back unhurriedly through the clear night, carrying on a mild conversation about nothing much which required only the minimum of answers and certainly didn't provoke her once. He got out at his aunt's house and saw her inside, at the same time wishing her goodnight in a manner which reminded her strongly of an elder brother or even a kindly uncle.

Undressing slowly, Prudence reflected that if this was armed neutrality it was going to be very dull.

She made suitable replies to her aunt's questions, rather coyly put, the following morning. Yes, she had had a delightful time, dinner had been delicious, the restaurant quite charming…

'Dear Haso is such a pleasant companion?' suggested Aunt Beatrix.

Prudence said cautiously that they had had a lot to talk about.

'Naturally. I expect he'll take you out again before we go to Guernsey.'

'What about Christabel?'

'She's in Italy, dear, visiting art galleries. She thinks that culture is very important, especially for a person of her kind…'

'What kind is she?' asked Prudence, allowing curiosity to take over.

'*Adel,* dear. Her position in life is very important to her. If—and I say if—she manages to get herself married to Haso, which I for one very much doubt, she will do her best to make him take his proper place in society.'

'But he's got a place—he's a medical man, and from what I can discover very well thought of.'

'He is also from *adel*, but we as a family have never considered that important.' It was Aunt Emma who spoke. 'Haso is the head of the family now, but he doesn't use his title, and although we have friends all over Holland, we make no push to go into social circles.'

'Well, well,' observed Prudence, 'I do live and learn, don't I?'

Haso came two days later, kissed his aunts, nodded

coolly to Prudence and observed, 'Well, everything is arranged, Aunt Emma. You have a late morning flight from Schiphol the day after tomorrow. Wim can drive you down. You'll be met at the airport and taken to your hotel. I've booked rooms for two weeks as you asked. I've arranged with the hotel to see to your return flight. I dare say Prudence can deal with that for you.'

He looked at her. 'I presume you will be coming back here? I don't think the aunts should travel on their own.'

'Pretty will be with them, and Aunt Emma's maid as well. I intend to fly back to England—I have to take a job, you know.'

'I can't see that a few days more will make much difference to that. You can fly back a couple of days later. You are, after all, in charge of them.'

Prudence had a scathing answer to that, only it wasn't uttered. She caught sight of the two elderly ladies watching her with scarcely concealed anxiety; to refuse to escort them back home would be more than unkind. She said with a serenity she didn't feel, 'Very well, I'll come back here, but I should be glad if arrangements could be made so that I could leave for England on the following day.'

He had got his own way, he could afford to be magnanimous. 'Give me a day or so's warning and I'll arrange that for you.' He got up to go. 'Give me a ring if you have any problems. My best wishes for a pleasant holiday. I've written to a colleague of mine at the hospital, his phone number is with the tickets.'

He had gone; the aunts fell to discussing what they

should take with them and Prudence sat on a window-seat, telling herself she was glad she wouldn't see him for at least two weeks, and then only briefly, before she went back home. It was a surprisingly lowering thought.

It was almost impossible to have any thoughts of her own for the next twenty-four hours. Pretty and Sieke were pleased enough to be going on holiday, but until they arrived at the hotel they had plenty to worry them. The aunts were by no means relaxed travellers, although they had journeyed widely. They changed their minds a dozen times as to what they should take with them, insisted on Prudence phoning to make sure that Haso's meticulously arranged journey was indeed without any chance of hold-ups, and drove the kitchen staff off their heads with instructions as to what should be done during their absence.

It was with relief that Prudence stowed her two elderly companions into the back of the Mercedes and then got in beside them. Pretty sat with Wim, but Sieke, being on the small side, was squashed in the back. Aunt Emma complained bitterly about the lack of space, but even she had to admit that Wim wouldn't be able to drive two cars back to Friesland. Both ladies were a little out of temper by the time they arrived at Schiphol, but since Sieke and Pretty were there to deal with the luggage and Prudence shepherded them to a quiet corner where they could drink their coffee in peace, by the time their plane was called they had recovered their good humour.

The flight was accomplished in comfort; there was no lack of attention on the part of the stewardess, who plied them with drinks, magazines and offers of cushions. When they arrived there were two cars waiting for them, the second for Pretty and Sieke and the luggage, so that the aunts could be driven in comfort the few miles to St Peter Port and the hotel.

The sun had come out after a rather gloomy morning and the road, winding between villages, was fairly empty of traffic. The hotel, when they reached it presently, looked pleasant, a Georgian mansion halfway up the outer slopes of the town, facing the harbour below and the open sea with Herm island in front and a few miles away Sark behind it. You could see Jersey on a fine day, volunteered the driver.

Haso had done his work well; they were received warmly, ushered to chairs while Prudence dealt with the desk work and then led up the wide staircase to their rooms. Haso again, thought Prudence, following behind with Sieke and Pretty, burdened with wraps and travel bags, hard on her heels, for the rooms were splendid, facing the sea, most tastefully furnished and, as far as she could see, having every comfort. Her own room, close by, although smaller, was just as comfortable. Pretty and Sieke were led away to the room they were to share on the floor above, and Prudence thoughtfully ordered a tray of tea before the aunts thought of it first.

Much refreshed, the aunts made themselves comfortable with books while Prudence made the telephone call to Haso which he had asked her to do in a manner decisive enough for her to waste no time about doing so.

His voice in her ear gave her the impression that

he wasn't pleased to hear hers. She said without pre-
amble, 'We're in the hotel and very comfortable. We
had a good flight and your aunts are delighted with
everything.'

She was surprised when he asked, 'And you,
Prudence—are you delighted?'

'Me? It all seems very nice...'

'Well, of course. So it should be—I'm not there.'

She couldn't think of an answer to that and he
didn't seem to expect one, for he said, 'Give my love
to the aunts and look after them well. Goodbye, Prudence.'

She hung up pettishly. Of course she would look
after his aunts, wasn't that why she had been invei-
gled into coming? She gave them his message, made
sure that they were content to sit while their unpacking was done, and repaired to her own room, where
she stood at the window for some minutes, staring at
the splendid view and not seeing it, as it was completely obscured by Haso's image.

She bestirred herself at length. 'This won't do,' she
admonished herself as she started to unpack. 'Anyone
would think I miss him!'

Which, of course, she did, although she wasn't going to admit that, not even to herself.

The hotel was not quite full, it was too early in the
season; they dined at a table in the big window overlooking the harbour, and here again Haso had seen to
things. A tasty variety of dishes was offered Aunt
Beatrix with due regard to her diabetes, and presented
in such a way that she could find no fault, and Aunt
Emma, who enjoyed her food, was pleased to com-

pliment the floor manager as they left the restaurant. Prudence saw them both safely to their beds, made sure that Pretty and Sieke were comfortable in their room, found a woolly jacket and took herself off for a walk before bedtime.

A few minutes' walk downhill took her to the boulevard, and she walked briskly towards the centre of the town. Castle Cornet at the end of its pier looked interesting, but it would have to wait for another day when she had more time. Now she contented herself with walking as far as the town church with a quick glimpse of the arcades and shops in the narrow high street. Very continental, she reflected, retracing her steps, but she doubted if the aunts would want to spend any time there. In the morning she would see about hiring a car so that she could drive them around the island. That was something Haso had forgotten to do, she thought crossly, climbing into bed and falling at once into a dreamless sleep.

She was wrong. After breakfast, which she ate with Pretty and Sieke while the two elderly ladies had theirs in their rooms, she was handed a key at the reception desk and was told that the car hired in her name was parked opposite the bar entrance. The clerk pointed it out to her; a neat Renault, roomy enough to take the aunts in comfort.

She took the key and went to have a look at it. There was a map on the front seat, she opened it up and studied it; the island might be small, but it was full of roads. She sat down on the low stone wall which encircled the hotel gardens the better to study it.

The man who strolled over to her was youngish, not tall but slimly built and good-looking. That his eyes were a shade too close together was not notice-able unless one studied his face very closely.

'Just arrived?' he asked her, and added, 'Hello,' and held out his hand. 'Jerome Blake. I've been here for a few days—I've been before, as a matter of fact, so perhaps I could help you to plan your trips? It's a bit confusing at first.'

Prudence shook hands. 'How kind of you. I have two elderly aunts with me and I thought perhaps a drive of an hour or so at a time. They tire easily.'

He said easily. 'Ah—you're with the Dutch lady who came yesterday? And another lady?'

She didn't notice the searching look he gave her. 'That's right. We're here for a couple of weeks.'

'Then you can't do better than divide the map into four and explore each area in turn. There's plenty to see—potteries, a candle factory, a craft centre, the famous miniature church, and of course, the shops in St Peter Port.' He smiled widely. 'Perhaps they won't be too keen on shopping, but if you need an escort you have only to say, I'd be delighted to escort you. The shops are open in the evening.'

It was nice to have someone young to talk to, but he was going rather fast. She said coolly, 'Thank you, I'll remember that, but I don't expect to have much time to myself.' He looked so downcast that she smiled at him. 'I must go, but I expect I'll see you around.'

It was pleasant to meet someone who so obviously wanted to know her better, unlike some men she knew, reflected Prudence sourly, but she wasn't sure if she liked him. She dismissed him from her thoughts and went to see how her aunts were getting on.

That day and the next few days were spent agreeably enough. She drove her companions to various parts of the island, watched candles being made, potters at work, then visited the smallest church, and now and then encountered Jerome Blake, who, without saying much, managed to convey his wish for her company. It was one evening, after they had dined following a pleasant afternoon's drive along the south of the island, that he came across the wide floor of the lounge where they were sitting before the aunts went to bed. He wished Prudence a good evening and addressed himself to Aunt Beatrix.

'I wonder if your niece would care to look around the shops?' he suggested with a smile. 'They're open until nine o'clock, and perhaps she has a wish to buy something.' He turned to Prudence. 'I'd be delighted to accompany you.' His smile was open and friendly and she stifled her vague feeling of dislike.

'I'd like that very much.' She turned to her aunts and found them smiling.

'Of course you should go, Prudence. Certainly we must take some trifle back with us—see what you can find. We shall sit here until ten o'clock, and if you are not back Pretty and Sieke will see us safely to our beds.'

'I'll fetch a jacket,' said Prudence. The prospect of shopping was delightful; Aunt Beatrix was well stabilised and Aunt Emma, although she couldn't do much, was almost her old self. She went in search of

Pretty and told her she would be back some time after ten o'clock, and very much to her surprise she found that lady agreeable.

'For you've had no fun at all so far, Miss Prudence,' said Pretty. 'Sieke and me, we've had time enough to go into the town and enjoy ourselves while you've been driving the car here, there and everywhere. You go and enjoy yourself.'

So Prudence bade her aunts goodnight and joined Jerome Blake outside the hotel entrance, prepared to do just that.

It was unfortunate that Haso should telephone that evening. It was Pretty who took the call and, undeterred by his harsh voice demanding to know where Prudence was, gave a satisfactory report of his aunts and added, 'And Miss Prudence has gone off to spend the evening with ever such a nice man—gone to the shops, they have. The first few hours she's had to herself since we got here.' She sounded accusing. 'Driving Madam and Mevrouw around all day long and playing patience with them every evening—it's not natural!'

'Tell her I'll telephone tomorrow evening,' said the doctor, and rang off.

CHAPTER FIVE

PRUDENCE, happily unaware of Haso's phone call, spent the evening looking in shop windows. Jerome Blake was a good guide. He showed her the best shops in the high street and the arcade, pointed out the covered market where she might get the chance of visiting one morning, and took her away from the high street, up a narrow, winding street lined with boutiques, antique shops and expensive jewellers. The shops were shut, but there was plenty to see. She would, she decided silently, find time to come on her own before they went back to Holland. She hadn't much money with her, but she had her Access card, and the clothes were exactly to her taste.

They stopped for coffee on the way back, and Jerome treated her with just the right amount of casual friendliness to make her uncertain of her initial wariness of him. At the hotel he saw her into the reception lobby, wished her a cheerful goodnight and went away, with the casual hope that they might have a similar outing before she left.

Perhaps she had been too hasty in her judgement of him, she thought uncertainly as she got ready for bed.

Pretty gave her Haso's message at breakfast, but only the part of it concerning his intention of telephoning that evening. She thought it a great pity that the two of them couldn't hit it off; she was sure her madam had hoped they would have an instant liking for each other, instead of which they were at daggers drawn. Pretty and Sieke, discussing it together in their mixture of English and Dutch, agreed that it was a crying shame.

Haso wasted no time in niceties when he telephoned that evening. 'You were out,' declared his voice coldly.

She snapped back at him, 'Yes, I was—for the first time since we arrived. And since you feel the need to poke your nose into my affairs, I had a pleasant evening with someone—a man—who's staying at the hotel.'

He said with infuriating calm, 'I'm not in the least interested in your life, Prudence, and I'm not at all sure why you should be so edgy. You're free to do what you like and go out with whom you please if and when my aunts are in good hands other than your own.' Which made her feel foolish. She wasn't going to say she was sorry; she gave a succinct report on both ladies and waited to hear what he had to say.

Very little and that uttered in a tone which held no apology. Prudence put down the receiver and flounced back to the aunts, waiting to play their usual nightly game of Patience.

'Was that dear Haso?' asked Aunt Emma in her rather loud, clear voice. 'How good of him to telephone!'

Prudence sat down, her colour high. 'He sends you his love,' she announced. 'He just wanted to know how you both were.'

Aunt Beatrix said in a vaguely questioning way, 'That young man—Mr Blake?—came to say if you were free would you like to go for a walk, but I told him that we had been out for a good deal of the day and you were too tired.'

Prudence put two packs of cards on the table, biting back an angry retort. The aunts were dears, but they had no business interfering with other people's lives. She had seen Jerome Blake standing by the window in the second lounge across the hall. She said quietly, 'I'm going for a walk with him—just for an hour. I'm not in the least tired, and he's a pleasant companion. I'll be back before your bedtime.'

She smiled at their surprised faces and went in search of Jerome Blake, who was to be seen still standing at the window with his back to the room, looking out to the harbour.

She said unselfconsciously, 'The aunts made a mistake—I'm not in the least tired and I'd love a short walk. Will you wait while I get a wrap?'

He was flatteringly pleased to see her; his obvious pleasure in her company was something after Haso's brisk dismissal of her. Prudence went up to her room, leaving him to mull over his edifying thoughts. A very pretty girl and no fool, but better than that, owning two aunts who, according to the receptionist's guarded answers to his carelessly put questions, were extremely well-to-do, and although she was rather vague about it, she believed one of them had a title—a Dutch title, of course. He would have to be careful with the girl, of course, she wasn't the kind to have the wool pulled over her eyes, but there was a week still. He would have to find out exactly where she lived—presumably she would return to England eventually.

They went down the hill and turned away from the town to walk along the road leading to the Aquarium. The sun had set now, but it was still light and the sea was calm. A ferry had just come in and there was a good deal of bustle in the harbour, but their road was quite quiet save for other people strolling along it. Jerome was careful to keep the talk to trivialities to start with, before cautiously slipping in a question here and there, and Prudence, still smarting under Haso's brusque tongue, answered him without much thought. He observed casually, 'You won't like London after this and wherever you are living in Holland, will you?'

And she replied carelessly, 'Oh, but I don't intend to get a job there. I've had years of it, but now I've actually left I should hate to go back permanently. Of course there's nothing for me near my home—it's a very small village in Somerset. Someone suggested that I should get a job in Holland, and I must say that where I'm staying in Friesland is delightful, only living in hospital there, or even in digs, wouldn't be the same as living in a country house with a heavenly garden.'

Jerome murmured casually and skilfully changed the conversation; he could be amusing and he was certainly good company. Back at the hotel he bade her goodnight without any mention of further walks. Lulled by his friendly casualness, Prudence had already decided that if he asked her out again she would certainly go, unaware that that was exactly what he had been hoping for.

All the same, her last thoughts before going to sleep were of Haso. They were unsettling, but she was too sleepy to go into that.

They went to Herm the next day and, the aunts being what they were, Prudence had arranged to hire a launch for their sole use. A phone call from the reception desk had ensured that they lunched at the hotel and that a taxi was booked to convey them to the launch. It was quiet on Herm, the hotel manager told them, with a handful of charming little shops, the hotel and a pub. The island was small enough to enjoy walking—half a mile across and a bare mile and a half long, and there was the famous Shell Beach... He beamed at them, not knowing the aunts well enough to realise that they never walked more than a few yards at a time. Prudence thought wistfully of an afternoon's exploring; out of the question with her elderly companions. All the same, the trip would be interesting.

The launch had been booked for eleven o'clock, and Pretty and Sieke left Prudence still at breakfast in order to get the aunts ready for that hour. It was still only nine o'clock. She drank the last of her coffee and wandered out across the courtyard and into the garden before the hotel. It was going to be a lovely day, and she perched on the side of a chair and admired the view. She didn't hear Jerome until he was beside her.

'What a heavenly morning!' she exclaimed, and

smiled up at him. 'We're going over to Herm for lunch.'

'The launches will be pretty full,' he warned her.

'Oh, I've hired a launch just for us,' she explained. 'My aunts couldn't go otherwise. Have you been there? Is the White House a good hotel? We're lunching there.'

'Excellent, yes. I've been there several times. I would have enjoyed showing you the Shell Beach; there are some delightful walks too.'

'Yes, well... I don't suppose I shall have the chance to explore, but I'm looking forward to it all the same.'

'At least you'll go in comfort.' Jerome gave her a sharp glance. 'Not many people go to the expense of hiring a launch for themselves.' He saw her faint frown and went on smoothly, 'I don't suppose it occurs to them, and it's well worth it; the queues for the returning boats can be quite long towards the end of the afternoon.' He moved a little away. 'Well, I must have breakfast, I'm going over to Catel to see some friends.'

Mentioning friends gave him a more solid background, and Prudence said at once, 'Oh, how nice for you! You must know the island very well.'

'Like the back of my hand,' he said lightly. As indeed he did, for he came most years, staying at good hotels, seeking out the well-to-do, intent on what he jokingly thought of as heiress-hunting. This time, he thought smugly, it looked as though he might have found her. Obviously the darling of her aunts, good-looking as well, and what he had gleaned so far led him to believe that she was well heeled. Her clothes were expensive, too.

He ate a hearty breakfast, well content.

Herm was delightful; the aunts, fortified by coffee at the hotel, strolled round the few shops—a boutique selling charming clothes, a small pottery selling non-tourist glass and china, and an even smaller shop selling postcards, paperbacks and all the trifles which hotel clientele might need.

They made their purchases, gave Prudence a pretty scarf she had admired and went at their own pace back to the hotel, where they lunched in comfort. Prudence had taken the precaution of warning the manager that Mrs Wesley required a diabetic meal and had suggested a suitable menu, so that, confronted by the well-planned dishes which she was unable to take exception to, Aunt Beatrix was able to bear the sight of her companions enjoying a lobster with rich mayonnaise followed by an even richer Charlotte Russe.

They consented to rest after this, sitting in comfortable chairs in the shade of the garden, but Prudence's hope of going off by herself for an hour was doused by their suggestion that she should read aloud from the newspaper they had bought with them from the hotel. A suggestion from the aunts, however graciously put, was tantamount to an order from anyone else: Prudence opened *The Times* and began on the proceedings in Parliament, constantly interrupted by Aunt Emma, discoursing on the politics of her own country.

They had tea presently and then returned to the launch, where its owner sat, smoking his pipe. He had

had a nice peaceful day with a good lunch at the pub, satisfied that he had made three times as much money as he usually did and had been able to take it easy at the same time. He handed the ladies into the boat and took them back to St Peter Port, taking care not to go at any speed, Aunt Beatrix having assured him that she was prone to seasickness.

There was a taxi waiting for them; Prudence had been instructed to ask the receptionist at the White House to phone over to Guernsey and arrange for one to meet them. Prudence had felt quite apologetic about it, but the aunts took it as a matter of course that their way should be smoothed for them. She surveyed them with affection as she accompanied them into the hotel. They had enjoyed their day, and despite their absorption in their own comfort they were quite incapable of being unkind to anyone. 'Delightful,' observed Aunt Beatrix, 'and they say it will be another splendid day tomorrow. Should we take a drive, do you think?'

At dinner that evening they discussed where they should go. 'Perhaps an afternoon outing?' suggested Prudence. 'You've had a long day, a rest tomorrow morning might be a good idea.'

They agreed. 'And perhaps you would go to the town, dear, and get that rather nice gold chain that we thought might do for dear Cordelia. I'll give you a cheque and my card, as I can't quite remember its cost.'

There had been no sign of Jerome. Prudence went to bed feeling vaguely let down, but he was having his breakfast when she went to the restaurant in the morning.

'Another lovely day,' he observed. 'Are you driving somewhere?'

'Not until this afternoon.' She helped herself to orange juice and sat down at her table. Sieke and Pretty had already breakfasted, and Jerome brought his coffee over and sat down opposite her with a friendly, 'May I?'

'I'm going into the town, I have to get something for my aunts. They're a little tired after yesterday.'

'They enjoyed themselves? And you?'

'Lovely, only I would have liked to see the whole island.'

He answered easily, 'Oh, well, I dare say you'll come again. Are you walking into town? May I go with you? I need to go to my bank.'

It would be pleasant to have company. They set out presently, after Prudence had visited the aunts and made sure that they were rested and had all they needed. Armed with an open signed cheque, she joined Jerome in the foyer.

They went up the hill this time, away from the sea, through Hauteville and then down the steps by the Town Church. It was still early and, although the streets were pleasantly filled, they weren't crowded.

'The bank can wait,' said Jerome. 'Suppose you do your shopping first.'

The jewellers was on the corner of the arcade, its windows glittering with gold and gems. Prudence went in and was instantly recognised as the young woman who had been in previously with the elderly

lady who had liked a particularly expensive gold
chain. It was produced for her now—a lovely thing
of solid gold links. Jerome had come in with her, and
she turned to him now.

'Pretty, isn't it?' she said. 'And very well made.'
She turned back to the salesman. 'I'll take it, please.
I have a cheque and my aunt's cheque card.'

She bent to write the cheque and Jerome, without
appearing to do so, saw the amount—a very substantial sum, and paid without so much as a lift of the
eyebrows. He wandered away and inspected some
samples of silverware in another case. Only a few
more days, he reflected, before they would leave, and
although Prudence liked being with him he was clever
enough to know that circumstances had thrown them
together, not her choosing. He would have to go carefully, on the other hand he had very little time...

They left the shop and he suggested coffee. 'Yes,
please,' said Prudence, 'but wouldn't you like to go
to your bank first?'

'Yes, of course, just across the street here. I won't
be a moment—just to cash a cheque.'

He went inside, went to one of the desks and sat
down, picked up the pen and scribbled on the back
of a paying-in slip, just in case she had followed him
in. But Prudence was quite uncurious—besides, it was
none of her business. She crossed the street again and
studied the clothes in a boutique until Jerome joined
her.

He took her to a small café at the far end of the
high street and then led the way back to the harbour.
He made no demur when she said she should be get-

ting back, and they walked the length of the boulevard and up the steep hill to the hotel, where he bade her a friendly goodbye. 'A very pleasant morning,' he added. 'A pity you'll be leaving in a few days. I do hope you'll let me have your address in England; it would be nice to meet again some time.'

He was clearly clever enough to keep away from her for the rest of the day, but the following morning as she strolled across the garden after breakfast he came towards her. 'Off sightseeing?' he asked. 'Have you been to the Rose Centre? It's well worth a visit, rather early in the year, but all the same most interesting; your aunts might enjoy it. It's quite easy to find...'

Prudence went to the car parked close by and got out the map and spread it on the bonnet and together they studied it. 'I'd be delighted...' began Jerome, then stopped, aware that someone was standing beside him.

'Hello, Prudence,' said Haso.

She was furious with herself for blushing. It was shock, she told herself, eyeing him warily, wishing him good morning in a faint voice. But the look he bent upon her was positively jovial. 'A splendid day,' he told her, and looked at Jerome.

'Oh, well—yes. This is Jerome Blake, he's staying here and has been kind enough to advise me about trips.' She looked at Jerome. 'This is Professor ter Brons Huizinga, from Holland,' she added unnecessarily.

The men shook hands and Haso said, still very

friendly, 'I'm going to have breakfast before I see the aunts. I left quite early.'

'How did you come?' asked Prudence politely, a little uneasy because Jerome was so silent.

'Oh, I flew myself over. I'll leave you to tell the aunts I'm here, Prudence. Were you planning an outing with Mr Blake? Do go ahead; I'll spend the morning here with the aunts. We'll meet for lunch, shall we?'

He beamed at her and then at Jerome, rather like a benevolent uncle, and she seethed silently. The nerve of it, arranging the day to suit himself! He caught her fulminating look and his eyes danced with amusement. 'Enjoy yourselves,' he advised them with what she felt to be false kindness, then he turned and strolled away in the direction of the restaurant.

Jerome, beyond an odd word here and there, had taken no part in the conversation, but now he said, 'Has he got his own plane? He seems very young to be a professor. One of these brainy chaps, earning fabulous sums helping fools like me.'

Prudence was angry, she was upset too, and her feelings were hurt, although she hadn't had time to find out just why. She said snappily, 'Oh, he's clever, but he doesn't need to earn a living…'

She could have bitten her tongue out for saying that, but somehow Haso had made her feel foolish and, even worse, careless of his aunts' welfare.

Jerome was too clever to answer her, he said soothingly, 'Well, since you're free to do as you like this morning, shall we go along to the Aquarium? It's quite interesting, and we can follow the cliff path to

Fermain Bay and have coffee there and take a bus back. Or we could take the car...?'

'No, I'd like to walk. Shall I meet you in half an hour—you might have to wait a bit.'

'I shan't mind that, Prudence.' He made his voice sound sincere and she went a little pink.

She put the map back in the car, locked it and went up to the aunts' rooms. They were delighted with her news, but she had expected them to be more surprised. Perhaps when you got old you didn't feel surprised any more. 'I dare say Haso will want to look you over,' she pointed out. 'He said he'd be up to see you when he had had some breakfast. He flew over this morning early.'

She went away to her own room to tidy herself and find a pair of sensible shoes and her shoulder-bag. Somehow the prospect of a morning in Jerome's company left her uninterested. She told herself not to be silly; it was a splendid chance to let Haso see that not everyone shared his dislike of her. She went back to Aunt Beatrix's room and found him there, sitting on the bed, eating a croissant.

He got up when she went in. 'There you are. Anything to tell me? I've seen Aunt Emma—she's splendid, and so, I imagine, is Aunt Beatrix.'

Prudence's sharp eyes had seen the croissant. 'Did that come up with your breakfast, Aunt Beatrix? You haven't eaten one?'

How awful if she had. After days of watching almost every mouthful Mrs Wesley had had, it would be just her bad luck for something to go wrong just as Haso had arrived. And why was he here, anyway?

'Don't panic,' said Haso softly. 'I took this off Aunt Emma's tray. I'm sure you've kept a watchful eye on both of them. Many thanks, Prudence.' His voice was bland. 'Now off you go and enjoy yourself with Mr—Blake.'

Prudence flounced to the door, but before she could go through it he added, 'I thought we might go out for dinner this evening, but if you want to spend an evening with—er—Mr Blake, I'm sure we shall all quite understand.'

She didn't answer, nor did she look at him, but closed the door with exaggerated care and went down to where Jerome was waiting for her.

His obvious pleasure at seeing her was balm to her ill-humour, but after a while she found herself becoming impatient at his rather fulsome compliments and the number of questions he asked about the aunts' homes and when he said with careful nonchalance, 'Your aunts—they seemed very distinguished ladies—from Dutch nobility, I dare say?' he was answered shortly.

'Yes—at least of the lesser sort. What made you ask?'

'I'm sorry, I must seem inquisitive, I don't mean to be. I meet many people on my travels and I'm deeply interested in people, especially of other countries.'

A reasonable answer, but it had grated on her ear. However, he laid himself out to be pleasant, and Prudence decided Haso's sudden appearance had made her edgy and peevish. She said suddenly, 'I'm sorry, I'm not much of a companion this morning.'

'I hope we're friends enough for that not to matter,' he told her, adding quickly, 'Have you seen Candie Gardens? They're delightful—we'll have coffee in Smith Street and go there if you like, it's only a short walk from the coffee house.'

The gardens were quite beautiful. They wandered round, stopping to examine the flowerbeds and admire the view out to sea, until Prudence said reluctantly that she had promised to be back for lunch.

Jerome took her through the old town, past the college and down Constitution Hill by the steps into Market Street, and then, since there was a little time to spare, led her through the market, between the stalls of fish and meat and vegetables, and in the flower market at the end of the building bought her a bunch of roses. She thanked him prettily, feeling a little uneasy at the proprietorial air he had suddenly adopted towards her. She had enjoyed his company, but she felt vaguely relieved that she would be saying goodbye to him in a few days. He was attentive, well mannered and most amusing, and yet there was something about him that she was uncertain about. She put the idea away from her and chatted a little too brightly to cover her uncertainty, but she found herself without words when they reached the hotel, and Jerome said with casual friendliness, 'You'll be too busy packing up tomorrow to spare time for me—would you come out to dinner this evening? There's a delightful hotel—the Bella Luce—in Moulin Huet valley. We can drive there—it's only a matter of three or four miles. I believe you went that way with your aunts to the pottery...'

'Yes, it's very pretty there.' Prudence hesitated, on the point of refusing him nicely, when she saw Haso striding towards them. There was a little smile lifting the corners of his stern mouth and his eyebrows were raised in what she felt sure was mockery of herself. She said on an impulse, 'I'd love to come, thank you very much. Where shall we meet?'

Haso was near enough to hear her. 'Why not the bar?' he enquired genially.

Jerome said stiffly, 'Prudence is dining with me this evening.'

'Splendid—there are some very good restaurants on the island, so I'm told. Prudence, the aunts are in the second lounge waiting for you. I'll collect them and see you in the bar in ten minutes or so.' Haso turned to Jerome. 'You must join us—I insist.' He bent a benevolent smile upon Jerome. 'Ten minutes suit you, too?'

He nodded and strolled away, and Prudence said, 'I'll see you presently,' and made her escape to her room, where she wasted five minutes of the ten sitting on her bed wondering about Haso's excessive benevolence. She came to the conclusion that he was making amends for his rudeness.

It seemed as though she was right. In the bar, sitting round one of the tables with the aunts and Jerome, he became the genial host. It surprised her very much when he started talking about his life in Holland. He said nothing about his work as a surgeon, but he was more than loquacious about the aunts' homes and went on at great length about his house.

'It's really a castle,' he explained, 'and full of

treasures—of course, it costs the earth to maintain, but the family have had possession of it for hundreds of years. My aunts' homes are old too, and of course, the family own a good deal of land.'

Prudence could hardly believe her ears. This boastful Haso wasn't the man she knew. She glanced at the aunts to see if they had noticed anything, but they were sitting there, nodding their agreement and sipping their tonic water, looking so placid that she wondered if she had never known the real man Haso until now. She studied his face; it was quite bland and his voice offered her no clues, and she was very relieved when they went up to the restaurant, leaving Jerome to speak to some other guests.

Over lunch the aunts debated as to how they should spend their afternoon. 'If we're going out this evening I think you should rest until tea time,' suggested Haso. 'I have to go out, perhaps Prudence will keep you company?'

'Yes, of course. I'll finish the novel I've been reading to you—we can have tea in the lounge and have a game of Patience afterwards, if you would like that.'

'We'll go out about half-past seven,' said Haso. 'What time are you going, Prudence?'

She eyed him across the table. 'Jerome suggested about eight o'clock.'

'You're not going far?' he asked casually.

'No, but one can't go far anywhere on Guernsey.'

He made a non-committal answer and asked if Pretty and Sieke were enjoying themselves.

'I imagine so,' observed Aunt Emma vaguely. 'They like their lunch in the bar and I believe they breakfast here with Prudence. I don't know about dinner...'

'They have it here,' said Prudence, 'before we do.'

The aunts elected to rest in Aunt Emma's room; there was a chaise-longue upon which Aunt Beatrix allowed Prudence to make her comfortable, while her sister lay on the bed and Prudence sat between them. She began to read, but within twenty minutes or so gentle snores allowed her to close the book and stroll out on to the balcony to sit in the sun and do nothing.

She was getting lazy, she reflected, and used to the kind of carefree life which she was never likely to enjoy. She began to think about a job; in a few days she would be back in England and would have to look for work without delay. The thought was disturbing; hospitals and nursing seemed to be in another world. Perhaps she should never have accepted Aunt Beatrix's invitation in the first place. By now she would have been safely in Scotland or somewhere similar, running a ward efficiently and perfectly content— well, almost perfectly. But if she had done so she wouldn't have met Jerome. Or Haso.

She was aroused from these unhappy thoughts by Aunt Emma requesting a glass of water, and, since she was awake and felt like a chat, Prudence returned to her chair and listened patiently and with affection while her aunt made sweeping statements about politics, the world situation and education, which was her idea of a chat. Prudence replied when necessary and allowed her thoughts to wander, but somehow they always returned to Haso.

She wore the corn-coloured silk dress that evening,

and the pearls Mrs Wesley had given her on her eight-
eenth birthday, unaware that in Jerome's eyes she presented a picture of moneyed elegance. She looked
particularly lovely, for she had met Haso on her
way—the aunts, as so often happened, were hopelessly unpunctual—and he had eyed her with one of
his mocking smiles. 'You look…' he hesitated, 'beautiful. Also well heeled.'

Prudence said a little stupidly, 'Oh, but the pearls
were a present from Aunt Beatrix, and I spend far too
much money on clothes instead of saving it.'

He looked her up and down deliberately. 'Money
well spent, my dear—although you'd look good in a
potato sack. Have a lovely evening with your Mr
Blake.'

'He isn't my Mr Blake, and you're being hateful
again!'

She swept past him, and when she saw Jerome,
gave him a dazzling smile; she might not be quite at
ease with him, but at least he didn't poke fun at her.

Jerome was no fool; he set about lulling her into a
sense of confidence in himself; he talked lightly of
nothing much as they drove to the hotel, and, when
they were there, sat her in the bar and kept the conversation to generalities. The restaurant was nicely
filled and they had a table by a window with a splendid view. The meal was delicious—cold watercress
soup, followed by *poulet à l'estragon* eaten with a
fresh mushroom salad, and strawberries and thick
Guernsey cream. Jerome had chosen a Muscadet, very
dry and light, and the good food and the wine eased
away the last of Prudence's vague feeling of disquiet.

They had their coffee at the table and then, since it was still light and a lovely evening, they strolled into the grounds of the hotel. Jerome didn't put a foot wrong—there had to be really the right moment, but that wasn't yet; he looked at the pearls—undoubtedly real—and the dress which certainly hadn't come off the peg, and bided his time. He had sensed her reluctance to spend the evening with him despite the dazzling smile, and he thought he had overcome it. Presently they got into the car and drove back to the hotel, taking the small lanes and not hurrying.

It was almost eleven o'clock when they got out of the car, and still pleasantly warm. 'I always think the view at night over the harbour is something to remember.' Jerome spoke casually, and Prudence strolled across the grass to the low stone wall overlooking the bay, hardly noticing when he joined her, for she was wondering if the aunts and Haso had enjoyed their evening together; the thought that she would have liked to have been with them even if she had quarrelled with Haso swept everything else out of her head, so that she didn't quite take in what Jerome was saying when he spoke. He sounded serious and at the same time strangely urgent.

She turned to look at him in the dim light from the hotel lamps. 'I'm sorry—I was thinking. What did you say?'

It was annoying to have to repeat everything once more. He gave a little laugh. 'Prudence, I'm in love with you—I know we haven't known each other long, but with me it was a case of love at first sight. Will you marry me? I know I haven't much to offer you.'

He had never told her what he did for a living and he wasn't going to now, because in truth he did nothing, relying on a small inheritance and his wits. 'But money isn't important—besides, I have contacts, and with your money I could set myself up.' He added rather belatedly, 'We could be very happy.'

Prudence had listened to him, astounded, unable to utter a word, so that he took her silence for delighted surprise. When she gave a small, gasping laugh he put an arm round her. 'You must have known how I felt?'

'No, I didn't. What makes you think I have money, Jerome?'

'Your aunts...my dear girl, it sticks out a mile! Personal maids, special launches, and that Professor—their nephew, isn't he?—with his own plane—besides, he made no secret of the fact, did he? And you're their niece...'

She slid from his arm. 'But I'm not—I'm no relation—they're old friends of the family. I haven't any money at all, Jerome.'

He didn't believe her. 'Perhaps not now—but you're bound to get something...'

She stood looking at him, finding it hard to believe that their conversation was actually taking place; it sounded like a third-rate novel.

She said clearly in a cool voice, 'Jerome, shall we forget all this? You've been wasting your time. I think you wanted to marry me for my money, only I haven't any. You'll have to believe that, and even if I had I wouldn't marry you if you were the last man on earth.'

She turned away, and he put out an arm and swung her round. 'You're right, you've wasted my time, but I'll give you something to remember me by...'

He pulled her close and she said icily, 'Let me go, Jerome!'

He was too angry to listen, he dragged her closer, and she lifted her hand and slapped his face—a mistake, perhaps, because he swore and tightened his hold.

'If I were you,' said Haso from the darkness of the trees behind them, 'I should let the lady go. For one thing, she is no sylphlike creature to be easily crushed, and for another I would be constrained to make you.'

Jerome loosed his hold so smartly that Prudence almost lost her balance. She hadn't been particularly scared, and now she was furiously angry—Haso had made her sound like some muscular athletic type squeezed into size twenty! She wanted very much to go somewhere quiet and very dark and have a good cry. She said loudly, 'There's no need to do anything of the sort, Professor. Mr Blake must realise that to go away as quickly as possible is the only thing to do.'

'Go indoors,' said Haso in a soft voice that demanded instant obedience.

Prudence went without a word. The lounges and hall were empty, guests had either gone to bed or were still out in the town. She wandered round and round the wide hall, carefully not looking out into the dark garden. She could have gone to her room, but that would have been cowardly. Haso thought nothing of her, he would think even less if she ran away from him. It was none of his business, anyway, she thought crossly, and when a moment later he came in through the door she said so, giving him a defiant look. Temper had given her a splendid colour and she was breathing rather fast.

Haso leaned up against a marble stand holding a pot plant. 'No, I know—the Jeromes of this world are no match against you, Prudence, but since I met the fellow I've been wanting to knock him down.'

'Whatever for?'

'It's time you grew up, dear girl. He's an adventurer, on the look-out for easy money, and he thought he had found it. Had you fallen in love with him?'

'Me? In love with him?' Her voice was an indignant squeak. 'You must be joking!' Suddenly she wasn't angry any more, only forlorn. 'But it was nice to have someone to talk to and he—seemed to like me.' She stood in front of Haso. 'Something always goes wrong when I see you.' She added like a child, 'We had a lovely dinner.'

Somehow that was the last straw. She burst into tears.

CHAPTER SIX

FOR the second time in half an hour Prudence found herself in the arms of a man, but this time she made no attempt to free herself. On the contrary, she laid her head against Haso's massive shirt front and snivelled and gulped, while his great arms held her with a comfort which was reassuringly avuncular.

She wept for a minute or two until Haso released an arm to fish out a handkerchief and mop her face. 'Now blow,' he told her, and when she had done so, 'Feel better now?' He smiled very kindly at her woebegone face. 'Now come and sit down. I'm going to fetch us a drink.'

He steered her into the lounge and sat her down, leaving her alone in the quiet room. He was back within minutes, carrying a small tray. He set a glass on the table before her and said, 'Drink up.'

'What is it?'

'Brandy.'

'I never drink brandy.'

'There's always a first time. Drink up!'

Prudence took a sip and choked a bit. She looked into her glass and mumbled, 'Did you fight?'

He laughed. 'No, we had a talk. He won't bother you again, Prudence.' He gave her a searching look. 'It will be your last day tomorrow. I think we might take the aunts on a final tour of the island, don't you?'

She nodded and took another sip of brandy, not looking at him.

'I'll see you on to the plane before I leave, but I dare say I'll be home before you. When do you want to go back to England?'

Clearly he would be glad to be rid of her. 'As soon as it can be arranged, please. Aunt Beatrix is staying on for a while, isn't she? She's quite used to her diet now and very good about taking her pills.'

'Good. Toss off that brandy and go to bed.' Haso searched her woebegone face; it was still lovely, despite a pink nose and puffy eyelids. 'It will be all right in the morning.' His voice was gentle.

She stood up and he got up, too. 'Goodnight, Prudence.'

'I—I haven't thanked you—I'm most grateful, and I'm sorry I cried…'

'Think nothing of it.' His smile was gentle, but she sensed impatience. She wished him goodnight and left him there.

She didn't sleep very well, but she went to breakfast pale but composed, hopeful that there would be few people in the restaurant. Only a handful, as it turned out, and that included Haso, sitting at her table, studying the menu. He got up as she reached him, wished her a placid good morning and beckoned to the waiter. 'Tea?' he asked her. 'I think we might have coffee in town. The aunts won't be ready much before half-past ten, and I want to buy a present for Mama—perhaps you would help me choose it?'

She was grateful to him for making it easy for her. 'Yes, I'd like tea and I'll willingly help you with the present.' She was sipping her orange juice. 'Have you anything in mind?'

'A piece of jewellery, perhaps. What are you eating?'

Prudence gave her order and buttered some toast. 'I bought a charming gold chain a few days ago—the aunts wanted it for your mother...' She stopped, while colour flooded her face. She stared down at her plate, remembering that Jerome Blake had been with her, and Haso, watching her, read her thoughts. He said quietly, 'Then it mustn't be a gold chain. She likes brooches.'

He led the talk to generalities, not appearing to notice that she hadn't much to say for herself, and when they had finished he said, 'We'll drive down, there should be somewhere to park at this time of day. Will ten minutes do for you to take a look at the aunts?'

She nodded, glad to have her morning arranged for her. The aunts were happily occupied in overseeing the packing of their clothes ready for the following day; Prudence went through the routine of checking their pulses, Aunt Emma's specially, and checked Aunt Beatrix's diet and pills, but really she wasn't needed any more. She found Haso outside the hotel, sitting on the wall which enclosed the lawn, smoking his pipe and reading *The Times*, and just for a moment she thought how nice and safe he looked. She wasn't quite sure what she meant by that; all she knew was that dislike had nothing to do with the feeling of being in a pair of safe hands.

He was a man who could find a place to park his car in without any fuss. They left it in the narrow side

street and went to the jewellers where she had bought
the gold chain. Prudence would have liked to have
lingered at the windows, but he urged her inside and
requested the saleswoman to show him some
brooches, and when he was asked if he had any pref-
erence, simply said, 'Oh, diamonds, I think,' and then
to Prudence, 'This is where I need your advice.'

Privately she considered that he was quite able to
decide for himself, none the less she bent over the
selection set before them. After a short time Haso
said, 'Well?'

She poked gently at a diamond bow, a dainty trifle
about an inch and a half across, set with diamonds in
a ribbon pattern. 'I like this, but perhaps your mother
has different tastes from mine.'

'I like it too, and I think she will. We will have it.'

The assistant went away to get a box in which to
pack it, and Prudence wandered off, not wishing to
be nosy about its price. It would be by no means
cheap, of that she was quite sure.

They had coffee and then went in search of a pipe
for Wigge and chocolates for the maids, and by then
it was time—more than time—to return to the hotel
and collect the aunts.

Haso drove them round the island and took them
to lunch at La Frégate Hotel, tucked away on the far
side of St Peter Port. Les Cotils was quiet and the
hotel was dignifiedly quiet with a restaurant overlooking the sea and delicious French food. With an
eye to Aunt Beatrix they chose *tomates suisses*, then
jellied chicken with a green salad. Strawberries and
cream rounded off their meal, although Aunt Beatrix,

denied the cream, was inclined to be petulant. She was slightly mollified when Haso lightly pointed out that she could have all the coffee she wished for.

After lunch he drove them to Cornet Castle, and after settling his aunts in chairs in a sheltered spot beneath the walls, he climbed up to the topmost viewpoint with Prudence, where they stood side beside each other, not speaking, watching the launches crossing and re-crossing to Herm and Sark.

Prudence hung over the wall to catch a glimpse of the aunts below.

'Have you been here before?' she asked.

'Several times. I've sailed over once or twice, but now I have the plane I can get here in an hour or two. I stay at La Frégate: no radio, no television, utter peace and quiet, but of course it would have been too hilly for the aunts. The de Havelet is pretty good, though.'

'We've been very comfortable, and it was pleasant for the aunts because they could sit outside in the garden and watch the harbour.'

He said abruptly, taking her by surprise, 'Blake went early this morning.'

How she hated herself for blushing, but she answered composedly enough. 'I was a bit scared of meeting him...'

She was even more surprised when he asked blandly, 'Do you suppose we are beginning to like each other a little?'

She said hesitantly, 'You've been very kind to me and I'm so grateful, really I am.'

'But it hasn't altered your opinion of me?'

'It's difficult to explain.' She turned to meet his look. 'I don't know you, do I? And whether I like you or not doesn't really matter—we're most unlikely to see each other again once I return to England, but I can have an opinion of you whether I like you or not. I think you're a kind man who takes good care of his family and his patients. I—I hope you'll be happy—you and Christabel—when you marry, living in your lovely home.'

She faltered then, because Haso was smiling his small mocking smile, his eyes hooded. 'What a pretty speech!'

Prudence turned away. 'You're impossible!' But after a few steps she stopped. 'I'm sorry, I didn't mean that, only you make me cross. I really do hope you'll be happy.'

He said gravely, 'You are a nice girl, Prudence. Why aren't you married?'

It was strange that he should annoy her so much, and within minutes it was forgotten. 'Aunt Maud is always asking me that...'

'And what do you tell her?'

She laughed a little. 'Why, that I'm waiting to be swept off my feet. I know that's silly—I'm not the right size or shape for that, but it must be marvellous to be showered with roses and diamonds and champagne. Not that it ever happens outside romantic novels.'

'No? Don't be too sure of that, Prudence. Now how about tea? Shall we go back to the hotel, or would the aunts enjoy it at one of the cafés?'

'Perhaps the hotel would be best, then Aunt Beatrix

won't be tempted to eat cakes. You're pleased with them both?'

'Yes. Aunt Beatrix tells me that she intends staying in Holland for another week or two. Pretty will stay too, of course. But she and Aunt Emma should be all right now. They're remarkably tough, you know.'

They started back the way they had come, and found the aunts quite ready to return for their tea. And after that Prudence had no more chance of talking to Haso, for although they met at dinner the talk was general and no mention was made of their journey.

There was no hitch in the morning; the aunts were shepherded into the car and, with Prudence sitting beside him, Haso drove to the airport where he saw them as far as Passport Control, bade them goodbye, gave Prudence a rather casual nod and waited until they were out of sight. Prudence, taking a last look, resisted a strong urge to rejoin him, which, considering they had parted coolly, was ridiculous. In any case, she reminded herself, he would be returning to Holland that same day.

She took Aunt Emma's arm as they went on board and settled both ladies comfortably, a lengthy task, before sitting down herself on the opposite side of the gangway.

Aunt Beatrix wriggled majestically in her seat-belt. 'How fortunate that this is a short flight,' she observed in resonant tones. 'I really don't care for flying. I shall ask Haso to drive me back to England.'

'He might be too busy,' suggested Prudence.

'I'm sure he will find time for me, my dear. A few

days in London would make a nice change for him
and give him a rest from the van Bijl girl.'

There weren't many passengers, but those there
were were listening avidly to Aunt Beatrix's observations. It was a good thing that the noise of the en-
gines drowned whatever else she had had in mind to
say. Prudence offered her a book, her special reading
glasses and the smelling salts she refused to travel
without. Aunt Emma wanted a cushion for her head
and professed herself ready for a brief nap, but first
she needed something to drink… They would be landing before the two ladies had had their needs satisfied;
Prudence thought enviously of Pretty and Sieke, who
Haso would have as passengers in his plane. She
might have gone in their place, she thought peevishly,
and they could have travelled in the plane with the
aunts. If Haso had liked her enough he would have
suggested that, she felt sure. As it was, here was another proof, if proof were needed, that he didn't like
her.

She brooded about it for a little while and then
dismissed it from her mind and concentrated on her
plans for getting a job. The moment they were back
she would ask Haso to arrange a flight for her to return to England, and if he showed a reluctance to help
her then she would do it for herself.

Wim was waiting for them at Schiphol, transferring
them and their luggage with practised ease to the car
and then, driving at exactly the speed the aunts liked,
transporting them back to Aunt Emma's house.

The household had assembled to meet them, and

Prudence was surprised to see Pretty and Sieke waiting in the hall.

'Such a lovely trip,' said Pretty to Prudence. 'You've no idea, miss—landed in the doctor's grounds and got driven back here.' She sighed. 'I'll miss it all when we go back to London.' She eyed Prudence's pretty face. 'You too, miss?'

'Well, it's all a bit different, Pretty. I'll be glad to see my aunt again, though.'

'That's what the doctor said,' Pretty told her as she slid away to help with the various bags and wraps being brought in from the car.

Prudence went to her room and surveyed the cases Wim had already taken there. There wasn't much point in unpacking; she emptied her overnight bag and went downstairs again, just in time for Sieke to tell her she was wanted on the telephone.

Haso had wasted no time. 'You wanted to go back to England as soon as possible? I have to go to London the day after tomorrow—I'll give you a lift. Be ready to leave by nine o'clock in the morning, will you? I'm taking the car.'

He didn't wait for an answer. Prudence stared at the receiver in her hand frowning fiercely. 'Well, of all the rude, arrogant men!' She replaced the receiver and the phone rang again before she could take her hand away. She picked it up, her 'Hello' icy. If he was going to apologise, he had better make it very civil. A woman's voice, speaking very strongly accented English.

'Professor ter Brons Huizinga wishes me to regret

that he could not finish his conversation; he was requested most urgently in the operating theatre.'

Prudence said 'Thank you,' and, since the voice had no more to say, hung up again. It was Haso's fault, of course; he made so light of his work that one tended to forget that he did any. Rather put out, she went off to see if the aunts needed her, and at once became immersed in the search for one of Aunt Emma's diamond ear-rings which had unaccountably disappeared, to be found presently, lodged in her hair.

There was no sign of Haso the next day, although Christabel arrived during the afternoon. The aunts were still resting, so it fell to Prudence's lot to entertain her. Not that there was much entertaining necessary; it was soon obvious to her that Christabel had come to discover exactly what Haso had done while he was in Guernsey, and since Prudence gave her only bare bones of news about their activities there, she gave up her questions presently and said sweetly, 'Haso was so glad to get home—he does miss me so much if he has to go away. It I hadn't been in Italy I would have gone with him. We do so much together, you know.' She shot Prudence a sly glance. 'It's so important really to know each other before marriage, don't you agree?'

'I dare say,' Prudence managed to sound offhand, 'although I don't see any point in waiting around once one has made up one's mind.' She added naughtily, 'Perhaps Haso hasn't made up his.'

Christabel went red. After a pregnant pause she said, 'I hear you are returning to England tomorrow.'

'Yes,' said Prudence cheerfully. 'Haso's giving me a lift—but of course he would have told you that.'

It was only too evident from Christabel's face that he had done no such thing. She said stiffly, 'Haso has been at the hospital since he got back—he is a very important man, you know. We shall see each other this evening.'

Prudence was feeling reckless. 'Why don't you come to England too?'

'Quite impossible; I have several engagements I cannot cancel.'

'You lead a busy life?' asked Prudence innocently. 'You have a job?'

The other girl gave what in anyone else would have been termed a sniff.

'Certainly not! I have no need to have one, but I have many friends and a full social life.'

Prudence nodded. 'It must be exhausting,' she observed, still very innocent. 'Of course, when you marry, you'll have to give that up, I suppose?'

'Certainly not. Haso has no need to work; he will retire…'

'Now you do surprise me, although I expect one should be prepared to sacrifice a good deal for someone one loves.'

Prudence smiled kindly at the somewhat discomfited Christabel, feeling that she had at least kept up her own end. All the same, it was a relief when Aunt Beatrix came in. She greeted Christabel with chilly politeness, sat down and asked, 'Are you stopping for tea? My sister will join me in a moment. Prudence, will you ring for Wim?'

Christabel declared that she had to get back. 'Haso will be expecting me,' she explained coyly. She made her goodbyes prettily, adding to Prudence, 'We are not likely to meet again, I think, but I am sure that if there is news of you, Mevrouw ter Brons Huizinga will tell me.'

Prudence said benignly, 'Oh, I'm positive that nothing I do will be of interest to you—not once I'm back in England.'

When Christabel had gone, Aunt Beatrix observed thoughtfully, 'You dislike each other, you and Christabel? Of course, she is jealous. She has been so sure of Haso and now she has met you she is filled with doubt.'

Prudence busied herself with the tea-things. 'She has no need to be! Haso and I don't get on at all, you know.'

Aunt Emma had her mouth open to speak when her sister said smoothly, 'Oh, well, it would be a dull world if we all liked each other. I will take a slice of that chocolate cake, my dear. Are you ready to leave in the morning? We shall miss you very much, you have been so kind and caring of our needs. You must come again…'

'I shall be working,' said Prudence cautiously.

'Then you must come and stay with me,' declared Mrs Wesley. 'We will go to the theatre and visit art galleries together.'

The talk became general, and presently Prudence wandered off into the garden. It looked delightful, and she wished she could have seen the gardens at Haso's home just once more and said goodbye to his mother.

She strolled back to the house and found that lady sitting in the drawing-room with her aunts, which delighted her so much that she hurried forward to say, 'Oh, Mevrouw ter Brons Huizinga, I'm so glad to see you—I was only just now wishing I could say goodbye.'

'You return so quickly, my dear, and there has been so little time. But I hope it is not goodbye, only *tot ziens*. I would like you to see the gardens in a month's time—they will be beautiful...'

'I'd like that too, but I really do have to get a job.'

'Yes, I understand that and I hope you will find something to your liking.' She got up. 'Well, I must go back home. Haso will be here in the morning. Such a pity that he has appointments in London and that he will have no time to visit your Aunt Maud.' She sighed. 'He works too hard.'

She kissed Prudence, embraced Beatrix and Emma and went out to the car where Wigge was waiting for her. As he opened the door Mevrouw ter Brons Huizinga turned to Prudence. 'I hear that Christabel came this afternoon. I thought she would.' She nodded her elegantly coiffed head, then got into the car and was driven away, and Prudence, watching the car disappear through the drive gates, felt regret because she wouldn't see her again.

Prudence got up early the next morning, had breakfast, had a quick breath of air in the garden and went to say goodbye to the aunts; a protracted business while they reiterated their thanks, renewed their wish to see her again as soon as possible and handed her several small packages.

'For dear Maud,' said Aunt Beatrix, 'with our love—and these are for you, Prudence. Have a safe journey—dear Haso is such a good companion.'

A remark which Prudence accepted with reservations. With a final kiss she went downstairs to the hall. It was almost nine o'clock, and she intended to start off the day well, whatever happened to the rest of it.

Haso was in the hall, sitting on the edge of the wall table, drinking coffee and talking to Pretty, but he put his cup down when he saw Prudence and went to take her parcels.

'Good morning. You look like a Christmas tree. You're ready?'

'Quite ready. Could these go in the boot?'

He nodded, dropped a kiss on Pretty's gratified cheek and led the way out to the car. Wim was there, so was Sieke, and Prudence was touched at the kindness of their goodbyes. They both called *'Tot ziens'* too as she got into the car beside Haso, and she turned and waved as he drove away from the house. Regret washed over her at leaving, but she was a sensible girl, she dismissed the nebulous thoughts that filled her head and asked briskly, 'Whereabouts do you want to drop me off? If you're going straight to London, perhaps you wouldn't mind going to Waterloo. I can pick up a train...'

'Near Tisbury, isn't it? I'll take you there.'

'Oh, well—but what about whatever you were going to do in London?'

'That's the day after tomorrow. I'll have time to kill.'

'That's kind of you, but there's no need.'

'None at all. We're catching the night ferry from Vlissingen; it will get us to Sheerness early in the morning and we should be at home by midday.'

After that he had little to say until they stopped for coffee, and then they only talked trivialities. Prudence, sustaining a tepid conversation, was glad when they drove on, for sitting silent in the car was far less awkward than facing him over a café table.

They reached the terminal with barely ten minutes to spare, so that once Haso had got their cabin tickets they drove on board. There weren't a great many cars in the vast deck. He took out their overnight bags and led the way up to the reception desk, got their keys and saw her to her cabin. 'I'll meet you by the Purser's office in ten minutes,' he told her. 'We'll have a meal before the restaurants get too busy. Do you want anything from the duty-free shop? Sherry for Aunt Maud, perhaps?'

He wandered away, and Prudence took a few things out of her overnight bag, did her face, combed her hair and went back to the Purser's office. Haso was there, standing at one of the windows watching Vlissingen slide away into the deepening dusk. He said as she joined him, 'You have been this way before? I prefer the hovercraft, but driving to Calais takes up too much time. Flying is the best way, of course, but I need the car...'

'Because of me? I do hope not?' She was feeling suddenly guilty.

'No. I am going to Birmingham before I come back. Shall we go in?'

The food was good, and Haso, whatever his secret feelings about her might be, was an excellent host. Prudence, quite forgetting that they didn't like each other, readily consented to stroll round the deck before she went to her cabin, indeed she so far forgot herself as to tell Haso that Christabel had been to see her.

They were standing at the rail watching the distant lights on the horizon. Haso didn't say anything for a few moments. 'To wish you goodbye?' he asked casually.

'Well, yes,' explained Prudence chattily; she was finding it so much easier to talk to him in the semi-dark and fortified by the excellent wine they had had with dinner. 'And to warn me off.'

Haso said softly, 'Oh, really—why was that?'

His voice was so gentle that she went on happily, 'Oh, she had the ridiculous idea that I was taking up too much of your interest. So silly!'

'Indeed, yes.' His voice was silky. 'And even sillier of you to imagine such a thing happening.'

With horrid clarity she recalled what she had said. She said waspishly, 'My imagination doesn't stretch so far. The mind boggles...'

She couldn't see his face, but his laughter sounded mocking. 'I think we had better say goodnight, Prudence, but before you go, do tell me one thing. If you had been taking up too much of my interest, would you have liked that?'

'That's a hypothetical question and doesn't need an answer. Goodnight.'

She turned to go, but he caught her by the shoulders and turned her round to face him. 'This won't need a answer either,' he said, and kissed her on her surprised mouth.

He had done it to annoy her, she assured herself as she got into her bunk, quite prepared to lie awake and get into a rage just thinking about it, but she had to admit that she had enjoyed it; she was still thinking about it when she fell asleep...

They met in the restaurant for breakfast, half an hour before the ferry was due to dock, and if Prudence had expected to feel awkward she had no need; Haso wished her a cheerful good morning, advised her to eat up without waste of time and applied himself to bacon and eggs. And, true enough, there was only just time to finish their meal before they were required to go down to the car deck and disembark, so that conversation was unnecessary and time-consuming. The business of going through Customs and Passport Control was quickly done; within fifteen minutes they were driving through the uninspiring town of Sheerness and then the flat, dull fields beyond, until after some time the Kent countryside presented its pretty face. But that was lost again as they flashed up the motorway, circumvented London to the south and joined the M3 to take, after some time, the A303. The Daimler made light of the distance and Haso drove fast in a calm, almost lazy fashion. Prudence, busy with her thoughts, had long since given up attempts to hold a conversation; it seemed to her that they were turning off on to the narrow country road to Tisbury in no time at all. She should have felt pleasure at that, but she was conscious of disappointment that the

drive had seemed so short and that they had had so
little to say to each other and what they had said had
been hardly friendly. She remembered his kiss and
blushed.

'Why are you blushing?' asked Haso hatefully.

'I'm not. You need to turn off here and go through
Hatch…'

'Yes, I know. I looked it up on the map.'

She held her tongue with difficulty; after all, he had
driven her all the way to her home. He could just as
easily have left her at Waterloo station.

The village, when they reached it, looked charming. Old Mrs Giles, stomping along the road to the
post office, saw them, recognised Prudence and
stopped to wave, and, as they passed the pub, Mr
Grubb the landlord was at the bar door taking a breath
of air. He waved, too. It was lovely to be home,
thought Prudence, refusing to admit to herself that the
pleasure was tinged with regret.

Aunt Maud was at the open door as Haso stopped
the car, and she trotted over to put her head through
the window. 'Darling, how lovely to see you again!'
She beamed at Prudence, planted a kiss on her cheek
and turned her attention to Haso.

She eyed the vast man sitting quietly, smiling a
little, and said in tones of deep satisfaction, 'So you're
Haso. How very nice!' She put out a hand and had it
engulfed in one of his. 'Come in—lunch is just about
ready. You're staying the night, of course—your
room is ready for you.' If she heard Prudence's quick,
indrawn breath, she made no sign.

'Thank you, Miss Rendell. I should like to stay until tomorrow morning. Where can I put the car?'

Prudence had got out and was standing uncertainly while her aunt directed Haso round the side of the house. 'There's a barn there—Prudence's Fiat is in it, but there's plenty of room.'

He got into the car again and drove away, and Aunt Maud put an arm around Prudence. 'What a very nice young man,' she commented, 'and how kind of him to bring you back.'

'He had to come to London anyway,' said Prudence, so sharply that her aunt looked at her.

'Yes—well, dear, it was thoughtful of him, just the same. Come indoors, I'll put the lunch on the table while you tidy yourself. I've put Haso in the room overlooking the garden at the back.'

Watching the Daimler disappear down the lane the next morning, Prudence told herself she was glad to see the last of Haso; he had been charming to Aunt Maud, patiently related all the news of his aunts, passed on the kind messages from his mother and presented her with two bottles of excellent sherry. Moreover, when she had suggested that if he should come to England again, he might like to visit her, he agreed to do so with flattering readiness. But his manner towards herself left much to be desired, she considered; he had been casual and at the same time quite sickeningly polite. His goodbyes had been brief with no mention of their meeting again.

Prudence went back into the house and began to clear the breakfast things ready for Winnie, the elderly woman who came each day to 'do' for Aunt

Maud. Aunt Maud, sitting by the window looking through her post, looked up as she went in. 'The house seems empty now Haso has gone. I like him.' And, since Prudence didn't give more than a mumble in reply, 'You didn't find a man to sweep you off your feet while you were in Holland, dear?' she asked placidly.

Prudence thumped a tray-load of china down by the sink. 'No—no roses or champagne or jewels, and no serenades.' She sighed. 'Perhaps I'd better take up with Walter again.'

Aunt Maud said with ill-concealed satisfaction, 'He's found another girl, dear. Remember Marcia Greenaway—old Mrs Vine's great-niece?'

'She has glasses and wears the most frightful clothes…'

'Yes, dear. She also has money.'

Prudence sat down on the kitchen table and swung her very nice legs.

'Oh, well, I'll have to carve a career for myself, won't I?'

'That reminds me—there was a letter for you. It came yesterday, so I didn't send it on—somewhere in Scotland.'

A post she had applied for and forgotten because no one had replied. Now it seemed they were only too anxious to have her. Aberdeen seemed a long way away, but the job was a good one—Sister in charge of the women's surgical floor. She remembered how disappointed she had been when she had heard nothing after she had applied for it, and now she had the chance of getting it she felt no interest in it at all.

Her visit to Holland had unsettled her. If she had refused Mrs Wesley's invitation she wouldn't have felt so unsettled—she wouldn't have met Haso either. It was surprising to her that she thought of him so much, since they had never become friends. She sighed so long and loudly that her aunt, sitting close by at her writing-desk, turned to give her a searching glance. Quite obviously Mrs Wesley's plans concerning Prudence and Haso hadn't been successful. Perhaps, thought Aunt Maud, something could be done about that, given the opportunity. She sent up a fervent prayer, rather muddled, but to that effect, and, being a lady with a strong belief in the powers of the Almighty, nodded with a feeling of satisfaction when the phone rang, and it was Haso's voice at the other end.

She listened to what he had to say. He had had a phone call from Aunt Beatrix begging him to get Prudence to go to the flat. She had decided to stay a few more weeks with her sister, and she was concerned that the flat might be neglected. If Prudence would be so kind as to contact the cleaning lady and see that the place was aired and dusted...

Aunt Maud passed on this news with a pleased smile, but Prudence frowned. 'Why didn't she telephone me instead of Haso?'

'I really don't know, my dear. He kindly offers to come for you and drive you up to the flat—he'll be in London for a few more days. He wants to know at once so that he can reassure Aunt Beatrix.'

'I'm going to accept that job in Aberdeen,' said Prudence, a remark which appeared to have no bearing on the matter in hand, but which Aunt Maud understood very well.

'Yes, dear, but you could answer the letter when you get back—I dare say that whatever Aunt Beatrix has in mind can be dealt with in a day or two at the very most.'

Reasonable enough. 'All right, I'll go, then. When?'

Aunt Maud picked up the receiver. 'This evening, dear, about six o'clock.'

There was one thing Prudence had learned about Haso, if he said six o'clock he meant just that; she was ready and waiting with her overnight bag when he drew up silently before the front door. They were away within ten minutes, his regretful refusal to stop for coffee mitigated by the kiss he planted on Aunt Maud's cheek. 'I'll drop Prudence off the day after tomorrow on my way to Birmingham.' He waved and drove off without further comment.

'If you're going to Birmingham,' declared Prudence, 'you'll be miles out of your way. I'll come back by train.'

'I shall bring you back, so don't let's argue about it, my girl.'

'I'm not your girl!' snapped Prudence, and, following a train of thought asked, 'How's Christabel?'

'As beautiful as ever.' He added blandly, 'We should be in town soon after eight o'clock. I'll see you into the flat and come back in half an hour—I've booked a table for dinner at the Connaught.'

'I'm not wearing the right clothes—besides, I like

to be invited, not told.' Here he was annoying her already, and they hadn't been ten minutes on the way.

He slowed to give her a good look. 'Just right for the Grill Room.' He held her look for a moment and she went pink. She had indeed spent some time and thought as to what to wear; the coffee-coloured crêpe-de-Chine outfit she had decided upon was charming, just right for a summer evening in town. She glanced with deep satisfaction at her shoes—Raynes and a wicked extravagance. Tomorrow, she reflected, she would find time to do a little shopping. She had brought only a cotton skirt and top with her, not suitable for shopping in town—or going out to lunch with Haso? said a little voice at the back of her head. Prudence dismissed the thought with a frown; dinner would be bad enough.

They made good time, and Haso saw her into the flat before driving off with the reminder that he would be back within half an hour. The flat looked pristine; well dusted and polished, and someone had left milk, bread, and eggs in the fridge. She supposed Aunt Beatrix had forgotten the arrangements she had made with the cleaning lady. Prudence put her things in the bedroom and went to the telephone. Mrs Briggs was at home and said that yes, of course she would come in the morning, and was there anything special?

Prudence explained, and arranged with Mrs Briggs to have a chat in the morning—before ten o'clock, she had added, with a thought to her shopping.

She had time to do her face and hair before Haso returned. She was hungry by now, and since she was to be given a good dinner she promised herself that she would do nothing to annoy him. She greeted him, therefore, with a sweet smile, offered him a drink, which he refused, and accompanied him out to the car, fortunately unaware of his secret amusement.

CHAPTER SEVEN

PRUDENCE had to admit that the splendid dinner which Haso gave her was well worth her efforts to be a perfect companion. Tarte Valentoise, hot from the oven, the Gruyère cheese, blending just so with the tarragon mustard, made an excellent hors d'oeuvre, pâté de saumon, served with shrimp sauce, followed by fillets of lamb accompanied by a fresh tomato puree and tiny potatoes, and all washed down by Chablis Grand Cru.

It seemed a pity not to sample the dessert Haso recommended. Soufflé aux marrons was, she had to admit, out of this world. Haso, contending himself with the cheeseboard, agreed that he had noticed that most women liked it, a remark which somehow rather spoilt her enjoyment of it.

Still, she was determined to maintain her role of agreeable companion; she listened attentively to all that he had to say, made only the most innocuous remarks if asked to give her opinion and in general behaved so unlike her usual self that the gleam of amusement in Haso's eyes became very pronounced. And when he took her back to the flat and she paused at the entrance to thank him for her delightful evening he listened to her little speech with a faint smile.

'Delightful, but surely hard work for you, Prudence, biting back the tart remarks I've come to expect from you and drinking in every word I uttered like a teenager at a pop concert. I dare say if I'd switched over to Latin it would have been all the same to you.'

She glared at him. 'You're beastly; quite the nastiest man I've ever met! I hope I never have to see you again!' Her voice, despite her best efforts, had become regrettably shrill.

'In that case, let us say goodbye, by all means.' He bent quickly and kissed her hard, turned on his heel and left her standing alone in the empty hall. She stood looking at the closed door for a few moments, then went up to Mrs Wesley's flat, where she sat down on one of the opulent sofas and had a good cry. Because she was so very angry, she told herself, and how dared he kiss her like that? She stopped being angry for a minute or two while she pursued the interesting thought that Christabel wouldn't have liked it at all—a chaste peck on the cheek was probably all Haso was allowed. 'And served him right,' said Prudence loudly, and fell to wondering why he had kissed her.

It wasn't until the next morning, sitting waiting for Mrs Briggs, that she realised she would have to find her own way back to Aunt Maud's the next day. It really had been a final goodbye last night, although Haso might come round to apologise. Unlikely, she decided as she went to admit Mrs Briggs.

Over coffee, sitting at the kitchen table, they discussed the members of Mrs Briggs' family at length, agreeing that the windows should be cleaned and the sweep booked before Mrs Wesley returned. Prudence

made sure that Mrs Briggs was receiving her wages
weekly from her aunt's solicitor and that she would
continue to go to the flat twice a week, then she bade
the lady goodbye before locking the door after her
and embarking on a morning's shopping. It was surprising how quickly the paucity of her wardrobe was
borne in upon her once she entered Harrods' doors,
and as usual, she spent rather more than she could
afford, reassuring herself with the fact that she would
be working again in the near future. She bore her
parcels back to the flat after a sketchy lunch, then
made tea and tried everything on. Repacking the
things neatly, she remembered that she would have to
carry them all as well as her overnight bag, although
she would get a taxi to Waterloo and another one at
Tisbury, both of which would make further inroads
into her depleted purse. She wandered into the kitchen
and examined the contents of the fridge; unlike the
previous evening, she would have to cook her own
meal.

She was doing a final check of the flat before she
left the next morning when the doorbell rang. There
was a young man on the doormat with an envelope
in his hand. He thrust it at her and said awkwardly,
'My name's Ted Morris—in the Professor's team,
you know. He asked me to give you this.'

He had an ingenuous face and a thatch of red hair,
and she liked the look of him. 'I'm just leaving, but
come in while I read it, will you?'

She wondered why Haso had written to her, and
opened the envelope a little impatiently. If it was an
apology, he was wasting his time...

The note inside was brief and businesslike, informing her that the bearer would drive her back to Aunt Maud's house, adding unforgivably, that it was hoped she would be civil to the boy and not make difficulties.

Prudence swallowed powerful rage. 'You know Professor ter Brons Huizinga?'

'Well, as I told you, I'm in his team—I'm only a houseman.' He beamed at her. 'But I live in Wiltshire and it's my weekend off...if you don't mind?'

'How very nice of you. I was dreading the train journey. You're sure it's not taking you too much out of your way?'

Her smile made him her slave. 'Good lord, no—only a mile or so, it'll be nice to have your company. I'd do anything for the Professor—he's a splendid man; we don't see nearly enough of him.'

'What a shame,' observed Prudence warmly and mendaciously. 'I'm all ready to leave—unless you'd like a cup of coffee?'

'I'd rather get on, if you don't mind—I'll just about get home for lunch if we go now.'

He picked up Prudence's bag and she locked the door behind them. 'Where do you live in Wiltshire?' she asked.

'Just outside Warminster.'

In the car he confided that his free weekend was a surprise. 'I'm not due for another couple of weeks, but the Professor said he'd have to come back in three weeks, and he'd like me there.' Out of the corner of her eye she saw him swell with pride. He could be right, of course, but be that as it may, she thought she detected Haso's manipulating hand in the turning of events to suit himself. And anyway, she reflected pettishly, he had taken her wish never to see him again seriously. The thought gave her singularly little satisfaction.

Ted drove well, and it was still early in the day. They made good time, stopped for coffee at Fleet and sped on down the motorway to the A303, turning off to go through the charming village of Hindon and so to Tisbury and presently to Aunt Maud's house, and in that time Prudence had heard a great deal about Haso. It seemed he specialised in abdominal surgery and was a very respected surgeon, already with some international fame. And a splendid teacher, concluded Ted enthusiastically. Prudence, murmuring suitably at intervals, came to the conclusion that she hadn't known the real Haso at all. Not that that mattered, she reminded herself. She had turned the page on him and his rudeness.

Ted refused more coffee, declaring that his mother would be expecting him. He bade Aunt Maud goodbye, shook hands with Prudence and hoped to see her again, then took himself off, leaving Prudence to explain why Haso hadn't brought her back.

'I think he must have been busy,' she said carefully, 'but it was awfully kind of him to get Ted to drive me down.'

'Perhaps he'll find time to come and see us before he returns to Holland.'

'Most unlikely,' declared Prudence, so sharply that her aunt gave her a thoughtful look.

It was very nice to be back home. Prudence un-

packed her overnight bag and spent the rest of the
day tidying away the clothes she had had no time to
see to before she had gone to London. That very evening she sat down and wrote to the hospital in Aberdeen, if she was still wanted she would have to set
about getting references and even go for an interview
if that was required. It was rather a long way away,
and suppose she didn't like it when she was given the
job? She reminded herself with some scorn that it
would be a challenge and it was about time that she
started doing an honest day's work again. That night,
just before she slept, she found herself recalling
Haso's home with something very like homesickness.
It took quite an effort to concentrate on the new job
in Aberdeen.

The next day, with the letter posted, she felt better,
now she had something definite to look forward to.
With commendable zeal she turned out her wardrobe
and drawers, washed and ironed and mended, helped
around the house, shopped for her aunt and drove her
on several visits to friends. Most of Aunt Maud's
friends were elderly, as was to be expected, and Prudence, sitting in a variety of drawing-rooms, patiently
answered kindly questions about her work and thinly
veiled ones as to when she was going to marry and
whom. These were usually followed by arch references to Walter, who, it seemed, to her surprise,
hadn't told anyone that he and she were no longer to
be married. She was careful to answer politely, for
the questions were meant well and she had known
most of the questioners all her life, but their questions
set up a train of thought which she was hard put to

dispel. She was, after all, twenty-five, half-way to thirty—suppose she never met a man she wanted to marry?

She had an answer to that a few days later. On the day that she had received a letter from Aberdeen offering her the post she had applied for. She had been down to the village to Mrs Legg's to buy some stamps and a few odds and ends for Aunt Maud and happily had a gossip, although the gossip was mostly on Mrs Legg's part; she thrived on it. Prudence went in through the side door, down the passage to the kitchen, put her purchases on the kitchen table and crossed the hall to the sitting-room. Aunt Maud had gone to the Manor to Mrs Vine, to visit her as she had taken to bed with arthritis, and Ellen and the daily woman were upstairs having what they called their weekly turn-out.

It was a fine morning, the doors to the garden were open and the room was cool, smelling faintly of furniture polish and the pot-pourri which Aunt Maud made for herself each year. There was also somebody in it—Haso! Standing with his back to the room, looking out on to the garden.

He turned round as Prudence went in and stood looking at her, saying nothing, and she stared back for what seemed aeons of time—in fact a mere few seconds, but time enough for her to discover something. It hit her with all the force of a shower of cold water and the shock just left her without breath. Here was the man she wanted to marry, and why had it taken her so long to discover it? Her eyes searched his face, calm and expressionless but with lines of fatigue etched deep. Her instincts was to rush to him and fling herself into his arms, but common sense held her back, and a good thing too.

'I am here on my mother's behalf.' His voice was chillingly impersonal. 'She's very ill—a totally unexpected appendix followed by peritonitis. She's in hospital, but wishes to return home. Above all, she wishes for you to nurse her.'

Prudence took a few steps towards him and then stopped. 'Oh, Haso, I'm awfully sorry; she's such a dear...but why me?' She added a little wildly, 'Anyway, I can't—I've just accepted a post in Scotland—they wrote today.'

'Which hospital?'

'The Royal General in Aberdeen.'

She watched him cross the room to the telephone and pick up the receiver. She listened unbelievingly as he dialled a number, then asked, 'The Royal General? Put me through to the Principal Nursing Officer, please.' And then, 'It's Professor ter Brons Huizinga here—Miss Thursby? I've a favour to ask of you. I believe that you have accepted a Miss Prudence Makepeace for a Sister's post. Can it be cancelled?' There was a pause while he listened. 'Urgent family reasons. My mother is seriously ill and has set her heart on being nursed by Miss Makepeace. Yes—a matter of a fifty-fifty chance—peritonitis; I'm very worried indeed.'

Prudence opened her mouth several times to interrupt. She had just formulated a suitably quelling remark when he went on, 'You will? My everlasting thanks. I believe I have a consultation at your hospital in about a month's time—I shall express my thanks to you then.'

He put down the receiver. 'That's settled. How long will it take you to pack?'

She gaped at him. 'What do you mean?' She loved him, of that she was quite sure now, she would go through fire and water for him, but she would not be bullied. 'Pack?'

'Don't waste time, Prudence. I'm not asking you to do me a favour, I'm asking for my mother. I'm only too well aware of your opinion of me, but for my mother I am prepared to go to any lengths. She's very ill and she asks for you. I've cancelled your appointment at the Royal General and I'm taking you back to Holland with me. I'm asking you to come— as a nurse, Prudence. My mother likes you, I believe you may be able to give her the help she needs to recover.'

His voice was still cold and expressionless; it must have cost him something to have sought her out. She longed to go to him and put her arms around him and tell him that she loved him—something quite impossible. Instead she said quietly, 'Very well, I'll come. May I have half an hour to pack and phone Aunt Maud? She's over at the Manor.'

'Shall I drive over and bring her back?'

She was already at the door. 'That would help. How long should I be gone for?'

Haso said bleakly, 'That rather depends, doesn't it?' He had followed her to the door. 'We shall know within a few days, but shall we say two to three weeks? She is most unhappy in the hospital, I believe she may do better once she's home.'

They went their separate ways, and presently, as Prudence was packing, Aunt Maud joined her. 'Darling, how fortunate that Haso reached you before you'd gone to that job! Poor Cordelia—such a dear woman, and he is so devoted. Ellen is getting a quick meal—sandwiches and coffee, for you both. I believe he plans to fly back this afternoon. He flew over and hired a car to get here.'

Prudence was still trying to put first things first. Never mind that she fallen in love, she had to pack sensibly, remember her passport and her money, answer Aunt Maud coherently and remember to treat Haso with a cool sympathy and be willing to do exactly what he wanted. Afterwards, in the unforeseeable future, she would have time to sort out her own problems. Her mind shied away from them and she concentrated on listening to Aunt Maud's gentle voice. 'One case, dear? I don't suppose you'll wear aprons or something while you're nursing Cordelia.'

'Well, Haso will have to get them for me; I haven't any. Aunt Maud, I'm so sorry to dash off like this, but really I had no choice...'

'Of course not, dear. What's to happen to your job in Aberdeen?'

'Haso cancelled it—without telling me first.'

'His mother must really be very ill,' observed Aunt Maud.

Prudence slammed the case shut. 'And Haso is very ruthless. What about me and my future?'

Aunt Maud studied her neatly shod feet. 'Well, we'll have to see, won't we, dear?'

Haso was standing at the sitting-room windows, staring out at the garden. His 'There your are,' Prudence considered totally undeserved; she had been exactly twenty-five minutes, but because her heart ached for the weariness in his face, she said nothing, only went to the tray on the side-table and poured their coffee.

'You'd better eat something,' she told him briskly, 'then we shan't need to stop on the way.'

He smiled at that. 'I hadn't intended to do so, but you're quite right.'

Their brief meal over, they went out to the car, an elderly Ford, bade Aunt Maud goodbye, and drove off. And if we get to Heathrow under four hours in this old crock, I'll eat my hat! thought Prudence.

However, they weren't going to Heathrow. She discovered quickly enough that he was heading for Shaftesbury, and then remembered that he flew his own plane. There was a small airfield to the south of the town; he would have landed there. She was right; he skirted the town when they reached it and took the Blandford road, to turn off after a mile or so, taking the narrow road along the top of the hill until they reached the airfield.

All that while he hadn't spoken. Now he got out first, opened the door for her and got her case and said, 'Wait here, will you?'

The car was handed back and he picked up her case. 'The plane is over there.' He nodded to a corner of the field. 'If you'll get in, I'll get clearance.'

He was gone for twenty minutes or so, which gave her time to sort out the chaotic thoughts seething in her head. They were almost swamped by the one overriding all the others: that she loved him and as far as she could see there was nothing to be done about it. He didn't like her, and what was more he was on the point of marrying the awful Christabel; worse than that, she had expressed a wish never to see him again, and if he hadn't needed her because of his mother's illness that would have been the case. She felt the beginnings of a headache just thinking about it. Better not to think.

Presently Haso returned, got into the plane, asked her if she was all right in the same expressionless voice, saw to her seat-belt and started the engine. Suppose she had said that she wasn't all right, Prudence wondered idly, would he have allowed her to get out and go back to Aunt Maud's? She thought not.

When they were airborne she ventured a glance at his profile. It was stern and gave away nothing of his feelings. She gazed lovingly at it and then looked away as he turned his head. 'It will save time if I tell you about my mother. It should take us about three hours to reach Kollumwoude. You will get my mother's room ready for her—everything we might need will be there. I shall go straight to Leeuwarden, and if it's possible bring her back by ambulance. Now, the case history...'

The onset had been sudden, although it seemed that his mother had had a dull, niggling pain for some weeks and had said nothing about it. Haso had been in Amsterdam, operating, when he had had a message from the faithful Wigge, and by the time he had driven himself back home his mother was in great pain and Wigge had most sensibly sent for a colleague of Haso's, who had diagnosed appendicitis and arranged for his mother to be taken at once to Leeuwarden Hospital. But before they could operate the appendix had burst and she had developed peritonitis. 'She had surgery, antibiotics and drainage,' went on Haso in a voice rigid with control. 'She has been very brave but she is exhausted. You have to give her the heart and strength to recover, Prudence.'

Prudence thought of Mevrouw ter Brons Huizinga, so happy in her garden, so kind, and the least deserving of such a catastrophe.

'I'll get her well again,' she promised.

'Thank you! Now, this we will do for her treatment...' Haso detailed it calmly, just as though he had been on a ward round discussing any one of his patients. Prudence listened quietly, interrupting only when she wasn't quite sure about something, and by the time he had made everything clear they were nearing Leeuwarden airfield. Haso began his descent. 'I told Wigge to leave the car here. We'll go straight home.'

He taxied into a corner of the airfield, helped her out of the plane, fetched her case and started towards the airport. It was quite small and not busy; within fifteen minutes they were free to leave and go to the car park. The Daimler was there; Prudence would have been surprised if it hadn't been, knowing Haso. She got in beside him without a word and sat silently

going over in her mind all the things she would need
to do when they arrived.

Wigge was at the door when they arrived. He ushered her in with a welcoming smile and said something to Haso.

'My mother is holding her own. I doubt if she'll
be fit to move until tomorrow. I'm going to the hospital now. You will stay here, Prudence, and see that
everything is ready for her. Wigge will look after
you.'

Upon which somewhat high-handed remark he
went back to the car and drove swiftly away. Prudence stood in the hall, looking at the door through
which he had gone, wanting to comfort him, to dispel
the stony calm of his face.

Wigge patted her on the arm and gave her a
comforting smile, picked up her bag and led the way
upstairs. There were several doors opening on to the
gallery and corridors on either side, one leading to
another small staircase, the other to the wing to one
side of the house. Wigge opened the door to one side
of the staircase and ushered her inside, put down the
case and beckoned her to go through a door on the
opposite side of the room. The bathroom they passed
through had everything that a woman could wish for,
but Prudence was given no time to look around it.
Another door led to a large room which had been
cleared of all but the most essential furniture. There
was a hospital bed against one wall, a small desk at
the window, two small easy chairs ranged against one
wall, a drip stand, a small trolley and a plain table
with a cloth. Prudence reflected that once her patient

was installed a few flowers wouldn't come amiss, and
a prettily shaded lamp or so would help remove the
severe hospital aspect. But Wigge was still walking
ahead of her, to open another door—another bathroom, well stocked with everything she would need
for Mevrouw ter Brons Huizinga. She made her approval felt and went back to her room.

'*Koffie?*' Wigge beamed at her and, when she nodded, said, '*In Eetkamer?*' And at her second nod he
made his stately way downstairs.

The room was charming and held every comfort,
its cream walls a splendid background for the peach
and grey brocade of the curtains and quilted bed-
spread. Prudence's feet sank into the cream carpeting
as she inspected the mahogany bed, the tallboy, the
table and triple mirror between the two long windows.
There were even one or two English novels on one
of the bedside tables. And flowers—little bowls beautifully arranged. Someone, she had no idea who, had
taken care to see that she should feel welcome.

She would have liked tea, but the delicious coffee
was welcome, accompanied by small sweet biscuits.
She felt hollow inside and hoped there would be a
more substantial meal later. She was polishing off the
last of the biscuits when the telephone rang and
Wigge came, soft-footed, to answer it.

It was Haso. 'My mother is holding her own very
well; she will be brought back home tomorrow afternoon—be ready for her then. You have all you want?
Do ask Wigge for anything you need—his English is
sparse, but he understands simple words. Be kind
enough to ring Aunt Emma and tell her that my

mother will be home tomorrow, but may see no visitors.' There was a short silence. 'Goodbye for the moment, Prudence.'

She hadn't had a chance to say a word. She hung up and went to unpack and hang up her few clothes, and found that someone had laid several white overalls on the bed. What was more, they fitted her.

Downstairs again, she telephoned Aunt Emma, a lengthy business, as Aunt Beatrix had to have her say as well; she passed on Haso's message, listened patiently to the two ladies' agitated replies, interlarded as they were with their own symptoms and uneasy anxiety, spent several minutes reassuring them as to their state of health, and rang off, promising to let them know any further news.

It was heartening to find Wigge at her elbow with a glass of sherry on a tray, and to make out, from his splintered English, that dinner would be served within a very short time.

Prudence drank her sherry, remembered that Aunt Maud had to be rung and had a brief conversation with her, and, bidden by Wigge, crossed the hall to the dining-room. It had been difficult to examine it thoroughly when she had lunched there with Mevrouw ter Brons Huizinga and Sebeltsje. Now she had the leisure to do so as she sampled the vichyssoise soup, the poulet chasseur with its accompanying dish of tiny young vegetables, followed by crème soufflé à l'orange, washed down by a white wine served by Wigge. It was a large room with an ornamental plaster ceiling, panelled walls, and furnished with a vast sideboard with a good deal of marquetry, an oblong table of some size with chairs in the Chippendale style, and a long case clock also covered in marquetry, and all of them in mahogany. There were a great many paintings on the walls, but those she decided she would examine at close quarters at some later date. It was a beautiful room, cleverly lighted with wall sconces and a delicate chandelier, and the velvet holly-red curtains gave it warmth. She drank her coffee at the table, wished Wigge goodnight and went up to her room, to lie in a hot bath, extravagantly laced with bath essence, wondering what the next day would hold for her.

It held a great deal—the morning, spent in a leisurely inspection of the garden, the answering of various telephone calls from members of the family, coffee taken on the veranda, gave her no indication of the rest of the day's activities. After a delicious lunch she had gone to her patient's room, made sure that everything was in readiness for her return and then changed into one of the overalls. There had been no messages, so presumably Mevrouw ter Brons Huizinga was considered well enough to return to her own home. Prudence went over the essential details of her illness, given so succinctly by Haso, and then sat down to wait. It was another lovely day. She settled herself by the window and looked out on to the gardens and thought about Haso.

Haso arrived first, bade her an impersonal good day, asked her if she had everything she needed, went away to talk to Wigge and the cook, and was back in the hall where Prudence was waiting. 'Better if you are already in her room,' he suggested, so she went obediently back upstairs.

His calm, cool manner towards her was to set the pattern of their relationship, she supposed, and indeed it would be the best, for they would have to meet and talk in a professional capacity for the next few weeks. Somehow, she would have to learn to hide her own feelings and present a similar manner towards him.

The ambulance arrived, and Mevrouw ter Brons Huizinga was borne upstairs and laid gently in her bed, with Haso standing in the background, not interfering, but letting Prudence oversee this delicate operation and then make her patient comfortable. She was appalled at the wan features, the sunken eyes and weary lines on Mevrouw ter Brons Huizinga's face. She was indeed, it seemed, very ill, and just for a moment Prudence wondered if Haso had been wise to allow his mother to return home, but then she opened her eyes and looked straight at Prudence. 'Just what I have wished for,' she whispered. 'Now I shall get better—home and Haso, and you, my dear.'

Prudence murmured soothingly and set about connecting up the drip ready for Haso to insert it; it was only the fourth day after her operation, and so far her patient was barely holding her own. It was going to be an uphill fight, but Haso's mother, unless she was very much mistaken, was a strong-willed and determined person; if she set her mind to getting well again, she would, only it was going to need a lot of help from all concerned.

The rest of the day was taken up with numerous nursing duties which she carried out meticulously.

There would be another nurse, of course, but Mevrouw ter Brons Huizinga had begged her to stay as evening turned into night, so the two of them had done what was necessary and Zuster Helsma, a cosy, middle-aged woman with, thank goodness, a working knowledge of English, had gone to her room to sleep and return to duty in the early hours of the morning when Prudence would take time off and return to take over again later in the morning.

The household had been well organised. She had gone to her dinner while Haso sat with his mother, and around midnight Wigge trod silently from the kitchen and tapped gently at the door. When she opened it, he indicated a tray of coffee and sandwiches on the table outside, and went just as silently away again. The old house was quite quiet, but Prudence sensed that a good many of its occupants were awake. Haso came from time to time, professed himself satisfied, cast an eye over Prudence's neat charts, told her in the calm, flat voice she had begun to dislike that should she need him he would sleep in the adjoining dressing-room, and that he was to be called immediately she felt it necessary. He assured her that a routine would be worked out in the morning so that she and Zuster Helsma had their share of off duty, and then he went away again.

Mevrouw ter Brons Huizinga woke from time to time, was made comfortable and slept again, while Prudence kept her quiet vigil by the bed, checking pulse and drip and blood pressure; she was very tired by now. At intervals Haso came in, and at three o'clock, when Zuster Helsma took over, he injected a sedative, pronounced his satisfaction as to his mother's condition and went away.

Prudence, sinking fathoms deep into sleep shortly afterwards, barely had time to wonder if he was sleeping too. She doubted it.

She was up again soon after seven o'clock, fresh and neat in her white overall, ready to do battle on her patient's behalf. Mevrouw ter Brons Huizinga was showing signs of doing battle for herself; there was a slight improvement as the day wore on, and the bleak chill of Haso's face held a tinge of warmth. Prudence spent her brief off duty strolling in the gardens with Prince as escort and, just as on the previous evening, stayed with her patient until she had fallen into a restful doze, so that it was in the small hours when she finally got to bed herself, to sleep the sleep of someone who had done a good day's work and knew it.

The days went by. Haso had his work, but every minute he could spare he spent with his mother, and the improvement by now was marked. She was able to take fluids now, and each morning she was lifted from her bed and sat in a chair by the window, well wrapped up while her bed was made. She was a shadow of her former self, but at least the shadow was beginning to have substance.

For the first time, she was allowed visitors—Aunt Emma and Aunt Beatrix. Prudence, ushering them into the bedroom, warned them that five minutes was to be the limit, and indeed ushered them out again exactly on time, much to their surprise. 'Really, dear,' observed Aunt Emma, 'surely my own sister-in-law...you are remarkably severe.'

Prudence eyed the two ladies tiredly. 'I'm sorry, but Mevrouw ter Brons Huizinga is still very weak. Next time, perhaps a little longer.'

'Well, of course, dear, you know best, I dare say. Poor dear Cordelia…' She looked at Prudence. 'You look a little peaked, child. You should get out more.'

Two days later there was another visitor—Christabel, a cool, chic vision in white, laden with grapes and hothouse flowers and a pile of magazines.

She greeted Prudence in the hall, where Wigge had prudently asked her to wait. 'I must say Wigge forgets himself, leaving me standing here. I've come to see Mevrouw ter Brons Huizinga.' Her hostile gaze swept over Prudence's severe uniform. 'You're her nurse, I suppose. I'll go up myself now.'

'She's sleeping and still ill. Perhaps you'll come again in a few days' time. I couldn't possibly wake her.'

'Nonsense! She will be delighted to see me. I dare say she needs cheering up.'

'Not while she's asleep,' pointed out Prudence. 'So sorry…'

Suddenly Christabel cast her a look of dislike. 'No wonder Haso's so gloomy these days; he must hate having you in the house!' She thrust the flowers and grapes into Prudence's arms. 'I shall complain to him.'

'You do that,' Prudence, made irritable by lack of sleep and long hours, snapped back. 'I couldn't care less. I'm here as his mother's nurse and I merely obey orders.' She added, 'And you can take these magazines back with you; my patient isn't able to hold anything heavier than a hanky at present. You might have realised that if you'd thought about it.'

They glared angrily at each other before Christabel turned on her heel and walked out to her car. Wigge, appearing from nowhere as usual, closed the door after her, smiled at Prudence and asked in bad English, 'I bring tea?'

'Oh, please.' She went back to her patient, who was awake, sitting up against her pillows, her head turned towards the windows so that she could see the gardens. Prudence gave her a drink and smiled at her. She smiled back and said, 'I feel better—stronger too. Your doing, Prudence.' And when Prudence smiled and shook her head she added, 'If Christabel calls, I do not wish to see her.'

'She came just now. I asked her to come back later.'

'Much later, I think.' Her blue eyes scanned Prudence's face. 'You're tired and Christabel has annoyed you. When will Haso come again?'

'This evening, I believe, *mevrouw*. He had to go to den Haag. Are you too warm? I'll bathe your face and hands, then perhaps you can take a nap?'

Haso came later. He nodded to Prudence, read the charts and sat down by the bed. 'Do go and have dinner, Prudence. When does Zuster Helsma come on duty?'

'Round about midnight.'

She waited a minute to see if he had anything further to say, and when he remained silent, went downstairs to her meal. Wigge was waiting for her in the small breakfast-room behind the drawing-room, the table nicely laid ready to serve the delicious food the cook sent up each day. He poured her a small glass of sherry and offered this to her with a paternal air which she found very comforting. He had taken upon himself the duty of looking after both her and Zuster Helsma, and, although there were servants enough, it was always he who saw to it that they had all they wanted.

Prudence sat alone at the table, carrying on a desultory conversation with Wigge, each of them trying out their very sparse knowledge of the other's language. But she didn't stay long; Haso would be tired after his day's work, and indeed, after a few words he went away, saying as he went through the door, 'If you are not too tired I should like to speak to you when you come off duty, Prudence. I shall be in the study.'

There had hardly been time for him to have seen Christabel, but she had a nasty feeling that that was why he wanted to see her. She dismissed him from her mind with some difficulty and applied herself to her nursing duties, and later, when Zuster Helsma took over and their patient slept, she went downstairs, aware that her nose shone, her lipstick had long ago vanished and her hair was a riot of curls, but not caring; Haso wouldn't notice, and presently she would go to bed.

She knocked and went in and found him sitting behind his desk, writing. He got up, offered her a chair and said coldly, 'I won't keep you long. I saw Christabel this evening, for only a few minutes, but she was very upset at your rudeness this afternoon.'

Prudence turned large eyes to him. 'Was I rude? You would have wanted me to wake your mother to listen to Christabel's silly chatter when she was enjoying a refreshing sleep?' She saw his eyes flash and added, the bit between her teeth now, 'And do tell her not to bring any of those glossy magazines—your mother can't possibly hold them. Really, she should have the wit to know that. Now you can blast me; I'm too tired to listen, anyway.'

She sat, her hands tidily in her lap, and watched his face. Poor dear, she thought, he's so tired too. If he had liked me just a little, we could have talked so comfortably together.

'You have played a major part in saving my mother's life and she depends on you. I am grateful for all that you have done, but if it were not for that dependence I would suggest that you returned home. You are a very unsettling girl, Prudence. I trust you implicitly as a nurse, but I'm not sure that I do as a woman. I cannot lose sight of the fact that it was I who urged you to come here, very much against your wishes, too. I'm very sorry for that, but I would do the same again, you know. However, I cannot have you disrupting my life. Just as soon as my mother is recovered, you are free to go.'

Prudence stood up. 'Well, thanks for nothing!' Just for the moment her love was swallowed by rage. 'Free to go? To a job I haven't got because you cancelled it? I said once that I never wanted to see you again, and I meant it, only you came along, arranging things to suit yourself. Now I'll say it once more, and mean it—my goodness, how I mean it!'

She swept out of the room and up the staircase and into her room, where she flung herself on to the bed and had a good cry. Rage and love and misery, nicely mixed.

CHAPTER EIGHT

BEYOND a rather pale face, Prudence showed no signs
of a prolonged weep and an almost sleepless night.
She attended to her patient's needs once Zuster
Helsma had gone off duty, meanwhile chatting of this
and that, which belied the strong feelings churning
around inside her. When Haso came to pay his morning visit she wished him good morning calmly, although a little colour crept into her face. He gave her
a cool stare as he went in, discussed his mother's
progress in a placid voice, and suggested that Zuster
Helsma might leave within the next day or so. 'For
you sleep well, Mama, do you not? And now that you
are walking a little, you will find that you will regain
your strength rapidly.' He glanced out of the end window. 'It's a splendid day, would you like to sit in the
garden? The stairs will be excellent exercise for you.
Also, Sebeltsje is quite well again after her cold; she
will be coming to see you. Rina and Tialda are coming tomorrow. They were at the hospital with you,
but I don't expect you remember that.'

'How nice, dear. They're not bringing the children?'

'No, my dear. Perhaps next week, and not all at
once. And you are to say if you get too tired.' He
gave Prudence a cool stare. 'I think that we might

dispense with Prudence's kind services in another week.'

'So soon? Just as I am beginning to enjoy her company. But of course, you want to get back to your work, my dear.' She smiled at Prudence. 'I expect you have a job waiting for you.'

Prudence managed a bright smile. 'Well, this hasn't seemed like work; it will seem very strange to be in hospital again.'

Even stranger if she were to find a good job at the drop of a hat. She cast a smouldering look at Haso, and encountered an amused look.

'Since Rina and Tialda will be here with you tomorrow, I should think Prudence might have some long-overdue time to herself. They should be here soon after eleven o'clock, I doubt if they will go again much before four or five o'clock. Consider yourself free to do as you like, Prudence. There is a car if you want to drive anywhere.'

She thanked him politely. She didn't want a car, she wanted to walk, or better still, bike along the narrow roads and enjoy the quiet scenery and the sunny weather. Of course she had had off-duty, shared with Zuster Helsma, but they had taken it in turns when and where they could, and never more than an hour or two at a time. It would be delightful to have hours of time all to herself.

Haso went presently and she set about getting her patient ready for an hour or two in the garden. It was a slow business getting there, but Haso had said that his mother was to use the staircase, and that lady was determined to do so. She had her reward once Prudence had settled her in a comfortable chair under the trees at the side of the vast lawn. The flowerbeds were at their very best, it was pleasantly warm and the birds were singing.

'Now I really do feel better,' declared Mevrouw ter Brons Huizinga, drinking the nourishing milk she detested without a murmur. 'Might we not have lunch out here?'

'Why not?' agreed Prudence, 'Just as long as you tell me when you begin to feel tired. Shall I ask Wigge?'

It entailed a good deal of coming and going by Wigge and the maids, but they were so delighted to see the mistress of the house looking almost herself once more that nothing was too much trouble. Bouillon, jellied chicken, puréed potatoes and a crème caramel were borne from the kitchen and set on a daintily laid table with Wigge hovering over them, anxious that his mistress had everything she most fancied. Mevrouw ter Brons Huizinga, who had been inclined to peck at her food, ate a splendid meal, due, she told Prudence, to being outside in her beloved garden. All the same, she was willing enough to climb the staircase once more and be tucked up again in her bed for a nap, and presently Prudence made her way to the balcony and later made her comfortable there where they had tea together.

A very satisfactory day, thought Prudence, getting into bed later, from the point of view of a nurse, but less so from the point of view of a girl in love with a man who didn't care two pence for her. There was no profit in thinking about that; she turned her thoughts to the pleasant time she would have on the morrow.

It was already warm when she got up in the morning, with a hazy sunshine which dimmed the blue sky. She went along to her patient and was kept busy until Haso's two sisters arrived soon after ten o'clock, and hard on their heels Zuster Helsma. Mevrouw ter Brons Huizinga, escorted into the garden again, introduced her daughters, begged Prudence to go quickly and not lose a minute of her free hours, then settled down to a cosy chat with her daughters while Zuster Helsma, after a quick priming from Prudence, poured the coffee. 'I'm to go and return to my former job at the end of the week,' she told Prudence, 'and you'll be going a day or two later; the Professor told me yesterday.' She gave Prudence a questioning look. 'Are you going back to England?'

'Oh yes, I've got to get a job. Where do you work?'

'I work in Leeuwarden—the Professor borrowed me. I shall go back to my ward.'

Lucky girl, thought Prudence, getting out of her overall and into a cotton blouse and a matching skirt. She didn't waste time in worrying about her future, but hurried down to the kitchen where she found Wigge and, after a few false starts, managed to make him understand that she wanted to borrow a bicycle. He nodded in approval; a bicycle to a Dutchman is a second pair of legs, and in many ways superior to a car. He went with her to the garage behind the house and wheeled out an elderly model which Mevrouw ter Brons Huizinga, at a much earlier date, had used. It was high in the saddle and the brakes were on the

pedals. Prudence, settled in the saddle, felt rather as
though she were on a throne, but the machine had
been kept in good order. She took a quick turn round
the yard before the garage, waved to Wigge and pedalled off.

She wasn't at all sure where she was going, so she
stopped to read the first signposts she saw and wished,
too late, that she had asked Wigge for a map. The
names were in Friese as well as Dutch, but that
merely rendered them doubly difficult. Dokkum
wasn't too far away, she knew that, but she wasn't
sure in which direction. She could of course go back
to the house and ask Wigge; on the other hand it
might be fun just to bike around and find her own
way. The signpost had three arms. She chose the one
on the left, going, if she had but known it, away from
Dokkum. The road was narrow and made of bricks,
and here and there they had sunk so that she wobbled
a good deal, but the fields on either side were green
and the horizon was wide, with no sign of a village.
Well away from the road she could see farmhouses
with their great barns at their backs, and there was a
narrow canal running beside the road. She could
glimpse water ahead of her, and presently came to a
small lake, ringed with bushes and a line of trees. She
got off her bike and stood looking around her, de-
lighting in the peaceful scene. There were coots darting between the rushes at the edge of the lake, and a
solitary small boat with a man fishing. He was too far
off to notice her and there was no one else in sight,
nor could she see any signs of a village. She got on

her bike again and pedalled on, reflecting on the pos-
sibilities of lunch at the first café she came across.

Only there were no cafés, no houses or farms either; the country on either side of her looked empty
save for cows and the occasional farm horse. She
came to a crossroads, but there was no signpost, so
she kept straight on. The canal had wandered off on
its own and the brick road had become even narrower.
Not suitable for cars, she decided, and probably too
unimportant to have signposts either. But it must lead
somewhere…

Apparently not, although she passed a solitary
farmhouse and then, just as she was beginning to get
worried as to where she was, she saw a man standing
by the side of the road. A farmer, she guessed, with
an ugly-looking dog beside him, but at least he would
know the way to somewhere. She conjured up her
smattering of Dutch, got off her bike, gave him good
day and for lack of suitable words, asked, 'Dokkum?'

She repeated herself as he stared at her, and she
wondered if Dokkum had a Friese name as well. But
this time he took the pipe out of his mouth and waved
an arm in the direction of a lane a few yards farther
along. It looked to her eye to be even less likely to
be going anywhere than the one she was on, so she
asked, 'Dokkum?' once more and pointed to the lane.

The man nodded and she thanked him and got back
on to the bike. Perhaps it was a short cut.

It was borne in on her after fifteen minutes or so
that, even if the lane went to Dokkum, it was by no
means a short cut. She passed a couple of cottages,
but if she had seen anyone she knew she would never

make herself understood. She cycled on, turning over the odd Dutch phrases in her mind, trying to put together something which would make sense when she next saw someone to ask.

She had been too preoccupied to notice that the hazy sunshine had become overshadowed by clouds, and looking over her shoulder she was dismayed to see that the sky behind her was an ominous black. It had grown very still too, and not a bird was singing. A low growl of thunder broke the quiet, and a drop or two of rain fell heavily. Prudence, who hated storms, looked about her in the hope of seeing a farm or a cottage, but there was neither, so there was nothing for it but to go on.

A louder rumble and then a flash of lightning, followed by a resounding clap of thunder, made it all too certain that she would get soaked to the skin and probably die of fright as well. She hurtled round a bend in the lane, obscured by an enormous tangle of shrubs, and braked wildly at the sight of a cottage at the side of a neat small plot of vegetables. She almost fell off her bike and hurried across to the stout wooden door. There was no knocker, so she thumped urgently, and when the door opened said just as urgently and in English, 'May I come in? Unfortunately I'm lost, and it's raining.'

At that moment there was a vivid flash of lightning, followed by a clap of thunder so resonant that she shot thankfully into the narrow passageway. It was only after the hideous din had died down that it penetrated her deafened ears that she had been answered in English. The speaker was an old man, tall and bent,

with a shock of white hair and a formidable nose, and
as he stood aside for her to go further into the cottage,
Prudence paused. 'You are English?'

'No, no, my dear young lady, a retired schoolmas-
ter. Pray come in and make yourself comfortable until
the storm is over.'

'Thank you, you're very kind. You see, I'm lost—
a man on the other road——' she waved a vague arm
'—pointed to this lane. My Dutch is hopeless—I just
asked for Dokkum. But it seems an awful long
way…'

'It is, and in the opposite direction.'

'Then why did he point this way?'

'Perhaps because my name is van Dokkum.'

He had opened a door in the narrow passage and
she went past him into a small room, with a window
at both ends and a door at the side.

'Oh, of course, he thought I'd come to visit you,
Mr van Dokkum.'

'And I am delighted that he did. A visitor is something of a rarity.'

He swept a pile of books off a chair and begged
her to sit down. 'You must forgive the untidiness, but
I like to be able to lay my hands on any book I need
without having to search for it.'

Prudence surveyed the chaos around her and wondered how he found anything at all among the dozens
of books piled on every available surface.

He saw her startled face and said simply, 'I am
writing a book, Miss Makepeace.'

She turned a surprised face to him. 'You know me?
I don't remember meeting you…'

'We have never met, but news travels fast in this part of the world. The baker—you know—he calls at Haso's house and his aunt's house, and then he comes to me. He was right too; he said you were the prettiest girl he had seen for a long time.'

Prudence blushed. 'Thank you, *mijnheer*. You have lived in England?'

'For some years, a long time ago. My English has become rusty, I think.'

She shook her head. It wasn't that—pedantic perhaps, and a little old-fashioned. She told him so, pleasantly, liking him very much.

The rain was torrential and the storm, at its height, thundered and raged around the little house, but she was barely aware of it. Her host fetched coffee from the small kitchen beyond the door, and they sat drinking it while they talked as though they had known each other for a lifetime.

Presently the rain eased off and the thunder diminished to a distant mutter. 'If you would tell me which way to go, I'll be on my way,' said Prudence. She glanced uneasily at the *stoelklok*, on the wall. 'I said I would be back about three o'clock.'

'An hour's cycling if you go back the way you came. You will have to go to Dokkum another day. But you cannot go before you have shared my lunch. You will be doing me a kindness, my dear. I see few people and it is delightful to talk to you. Surely another hour would not matter? Besides, you should wait for a little while, the storm may return.'

Another hour surely would not matter, it was already almost two o'clock and she was hungry. She agreed to stay and, since Mijnheer van Dokkum refused help, examined the books overflowing the bookcases.

They lunched off rolls and ham and a bowl of strawberries from his garden, and washed them down with more coffee, talking all the time, so that when Prudence next looked at the clock it was to find that it was already half-past three. An hour's cycling before her too, but she couldn't just get up and go like that. She helped him clear away the dishes and was setting the table to rights once more when the cottage door opened. She had her back to it, and the storm, circling back again, was a continuous rumble, so that she had heard nothing. Haso's casual 'Hello' sent her spinning round to gape at him, her pretty mouth half open.

She said the first thing that entered her head. 'How did you know I was here?'

His voice was bland. 'I asked around.'

'But I didn't see anyone—at least, only a man fishing on the lake and another man with his dog.'

'Both of whom gave me an accurate description of you—a big girl with flaming hair.'

'Well——' began Prudence coldly, to be interrupted by Mijnheer van Dokkum, who came from the kitchen with outstretched hand.

'Haso, how delightful—two visitors in one day...' He cocked an eye at Prudence's pink cheeks. 'Looking for this young lady, were you? She was caught in the storm as well as lost and most happily arrived here. You have not been anxious about her, I hope?'

Haso had shaken hands and stood listening to the

older man. 'Prudence is well able to cope with events, *meester*, although a local map might have made things easier for her.'

There was a silky tone in his voice which prompted her to say sharply, 'It wasn't suggested, nor did anyone enquire as to what I intended doing. However, Mijnheer van Dokkum had kindly explained how I can get back, so I'll be on my way.'

'I'm taking you back in the car,' said Haso.

'Thank you, but I have a bicycle, Wigge lent it to me.'

He said patiently, 'Yes, I know. You will come back in the car—someone can fetch the bike later on.'

'But I want to cycle back...'

Mijnheer van Dokkum stood equably between them, enjoying himself. 'There is still coffee in the pot, let us have a cup and settle the matter sensibly.'

He had an air of authority which it would have been hard to ignore. Prudence sat down with her shoulder turned to Haso and looked out of the window. A sudden flash of lightening made her turn her head sharply to encounter Haso's stare. Because it was intolerable to sit there under it, she asked, 'You know Mijnheer van Dokkum?'

'He was headmaster of my school. He is, as you may have gathered, a learned man, and a very old friend.'

Their host came back with three mugs on a tray and sat down at the table. He waited until a resounding clap of thunder had spent itself, then observed, 'It would be foolish to cycle in this weather, my dear. The baker comes tomorrow and he will put it on his roof and leave it at Haso's home as he goes past. It will be quite safe here tonight.' He turned to Haso. 'And how are things at the hospital? Busy, I suppose?'

Haso was leaning against a window-sill, looking placid. 'Yes—it doesn't matter what we do to improve things, there's always a waiting list. It's worse in Amsterdam, of course.'

'You have visited our hospital?' Mijnheer van Dokkum asked courteously, and smiled at Prudence.

'No, I haven't…'

She hesitated and Haso said blandly, 'Prudence has had no opportunity to do so. Her pretty nose has been pressed quite ruthlessly to the grindstone. I dare say, if she wishes, I can arrange for her to go round some of the wards either in Leeuwarden or Groningen.' He crossed his long legs and studied his well-shod feet. 'She will be going back to England very shortly. Mama has made a splendid recovery.'

She had no answer to this, and Mijnheer van Dokkum filled an awkward silence by enquiring after Prince.

'He's in the car. I didn't bring him in—he might make havoc of your papers.'

'Very thoughtful of you.' The old gentleman turned to Prudence. 'You have met Prince, of course?'

She nodded. 'He's gorgeous!' She caught Haso's almost satirical eye and added defiantly, 'I like all dogs.'

Haso put down his mug. 'Shall we go? That book you wanted, *meester*, I'll bring it over at the weekend.

And it's time you dined with us again. Mama will be so delighted to see you.'

'I'll look forward to it, Haso.' They shook hands and Prudence, not quite knowing why she did it, kissed the old man on his cheek. 'I'm so glad I met you,' she told him.

He had her hand in both of his. 'And I am looking forward to seeing you again,' he told her with the air of a man who was sure that he would. There was no point in refuting this; she murmured something or other and went outside with Haso, to be hurried across the vegetable plot and into the Daimler, where Prince welcomed her with a good deal of panting and whispered barks. She pulled his ears gently and asked him how he did, then sat silent while Haso drove the Daimler down the lane until an open gate into a field allowed him to turn the car. Mijnheer van Dokkum was standing at his door as they went past his little house, and she waved and smiled. She had enjoyed every minute of his company and, even though the afternoon hadn't been quite up to her expectations, it hadn't held a dull moment.

She stole a glance at Haso, but he looked so stern that she decided not to ask him why he had come looking for her to change her mind as a sudden thought struck her. 'Your Mother isn't...she's all right? But Zuster Helsma is there.'

'Zuster Helsma returned to the hospital a couple of hours ago, there's an outbreak of gastro-enteritis on the children's ward.'

'So that's why you came to look for me!'

His 'No' was decisive. It left her puzzled.

The Daimler made short work of the journey back. Prudence looked out of the window, with Prince breathing heavily down the back of her neck. Haso had no wish to talk, so she kept silent. It was magic sitting beside him, but she was profoundly unhappy as well. She would go home and never see him again. She would have to learn to forget him, although that might be difficult, since Aunt Beatrix would pass on news about him from Holland to Aunt Maud, and it would filter through to her. Especially interesting news such as his marriage to Christabel. She heaved a great sigh, thinking about it, and Haso said sharply, 'What's the matter?'

'Nothing, nothing at all.'

He turned into the drive and stopped before his front door and got out. Prudence was still fumbling with her door when he opened it and then turned away to do the same for Prince. Still without speaking they went into the house, to be met by Wigge. He smiled at Prudence, said something to Haso and went to open the drawing-room doors.

'My mother is still downstairs. She will be interested to hear of your meeting with Mijnheer van Dokkum.'

She went past him into the room—and came to a halt. Mevrouw ter Brons Huizinga was still sitting by the window, and there was someone with her—Christabel.

The girl looked immaculate: creaseless silk dress, not a hair out of place, exquisitely made-up. Prudence, only too aware of her own damp, grubby dress, her tousled hair and shiny nose, went slowly red under Christabel's sneering amusement, but she put up her chin and crossed the room to her patient, who had sat up and exclaimed delightedly, 'There you are, my dear! We were a little worried, but I knew Haso would find you.'

'Yes, I'm sorry that I didn't come back sooner. I didn't know that Zuster Helsma had to return to hospital...'

'Was that the reason Haso gave you?'

Mevrouw ter Brons Huizinga sounded amused and Christabel said loudly, 'What other reason could there be? She's a nurse, isn't she? And it's her duty to be with you.'

Haso had come into the room and was standing before the great fireplace with Prince beside him. He said quietly, 'What a good thing there are those of us who fulfil that duty.'

Christabel looked at him doubtfully. 'I don't understand you, Haso.' She gave a little laugh. 'I must go—there's the van Rijns' dinner party this evening. You're going, Haso? Call for me at half-past seven, will you?'

'Very well.' He glanced at his watch. 'You must excuse me, I have some telephone calls to make.'

He and Prince went away, and Christabel gave a little titter. 'I'll say goodbye, *mevrouw*, what good fortune that I was able to take the place of your nurse for a few hours. We had such a pleasant gossip—we share so many acquaintances, don't we?'

Mevrouw ter Brons Huizinga said quietly, 'Indeed, yes. Goodbye, Christabel.' She gave a gentle sigh as the door closed. 'Come and sit down, dear, and tell me about your afternoon.'

Prudence sat, pushed a few unruly curls back from her forehead and gave an account of her adventures. 'I liked Mijnheer van Dokkum,' she finished. 'Isn't he lonely, living in that little house by himself?'

'I should imagine that, writing the profoundly clever books he is engaged on, he might prefer to be alone.'

'But surely someone must do the housework and cook? And what about typing his script?'

'Oh, Haso arranged for someone in the village to go once a week and put clean sheets on the bed and tidy up, and as for the typing, he collects each chapter as it is written and takes it to Leeuwarden to be typed.' Mevrouw added unexpectedly, 'Was Haso very angry?'

Prudence's charming face pinkened. 'I—well, yes, I think so, but he... It's rather difficult to tell, isn't it? I'm sorry I went so far and got lost; it was silly to go out without a map and I didn't notice the time.' She looked anxiously at her companion. 'You were all right? Did Zuster Helsma have to go soon after I went?'

'About an hour, dear. But I had Rina and Tialda. They would have stayed, but Christabel came to see me.' And, at Prudence's look of enquiry, 'They dislike each other—so unfortunate! I was only glad that Sebeltsje wasn't here. She is apt to speak her mind; her sisters are more restrained. You see, they try to like Christabel for Haso's sake, but of course Sebeltsje has no such idea. She has told him several times that he is making the mistake of a lifetime if he should marry her. I have told her many times that she has no need to worry about that, but she is devoted to him and wishes only for his happiness.'

'She doesn't think Christabel would make him a good wife?'

'And you, what do you think, Prudence?'

Prudence took a long while to answer. She said after much thought and carefully, 'Well, it's hardly for me to say, Mevrouw ter Brons Huizinga,' and then was appalled to hear herself say, 'No, of course she's not the wife for him; she's vain and selfish and she doesn't love him, not the kind of love that will wait up for him when he's late home and see that he's fed and cared for when he's dog-tired, and look after his house and see that it's run as he likes it to be, and listen to him when he wants to talk, and not fuss about her clothes all the time...' She stopped, aghast, and saw that his mother was smiling at her.

'You have put it—how do you say?—in a nutshell. One may not interfere, however much one wishes to, one can but hope for the best.'

Prudence stammered a little. 'I'm sorry, I shouldn't have spoken like that, it isn't my business. Perhaps he sees something in Christabel that we can't...'

His mother nodded. 'Oh, yes, dear—or rather, he didn't see it quite as quickly or clearly as we did.' She smiled. 'What a relief!' she observed. 'You know, dear, I think I'd like to go to bed and have my supper sent up. I feel specially well, but I have a great deal of thinking to do.'

So Prudence dined alone, with Wigge hovering

attentively. There was no sign of Haso; he would have gone to his dinner party by now and she would be in bed long before he returned. Tomorrow, she promised herself, she would ask him when he wanted her to leave, and arrange her flight back to England. The sooner she was away, the better. She wished Wigge goodnight, paid a brief visit to her patient and, since there was nothing to prevent her doing so, decided to go to bed with a book.

She had bathed and was sitting in her dressing-gown, brushing her hair, when Sieke brought a message. Mevrouw wondered if Miss would very much mind reading to her for half an hour; her brain was too active for sleep and something soothing, read aloud, might quieten it.

It took Prudence a minute or two to understand what was wanted of her. Her Dutch was coming along nicely, although she found speaking the language difficult, but Sieke was adept at sign language and Prudence picked out the essentials, put down her hairbrush and went along to Mevrouw ter Brons Huizinga's room. That lady was sitting up in her bed, looking pleased with herself.

'You don't mind, dear? Something tranquil? *Pride and Prejudice* perhaps... I have always enjoyed that bit where Mr Darcy refuses to dance with Elizabeth.'

'Oh, right at the beginning—shall I read it to you now?'

Prudence went to the little bookcase in a corner of the room, found the book and settled down to read. She had read for ten minutes or so when her companion observed, 'They are very alike—Christabel and Miss Bingley.'

Prudence stopped reading. 'Well, yes, I think perhaps they are…'

'Miss Bingley didn't get Mr Darcy, though, and nor will Christabel get Haso,' went on Mevrouw ter Brons Huizinga with relish. 'They both made the same mistake—they didn't know their man.'

She looked at Prudence, expecting an answer. 'Well,' said Prudence slowly, quite forgetting that she was talking to Haso's mother, 'he can be very tiresome, you know—that bland face—one never quite knows what he's thinking, and he has quite a nasty temper, he needs someone to dilute him. But he's utterly dependable, isn't he? And kind…' She amended this, 'Well, kind to the people he likes and loves.'

'He has been unkind to you, my dear?'

'Oh, no. Just overbearing and dictatorial and impatient…' Reason had taken over her wandering thoughts. 'Oh, good heavens, what have I been saying? I—I do beg your pardon, *mevrouw*, I must have almost lost my wits—please forget what I said. It was unpardonable of me. Haso's your son and he is devoted to you, and I had no right to criticise him.'

Her patient appeared quite unshaken. 'Yes, dear, I know he is, but I think that of all the people he knows, you have the most right to criticise him.'

Prudence decided not to think about that. She said hastily, 'Shall I go on reading?'

Just in time; Mr Darcy and Elizabeth Bennett were crossing swords in the ballroom when she heard a faint sound behind her and turned her head to see Haso standing in the doorway.

He strolled into the room and she stood up, closed the book and put it back on the shelf and edged towards the door. But his genial, 'Don't go, Prudence,' brought her to a halt. 'Can you not sleep, Mama? Would you like a little something to help—a sleeping pill?' He looked at Prudence, taking his time about it. 'Although I should imagine that Prudence is a better alternative.'

Indeed she looked quite beautiful, with her hair in a bright tangle of curls and the dressing-gown Pretty disapproved of doing very little more than enhancing her splendid figure.

It annoyed her very much that she was blushing, but she looked away from his bright stare and addressed herself to Mevrouw ter Brons Huizinga.

'You're quite comfy? There's nothing more that you need? Then I'll go to bed, *mevrouw*. If you need anything later on, you'll ring?'

She went to the door. 'Goodnight, *mevrouw*, goodnight.' The second goodnight she addressed with a distinct cooling of tone to Haso, and his firm mouth twitched, although his own goodnight was casual. She went through the door in a hurry, forgetting to shut it behind her, and she went to her room, where she brushed her hair once more, stared for a long time at her reflection in the looking-glass, went over—word for word—what Haso had said, which wasn't much, she had to admit, and went to bed.

Just as she was on the verge of sleep, she shot upright against her pillows. She had forgotten to tell the cook that her patient had expressed a desire for a coddled egg for breakfast in place of the usual scrambled egg, sent up without question each day. She got out of bed, put on her dressing-gown once more, and found a pencil and some paper. Her Dutch conversation was scanty, but she could pen a simple message as long as the reader wasn't fussy about the grammar. With her note in her hand, she opened her door and crossed the landing to the staircase. Mevrouw ter Brons Huizinga's door was ajar. Her patient's voice was soft but very clear; moreover, she was speaking English, and Prudence could hear her very plainly.

'Such a dear girl,' declared her patient. 'I can never repay her for her care and kindness.'

Prudence had been well brought up; one didn't listen to other people's conversation, and anyway, listeners never heard any good of themselves. She did her best to turn a deaf ear and put a foot on the first step, but she couldn't help hearing Mevrouw ter Brons Huizinga's voice, although the only word she could distinguish was 'Christabel' uttered urgently, to be followed by Haso's decisive voice, 'Of course I intend to marry her, Mama.'

She took another reluctant step, shamelessly listening now, but quite unable to hear what his mother was saying. However, she couldn't fail to hear every word Haso said in reply, 'Love her? Marry her?' He laughed, but he didn't sound amused. 'She's only looking for a wealthy husband and a lazy, empty life. Oh, I know I brought her here and for a time I suppose I found her amusing... There was someone else before we met.' Walter, thought Prudence.

He must be moving round the room, she decided dully, for his voice had become a murmur. She stood very still, going over every word he had said: each one of them hurt like a knife wound and she felt hot and cold at the shameful thought that Haso looked upon her as a scheming woman. She had become resigned to his dislike, but all the time he had despised her...

His voice, suddenly nearer, sent her scuttling soundlessly back to the gallery, but not before she heard him say, 'It's a pity I must be in Amsterdam tomorrow and won't be able to see her—I'll do so as soon as I come back.'

He would see her if he came through the door. Prudence slid silently into her room and closed its door, to stand with her back to it; listening, she heard Haso bidding his mother goodnight and then his footsteps going down the staircase.

For the moment rage was uppermost in her mind, and a strong wish never to see him again. Unhappiness would come presently—but before she gave way to that she must make plans.

CHAPTER NINE

TO GET away as quickly as possible was more important than anything else. To do it without calling forth a lot of enquiries, Prudence would need an urgent summons from Aunt Maud. If she received it the following morning, she would be away by the evening. How fortunate that Sebeltsje was coming to spend a few days with her mother and could take her place. Mevrouw ter Brons Huizinga no longer needed a nurse; her maid was a sensible woman and there were ample domestic staff. Prudence hated leaving her patient, but there was no reason why she shouldn't. Besides, if she went away, there was a better chance of her patient and Christabel becoming friends.

There was a phone by the bed; she dialled Aunt Maud's number.

Her aunt's voice came very clearly over the wire. 'Prudence? How nice to hear from you, my dear!'

Prudence didn't mince matters. 'Aunt Maud, I have to have your help, only I can't explain now. I want you to telephone me here in the morning, early, and ask if I can come back to England without delay. You can be ill—never mind what, but you need me to nurse you...'

Aunt Maud was no fool. 'You're running away, dear.'

'Yes, but I want to do it nicely and nobody must know. Aunt Beatrix is staying in Holland for another few weeks, so there's no fear of anyone finding out.'

'And you can't tell me why?'

'No, Aunt Maud. Only that I've not done anything wrong; it's just that I have to get away from here very quickly.'

'Ah—you've met someone who's swept you off your feet?'

'Yes. Oh, Aunt Maud, you must help me!' Prudence swallowed back threatening tears. 'Mevrouw ter Brons Huizinga is quite well again, and her daughter will be here to help.'

'And Haso?'

'He's away. He's going to Amsterdam.'

'You want to leave while he's away?' Aunt Maud added quickly, 'I'm not prying, dear, and of course I'll help you. Would pneumonia do, or perhaps a mild stroke?' And, when Prudence didn't answer, 'A stroke sounds more urgent, but then of course I wouldn't be able to telephone to you—a broken leg, I think. I'll phone early in the morning and expect you when I see you. And, Prudence—I'm so sorry!'

Prudence mumbled her thanks, got into bed and after a short bout of weeping fell into a troubled sleep. She awoke early, paid her customary visit to her patient and was almost dressed when Wigge tapped on her door to tell her she was wanted on the telephone. 'A call from England,' he told her in the slow, basic

Dutch he used when addressing her, and gave her a look of concern.

It was Aunt Maud, acting her part so well that just for a moment Prudence almost believed she had broken a leg. 'I'll come as soon as I can,' she said for Wigge's benefit, as he was hovering behind her.

That made it easier for her. It wasn't difficult to make him understand that she would have to return to England as soon as possible to look after her aunt. He received the news with a sympathetic shake of the head and an offer to get her a seat on the first available plane. She thanked him warmly, feeling mean, and went to tell her news to Mevrouw ter Brons Huizinga. She felt even meaner doing this, for that lady was instantly all sympathy and full of helpful suggestions. Wigge would drive her to the airport, and had she got enough money, and was there anything she needed to take with her?

Prudence went to finish dressing, feeling like something nasty under a stone. All the same, her plan was working; she would be gone by the time Haso got back. For her peace of mind, it was a good thing that she didn't know he had telephoned while she was getting her patient ready for her breakfast, and Wigge had told him she would be returning to England as soon as a seat could be booked on a flight.

Haso had listened carefully to Wigge and then talked at some length, and Wigge had listened in his turn and then put down the receiver. He thought it all a little puzzling, but it would never have entered his head to do anything but what he had been asked.

Accordingly, he waited until Prudence had settled her patient and then sought her out. There were no seats available, he had tried every available source, but he had booked her on an early morning flight the next day. The ferries, he pointed out in his painstaking mixture of Dutch and English, wouldn't save any time at all; there was no time for her to catch the day boat, and the night boat, coupled with the train in England, would get her back several hours later than the early morning flight.

She agreed reluctantly, comforting herself by the thought that Haso wasn't due to return until the following evening anyway. She would be back home by then. She thanked Wigge and went away to tell Mevrouw ter Brons Huizinga and accompany her to the garden, where they were presently joined by Sebeltsje and Prince.

The day, from Prudence's point of view, dragged; she packed the cases, counted her money and went with Sebeltsje and Prince for a walk in the grounds, to find when they returned that Christabel was there, sitting by Mevrouw ter Brons Huizinga, regaling her with an account of a concert she had been to on the previous evening. Her companion, too polite to show boredom, none the less looked glassy-eyed, and Prudence made haste to suggest tea while Sebeltsje exclaimed, 'Oh,' and then in Dutch, 'You here again? Haso is away.'

Prudence did not wait to hear Christabel's reply, but went to find Wigge, and when she got back Chris-

tabel was asking her hostess how much longer she
would need her nurse.

Mevrouw ter Brons Huizinga spoke in English.
'Prudence goes home tomorrow. Her aunt in England
is ill and needs her. We shall all miss her.'

'You won't be able to say goodbye to Haso,' observed Christabel with satisfaction. 'But then, of
course, you really don't need to—you're only the
nurse.'

This unforgivable remark was met with a stony
stare from her three companions, and an icy silence
broken by Sebeltsje's outraged voice, 'What a very
nasty remark to make—but then you always were
spiteful. I dare say Haso will go over to England and
see Prudence when he gets back.'

Christabel went an angry red. 'What nonsense!
Why should he do that?'

'Good manners, Christabel. But you wouldn't
know about that, would you?'

Christabel flounced out of her chair. 'I won't stay
for tea. It's to be hoped that when I am Haso's wife,
we shall achieve a better relationship.'

Sebeltsje opened her eyes wide. 'Never tell me he
has proposed...?'

Christabel opened her handbag, inspected the contents and said carefully, 'He will do so.' She closed
the bag and glared at Sebeltsje. 'I will say goodbye.'
She shook Mevrouw ter Brons Huizinga's hand, ignored Prudence and with a brief 'Tot ziens' to Sebeltsje, walked away.

No one spoke until they heard the car drive off.

'Tiresome girl,' observed Mevrouw ter Brons Huizinga.

Her daughter asked anxiously, 'Do you suppose Haso has asked her to marry him?'

'My dear, how would I know?' she replied. 'In any case, there is nothing we can do about it.'

A remark which made Prudence long for the next day, so that she might go away and never come back again, never see or hear of Haso again as long as she lived.

Mevrouw ter Brons Huizinga declared that she was tired after dinner, and when Prudence had seen her safely into her bed, she and Sebeltsje decided to go to bed too. Prudence was to go early in the morning and she still had a few things to pack. But although she had said she was tired, she loitered around the pretty room for a long time, only to go to bed at last and lie awake, thinking of Haso. When at length she fell into sleep, it seemed only a few minutes before she was wakened.

It was another glorious morning. She dressed quickly, fastened her case and peeped in to see if Mevrouw ter Brons Huizinga was still asleep, and, since there was still ten minutes before she needed to go to breakfast, she trod quietly through the house and made for the gardens. She took the narrow path to the swimming pool and went to sit down on the seat by it. This, she reminded herself, was where she had first met Christabel.

'And I called it a paradise for two,' she told a sparrow waiting hopefully for crumbs.

'How very apt!'

She gave a squeak of surprise as Haso sat down beside her, and Prince flopped down and leant his great head against her. She said foolishly, 'But you're in Amsterdam...'

He ignored that. 'Wigge tells me you have to go home to nurse your aunt. I'll drive you there.'

She looked at him with startled horror, and his blue eyes gleamed with amusement. 'No, no, there's no need, really there isn't. I've got a seat on a morning flight—it will be quicker.'

'On the contrary. We will have breakfast and be away within the hour, drive down to Calais and cross over to England by hovercraft. We should be at your home by tea time. Is your aunt in hospital?'

'Yes—no. There's absolutely no need!' She tried to keep the panic out of her voice.

Haso said silkily, 'But I must insist, Prudence; it's the very least I can do after the care and kindness you have shown to my mother.'

Prudence stared down at Prince's ugly face and wished the ground would open and swallow her. She tried again, 'I would prefer to go alone by plane.'

He got to his feet. 'We'll say no more about it. Come, Wigge will have been getting breakfast ready for us, and then we can be on our way.'

It was now or never. Prudence opened her mouth, confession on the tip of her tongue, but he forestalled her. His brisk, 'Come along, then, Prudence,' drove the half-formed sentences from her head. Haso took her arm and marched her into the house. Wigge was waiting in the hall, even at that early hour shaved and dressed immaculately. He opened the door of the small room behind the dining-room, where Prudence had had her meals during the time her patient had been bedridden, and stood aside, his *'goeden morgen'* uttered with his usual solemnity, but he looked smugly pleased with himself.

Prudence went past him and then stopped suddenly. The room was awash with roses, pink and red, yellow and white, massed in a great bowl in the centre of the table, arranged in huge bouquets in vases wherever there was a place to set them, and the jardinière under the window overflowed with them. Her lovely mouth opened in surprise and her eyes widened. They widened still further when she saw the champagne in its silver bucket on the table.

Haso had shut the door behind him and was leaning against it, watching her. 'Do you remember Cornet Castle?' he asked. 'I asked you why you were not married, and you expressed a wish to be swept off your feet, showered with roses, champagne and diamonds. I have done my best at rather short notice, my dear—my very dear girl.'

He came to stand before her and took her hand in his, and opened his other hand to show her what lay within it. A ring, a glowing and exquisite sapphire surrounded by diamonds in an old-fashioned gold setting. 'And this.' He slipped it onto her finger and caught her hand close again.

Prudence, mouth and eyes wide open again, looked at the ring on her finger and then at Haso's face. The look on it would have satisfied the most doubtful of girls, and her heart raced with sudden excited happiness. All the same, there was a question which had to be answered teetering on her tongue. But she couldn't utter before he spoke.

'I saw you on the stairs. You're a big girl—thank God for that—and light on your feet, but I believe I would hear your footfall a hundred yards away. You heard at least part of the conversation Mama and I were having, but not the whole, and you, being you, jumped to conclusions. It seemed to me that you might do something silly...' His tender smile belied his words. 'I warned Wigge to keep an eye on you. He phoned me the next morning and I told him to delay booking your flight, and came back...'

'Christabel...' Prudence interrupted urgently. 'She said...'

'Believe me, my darling, I have never been in love with her—any talk of that or of marriage was fiction on her part. I knew it, of course, but until I met you I didn't bother to do anything about it. She was an amusing companion, someone to take about while I waited until I met the girl I wanted for a wife. You, my darling girl. I went to see her yesterday—as you no doubt heard. She wants only an easy future and plenty of money. If I know Christabel, she is already spreading her net wide.'

Prudence looked up into his calm face, but it was not so calm, she saw, while excitement bubbled inside her. He was looking at her in that same very satisfying manner. She savoured it for a long moment before asking, 'Your mother...?'

'Loves you—so do my sisters. They can't wait to see us man and wife.'

'Aunt Maud? I phoned her...'

'So did I. My darling silly little goose, how I do love you. Will you marry me?'

Haso had let her hand go at last and taken her in his arms, and even if she had wanted to answer him she had no chance, for he started to kiss her with the air of a man who had waited a long time for something, and now that he had it was in no hurry to give it up.

FALLEN IDOL

Margaret Way

Dear Reader,

I was born, bred and have lived for almost the entirety of my life in the beautiful river city of Brisbane, capital of the vast state of Queensland, the Sunshine State and the tourist mecca for Australia. Brisbane is surrounded by seven tree-clad hills that at the height of summer float a blue eucalyptus haze over the city, making us all soporific like the koalas that live and mate in the branches. My hometown to me is a place of golden heat, of cloudless cobalt blue skies, friendly, caring people (a well-known English journalist once described us as "cuddly as koalas"), hectic tropical blossoming, pawpaw and mango trees in every backyard and an annual burst of glory November/December when the great shade trees—the jacarandas and the poincianas planted so prolifically all over the city—burst into flower. I have seen whole hillsides blanketed in violet, streets so densely lined with poincianas that they form a rosy umbrella. At such times it's like seeing some fantastic impressionist painting come to life.

My love for my country, my own state in particular, inspired me to write. In my romances I seek to convey a sense of place. I want my readership to enjoy all my country has to offer, even if it is only through the pages of a book. In turn, my writing career has afforded me the ideal life-style. I've always been there for my family and I've been able to choose my own working hours, whether it be a late 11:00 a.m. start or a 2:00 a.m. finish. I've enjoyed it immensely, and the pleasure remains.

I'm a voracious reader, a novel a day. I read every printed word my eye falls upon. I did as a child, happily lapping up the blurb on the back of the cereal packets or the advertisements lining the old trams as I rode back and forth to school. I've led a happy life and a sad life, like most of us, but I wouldn't have missed it. If life isn't exactly a celebration, it's one heck of an experience.

I hope you enjoy *Fallen Idol,* which has to be a particular favorite of mine. My warmest regards to my readership—so many of you so loyal.

Margaret Way

CHAPTER ONE

IT WAS the night of her twenty-first birthday party and
Claudia stood by the balustrade looking down at the
floodlit garden. It was springtime and the terraces
were aflame with colour; great drifts of azaleas, hundreds of them, running right down the hillside to the
river; a vast sweep of velvety, green lawn and the
boundaries of their large property bordered by jacarandas, exquisite in their flowering. Hundreds of camellias had been stripped from the bushes to float
across the jewelled surface of the swimming pool, a
glorious variety of shapes and colours. She wore
white camellias in her hair, one perfect bloom behind
each ear. She was a true platinum blonde and for tonight her long hair had been drawn back off her face
and arranged in shining, intricate coils at her nape. It
was her own idea to use the camellias. They were her
favourite flowers and if they looked marvellous in her
hair, she didn't seem to care.

In a short while the first of their guests would be
arriving. Her father had hired people to take care of
the parking. Two hundred invitations had gone out.
She could see Fergy making a last minute inspection
of the big striped marquee that had been erected to
the right of the pool area. This was to serve as an
additional bar and buffet area and the entrance had

been flanked by two enormous brass bound timber planters bearing magnificent clusters of the rhododendron Cleopatra in a brilliant red.

It should be one of the happiest nights of her life, but Claudia's happiness had been shattered months ago. Then she had discovered Cristina, her stepmother, was having an affair with Nick. Of course they had denied it vehemently. Nick, especially, had been furiously angry. He had even slapped her and she wouldn't forget *that* either as long as she lived.

Dominic Grey.

Her father's protégé. The brilliant young architect who had been accepted straight out of university into one of the most prestigious architectural firms in the country. Nick's was a great success story. Her father had often said Nick had been born knowing more than most architects could squeeze into a lifetime's practise. He had been so impressed with Nick he had taken him on as his personal assistant. Now after seven years, Nick was a full partner and a legend on his own.

Legends. Legends and idols. Ever since she had first met him at the tender, terribly impressionable age of thirteen, Claudia had idolised Nick. He was so much more than a highly gifted young man. He was remarkable in so many ways. There was a tremendous vitality, *awareness,* a certainty in him that her father called the certainty of natural genius. Nick was only a young man, yet men like her father at the very top of their profession listened to him when he spoke; took his drawings into their hands with the kind of attention only given to a master, rarely an apprentice.

Damn you, Nick!

Once when she and her father had been sitting quietly together he had told her Nick was the son he had always longed for... 'Understand, darling, you're as perfect a daughter as I could ever wish for, but *Nick!* You'll have to grow up quickly and marry him, my angel!' her father had joked. A joke, yet *not* a joke and Claudia had laughed sadly. She knew what Nick meant to her father. She had seen the deep affection and pride growing. Grant Ingram was a man who *should* have had a son. Though he had never, up until that moment, spoken of it Claudia had been aware of his sense of loss. A man like her father needed a son to follow after him; a son to inherit all that he had built up. Though she had always been an excellent student and majored in Fine Arts at university she had not inherited her father's gift. She loved houses and architecture and anything to do with the Arts, but she had no *special* ability. As the only daughter of a rich and cultured man she had been taught all the extras. She moved beautifully from long years of ballet, she spoke beautifully as was expected of her and doubly secured from Speech and Drama; she played the piano extremely well. She also played tennis, golf and squash. She rode well and she could swim like a fish. She did most things well but she could never take over where her father had left off. She was a girl. A precious ornament. There had never been, nor was there now, any pressure put on her to shine and succeed. It was enough that she had inherited her mother's blonde beauty and graceful manner. There was no need for her to make her own mark. Her father would leave her very comfortably off. *He* had made the money. *She* could spend it. It would have been a far different story had she been a boy. Her father would have expected great things of a son. He would, most probably, have been hard on him. Claudia was valued differently. It was her goal to marry someone like Nick so her father would have the son he had always wanted. Claudia did not begrudge her father his deepest wish. She understood his unfulfilled longing and could have wept for him. But Nick had always been out of reach. And now? Her idol had fallen.

Claudia turned away from the balustrade and walked back into her bedroom. She was seized by the most powerful melancholia, an intense desire to turn back the clock. It would be a difficult evening to get through. She could not possibly disappoint her father. He had gone to so much trouble and expense. Even Cristina, perhaps guiltily, had made a great effort to help out.

Cristina.

At first she had been rather shocked her father had married a woman nearly twenty years younger than himself. 'Mind you, love, they all do!' Fergy had said. Grant Ingram had told them he was marrying Cristina a short week before the actual ceremony. 'None of our business, I expect,' had been Fergy's next comment. 'I daresay the real reason is, he's hoping for a son.'

A *son.* How wonderful! A little brother. Immediately Claudia had felt better. But in four years, Cristina had refused point blank to stay home from her thriving interior design business and Claudia could swear her stepmother was scared silly of having a child. Once when Claudia had remarked happily that a mutual friend was expecting a baby, Cristina had exclaimed: 'How *dreadful!*' Cristina was a very glamorous creature. Not beautiful nor even strictly good looking, but impeccably elegant. For Cristina there would be no babies to perhaps ruin her tall, reed slim figure. Most people thought Cristina was a very impressive looking woman but strangely enough Nick had never looked impressed, though his penchant for mature women had always been too obvious. Beautiful women seemed to flash in and out of Nick's life, but he didn't seem to have much time for young girls.

'I really can't stand their conversation,' he had once told Claudia lightly. 'Except you, Claud, darling, and you're that way because you're your father's daughter.'

Yet in the midst of it, Nick and Cristina had had an affair.

Claudia became aware she was staring sightlessly at her reflected figure. She willed herself to pay attention. Her dress was exquisite. A rustling silk taffeta, ribboned and ruffled, the tiny bodice strapless, the skirt tiered to the floor, exaggerating the narrowness of her waist and making her look very feminine and fragile. This was the way her father liked her to look. At her ears she wore his present: diamond and pearl drop earrings. They were superb. She had intended wearing her mother's pearls around her throat but decided at the last minute they were too much. Her skin was already lightly gilded by the sun and her eyes looked very green, taking on the depth of the glossy leaves that sprayed out from the white camellias. She looked the very picture of innocence yet she was guilty of downright hatred in her heart. Hatred and deceit.

Yet how could she tell her father? 'Look here, Daddy, the Nick you love so much is sleeping with your wife.'

Claudia laughed aloud in a paroxysm of grief and irony. They'd both been super discreet since then. Nick took good care never to be left alone with Cristina for a moment. There was no use thinking about what they could manage when every back was turned. Grant Ingram suspected nothing and his daughter, burning with anguish, kept quiet. Yet the nightmare of that June afternoon came regularly…

Nick's car wasn't in the drive or the garage so there was nothing to warn her. She was home early from university thrilled with the 'excellent' on a rather difficult assignment that had just been handed back to her. With a few extra hours up her sleeve she intended to get in a game of tennis at the club. She ran up the stairs and used her own key on the front door so as not to disturb Fergy. Her father called Fergy their major domo. She was much more than a housekeeper. Fergy had been responsible for the smooth running of the household since Claudia's mother had been killed in a freak riding accident when Claudia was barely seven. Fergy had come with Miss Victoria and she had remained to look after her beloved Miss Victoria's daughter. In the Ingram household Fergy was a very special person indeed. Not even Cristina had been able to change that. Not that she tried very hard. It suited Cristina as well to have someone as dedicated and competent as Fergy to look after a very large house and garden, do the hiring, firing, answer the routine mail. Cristina had her own life and Fergy had the admirable knack of disappearing when she wasn't wanted. After he and Cristina had been married Grant Ingram had built Fergy her own self-contained bungalow in the large garden so Cristina would have no sense of sharing her home with another woman. He had talked it over with Fergy first and Fergy had told him bluntly it would suit her as well. 'I just hope, for God's sake, when I come home late one night, I remember.'

Fergy would probably have had a heart attack had she chanced on Nick and Cristina that winter's afternoon. Fergy's manner with Cristina was always crisply friendly, but she had the greatest affection for Nick. Seeing Nick with Cristina would have blown her mind. But Fergy, that afternoon, was visiting a nursery with Bill, their gardener, as Claudia belatedly remembered, which accounted for the extreme quietness of the house.

Claudia often wished afterwards she had called out. Her own relationship with Cristina was friendly enough and she had seen Cristina's smart, new Mercedes coupé in the garage (a present from her trusting husband), but up the stairs she went, her own life so crowded with activities she often acted as though she didn't have a moment to spare.

Just as she reached the first landing she saw Nick coming very quickly along the gallery and she had looked up at him in blank astonishment. He was singularly handsome. Very tall, very lean, very dark except for eyes that at times could look like pure silver. No one had Nick's quality. The authority. Yet as Claudia watched him she was surprised by the grimness of his demeanour. It even gave her a momentary pang of fear. So *that* was how Nick could look! For her, he always smiled.

They were almost on a level before he saw her and he recovered in an instant, startlingly charming while the world spun around her. For even as he spoke, Cristina came running along the gallery crying out his name. Not Nick as they all called him but, *'Dominic!'* with ardour and quickened breath. Cristina with a mist-green silk robe half falling off her, her body trembling, her hazel eyes filled with tears.

Claudia knew she would never forget it if she lived to be one hundred years. She could even recall the fragrance Cristina had worn that day and never since. It was so terrible. So shocking. So wrong. Nick and his fatal charm. Nick without dignity. Without humour.

With his figure swimming uncertainly before her eyes, Claudia had reacted, over-reacted, and Nick had told her bitingly he wasn't going to be damned by a schoolgirl's hasty judgment. She wouldn't forget that either. For all her surprisingly poised manner Claudia knew he had divined her secret; she had a very tender feeling for him and it had always touched her he was very gentle with her. But never then. Her coolness had turned to turbulence and at one stage he had slapped her so her head flew back and cleared of its faint hysteria. And then he had tried to hold her. *Hold* her! She *hated* him. More, much more, than she despised Cristina.

'Claud, Claudia, take it calmly,' he had urged her, his mouth near her ear, but she had broken away from

him, white-faced while Cristina in her beautiful robe
had cried over and over again Claudia was mistaken.

But Claudia had known. Perhaps she had always
known since Cristina had first laid eyes on Nick. Then
her startled gaze had flickered and fallen. 'I mean he's
too much!' she had drawled to Claudia afterwards,
but to the sensitive and perceptive Claudia it was easy
to see she was unusually excited. Where her husband
was all sweetness, Nick was certainly spice. Nick, the
fallen angel.

It was the end that day of a girlish passion; the
beginning of something else. The end of a carefree
life; the beginning of terrible tensions. There was no
anger left in her now. Only bitter disillusionment and
a watchfulness that had forced her stepmother into
toeing a straight line. They were all really enemies
but like good actors they could assume smiles when
Grant Ingram was around. What *was* life if one
couldn't be civilised? What *was* infidelity for Heav-
en's sake!

'Claudia?' Fergy tapped on the door first, then
came her head. 'Say, what's the matter, kiddo?'

'Why, *nothing,* Fergy!' Claudia turned brightly.

'You can't fool me, love.' Fergy looked at the girl
very closely. 'I expect moments like these you feel a
little sad?'

'Yes.'

'If only your mother had lived to see you!' Fergy
circled around admiringly. 'You're not wearing her
pearls?'

'I'll show you.' Claudia picked up the lustrous double strand and held them to her neck.

'Too much!' Fergy confirmed. 'I like the camellias

in your hair. A lovely touch. Your daddy will be very proud.'

'I hope so.'

'Cheer up, love,' Fergy told her dryly. 'You're the precious pearl in the Ingram collection.'

'I've *other* things to offer, Fergy.'

'Hold on to that, kiddo. It's your father's nature to equate *his* women almost exclusively with looking great. If you'd been plain you would have been a terrible failure. However, you ain't. Only the servants are ugly around here.'

'*Servants!* What a stupid word. Why, this house would grind to a halt without you. We're utterly dependent on you, dearest Fergy.'

'This is *my* home, love, because it's *your* home. Anyway, your father is an important and very amiable man. Who am I to complain? Now *you,* I can understand your complaints. You're a highly intelligent girl not a beautiful doll to hang clothes on. Incidentally, the dress is ravishing.'

'You look lovely too.' It calmed Claudia just to have Fergy around and she did look most beautiful with her dear, kindly, so familiar face. She was now approaching sixty and her tanned skin was very lined but Fergy continued to radiate good humour and energy. Tonight she was wearing a most unusual creation of her own choosing, something like an Eastern robe, and her hair, usually cropped like a boy's, had been permed into a sea of little snails.

Claudia bent down and kissed her. 'I can never thank you, Fergy, for all you've done.'

'Will you *stop!*' Behind her glasses, Fergy's eyes momentarily shone with tears. 'My dearest child, you are so much like your mother, you can't imagine. I know seeing you tonight will take your grandparents back.'

'If only I'd had brothers and sisters.'

'Too late now, darling,' Fergy said. 'The next patter of feet in this house will have to be *your* children. I'm sure your stepmama will never take herself off the pill.'

Claudia had to fight not to show her sudden distaste. Cristina, she was certain, would do anything for Nick. Would she ever forget how Cristina had *looked*. The straining and the passion in her hazel eyes, nipples surging against her thin robe, the recklessness that was in her. Cristina wanted Nick with a ferocity that had made her lose her senses, betray her husband in his own house. She would do anything Nick asked of her only Nick wouldn't be asking her to leave her husband. Far from it and Claudia could even feel pity for her stepmother. Cristina might be madly in love. Nick wasn't. For Nick women were sometime alluring. His real life was tied up with plans, houses, buildings, great edifices; a whole field of endeavour far more important than making love to women. Cristina like so many before her was doomed to dismissal.

Well done, Nick!

Her grandparents were the first to arrive—Sir Ross and Lady McKinlay. Before his retirement Sir Ross had enjoyed a distinguished career as an obstetrician and had received his knighthood in the early 1970s. The same year, rather terribly, that his daughter had been killed. The blow had been enormous. Sir Ross had retired a few years after and his wife Claudia, after whom Claudia had been so joyfully named, had withdrawn from community affairs where once she had played an invigorating role. It was only in recent times that she had become reinvolved in those organisations most dear to her heart. The renewed interest and bouts of fund-raising had had a most beneficial effect on her mentally and physically. Claudia McKinlay was the kind of woman who functioned best when many demands were made upon her, but Sir Ross had been drastically altered by his daughter's sudden, early death. Where both parents had suffered, Sir Ross had been especially vulnerable. Grief had turned to a kind of despair and this had resulted in a closing off of his once wide social environment, and there was not a thing his family or his many loyal friends could do about it. Only his granddaughter could have brought him out to a large party and when he saw her coming down the stairs towards him he discovered something that miraculously eased the dammed-up desperation in his heart. He could never truly lose his daughter, she was here; Victoria's greatest achievement. Moreover she would go on through family. Claudia would marry. She had grown up so much in the last few years. Now she was a woman with a woman's miraculous body. She could have a child. His great-grandchild. For the first time in a very long while Sir Ross realised he wanted to stay alive.

'Grandad. Nanna!' Claudia's lovely face reflected the depth of feeling she had for these two very special people. She was so proud of them. They had done so much with their lives. Really worthwhile things. She embraced each of them in turn, looking deeply into their eyes. Her grandmother was a tiny woman with fine bones showing sharply through her delicate skin. She looked ethereal until one put her to the test and then she was streets ahead of almost anyone half her age. Claudia always said her grandmother would walk the legs off her. The silver-haired fragility was all a disguise. Now she was wreathed in smiles that nonetheless hid a few tears. Family celebrations always had their emotional moments and Claudia was the living image of the daughter they had lost. For that matter it was easy to see where the family face had come from. Ross McKinlay was still a strikingly handsome man and his colouring and patrician features had been reproduced in his daughter and granddaughter as they would be again. It had long been one of Claudia McKinlay's little jokes that 'all Ross's patients fell in love with him', and for a little while many of them had, but it was the dreamy, idealised love that had little to do with real life. Anyway Dr McKinlay never noticed. He was too busy looking after his patients.

Tonight he held his granddaughter most tenderly and the terrible sorrow that had held him so long in its grip lifted suddenly off his heart; an uncanny experience that he later tried to explain to his wife, when knowing him so well she had already divined it and thanked God from the bottom of her heart.

By nine-thirty all the guests had arrived and the party was in full swing. Grant Ingram had designed his house for large scale entertaining and the big, brilliantly lit rooms, the spacious entrance hall and the terraces were filled with people, laughing, talking, fooling around the piano, dancing. Many of the guests were Claudia's own friends, but all age groups were represented; Grant Ingram's closest associates, Cristina's friends, long time friends of the Ingram and McKinlay families. All of them mingling happily, their pleasure accentuated by their very beautiful surroundings and the evening dress that everyone wore.

Cristina looked particularly stunning in a one-shouldered, toga-like garment the colour of sweet sherry. It went wonderfully with her dark auburn hair and her changeable, hazel eyes. Her hollowed out cheeks and high bridged nose gave her a look of distinction and her skin, lightly freckled without make-up, looked flawless under the bright lights. She was dancing with Mike Fairholme, a T.V. personality, and whatever she was saying it had Mike's full attention. He had even stopped dancing to be sure he caught it all.

Claudia, chilling a little, looked towards her father's group. They were all clustered around him almost in homage. Her father, well into his fifties, still had a boyish look about him, something that had to do with his wonderful enthusiasm and working in a field of great, cultural achievement. He had turned his head over his shoulder to say something to Nick who was standing with careless elegance his back resting against the fireplace, his handsome profile reflected in the eighteenth-century mirror. It was almost like father to son, the expression on her father's face, the affectionate attention Nick accorded him. Whatever the exchange Claudia saw her grandfather applauding and the interest and animation in his darling, distinguished face drove out all of the remaining chill. She had been so worried her grandfather would find this big party a trial, but somehow he seemed to be enjoying himself in a way none of the family had anticipated. Indeed she saw her grandmother reach over and clasp his hand and the smile he turned on her was sufficient to make Claudia feel a blaze of happiness. There were so many ways to love. She loved her father deeply. She adored her grandmother but a singular feeling flowed out of her to her grandfather. He looked wonderful in evening clothes. His face and tall, thin figure suited formal dress...

'Oh, Claudia, there you are!' A group of her friends came in from the terrace to sweep her away. So far she had only greeted Nick on arrival and there were so many people it would be possible to get right through the night without exchanging another word until he left. He was being particularly brutal to Cristina tonight, bringing Amanda Nichols with him, possibly the most decorative young widow in town, and a woman Cristina actively disliked. She would hate her now.

'Do you know you're the most beautiful creature here?' her friend Matthew Lewis told her languorously. He had danced her into a corner where there was a pocket of deep shadow. 'I think that Amanda baby is second best if you go for the older woman. They tell me old Nichols left her a packet. She must be wearing half of it around her neck. Nick's a bit of a swine bringing her, isn't he?' He went to kiss her tenderly under the ear, but Claudia drew back.

'What do you mean?'

'Oh—' Matthew looked a bit rueful now, 'one gets to be a bit bitchy on the periphery of the jet set.'

'Say what you mean.' Claudia brought up her hand and lightly hit him.

'I told you, darling, bitchiness really. Poor old Cristina is working hard to show she's not livid.'

'She has never liked Mrs Nichols,' Claudia said.

'Of course. But she's always liked *Nick*.' Matthew's blue eyes glittered as he let that drop.

'Really, Matthew...' Claudia felt her heart slow.

'I'm no fool, birthday girl. Come to think of it, it's quite understandable. Nick has bloody *everything*. He's spoken of at Uni as one of the *great* ones. None of us feel we can accomplish anything. Old Prof Barrett hardly ever talks of anyone else. I reckon he hangs his life on having taught Dominic Grey. And if you don't believe me...'

'I believe you.'

'And if that's not enough he can have any woman he wants. Lucky devil! It's a terribly elusive thing, isn't it, sex appeal? Now *you* have it. So much, I'm utterly helpless. Nick has it. God, it covers him like a shower of diamonds. Bloody unfair. Jill over there couldn't be sexy if she took off all her clothes. Yet she's a very pretty girl. You see it so many times. The haves and the have-nots. Some dangerous little chemical that's added at birth.'

'I hope you're going to restrict those kind of comments, Matt,' Claudia said, rather emotionally. 'You're talking about my father's *wife*.'

'Quite so, none of my business.' He rubbed his chin on the top of her shining hair. 'Anyway, Claudia, I'm only teasing you. I love you too much to try and hurt you.'

'You're not teasing, Matt. You're making one of your usual sharp observations. So Cristina finds Nick very attractive. She's not the only one.'

'*I'll* say! He could walk any one of them home.'

'So I don't approve of your linking their names together.'

Silence.

'Matt?' Claudia lifted her head beseechingly.

'Of course not, darling. I shouldn't have said anything. It's a good thing, mind, your father is so supremely sure of himself he's not paying much attention. Cristina's glances speak volumes. If she doesn't watch it quite a few people will become aware of how she feels. She's just walked across to Nick and put her arm through his.'

'Why shouldn't she? She's the hostess.'

'Nick looks like he's going to tell her to remove it.'

'Nick's great at putting people in their place.'

A tall, blond young man stepped in front of them. 'Say, Lewis, you can't monopolise Claudia all night. Claudia, they're playing *our* song.'

'What, from when you both went to dancing school?'

'You don't like her dancing with other fellas, do you?'

'You can read my mind,' Matthew replied.

'*Please,* this is a party.' Claudia moved away from Matthew's encircling arm and gave her hand to the determined Peter. Both young men were staring rather fixedly at each other, propelled by a faint hostility. Friends for a long time, their mutual interest in Claudia was transforming friendship into jealousy.

'I don't know why you like Matt so much,' Peter was now saying. 'I can see him being very ruthless in the years to come.'

Her father and grandfather took her in to supper.
There were little speeches, of course. Many toasts.
Claudia had to clear a few tears from her blazing,
green eyes. While their guests were drinking coffee,
her father insisted she play the piano, then settled
back to enjoy his daughter's accomplishment, the romantic figure she made at the big, black concert
grand, the light on her platinum hair, her slender arms
and naked shoulders, the tiered skirt of her lovely
dress billowing to the floor. Looking at her, he saw
Victoria and he knew Claudia's grandparents would
be seeing their daughter too. Something pressed on
Grant Ingram's heart, some appalling weight, but he
didn't allow it to settle for any time. It was all a
matter of survival and he had long since perfected the
knack of turning aside those intensely painful
thoughts that could upset his equilibrium. Claudia was
a splendid daughter and he could bask in her beauty
and feminine talents. As well, she was fantastically
dutiful in a day when young people challenged their
parents at every turn. All in all, he was an extremely
lucky man.

The champagne was flowing freely and now there
were quite a few open flirtations going on.

'You played beautifully tonight, Claudia,' Cristina
volunteered, gazing past Claudia's head to where
Nick was leaning attentively over Amanda Nichols to
hear what she was saying. Amanda was looking up
at him, eyes glowing, lips parted. She wore the same,
excited look Claudia had seen stamped on Cristina's
face.

Another young man managed to get past Matthew's
defences and whirled Claudia away. To anyone

watching she appeared to be having a marvellous time. Colour flowered along her cheekbones, her eyes brilliant, her mouth was soft with laughter; her whole aura was youthful beauty. Yet inside Matthew's talk had unsettled her. There were forces loose to destroy them all. Her father was such a proud man. He had lived a life untouched by any kind of scandal. Talk of Nick and Cristina coming to his ears would deal him a terrible blow. His judgment had always been impeccable. He had chosen Cristina as his wife. He had paid Nick the greatest tribute of all. He looked on him as a son.

Her partner left her for a moment to get them both a cold drink and Claudia walked out on to the terrace, savouring the cool air. Most of the dancing couples had flocked inside. Mike Fairholme was now at the piano and Cristina, who was really very clever, was giving her impersonation of Cleo Laine. If they could *only* go back in time. Back to the time before Cristina had fallen under Nick's spell.

Claudia moved farther down the terrace with Cristina's voice following her. It was a full-bodied mezzo. A *voice*, in the real sense. Why couldn't Cristina simply be happy with her father? The day they were married, she had been in floods of tears. 'Grant is the most wonderful man in the world!' she had cried emotionally. It made no sense at all. Indeed it was absolutely unthinkable. And at the bottom of it, deeper even than her fears for her father, her own bone-deep hurt...the anger and bewilderment. For all his sexual radiance she had thought Nick naturally fastidious. There were beautiful women certainly, but not in excess. They were more than beautiful, they were intelligent, successful women in their own right. No one could have called him an addicted womaniser.

'So this is where you've run off to?' a voice said.

She had spent most of the night hiding, now he had found her.

'Don't you like Cristina's singing?' He joined her, looking down at her steadily.

'I'm sort of very sensitive about Cristina,' Claudia said.

'You mean you're a self tormentor.'

'This is *my* night, Nick,' she said.

'How you've changed.'

'Haven't we all? *Terribly.*' She turned her head swiftly so the pearl drops moved against her cheeks. She could feel their burning; pink flags that would still be apparent in the muted, golden light.

'You like to sit in judgment, Claudia, don't you?'

'Once you could do no wrong. My father idolises you, Nick.'

'Oh, does he really?'

'You know he does.' His voice was the most dismal pleasure to her ears. Dark and vibrantly cutting.

'Do you resent it?'

'No.'

'You're certainly perfect. A very beautiful girl with no faults or foibles.'

'Why don't you just *go,* Nick,' she said.

'I want to wish you a happy birthday. I haven't even given you my present.'

'I don't want any present from you and you know it.' She moved farther away from him, staring out at the garden, the shining line of the river.

'No, you prefer to press your atrocious charges.'

'You know *exactly* what I think, Nick.'

'Yes, some cruel little goddess who calmly pro-
nounces judgment. That's really your style. God-
desses don't deal in justice or mercy. If a mortal dis-
pleases them they turn them into monsters. That's
what you've attempted with me. I'm only surprised
you haven't had me assassinated publicly.'

'And humiliate my *father?*' All her pent-up anger
broke from her. 'Have you broken it off now, Nick,
have you? Do you want forgiveness?'

'From *you?*' He caught her wrist and her heart
pounded high in her throat. 'Who are you to forgive
me anything? Grant Ingram's spoilt-rotten angel.
What experience have you of life to judge anyone?'

'Oh, no, no, *no,* Nick. You're not going to get out
of it that way. There are penalties one pays for taking
another man's wife.' She knew the moment she said
it she had pushed him into a terrible anger.

'What about his *daughter?*'

'She hates you.'

'I don't mind.' His handsome face was drawn into
an austere mask.

'Don't you touch me, Nick,' she warned him, assailed by pure terror.

'Because you couldn't bear it, or because you really want it?'

'You're mad.' She looked behind her, seeking to
escape but he closed the distance between them grasping her by the shoulders.

'No escape, Claud,' he said. 'This has been coming
for a long, long time.'

'You know what I think of you.'

'I don't give a damn.' His voice was devoid of all feeling as he pulled her into his arms.

She twisted her body in a long convulsion of fear and helpless rage but it only brought her closer to lying back in his arms. *'No!'* she was screaming inside but she knew she could never use her voice. Then his mouth covered hers and the stress was too much. She went limp. Her mouth open, panting for the breath he wouldn't allow her. Sensation was spreading out through her body, shooting along her nerves. He was destroying her like the expert he was, taking her innocence in a kind of joyless triumph. She had no choice but to submit as he savagely explored her mouth, his hand hard at her back, moving her breasts against him so that she began to feel alight with a dark excitement.

'Little hypocrite,' he said harshly. 'I don't even have to coach you.' He tore his mouth away and Claudia felt so soft and faint inside she seemed to collapse against him, while he, oddly enough, gathered her closer. 'You're crying,' he said. 'You should be.'

She could feel the glitter of tears in her eyes. 'I'm crying for both of us,' she said very shakily, aware she had so little control over her body, she could not then pull away from him.

'Confusing isn't it?' he said cruelly. 'Maybe a little more experience would make you less puritanical. *Puritanical,* God,' he laughed harshly. 'Ice on the outside and a fire within. Give me women like Amanda any day. They're *exactly* what they seem.'

She couldn't understand how she could feel so frail. How unbelievable that she should be clinging to

him when she was jolted through with fright and revulsion. Yet her limbs seemed to be aching for contact, one of her white arms stretched along his black
sleeve, her slender body heavy against his, his arm
pinning her around the waist, the other under her chin,
touching her throat.

'Do you want me to kiss you again?' His silver
eyes flashed. 'You're so damned good at it. Saintly
little Claudia with the fabulous mouth.'

She buried her head into the curve of his shoulder.
'Don't, Nick.'

'Oh, God, you couldn't be more *perfect.* I could
kill you, Claudia. I want to after I love you. Nobody
else in the whole world would treat me as you have.
No one else would damn me out of hand.'

She did it without thinking at all; let her body relax
against him, the need so insistent it counteracted her
will. Whatever he did, however terrible, he still had
this power.

'What are you doing, Claudia?' he asked tautly.
'Do you think you've found some other way?'

Lightheaded and dizzy she lifted her head. 'If I
could hurt you, Nick, I would.'

'How, angel? You can't even stand by yourself.'
His mouth came down, slid along her cheekbone to
the corner of her lips. 'Come on, Claudia, if you want
to play grown-up games.'

She gasped and went to cry out but he moved his
mouth over hers, abruptly, shockingly, taking charge
of her again. There was no warmth, no tenderness in
this at all, but a devastating seduction performed in
cold blood.

'Well, well, well, what have we here?' A familiar voice exclaimed happily.

The terrible difficulty lay in trying to speak. Claudia made an attempt and failed, being at that moment queerly disoriented. Her body couldn't even make the withdrawal from Nick's and he still held her against him with her shining skirt fanning out at the back of her.

Her father's expression said it all; a disbelieving *joy*.

'I've been trying to give her her present all night,' Nick said with a charming wryness.

'And have you?' Grant Ingram asked.

'Not as yet, sir.'

'Then I'm going to give you a chance to do so,' Grant Ingram looked from one to the other with an expression of the most intense indulgence. 'Don't be too long though, Nick. A lot of people are asking where the birthday-girl disappeared to.'

'Five minutes, Grant, and we'll be there.'

'Perfect.' He nodded to them, blue eyes glowing, and walked away.

'Oh, hell!' Claudia wailed.

'For God's sake, be *quiet!*'

'You let him think…'

'Okay, so what if I did?' he returned coolly. 'Your father has been living for the day when our relationship would change.'

'Oh, it's *changed*,' she said bitterly.

'Don't I know it.' He turned her so the light shone directly on her face. 'I've seen you grow from a delightful child into some terrible little avenging angel. I told you once, Claudia, that you'd made a terrible mistake but mistrust and condemnation are all I've ever had from you. Until *now*.'

She could have wept with her own helplessness. 'You wanted to bring me down, Nick.'

'Yes. You've been breathing too much rarefied air up in your ivory tower. I had thought you a frozen little witch but the heat you generate is staggering. You know what you are? You're a siren.'

'What utter nonsense! I don't belong in any such category.'

'You mean you don't *want* it to be true. You carry some idea of yourself that's shocked and outraged by the idea of passion. Your life is very cool and controlled and trouble free. You surround yourself with the sort of young men who won't endanger you. You offer them very little but that doesn't stop them falling very foolishly in love. I pity them, Claudia, because you're not at all kind.'

'And you *are*?' She looked up at him in anger and sorrow. 'I thought you cared about my father a great deal?'

'I do.' His voice was hard. 'I respect and admire him but the fact is he's never handled you properly. If he'd treated you more as a developing human being, an emerging *woman,* instead of some perfect porcelain figurine, like the Meissen he's so fond of, perhaps you'd be somewhat different. As it is, you're rather frighteningly rigid.'

'I saw you, Nick,' she said. 'I saw Cristina. Cristina most of all. Her face openly expressed *everything*. I may have my faults, but I'm not a fool. I always felt Cristina was attracted to you, but I never, ever considered she would allow her feelings to get the better of her.'

'There was a moment tonight when *you* were abandoning all your inhibitions,' he told her brutally.

'That's different and anyway, I deny it. I have no husband to consider. I'm betraying no one, only myself, kissing you. I have the greatest revulsion for what you've done. Maybe you've stopped—how can I say? The fact is Nick, you and Cristina are playing with fire. If you don't care about my father, *your* career could be ruined. You may be all kinds of a genius but my father is a very influential man.'

'I have a terrible urge to strangle you,' he said quietly. 'No matter what you thought you *saw,* I am not, nor ever will be, your stepmother's lover. I do not care to go on protesting my innocence. Even for you. All this panic and anxiety you're suffering, is self inflicted. It would have to be a massive, uncontrollable passion for me to start a relationship with another man's wife. I've never met the woman who could induce that in my whole life. I've met a silly, little girl with a psychiatric disorder who could bring me remarkably close to it. But not Cristina, *no.* Cristina does *not* turn me on.'

'You want me to believe you, Nick. It's a tall order.'

'I expect tall orders from my *friends.* I know damn well you wouldn't have got such a high university entrance rating without *my* help with your maths. I spent hours with you, you little brat. You may be high on the humanities but you sure as hell have no mathematical bent.'

'No one ever explained it like you did,' she said.

'Anyway didn't I thank you over and over. Didn't I tell everyone I would never have passed without you?' Her green eyes were full of tears. 'Oh, hell, Nick,' her voice broke. 'Why couldn't you just leave well alone. There are plenty of women to love.'

'Shall I take you up on it?' he demanded harshly. 'I won't go back to Cristina if I can have *you*.'

'What, destroy me as well?' her voice rose. 'No chance of that, Nick. I want someone a whole lot better than you.' She saw the violence in his eyes and she moved back. 'But I'll offer you a deal. I'll never go to my father as long as you keep away from Cristina.'

'Did Cristina tell you about *us?*' he asked with gentle menace.

'She denied it, as you know.'

'Ah, yes. But you were determined to have a crime. Name the villain. You're not so much preoccupied with what Cristina might have done as with *me*. All in all, you're rather an interesting psychological study. Are you determined to drive me out by fair means or foul?'

'I don't know what you mean.' Her lovely face was pale.

'Oh yes you do.' His eyes held her fast. 'I don't think there was ever a time I couldn't have picked you up and put you in my pocket. You were the most breathtakingly sweet little girl. I think when I first saw you, you stopped my heart. So gentle and sweet and serene. One thick, white-gold plait and big, wonderful green eyes. You were very special then. Now you're a terrible disappointment.'

Claudia was almost afraid to speak. He looked so

grim and bitter. 'We must go in, Nick,' she said. 'We're being missed.'

'As to that,' he said acidly, 'it might be helpful to stay here. I don't think your father wants anything more than to see you and me together. It would add something even more perfect to his collection.' He laughed bitterly. 'My, my, Claud, don't you look shocked. You're at pains to tell me *you're* not a fool. In all modesty I have a higher I.Q. We could get married. Then nine months later present your father with a grandson who would be as good as he and I put together. I know, darling. I *know*. Your father, much as he loves you, only has a tiny glimpse of *you*. He's one of those men who, in the most charming way possible, relegates women to the traditional, secondary role. *Service* is all very well. I don't think he really sees any point in a woman unless she is beautiful or like Cristina has the knack of presenting herself as very glamorous. There are no women associates in the firm. Jane Newcombe had to go to Harmann's.'

'Jane is a friend of yours,' Claudia defended her father's decision half-heartedly.

'Jane is a fine architect and she graduated top of her class. It was *our* loss. I told Grant this, but he brushed it aside. Positions should go on *merit*. You don't seriously think your father would have taken me on if I hadn't worn the old school tie. It helped too to have Lang Somerville as a grandfather. I'm only being realistic, Claudia. As fine an architect as your father is, he only works with people who are socially listed. He only employs people with a substantial background.'

'That *can't* be true!'

'What would *you* know? You've led a very privi-
leged life to say the least. Jane has had to fight for
everything she's got. You know nothing about battles.
You've had no shaping at all. Your father might as
well pick you up and shove you in one of those display cases he had built— ''Now here's a very valuable piece and that over there is my daughter!'' I'd
choose Jane over you any day but it's not as easy as
that.'

'I admire Jane, too,' she said helplessly. 'I know
she's clever and tough. Do you want me to be *tough?*'

'I don't want anything from you,' he said bitterly.
'I go insane when I see you.'

'You hurt me too,' she protested, so disturbed and
depressed there was an actual ache beneath her breast
bone. 'Please, Nick, we must go inside. It's impossible for us to talk any more. *Impossible.*'

'Then isn't it peculiar you want me to make love
to you? You can't stand it, can you?'

'No.' She had to admit it. It seemed such a trans-
gression. She could deal with Nick more easily as her
hero, not a fallen idol.

'Oh, God, what a little coward you are!' He slipped
his hand into his dinner jacket and when he withdrew
it he was holding a small article wrapped in crimson
and gold paper. 'There just isn't any way we can get
out of this. Happy Birthday, my angel. It's not what
you really need but it's all I'm allowed.'

'I don't want anything, Nick!' Her breasts were
rising strongly upon her narrow ribs. It was quite apparent she was agitated.

'*Take* it.' The air was electric. He held it out to her and as she took it their fingers touched.

Such a weight of desire came on her, Claudia had to drop her shining head. Desire and a sickening misery. 'Thank you,' she whispered shakily.

'Little fool.'

They had scarcely moved a few feet when Cristina bore down on them separating herself from the shadows. 'Nick, Claudia, you really will have to come inside.' Her little laugh had a jangly sound. 'What on earth are you nattering about anyway?'

'Are you sure you want to know?' Nick asked, very harshly.

'Aaah!' Cristina almost wheeled back against an arched pillar. 'You're not going to be happy, are you, Claudia, until you've torn us all apart?'

'I bleed for you darlin',' Nick said very suavely.

Claudia literally could not bear it. Without another word, she picked her full skirt up and fled. She wasn't worldly like Nick and Cristina. She was frightened of forbidden pleasures. Could one really toss infidelity off or did people like Nick and Cristina not recognise it? She could deal with nothing, *nothing*. Even Nick's kiss had tied her in knots. She brought up her hand and rubbed her mouth. It was pulsing with heat, glowing with natural colour.

'Oh there you are, darling!'

She could hear her father's voice and in the next instant he had walked through the open doorway and grasped her arm, linking it through his own. 'Well, what did Nick give you?'

'I haven't looked yet.' It sounded like a lament.

'Uum.' Her father pulled her to him and kissed her

cheek. His blue eyes looked at her with pride and approval. 'I expect you want to do that on your own?'

'Yes.'

'You've never hidden your feelings with me. You're very fond of Nick, aren't you? In fact I'd say he was about your favourite person.'

'*You're* my favourite person, Daddy,' she said. 'You're the best father in the world.'

'No question about that!' He laughed, highly pleased. 'Now where did Cristina get to?'

'She'll be here in a moment.' Claudia tried not to stiffen her body.

'I never realised she was so clever,' Grant Ingram murmured and drew his daughter back into the throng. 'Everyone really enjoyed her performance. Your grandmother was even trying to talk her into being the star turn at one of her functions. But you know Cristina. She absolutely refuses to be pinned down.'

At the sound of their approach, many heads turned.

'Grant, over here!' a woman's voice called. 'You've got to settle this argument.'

'Claudia.' Matthew was by her side. 'Mind if I sweep your daughter off, Mr Ingram?' he smiled.

'Enjoy yourselves,' Grant Ingram returned the smile benignly. Matthew was an utterly suitable young man but he wasn't for Claudia. 'Shall I take Nick's present for you, darling?' he asked. 'I'll just pop it in my pocket and give it to you after.'

Claudia's lovely face flushed pink. She passed the small package to her father and all the time Matthew didn't take his eyes off her. In a sense Grant Ingram was too self-absorbed to see the change in Claudia but Matthew did. She looked staggeringly beautiful and a little wild all at once. Something had taken possession of her. Someone. Matthew took Claudia's arm, his bright eyes darting around. A tall man came in from the terrace. Nick Grey. He too glanced across the room finding Claudia at once.

'So!' Matthew thought violently. 'If you think Claudia's going to be one of your casualties, Nick, you've got another think coming.' The muscles in his arm jumped and his expression tightened. For two years now he had been Claudia's friend. He had wanted her like crazy for all of that time. Now as he looked at Nick Grey's handsome, intense face he was shocked by his own jealousy. Claudia would need a little more convincing to see what kind of a man Dominic Grey was. There was always a great deal of talk about Nick. He was that kind of man.

CHAPTER TWO

EVEN with the Finals of her Honours course coming up, Claudia continued to go into the gallery. For the past two years she had been working *and* learning at a well-known art gallery run by Marcus Foley, connoisseur and patron of the arts, champion of the gifted unknowns and widely recognised as one of the most successful dealers in the country—certainly the most colourful. Marcus had once been a talented painter himself but once he recognised his own fatal facility he had turned his abundant energies to dealing and helping more gifted artists to achieve recognition. Therein lay his true genius and Marcus was enormously loved and revered.

Monday was the one day he allowed himself off and that was the day Claudia found herself a steady job; Monday, all day and Fridays until nine o'clock, though she never managed to get off until ten thirty or later. Not that she ever objected. What she was doing wasn't really a *job* at all. She *loved* it and she was very fond of Marcus who had been cast by nature in the baroque, rococo mould, or so it always seemed to Claudia. Yet Marcus had told her as a boy in England he had been violently unhappy though he never explained it other than to say he was always too small, too thin and too delicate to ever please his fa-

ther. It had been his mother, apparently, who had sent
him on a long holiday to her sister in Melbourne.
During that pleasant stay when he managed to grow
a foot and never suffered one asthmatic attack he expressed a desire to remain in Australia. His aunt, a
maiden lady and a very good artist, had been delighted and promptly sent her sister a cable explaining
the climatic conditions were having a surprisingly
beneficial effect on Marcus.

His parents had not answered at once though Marcus and his Aunt Estelle waited patiently, but eventually his father wrote to say Marcus could always
come back if he wanted. He did in fact return when
his gentle little mother died or as Marcus put it 'gave
up' and his father had only dimly recognised him
then. In the intervening years Marcus had turned from
an undersized twelve-year-old with a mop of light,
fuzzy curls into a tall, handsome, flamboyant creature
who could have stepped from a virtuoso painting de-
picting a very dashing and debonair young man of
fashion.

But even then his father could not accept him easily. 'The only thing I actually got out of him was I
had turned into something *vulgar* which was somehow to be expected now I had attached myself to
"that idiot Estelle".' At that point, apparently Marcus
had blazed into anger, socked his father and leapt on
to the first boat home.

Thirty years later he was still wonderfully impressive. He had legions of friends because he was extraordinarily kind and generous and he *enjoyed* people; probably women more. He had survived two
jumbled marriages and he lived in the golden hope of

finding, even now after all these years, the perfect mate. Certainly it was possible. There was no end of charming, flirtatious unattached women who wouldn't let him alone.

Claudia had to deal with one that very morning. Helen Villiers was a large, handsome lady who didn't really care about all the paintings she bought except it gave her the opportunity to talk to Marcus.

'Marcus not in, dear?' She went to the door of Marcus's very grand office and peered in as a double check.

'Not Mondays, Mrs Villiers,' Claudia smiled. Marcus had once been known to crawl under his massive desk to avoid detection by that very lady.

'How silly of me, I forgot.'

'Could *I* help you?' Claudia stood up and came around her own exquisite little bureau plat.

'I was just passing, you know,' Mrs Villiers lightly fanned her rose-scented body. 'I saw your stepmother the other day. I'd like to know her secret for always looking so special.'

'Effort and she's very well organised,' Claudia said.

'I fear I interrupted her—*lunch*. Nick Grey is still with your father isn't he?'

'Yes, of course.' Claudia kept her face cool and pleasant. 'Was Nick having lunch with Cristina?'

'I do hope I haven't let the cat out of the bag?' The slightly prominent blue eyes bulged.

'I'm not altogether sure what you're trying to say,' Claudia murmured, moving slightly away. She detested bitchy, troublemaking women and she had not thought Helen Villiers was like that until now. 'Cristina and Nick are quite friendly. He is always at our home. I don't see anything in the least unusual about their lunching together.'

'Of course not as she's so *happily* married.'

It was like receiving an unexpected blow in the stomach. 'You surely haven't come here, Mrs Villiers, just to tell me all this?'

'Good Lord, *no!*' Helen Villiers gave an odd little grimacing smile. 'How many women do *you* know mad about Nick Grey? Don't think I *blame* your stepmother for looking so...*unguarded.* He's an extraordinarily sexy man. I thank God he's much too young for me.'

'This is really a ridiculous conversation,' Claudia said. 'I don't know what Nick and my stepmother were discussing when you happened upon them but I'm pleased to tell you it could only have been something quite innocent. Probably Cristina fears my father is over-working. In fact this is very much the case at the moment. There's a very big project they're working on.'

'I've heard of it,' Helen Villiers returned blandly and Claudia saw her eyes widen as the entrance alarm sounded then someone came in the main gallery door.

'Why, hello!' Cristina stood there wearing a superb black linen suit teamed with an exquisite white blouse, very simple, very expensive gold jewellery, impeccably made-up, her mane of dark auburn hair wonderously arranged, an absolute stunner.

'Why—that's quite spooky!' Helen Villiers laughed gayly. 'We were just speaking about you.'

'Really?' Cristina raised one delicately painted brow. 'Oh, do go on.'

'I was just saying how marvellous you always look!' Helen Villiers eyed the younger woman archly. 'The other day for instance, when you were having lunch with Nick Grey, I said to the people I was with, "Cristina Ingram *must* be the best dressed woman in town." I'm sure you spend a fortune on your clothes.'

'Rubbish!' Cristina said curtly. 'I spend a lot of time *planning* my wardrobe. I *don't* spend my time buying almost anything my eye falls on,' her hazel eyes swept Helen Villiers over-dressed, matronly figure, 'and I don't indulge in a lot of torrid gossip. I believe you've told quite a few people you saw me having lunch with Nick Grey as though it was a cause for general concern?'

'Well it *was* a titillating scene,' Helen Villiers didn't falter although her firm cheeks flushed.

'Oh, *please,* Mrs Villiers,' Claudia intervened. 'This is most distasteful and really none of your business.'

'I expect you're very unhappy about it all the same.'

'Oh, look here!' Cristina said aggressively. 'We're not—I'm not and neither is Claudia—interested in your tawdry brand of gossip. I'm very fond of Nick, we *all* are.'

'You must be. You were touching him all the time.'

'I beg your pardon!' Cristina paled and for the first time her freckles became apparent.

'This is really rotten, Mrs Villiers,' Claudia said. 'Why are you interfering in our lives, acting so maliciously? Do you feel spiteful towards my stepmother and, if so, for Heaven's sake, why? I'm sure she's done you no harm. You scarcely know her.'

'I know *of* her. That is important.'

'And what does *that* mean?' Cristina almost shouted. 'You may very well regret this. I've never done anything I've been ashamed of in my life.'

'Obviously you think nothing of breaking up marriages,' Helen Villiers cried with a kind of suppressed venom. 'Do you know a Louise Baker?'

Cristina's own look of anger retreated in perplexity. 'I don't think so. *Should* I?'

'You don't know her husband Martyn?'

'Good grief, that cad!' Cristina shrugged him off contemptuously. 'What has all this to do with me?'

'Louise Baker is my niece.'

'My God, I hope she's not as boring as you are,' Cristina cut in furiously. 'It's true Martyn Baker caused me some embarrassment at one time with his highly unwanted attentions, but eventually I had him slung off my premises on his ear. I detest men who confuse pleasure with business and now that I think of it it might be as well to put you in hospital for a few weeks.'

'How *dare* you!' the older woman tottered backwards in alarm.

'I think an apology is in order, Mrs Villiers,' Claudia grasped Cristina's arm meaningfully. Cristina's hazel eyes were positively glittering and there was a high flush on her cheekbones. 'I think you were quite wrong about your niece and I *know* there is nothing reprehensible about a little show of affection. Nick Grey is as a son to my father which pretty nearly makes him *family* to us.'

'You swear you had no squalid little affair with my niece's husband?' Helen Villiers cried tersely.

'God give me patience!' Christina returned grimly. 'Just who do you think you are, madam, the public executioner? Martyn Baker is a common weasel, not a gracious, refined person like yourself though it seems you'd hang any poor devil who so much as looked at me. In essence he or your niece is a liar. Are you grasping what I'm saying?'

'Louise told me…' Helen Villiers stuttered.

'Louise is an idiot. Martyn Baker might be carrying on with half the town but not me. He came to me with some story about redecorating his home and of course I took him perfectly seriously. I get such enquiries all the time. Later I realised he was just wasting my time and had him tossed out by a Swedish friend of mine. He's the bouncer from over the road,' Cristina laughed harshly. 'As to having lunch with a good friend of the family's!'

'*Please.*' All at once Mrs Villiers seemed defeated. 'My niece has been so wretched. The anguish!'

'And we do feel sorry for her and for you, Mrs Villiers,' Claudia said rather tartly, 'but you do see you've made a terrible mistake.'

'I do.' Helen Villiers shed a tear in front of them, then she turned to Claudia appealingly. 'You won't tell Marcus, will you?'

'She certainly won't. *I* will.' Cristina glared her rage across the table. 'If you expect pity from me you won't get it. By the sound of it you've been going around the town trying to destroy my reputation.'

'No, *no!*' Helen Villiers threw out an arm towards Claudia. 'Tell her that's not so. I was merely having a discreet word in *your* ear.'

'Let me see you off, Mrs Villiers,' Claudia said. 'I expect we all make foolish mistakes at times.'

'I always felt you were such a *sympathetic* girl,' Mrs Villiers allowed herself to be drawn away. 'Marcus is totally devoted to you.'

'Wicked old bitch!' Cristina cried out in a ringing tone just as they reached the bottom of the stairs.

'I really did mean it about Nick Grey and your stepmother,' Helen Villiers suddenly said. 'I might have been wrong about Martyn, I suppose, he's such a degenerate character, but I know what a woman looks like when she's in love. Friend of the family indeed!'

'I am asking you, Mrs Villiers, not to discuss this.'

'Exactly.'

'My grandmother always says if you can't say something good about someone don't say anything at all.'

'Your grandmother, if we are speaking about Lady McKinlay, is far above your stepmother,' Helen Villiers replied.

'Ugly, unfounded rumours could hurt *all* my family. 'Well, I suppose…'

'Would you like me to give a message to Marcus?'

'Yes, dear.' Helen Villiers sighed and slipped behind the wheel of her car. 'I'm going away for a few days. I fear this has been all too painful. I'll ring him when I get back.'

Claudia could not bring herself to wave the woman off. Yet, however meddlesome Mrs Villiers was, she was no fool. It was getting to the stage where Cristina would have to wear a mask around Nick.

'Has the horrible old bitch gone?' Cristina demanded to know.

'Yes. I wish that hadn't happened. Mercifully no one came in to buy a picture.'

'I wanted to put one right over her head.'

'Damn it, Cristina,' Claudia cried. 'Can't you see what you're doing is dangerous? Are you going to throw up a good marriage, a good husband, so you can have some insane little affair with Nick?'

'Oh my dear...' Cristina blinked the furious tears back.

'I can't *believe* this of you. Of both of you,' Claudia exclaimed with appalled reproach. 'Daddy thinks the *world* of Nick. He thinks you're a very stylish lady. His *wife*. I think the shock would kill him.'

'It's my fault. All *my* fault,' Cristina said. 'God, don't you think I hate myself? Once I used to take a hard moral stand about things like this. I saw other women as being simple-minded fools but then I fell in love. I tell you, Claudia, I'm *spellbound*. I don't want to be, but I *am*.'

'You don't *love* my father?' Claudia asked in anguish.

'Of course I love him.' Cristina held a finger to her heavily mascaraed lashes. 'It's possible to love *two* men at the same time. What I feel for Grant is quite different. It's a beautiful relationship. I can see what I feel for Nick is a sin.'

'I certainly hope so,' Claudia moaned with heavy irony. 'You could wreck your whole life. I don't want to hurt you, Cristina. We were getting on quite well, but I must point out that Nick is not as committed to you as you are to him.'

'I know that.' Cristina was trying desperately not to cry. She had to go straight to work and she could not possibly ruin her makeup. 'There's no need to point it out, Claudia.'

'I think there is.' Claudia's young face was shadowed and upset. 'It must be pretty awful to fall desperately in love with the wrong person, but I suppose honour must help. You don't want to hurt Daddy, do you? Break up your marriage?'

'I wish I were dead!' Cristina said violently.

'I'd choose fighting it out any day. I feel sorry for you, Cristina, but I'm on my father's side. He would be badly stricken if some rumour came to his ears. He's not a jealous man but I think he'd be extremely *final* if he ever found out. You'd be on your own. You don't really believe Nick would go on seeing you?'

'Why couldn't he have been a perfectly *ordinary* young man?'

'My father would never have become interested in him. You must realise Daddy only surrounds himself with exceptional people. He believes you to be exceptional and it's quite true you're a very clever woman. You run your own business and you're very good at it. You look stunning and Daddy loves that. If you want your life to follow a certain style you'd better start telling yourself Nick is poison.'

'And what about you, Claudia?' Cristina asked oddly, a bitter little smile twisting her glossy mouth. 'You've been excessively attached to Nick ever since I can remember.'

'Not any more.'

'Disgusted with him, are you?'

'Yes I am. If you don't mind I'd rather not talk about Nick.'

'All right.' Cristina picked up her handbag. 'I daresay you're in love with him. Most women are.'

'Why did you come here?' Claudia asked. Cristina, although she enjoyed Marcus's company, rarely came to the gallery.

'I can't really talk to you at home. You're so *pure* and remote.'

'I also care what happens to you, Cristina,' Claudia said. 'We're not all that close but I do like you and admire you for your ability. You just can't imagine how I felt that afternoon...'

'You're such a child, Claudia. An adolescent. Wait until desire takes hold of you.'

'Maybe that's exactly what it is,' Claudia answered soberly. 'Desire. Not love. Love shouldn't be something frightfully destructive.'

'Well it *is*.' Cristina's whole reed slim body conveyed her titanic helplessness. 'Will you be in to dinner tonight?'

'No, I told Fergy, I'm going over to Grandad's tonight. Nanna has a meeting and I'm going to keep him company.'

'Then give him my love,' Cristina said with perfect sincerity. 'That woman has made me feel quite sick.'

'Me too.'

'Make yourself a cup of tea.' Cristina wiggled her fingers over her shoulder. 'I hope Marcus is going to join us Saturday night. He's such marvellous company.'

Claudia stared after her stepmother with an expression of almost theatrical perplexity. 'I'll leave him a reminder.'

'Good, dear. Take care. Remember what Marcus always says. If some lunatic comes in with a sawn-off shotgun and demands some of the paintings, let him have the lot.'

'I'll remember,' Claudia muttered in a strangled voice. These days she wasn't all that sure what *lunatic* meant. If she *had* to pick a word that best described her stepmother's behaviour it would have to be schizophrenic. Cristina was only in her early thirties so it couldn't be some raging hormonal imbalance, a mad desire to stave off loss of desirability with a particularly white-hot affair. This was actually Cristina's second *marriage*. Her first had ended abruptly at the age of twenty-four, the reason being, according to Cristina, her husband had been 'a terribly dull guy'. First of all, he was an accountant...

It was a slow day altogether after a very profitable weekend but towards late afternoon Marcus called in and everything blossomed for an hour.

'You seemed a little depressed when I came in,' Marcus observed in his wonderfully fruity voice actually handed on to him by his father.

'I suppose I was.' Claudia ran her fingers with absent reverence over a MacKennal bronze that had recently cropped up in a convent where it had served as a kind of paperweight. Reverend Mother had thought it a bust of the Madonna but when told that it was not had no objection to selling it to Marcus for an undisclosed price.

'Anything I can do?' Marcus looked up at her from

beneath his Mephistophelean eyebrows. 'I'm fond of solving knotty problems.'

'Very good at it too,' Claudia smiled. 'No, I don't think so, Marcus dear.'

'In love, are you?'

'Why ever would you say that?' Claudia burst out after a moment of profound silence.

'Come, come, Claudia,' Marcus looked at her with an expression of sympathy and a smile. 'I was at the party remember?'

'So?' She knew she was flushing badly.

'My dear child, I've known you since you were a little girl and your father used to bring you in with him so you could develop an "eye" early. I know every expression on your face. I know when you're happy, sad, worried and depressed. I also know when someone in particular is causing you a little heartache. Someone who has been at the centre of your life for a long time now. Someone *I* see as absolutely ideal for you.'

'You're wrong, Marcus,' Claudia shook her head.

'As a matter of fact, I'm not.' Marcus glanced quickly through a letter, then tore it up. 'Should have really stamped on it,' he muttered distastefully then returned his glance to Claudia. 'Nick cares about you a great deal.'

'Who says so?'

'My dear, I *know*. I should think everyone knows. Your father thinks the world of him, that's so, isn't it?'

'He would have liked Nick as a son.'

'Well, I wouldn't be unhappy with a son like that

either,' Marcus said mildly. 'The question is, dear girl, is it making you a little bit jealous?'

'Marcus!' Claudia's emerald eyes opened wide. 'You must be mad!'

'All right then,' Marcus spread his large, shapely hands. 'We have a mystery here. What is the problem?'

Claudia turned her head away. Nice as Marcus was, she couldn't tell him. 'I think Nick sees me as a little girl,' she side-tracked. 'He's quite a bit older and he has *never* been interested in my age group. Young girls have terrible conversation.'

'Quite right, they do, but they're so *pretty!*'

Claudia shook her head again, shoulders drooping, eyelashes coming down on her cheeks.

'Listen, my little one, your conversation is really very good. Incidentally *I* must take a little credit for it.'

'Of course.'

'Don't be cheeky.' Marcus turned away to check the security system. 'I'm not sure what's gone wrong between you and Nick but I wouldn't allow it to keep up if I were you. I think possibly Nick has *had* to get used to thinking of you as a child, or a young relative or whatever. It would never have done, for instance, not to allow you to grow up, finish off your education, allow yourself plenty of young admirers.'

'Marcus, *stop*. Turn around here and tell me what you're talking about?' Claudia pleaded.

Marcus did turn around, shaking his leonine head. 'I believe, my dear, you've got to work it out for yourself. Perhaps that would be best.' He reached out and touched Claudia's shoulder. 'What did dear old

Shakespeare say? "We that are true lovers run into strange capers".'

'*As You Like It,*' Claudia confirmed sighing. 'Speaking of strange capers, Mrs Villiers was in this morning.'

'Dear Lord!' Marcus's large, pleasantly rounded form shook from head to foot. 'Surely she knows I'm not in Mondays?'

'Probably forgot.'

'You didn't say where I was?' Marcus walked about, turning off the lights.

'So she could go out searching? No.' Claudia moved to help him. 'Actually she just wanted you to know she's going away for a few days.'

'That's scarcely *my* business,' Marcus said mildly. 'Why can't women be happy on their own?'

'How can *anyone* be happy on their *own,* Marcus? We must have someone to love. You have wonderful friends.'

'For which I'm intensely grateful.' Marcus stroked his luxuriant moustache. 'I can't say I blame her for chasing me. I'm an awfully good catch.'

This had the effect of making Claudia laugh wildly and after a moment Marcus joined her. 'Seriously, Claudia, I *am,*' he gasped when they sobered. 'Now, as you're going out to your grandfather's I'll put the De Maistre in the boot. It's a very interesting work. We were lucky to get it. It was sold at Christie's at the end of '74. Burnett wouldn't let it go until now.'

Marcus locked up and they walked in a companionable silence out to Claudia's little runabout. 'Have you arranged about the flowers for Friday?' Marcus asked, as he settled the heavy painting into the boot.

Friday evening they were having a showing of Allan
Brunton's new works; brilliant canvases alive with the
birds and flowers of tropical North Queensland.

'Actually I didn't ring the florist this time. I rang
the nursery. All the cymbidiums are out and I thought
they'd look marvellous in baskets about the place.
They'll pick up the theme of the paintings as well.'

'Good girl! So beautiful and so capable. Do you
know neither of my wives cared about having children and one simply can't be happy without children.'
For a moment Marcus's heavy, handsome face was
lost in melancholy, then it faded into something else.
'You didn't forget the Dixons, did you?' He held
open the car door and Claudia slid in.

'I haven't forgotten a thing. At least I hope not.
Remember Dr Kempf will be coming in in the morning.'

'Will she the old vixen!'

'She's a highly regarded critic.'

'Give me a man any day. They're easier to deal
with.'

'You love women, Marcus.' Claudia turned a smiling face to him. '"Bye, now. See you Friday. I've
left all my little notes for Jean. The orchids will arrive
Friday morning. They're going to set you back a bit,
but they'll look magnificent and we can always use
them again.'

Marcus leaned over and kissed her on the forehead.
'Say hello to your grandfather for me. I was so
pleased to see how much he enjoyed the party.'

'Yes he did, didn't he?' Claudia could still see her
grandfather's eyes on her as she had come down the
stairway. 'I really think his great sadness is passing.'

'Maybe he's seeing great promise for the future,' Marcus said perceptively. 'And that promise is in *your* hands. Which brings me back to Nick. Don't let misunderstandings get in your way. Nick no longer sees you as a small girl. Take my word for it. Why shouldn't you be his *wife?*'

'For one thing, he doesn't love me,' Claudia suddenly started the engine. 'And another, Marcus, you old matchmaker, I certainly don't love him.'

'It might help you to put it in gear.'

'Yes.' Claudia shifted the gear stick into Drive. 'I do hope Nick won't come on Friday.'

'Of course he'll come!' Marcus waved her off, having the last word. 'Nick wouldn't miss one of my showings for the world.'

CHAPTER THREE

A CROWD was fast gathering and Claudia motioned to one of the hired waiters to circle with drinks. That done, she paused, her eyes scanning the large gallery. The cymbidiums looked superb; pink, white, yellow, a very pale green and a rich, rust-red. The abundant flower spikes on some were easily five feet long and she could see from Marcus's beaming face they were proving just the decoration for the Brunton showing.

Above the exotic, waxy opulence of the flowers, the paintings radiated the splendours of the tropical North. As with Gauguin, colour was the *raison d'être* of Brunton's work and he had devoted the last four years of his working life exclusively to catching the atmosphere north of Capricorn; the peculiar brilliance of the light, the sheer abundance of flora, the flaring colours, the myriads of birds like precious jewels. Several of the largest paintings were already displaying reassuring red stickers; not that Allan Brunton, a man as spectacular as his paintings, needed all that much reassuring. Claudia had already overheard his declaiming to a lad who sought to engage him in conversation that he 'didn't give a damn whether anyone bought his paintings or not'. With another artist one might have wept torrents but such was Brunton's rank, dealer and buyer just had to laugh it off. 'Al-

ways feel he's never quite got the hang of civilisa-
tion!' Marcus often said.

One of their best clients, an enormously wealthy
elderly gentleman, 'a bit on the gay side' as Marcus
put it, was now whispering in his ear and several
minutes later Claudia was asked to affix a 'heavenly
crimson dot' to the very sumptuous No 28—'Hymn
to Tropical Beauty and Fruitfulness'. The price tag
was as arresting as the brilliant images and having
been in the client's home, Claudia couldn't conceive
of where such a very large painting might go. There
was no more wall space. It was even rumoured there
was some sort of gallery in the upstairs what-not.
There were handsome paintings in the kitchen, scattered along the garage walls, many a guest had been
known to come back enraptured from a visit to the
toilet. All at once Claudia decided it wasn't her job
to worry where the client's pictures might go.

Shortly afterwards her father and Cristina arrived
and perhaps twenty minutes before the 8 p.m. closing
time Nick called in. *Alone.* Cristina was in the middle
of a sentence as Nick pushed through the crowd but
as soon as her eyes fell on him, she suddenly flushed
and faltered badly. That she was flustered was so obvious Claudia felt extremely uncomfortable, but the
effect wasn't as bad as she feared because her father
swung around rather bewildered, then exclaimed
aloud in pleasure. 'Why, it's Nick! Damned if I knew
what was bothering you, darling.'

'Why, of course it's Nick,' Cristina said helplessly.
'I thought a woman over there was going to tip champagne all over his sleeve, it's such a crush!'

To Claudia's way of thinking it came out too contrived for words, but apparently her father needed little convincing.

'You'll have to excuse me,' she said and gave Nick a fleeting, wintry smile.

'I think this little show is going to be a success,' he said mildly as he greeted them. 'Won't you show me around, Claudia, instead of rushing away?'

'Yes, darling, that's your job,' her father pointed out with a sharp, amused smile. 'You don't have to *buy* one, Nick. That's carrying things a bit far.'

'A bit colourful for me,' Nick murmured detachedly. 'Excellent of their kind though, one has to admit.' He half turned to look at Claudia but she kept her green eyes on the painting right in front of her. There was a snake she suddenly realised in one of those rioting trees...brilliant eyes in a menacing triangular head.

'Where are you going afterwards, Nick?' Grant Ingram suddenly asked.

'As a matter of fact, home.' His silvery glance moved off Claudia and stopped at her father.

'Let's have dinner. Just the four of us,' Grant Ingram said. 'Cristina and I were going on but I'm sure they can find us a table for four.'

'I'll probably have to stay, Daddy,' Claudia said.

'Nonsense!' Grant Ingram's blue eyes were serene. 'Marcus won't mind in the least.'

'I don't know.'

'*I'd* like it,' Nick said and caught Claudia's hand firmly. 'Quickly, show me around before we go.'

She looked back over her shoulder as they moved off. Her father was smiling, but it was very hard to define the expression on Cristina's face.

'What can you tell me about this one?' Nick suddenly asked dryly and turned his attention to a strange, jungle scene.

'I don't *want* to go to dinner tonight, Nick.'

'Would you please speak a little louder, Miss Ingram. I can't hear you in all this din.' There was an expression of malice on his handsome dark face.

'Don't you *care* that Daddy might notice something?'

'Why do you have to keep calling your father "Daddy" in that little-girl fashion?'

'Because that's how I think of him if you want to know.'

'Why do you have to be some sort of goddamn little paragon?' he enquired. 'A veritable child of light!'

'Like it?' Marcus came over to clap him on the shoulder.

'It vaguely upsets me,' Nick said.

'Complex chap!' Marcus said rather sadly.

'Who, me or Brunton?'

'I meant Brunton but I suppose one would have to watch *you* carefully.'

Claudia stared up at Marcus aghast but to her relief he was smiling at Nick most affectionately.

'I haven't spoken to the Randalls since they came in,' she pronounced quickly. 'Excuse me, won't you, Nick?'

'Of course. Marcus can show me around.'

'Step this way, laddie,' Marcus boomed.

Of course there was no way of getting out of dinner. Her father expected it and what her father expected, her father got. Even if it turned out to be the very last thing in the world. Like Cristina and Nick.

There was not the slightest difficulty finding the best table even on a busy night. Her father commanded attention wherever he went. Accepted it as his due. Now as they all sat at a table together his eyes wandered with pleasure from his daughter in a lovely pale jade crêpe de Chine sheath dress, hand-sewn with beads and silver sequins, to Nick, lean and elegant in his impeccably cut dark grey suit, shirt and tie expertly chosen and in the traditional, classic style Grant Ingram most admired. Nick was a handsome man. But for all that, the chiselled features, the thick, black hair and stunning light eyes, were merely a bonus. It was the brilliance of his personality, his particular abilities that made him so sought after. He had a peculiar *drawing* power. For men and for women. Even Cristina who had said Nick was 'so dazzling he was blinding' had overcome her initial reaction. She was as fond of him as the rest of them. Perhaps not *Claudia.* Grant Ingram smiled indulgently on them both. His most longed-for wish appeared to be working out very nicely.

Claudia barely tasted a morsel of food but the others ate and drank with pleasure. Cristina was particularly scintillating, as if she had an excess of nervous energy she had to burn off. Her hazel eyes even had a hint of triumph in them as they rested on her step-daughter's still, downbent face. Claudia might be all those years *younger* but Cristina was still the more vibrant of the two; the more interesting, the more witty, the more able to hold and keep a sophisticated man's attention. That night all her old pennants were flying. She couldn't bear to lose her husband any more than she could bear to have Nick turn away from her in boredom. Nick was the most dangerous person in the world to her. In his company she felt as much on a high as any pathetic victim of an addiction. What he represented she didn't know but it was something she had missed.

The maitre d' came over to make certain they had enjoyed their meal and afterwards Cristina suggested they might make use of the small dance floor. Several couples were moving about in languorous abandon enjoying the immensely pleasing sounds that were emanating from the four-piece group.

'You're very quiet tonight, darling?' Grant Ingram said when he and Claudia were alone.

'I'm a little tired.' She smiled at him, trying not to see Cristina and Nick over her father's shoulder. Anxiety was there again, right around her heart. Cristina was in such a brittle mood tonight the whole thing could blow up in their faces.

'You're studying too hard,' her father told her.

'No wonder, it's close to exams.'

'I'm very proud of you, Claudia,' Grant Ingram smiled. 'What are you going to do with yourself when it's all over?'

'I have a few things lined up,' she said readily enough. 'I might even travel for a year.'

'You're joking, darling,' her father said lightly. 'I can see which way the wind is blowing.'

Can you? she thought sadly. In many ways her father only saw what he wanted to.

'My advice is, darling, don't go rushing off overseas. I guess I understand how you feel about Nick.

You've always been a child to his young adult, but these days it seems to me he's treating you as a *woman.*'

'That's the problem with Nick. He treats women like women and they *love* it!'

'He's never married any one of them,' her father said.

'Maybe he hates the idea of marriage,' Claudia said moodily. 'He told me once it was agony when his parents' marriage broke up. It was so bad for a time he had to go and live with his grandfather.'

Grant Ingram nodded. 'That's right. But it was a very long time ago, sweetheart. Nick was only a boy.'

'What *worse* time,' Claudia said. 'I don't think underneath all his surface charm Nick really *likes* women. He mightn't think they would be too faithful. He told me he blamed his mother for the break-up of his parents' marriage.'

'She was an extremely beautiful woman,' Grant Ingram said. 'It could be very difficult for any man to hold a woman like that. Grey is a good fellow but ultra-conservative, rather rigid in his thinking. If anything I would have to sympathise with Nick's mother. However much he blamed her he's very much like her. But that's just between you and me. Nick is all the Somerville side of the family.'

'And he's never forgiven his mother's defection.'

'What is it you're getting at, darling?' Grant Ingram asked just a shade testily. 'I think you're throwing up all kinds of silly defences. I'm totally convinced Nick is just about ready to settle down and nothing in this whole world would please me more than if he decided to settle down with *you.*'

'Why, *exactly?*' Claudia asked. 'Do you think he's the right person to make *me* happy, or is it because you love him dearly?'

Grant Ingram laughed a little ruefully. 'Every woman needs a man to take care of her. In terms of character, ability, ambition, I can't think of anyone I would rather see you married to. Do you resent my affection for Nick? Is that it, darling?'

'Ah, no,' Claudia shook her head. 'I understand the special relationship that exists between men. Father to son. Most men, I suppose, would wish for a son before a daughter. Of course they love their daughters, as you love me, but the really important thing in a lot of men's lives is to have a son. Preferably sons. It's perfectly understandable. A man relives his hopes, his dreams through a son. A lot of the time it could be a second chance. I suppose mothers do it too through their daughters but the male of the species is predestined to do great things,' Claudia shrugged a little ironically. 'I believe you think *Nick's* child, providing I was accorded the great honour of being its mother, would be the greatest architect the world has ever seen.'

'Damn it all, darling,' her father laughed. 'He *might* be. There's really a great deal to be said for mating the right couples.'

'I hardly dare mention *love.*'

'You love him,' Grant Ingram said soberly. 'I know you're still slightly in awe of him, but you're demonstrating your own style. You're a beautiful young woman. You're well educated, well bred. What more could a man want?'

'Plenty,' Claudia said fierily, marvelling at herself

for saying it. 'Actually it's *sexy* women men go for. Another woman might have plenty to offer but if she hasn't got *that* she's a non-event.'

'Personally I detest crude women,' Grant Ingram said. 'Certainly I would never marry one.'

At which point Cristina and Nick returned to the table, Cristina, flushed and brilliant-eyed, Nick looking rather taut and silent by comparison.

'I think we'll leave you two young people,' Grant Ingram said.

'But it's *early,* darling,' Cristina protested, rather tartly. She was as *young* as anyone, actually.

'I'm ready to go home,' Claudia said.

'You're not a bit of fun, are you?' Nick challenged her with a mocking smile.

'That's a little bit of her trouble,' Grant Ingram murmured and gestured to the maitre d' for the bill. 'She's too serious. No, stay here, darling, and enjoy yourself. Nick will bring you home.'

'I'm enjoying myself too, you know,' Cristina told her husband, opening wide her changeable eyes.

'Don't fret,' Grant Ingram told her. 'The evening's not over. It's just that I think these two have much to say to each other.'

'Oh, God, Grant!' Cristina groaned. How could *anyone* be so blatant in their matchmaking? Claudia and Nick had nothing to say to each other. Claudia was just a baby.

Yet Nick, the traitor, reached out and grasped Claudia's hand. 'I'm hoping to persuade Claudia to dance with me.'

'She looks tired,' Cristina snapped, a tone of voice

that made Grant Ingram lift his head from his credit card to frown at her.

'It's *relaxation* she needs,' he pointed out sternly.

Cristina wasn't brave enough to start up again. Grant was the most courteous and considerate husband in the world but he could be surprisingly stuffy when crossed.

'Have a lovely time!' Cristina said as they left, but her over-bright eyes made it plain she thought that impossible.

'Some days,' Claudia said, 'I feel like an old, old woman.'

'*How* old?' Nick lifted her hand to his mouth.

'Don't play games with me,' she said with icy disapproval.

'This is no place to kiss you in earnest.' His silver eyes sparkled in his handsome, dark face. 'Dance with me, Claudia? It will all be quite friendly.'

'I'm very glad my father had his back to you when you were dancing with Cristina.'

'It's a sticky problem, I'll admit.'

'You're tired of her, aren't you?' Claudia accused him, feeling so angry her hands were shaking.

'Keep that up and you might have to go in a strait-jacket,' Nick returned rather curtly. 'Do you want to dance or don't you?'

'No. I don't want you to touch me.'

'What a wicked lie!'

'You don't seem to realise I *mean* it.'

'Hush, you little fool.' He held her hand so tightly she couldn't pull away. 'If you don't want to dance, we'd better go.'

'It's the only way.' She was already standing, one

hand still in his, the other reaching for her evening purse.

There was no one in the car park. 'Get in,' Nick said briefly and with a crushing disdain.

'I should never have come.'

'I don't see what else a dutiful daughter could do,' he taunted her. 'And it's much too early to take you home. Your father is expecting us to dance the rest of the night away. One wonders why.'

Claudia wasn't listening. She was buckling her seat belt. This was the first time she had been inside Nick's new car, the Jaguar coupé, and she thoroughly approved of the high console down the middle. Not that Nick had any ideas of crossing over anyway. In the lamplight his expression was one of positive dislike.

'What about my place?' he asked as the big engine fired.

'I don't *believe* you.'

'I'm serious. I'll read you a bedtime story before I take you home.'

'I'd prefer it if you skipped the story.'

'Don't be such a kill-joy. Really, Claudia, you're turning into a terribly dull girl.'

'Because I wouldn't consider sleeping with you? Sorry about that.'

'Have I *asked* you?' he drawled.

'I'm sure you would given the chance.'

'*No.* It would be sacrilege. I see you as an object of *adoration,* Claudia. You're much too fine a person to ask into bed.'

'You mean you hate wasting time.'

'You disgusting little bitch.'

Never in all the years that she had known him had he called her such a name. She wasn't a bitch. She *wasn't*. She was carrying a terribly worrying burden.

'What's the matter with you now?' he asked harshly.

She couldn't answer because she was choking on a few involuntary tears.

'I'm sorry,' he said. 'I didn't mean it. I just made it up. You're an angel with a very pure *little* mind. My place, is it? No seduction scene. No kisses, caresses, no vicious words. I'll show you the plans for the MacAdam residence. You used to be interested in things like that.'

'I want to go home, Nick,' she near-whispered.

'My poor dear child, it would be much better for *all* of us if I kept you out for at least another hour. Consider your father's feelings. Cristina's. She seemed ready to explode.'

'You only *thought* she could play the game.'

'Who needs friends, Claudia, when I have you? I'm the victim of a bit of damning circumstantial evidence yet you've come down on me like a fury. Could it contain the element of a woman scorned?'

'No,' she said, sounding very young and shaken. 'I worshipped you for years and years. Another case of a fallen idol, I'm afraid.'

'For God's sake!' he said angrily and with a look of near despair, 'what the hell can I do if some fool woman finds me cataclysmically attractive? I'm as angry with the whole thing as you are. I've tried to reason with Cristina, but she persists. Maybe it's the bloody menopause!'

'What an extraordinary diagnosis,' Claudia offered

flatly, 'but try saying that to Cristina for a whole month. When it actually happens and it's a good way off, she'll think there's nothing left for her. When desirability fails, go jump off a mountain.'

'A bridge anyway. If she doesn't, I'll *have* to!' He was heading towards his own home and Claudia reminded herself cynically that it would be better if Cristina and her father thought she and Nick were enjoying a long evening.

'Expecting someone, Nick?' she asked as they drove through the tall, iron lace gates.

'I always leave the lights on when I'm not at home. A simple precaution.'

'What an extraordinarily beautiful old house this is,' she said quietly. 'I always expect to see your grandfather come out to greet us.'

'Yes,' he agreed a little curtly. 'It would trouble him a great deal to know what goes on in *your* mind.'

In silence they walked to the front door, a soft golden light streaming through the patterned lead-lights. It was a traditional Tudor manor house built by Nick's great-grandfather and its most outstanding feature apart from the wide swaths of leaded glass windows with inserts of European stained glass was the magnificent panelling brought intact from England in the formal dining room. The estate had passed to Nick after the death of his maternal grandfather, Lang Somerville, but it was much, much too big for one man, though Nick's grandfather had lived the last ten years of his life alone in it and quite happily. It had been his home and now it was Nick's.

'Well don't just stand there!' Nick knit his black brows.

'Oh, Nick...' Her voice sounded fearful and gentle.

'*I'd* never hurt you, Claudia.' There was the faintest smile in his eyes. He took her hand and led her into the drawing room turning on the light at the same time. 'Do you want to stay here or go into the library? It's a darn sight cosier.'

'Aren't you going to show me the MacAdam house plans?' She looked up at him worriedly, her eyes very large and lit with a desperately controlled excitement.

'Now?'

'Yes now.'

He looked down at her trembling hand in his. 'You used *not* to be afraid of me.'

'I only wish we *could* go back to before.'

'You've no right to behave like this, Claudia,' he said.

'And how can you be so *dreadful!*' She broke away from him then. 'I can't stay here, Nick. I can't be with you at all.' An emotional tear rolled down her creamy cheek.

'Claudia,' he said bleakly, 'it's not even midnight. I'll take you home then. Can't you talk to me for an hour?'

She put her hands to her temples, slanting her eyes back. 'I can't think of a single thing.'

He wasted no further time, closing the gap between them and wrenching her into his arms. 'Do you want me to strangle you, do you?'

'This violence is new,' she goaded him, shaken, shocked, acutely aware of the peculiar tensions that bound them.

He exclaimed under his breath. 'Is there anything else I *can* do with you?'

'Yes. Take me home.' A long pin had fallen out of her hair and now it slid in a heavy platinum coil down her back. The sight of him, the touch of his hurting hands was rousing a dark clamour in her blood, quickening into raw sensitivity her irreconcilable feeling for him.

'It makes no difference that I'm telling you you're quite *wrong?*'

'I *want* to believe you, Nick. You must know that.'

'Then there's only one way to show you.' The initiative was his and he grasped the long coil of her hair and forced her head back against his shoulder, pressing his mouth down on hers until she parted her lips on a moan of pain.

'Forget *everything* but this,' he said tautly, twisting her slender body even nearer so the pulses began beating ever more thunderously in her veins. She had imagined being kissed by Nick so often, but the reality was beyond anything she could handle. Even while her mind seethed in self-disgust, her body trembled and yielded independently, slow fire wrapping her around. He was so blindingly skillful in his heart-stopping role. A real-life sorcerer. She allowed him to explore her mouth a while longer, then with a convulsive movement she jerked her head away.

'I've got to hand it to you, Nick, you know how to make love.'

He just looked at her, hostility surfacing in his diamond-bright eyes. 'Curiously enough so do you, when I know you're still a virgin.'

'You're quite certain about that?' she snapped, points of colour staining her cheekbones.

'Yes. A virgin. Much too long.'

There was such an odd, menacing tone in his voice she closed her eyes and abruptly he lifted her, carrying her back to the wide sofa where he held her across his knees.

Tears of rage and panic dropped on to his hand. 'You promised me...'

'Shut up.' He answered so fiercely it checked her. 'You've got to understand something, Claudia. You can't goad a man beyond his limits.'

She felt his hand on her shaping her breast but before she had time to breathe or even cry out his mouth had descended again and it was far too sweet to avoid. Urgency poured into her veins so her heart thudded within her narrow ribcage. She lifted her arms, drugged with yearning, linking them around his head so his strong body trembled with the force of his reaction.

It was like trying to tame a prowling panther and in her excitement was a measure of terror. She had known Nick for so long but he was someone else now. A lover, sexual and angry. She thought she heard her fragile dress begin to tear, but then the zip was darting down her back and with a swift motion of his hand he had peeled it from her, flinging it so it flew through the air in a shimmering haze.

'Oh, *no,* Nick!' she cried breathlessly, her whole body suffused with heat. Without her dress in a flimsy slip she felt utterly bereft, raising one hand protectively across her body. She had always been shy with Nick. Couldn't he understand?

'I won't hurt you. Just a little,' he muttered, his lean fingers curving around her throat.

'*Nick.*' He seemed utterly unstoppable, a hard tension in his face.

'All the misery you cause,' he said grimly.

She knew in that instant he was about to seek her breast and she jerked back convulsively in a frenzy of emotion. She had never known such intimacy in her life, the terrible, awesome power of desire. She didn't think she could bear Nick's hand on her naked flesh but now her breasts were exposed and he was putting his mouth to their rosy peaks bringing her mortally, perilously within his power.

'You're so beautiful,' he murmured spreading his hands over the curve of her hips. 'All I've got to do is keep loving you.' His voice was filled with a kind of exultancy, a suppressed triumph and it burnt into her like a flame. She turned her head from side to side to clear it, shuddering as Nick brushed his hand down her body. Part of her wanted his overwhelming male aggression, the rest of her couldn't bring herself to surrender. She knew who she was. She knew what she wanted. Love and respect. Not a demonic desire.

With a tremendous effort she brought her body upright drawing her slender legs up so she was sitting like a child in his lap. 'Please stop now, Nick,' she begged him, breathing very deeply in an effort to slow her racing heart beat.

'You sound like a little girl.'

'You know I am. At least I'm—'

'Frightened?' Incredibly he was holding her in an attitude of protectiveness.

'I want the man I love to love only me.' She pressed her mouth against his throat, mournful and ardent. So stupid!

'Perhaps he does. Perhaps he's loved you for years.' He brought his hands upwards beneath her breasts, the tips of his fingers stroking the nipples.

'*Please* help me, Nick,' she whispered. When he did that her mind began to whirl out of control.

'Then tell me you believe me.' He pulled her head back so he could look into her eyes. '*Tell* me.' His silver eyes were blazing.

'I'll *try*, Nick.' Desperately she tried to appease him.

'You don't know *anything*, do you?' he asked harshly. 'No matter what you know of me you can't give me your trust. It's some deep-seated defence. Something a vulnerable little girl thought up to guard against her own longing. You've been in love with me since you were about thirteen years old.'

'*Nnn...no!*' She tried to pull back as he held her close to him, feeling like the victim of a mad obsession.

'You've wanted this at any time for years now.'

'No, Nick, I won't *let* you.' Her body jerked away from his hard domination.

'Sweet God!' he breathed. 'This is all more bizarre than I thought.'

With an expertise she hated he turned her and got her back into her flimsy garments, bringing her rather roughly to her feet where she stood with enormous eyes while he dropped her lovely dress over her head. He even ordered her curtly to lift her arms and turn around so he could adjust the zip. It was exactly as if she were a child or some colourless puppet.

'Now, goddammit,' he fairly shook her, 'I'm going to take you home. Is your blasted dress all right?'

'I don't know.' She looked at him so strangely, brushing tears from her eyes.

'I could beat you, Claud,' his voice sank to a whisper. 'Don't look like that, *please.*'

'I'm a disgrace, aren't I?'

'You idiot.' He brushed her heavy hair away from her face. 'You always knew I'd make love to you.'

'I think it was as hard for you as for me.'

'*Harder,* baby.' His dark face mocked her. 'You don't even know the half of it. What are you going to do about your hair?'

'Is it untidy?' She sounded frightened.

'As if it matters.' He stood there watching her very closely. 'I guess you're old enough to let your hair down.'

'I'd better fix it.' Colour emphasised the creaminess of her complexion. 'Daddy or Cristina might still be up.'

'You look fine. Leave it,' he said a little curtly. 'Seeing you kissed senseless might be good for them both.'

No one was up, however. Claudia slipped into the quiet house, turned off the exterior lights and climbed the stairs to her bedroom. Her father and Cristina had their suite in the other wing and all that mattered now was to reach the solace of her own room. In a sense she had always known what had happened tonight. What *would* happen if she allowed Nick to carry her off to where they would be quite alone. The scent of him still clung to her; to her mouth, to her skin, to her clothes. Hers was the worst kind of obsession, instilled too early. She could still feel his hands on her breasts, demanding, strong, clever hands. She had always liked just to look at them, the beautiful shape, the expressive elegance. How incredible they had touched her body. And with such authority! How incredible she had given in at all.

Silence along the long gallery. She opened the door of her own room, flicked the light switch then turned back to find the master switch that controlled the recessed lighting in the gallery. Another second and the main house was in darkness but Claudia thought she caught the glimmer of light from the far end of the long passageway. She didn't wait to make sure but hurried back into her room.

She found the slightest tear in her dress but it could be easily mended. In the bathroom she stopped for a moment before she slid her nightgown over her head. Normally she undressed without ever looking at herself; now she turned and looked at herself in the mirror, seeing her body as a lover might. Her skin was flawless over her entire body and she relived again how hungrily Nick had reached for her, his mouth and his hands. She pressed her arms around her own body, her green eyes huge and troubled. Nothing made sense, *nothing!* Could he possibly reach for another woman with the same fervour? Could he possibly be telling the truth after she had berated him so terribly? Yet even tonight Cristina had flaunted her power, leaning heavily against him as they danced, finally disentangling her hands, her hazel eyes overbright.

Claudia's soft mouth twisted in an expression of pain and disbelief. Was this some thoughtless cruelty of fate that Cristina had conceived a passion for a man who had merely been charming to her since she was the wife of his senior partner? It had happened before. Men and women had been known to fall madly in love without encouragement, just as they were tempted to want what they could not have.

Claudia dropped her pink nightgown over her head, reaching behind the door for her pink satin robe. Her hair was hanging long and heavy over her shoulders and she saw she looked different, pulsing with an inner light. These kinds of triangles were only for fiction. They were too terrible for real life.

A tap on her door, then the soft thud of footsteps in her bedroom made her heart leap to her throat. She hurried to the bathroom door and looked out in apprehension. Cristina in a marvellous burgundy nightgown and matching peignoir was standing in the middle of the room looking very severe and elegant...*odd*.

'Goodness, Cristina, you frightened me,' Claudia managed.

'I'm sorry, but I knew you wouldn't be in bed. I heard you come in.'

'Is something wrong?' Claudia slowly belted the silk cord around her waist.

'No.' Cristina paced a little aimlessly around the room, then suddenly she turned. 'Well, *yes*. I don't know how I can say this, Claudia, without sounding extremely interfering but I'm worried about you and Nick.'

It was so ridiculous Claudia laughed, albeit a shade hysterically. 'I suppose it makes a change!'

'Claudia,' Cristina said severely, 'I'm thirty-four years old. I've coped with failures, frustrations, my little triumphs, some defeats over a long period of time. You're just twenty-one and a very young twenty-one at that. You've led a very sheltered life. You've had little experience of the down turns in life.'

'I think all that has just begun to change,' Claudia said with a little flash of wry amusement. 'Why pick on tonight to give me a little...sisterly advice?'

'As it happens I'm feeling very uneasy about you and Nick,' Cristina continued incredibly. 'I know he's been perfectly charming to you all these years but you were only an infant. You're a young woman now and very attractive in a virginal kind of way. That kind of thing appeals to a great many men.'

'You amaze me, Cristina,' Claudia said. 'Haven't you got enough of a problem without taking on mine?'

'For God's sake, Claudia. I'm concerned about you!' Cristina hit the back of a Louis XIV chair with a small, clenched fist. 'Nick Grey is far too much for you to handle. He could hurt you badly.'

'I'm well aware of that, Cristina,' Claudia said coolly, though her whole body seemed tied in knots. 'What would you have me do?'

'It's because you're so young, so inexperienced,' Cristina said. 'I have a duty to you.'

A duty? my foot, Claudia thought.

'So why don't we both tell Nick to go find his pleasures elsewhere?' she said grimly. 'By the way, Cristina, he has sworn to me that there is not and never has been anything between you.'

'And you *believe* him?' Cristina stabbed at her hair wearily.

'You told me the same thing yourself.'

'Then I probably will again.' Cristina's husky voice changed to bitterness. 'If I can't help myself, Claudia, I can help you. Nick is a strange man. Cruel. Maybe what he felt for me has passed but it left me with a lot of scars. Now he has turned his attention to you. You with the white-gold hair and big green eyes. Yesterday you were just a child he could help with your homework, today he's seeing you with new eyes. It could be something serious. I feel it.'

'Are you jealous, Cristina?' Claudia asked, not with any challenge but a gentle need to know.

'Does it matter?' Cristina's eyes momentarily filled with tears which she blinked furiously away. 'Maybe I am, a little. How could I not be? But more importantly I have a few decent feelings left. I want to protect you, Claudia. Give you the benefit of my painful experience.'

'Maybe none of us can do that,' Claudia said. 'Don't upset yourself, Cristina. I've never seen you cry.'

'Oh I *cry!*' Cristina said bleakly. 'I cry until my eyes are red and swollen.'

'So might we all after we get burnt. You went after Nick, Cristina. You can't deny that.'

'Yes, but he was so *provocative!*' Cristina put out an appealing hand. 'I'm used to men. I've been very much admired in my time, but I've never met anyone remotely like Nick.'

'He's not good husband material,' Claudia said.

'Oh, God, I know that of course.' Cristina stopped her pacing and collapsed into the Louis XIV chair looking very haggard but still glamorous. 'I'm scared rotten the man I *really* love might hear something.'

'I would be too,' Claudia couldn't resist saying. 'You don't *act* scared rotten, Cristina. Scared rotten ladies don't cling to other men in full view of their husbands.'

'Grant had his back to us,' Cristina said. She looked up her face white with indignation. 'Don't you go making trouble for me, Claudia.'

Claudia stroked her aching forehead. 'I weep for you, Cristina. I'm not out to make trouble.'

'Oh, I *know* that!' Cristina threw out a distracted hand. 'You're a good girl, so it makes it all the more intolerable to allow you to fall into Nick's clutches.'

'Oh, well, I have.'

'You don't *mean* that!' Christina looked shocked out of her mind.

'If it makes you feel any better, I've been the same for the past eight years. I've always been gone on Nick, you know.'

Cristina stared at her stepdaughter for a moment, then laughed. 'But that was just a schoolgirl thing. I understand. We all have our crushes. I remember I was very taken with my maths teacher. In fact I could have taken him away from his wife but I was just a baby of sixteen or so.'

'Wasn't *he* lucky.'

'Look…' Cristina began.

It was impossible to be angry, only helpless and desolate. 'Please go back to bed, Cristina. I'm rather tired.'

'Did Nick make love to you?' Cristina asked, her eyes glowing strangely.

'As a general principle, Cristina, I think it's better *not* to kiss and tell.'

'He did, didn't he?' Cristina persisted.

'We can afford to,' Claudia pointed out sharply. 'He's not married and neither am I.'

'Oooh!' Cristina bent over like a woman in a wheelchair.

'I'm sorry if I've hurt you.' Instantly Claudia felt remorse. Cristina was obviously the victim of a powerful addiction. 'Why don't you go away for a little while, Cristina. You'll see things better. As they are. Daddy loves you and you've told me you really love him. That is as it should be. What you feel for Nick is some terrible fascination. It's unreal and *worse,* he doesn't *want* you.'

Cristina breathed in sharply her whitened face ghastly. 'How would *you* know?'

'I hope so, Cristina, for all our sakes.' Very fervently Claudia joined her hands. 'I know a lot of people don't seem to take their marriage vows very seriously, but Daddy does. If he heard *one* word about you and Nick, I think you'd be finished in his eyes. You see, my father has a thing about perfection. Women are sort of fantasy figures. All beautiful heroines. He could never tolerate second best. Surely you've seen what he's like? If you failed him I think he could cut you out of his life and never look back. He'd cut Nick out as well and terrible as it may seem he'd grieve more about Nick. Maybe I know my father better than you do. In *that* department I've a lot more experience. If you want your marriage and I know you do, you'll have to beat your feeling for

Nick. Or grit your teeth and bear it. It will go away. Everything needs feeding. Even love.'

'Maybe I feel things more passionately than you,' Cristina said in a coldly cutting voice. 'You're a very cool, reserved sort of person so you wouldn't know. I came here tonight to make you listen to me. I can see from your face Nick made love to you. I'm far from being a stupid woman. You look turned inside out. If you are, take your own advice. Give Nick up. Let him go to that Amanda woman. She'll have him. With pleasure.'

'And *you* have?' Claudia couldn't let it alone, though she heard the same thing over and over. Nick had accused her of condemning him out of hand and she had to admit she had thought him highly principled for years.

'I'm one of the *unfortunate* ones,' Cristina said. She didn't meet Claudia's eyes but dragged herself to her feet. 'Forgive me for all this, Claudia. I couldn't just step aside complacently and allow Nick to have you. In the end, we're *family.*' Her thin, but well-shaped mouth twisted. 'I guess a year from now we can speak about this and laugh.'

'I don't think so,' Claudia said painfully. 'It's a terrible thing to see an idol fall.'

Cristina's jaw tightened but she said nothing. As she passed Claudia she put her hand on her shoulder, pressing down on it with the palm. 'I've said it all, dear, and I feel terrible, but I'm prepared to do anything at all to keep you and Nick apart. You're meant for better things.'

Claudia didn't answer. There was nothing to say.

CHAPTER FOUR

A few weeks went by of relative calm. They were all very much preoccupied with their own affairs. Claudia was preparing for her exams and concentrating intensely; Cristina had been asked to handle the renovation of the Ashleigh Hotel, a small hostelry that had seen grander days and Grant Ingram was totally absorbed in a very big commission, the Kuhn-Culver Building for which Nick was his chief designer.

'I don't know why I bother cooking at all,' Fergy complained. 'Never a day goes by that someone doesn't ring to say they won't be home.'

Eventually the week of examinations went past and Claudia was left face to face with the prospect of doing nothing. Of course it was coming in to the holiday season and even Marcus closed the gallery for a full month starting from Christmas Eve while he flew off to London, Paris, Rome, combining business and pleasure and making annual visits to his major, expatriate artists. At the end of her examinations Claudia had planned on a lovely long holiday at their beach house, maybe asking three or four of her girlfriends but now she felt too worried and nervous to leave the house.

'What *is* wrong with you?' Fergy asked one afternoon when Claudia was making an attempt to help her clean the impressive collection of silver that usually adorned the sideboard in the dining room. 'You seem awfully restless these days?'

'This is mine, you know,' Claudia said, polishing the magnificent tray that held a Victorian tea and coffee service.

'I know, dear,' Fergy said mildly. 'For that matter most of the silver belongs to you. By rights, that is. It was left to Miss Victoria by her grandmother who in turn had been given it by her grandmother. Valuable it is too, especially that Garrard tureen.'

'I like all the plain things best,' Claudia murmured, polishing absently, 'like that lovely little cup. Too much ornamentation doesn't appeal to me.'

'To say nothing of its being harder to clean.' Fergy, in fact, used a large, high quality paint brush to facilitate her cleaning of the richly decorated pieces. 'Why aren't you going to the beach as you said?'

'Don't feel like it at the moment.'

'Why are you avoiding Nick?' Fergy finally asked.

'Good Heavens, I'm not!' Claudia's voice held an urgency that gave her words the lie.

'*Why*, dear?' Fergy persisted. 'I really think it's going on a bit too long.'

'I can't explain, Fergy. It's very difficult.'

'I'm ready for it,' Fergy said rather dryly. 'Part of it is you're worried about your stepmother.'

'*Fergy!*' Claudia said helplessly.

Fergy turned her shrewd blue eyes directly on the girl. 'I've been around a long time, precious girl. You don't *really* think anything much escapes me?'

'What is it you mean?'

Wry little lines bracketed Fergy's mouth. 'My eyesight mighn't be as good as it used to be but even then I've noticed Mrs Ingram finds our Nick *very* attractive.'

'How extraordinary!' Claudia said in that same distracted fashion.

'You mean that I noticed. How young you are, darling.'

'Cristina said the same. In fact, everyone says the same. How *young* you are, Claudia!'

'Who wouldn't turn back the clock!' Fergy sighed. 'Take no notice when your stepmother says it. Getting older is brutal for women. Some more than others.'

'Do you think Daddy's noticed?' Claudia asked fearfully.

'Not so far,' Fergy said. 'Your father has created a world of perfect order. Perhaps he doesn't *want* to see a flaw. Mind you, I wouldn't want to be your stepmother if she ever lets him down.'

'So what do we do?' Defeated herself, Claudia needed Fergy's support.

'About what, honey?' Fergy asked, smiling broadly. 'You don't think Nick is even vaguely attracted to your stepmother?'

Suddenly there was no support. No common knowledge. 'You don't think so, Fergy?' Claudia asked gravely.

'My dear, I don't think Nick likes your stepmother at all.'

'But he has always been charming to her.'

'As he is to everyone. Even *me*.'

'He really likes you, Fergy. You know that.'

'All right, he does.' Fergy smiled with pleasure. 'But what would you have him do, dear? He's very close to your father. In fact he's pretty well family. Not that his future would be at stake if he suddenly left the firm, but he owes your father a good deal. Brilliant or not it would have taken him a good deal longer to get where he is today. Another thing, your father hasn't a jealous, envious bone in his body. He's genuinely proud of Nick's great talents. He's even prepared to take second place which normally most men wouldn't do even for a son. Nick knows this. He's an orphan really, you know. He idolised his mother and she went off and left him…'

'There was no way she could *take* him,' Claudia pointed out defensively, 'and leave her husband.'

'Then she should have stayed with him,' Fergy said.

'I expect she felt terrible about it.'

'I don't condone her actions,' Fergy said. 'I remember her well. A glorious creature. Boyoboy was she beautiful! A female Nick.'

'How did she ever marry Nick's father?' Claudia asked. 'He's such a cold, remote man.'

'Basically I think he was just a very reserved, very sensitive person. It sounds so strange, I know when you think of him these days, but at the outset of their marriage no man could have been happier. He adored her. Worshipped her, if you like. But then she had a tremendous ability to *attract*.'

'Like Nick,' Claudia said very bleakly.

'Yes, like Nick,' Fergy was forced to agree. 'I don't know that it's an enviable gift. It's hard to lead an ordinary dull old life when you're immensely vibrant. Certain individuals have a powerful effect on others.'

'So you don't think Cristina's attraction is very serious?' Claudia tried to sound dispassionate.

'It would be *very* serious,' Fergy said sternly, 'if the attraction was mutual. I can't even dwell on it, but take it from me, sweetheart, Nick knows what he wants. *Who* he wants. There, isn't that a beautiful shine?'

The conversation should have reassured Claudia but it didn't. Shrewd and observant as Fergy was, her feeling for Nick and her underlying dislike of Cristina, for that was what it was, prevented her from seeing the truth. Nick was as guilty as ever Cristina was. Cristina wouldn't lie. One had only to look at her white, tormented face. Men were such absolute villains. They could lie beside one woman and tell her they loved her, then go off home and pretty well say the same thing. Other men even admired them for it. Maybe men had tremendously more powerful urges than women. Everyone said so. Fact or a darn good excuse.

Nick arrived one evening just as Claudia was waiting to go out. Fergy showed him in and they stood smiling, talking for a moment as Claudia came down the stairs. Immediately Nick looked up and Claudia wished to Heaven she knew what she could do to stop her heart from breaking.

'I'll leave you two to say hello,' Fergy said. Claudia had stopped dead on the stairs and even Nick had gone quiet.

'Daddy will be down in a few moments, Nick,' Claudia said politely. 'Won't you come into the library?'

'Where are you off to?' he asked, moving towards

her, his eyes moving slowly down the length of her body. She and Matthew were going to a party and she was wearing a very pretty short evening dress in a creamy, flower printed chiffon. A thin, V-shaped halter caught the brief bodice but the skirt billowed out from her small waist. She wore her hair loose as well, but drawn away from her face to the back of her head where it was caught high by a silk rose. She looked beautiful but somehow unhappy.

'Oh, just to a party,' she murmured, seemingly as absorbed in staring at him as he was in staring at her.

'You look like being beautiful doesn't make you happy,' he said.

'I don't think beauty is supposed to bring happiness. In human beings anyway.'

'Are you going to come down?' he asked, his lean handsome face turning hawklike.

'Yes, of course.' She moved at once but he stopped her when she was just a step above him and almost on line with him.

'It seems to me you're getting positively skinny.' His long fingers encircled her waist.

'You know what? I can't eat.'

'Really?' His eyes were so sparkling, so full of light they were pure silver. 'Doesn't it make you feel better I've mended my wicked ways?'

'Maybe it's because you're just too busy.'

'In fact I *don't* work twenty-four hours a day. Twelve, maybe.'

'Daddy tells me the Kuhn-Culver is going to be the best building in this city?'

'Including the Phillips we did last year.'

'Congratulations, Nick.' Her gentle voice was bitter-sweet.

'Little bitch.'

'Once you would *never* have called me that.'

His hard, mocking face softened. 'I guess you're right,' he said coolly. 'Just as once *I* had your respect.'

'Sad isn't it?' She looked intensely into his wonderful face. Everything was so clean cut and definite; sharply drawn black brows, thick black lashes, fine grained olive skin tanned to a dark gold, straight nose, clean jaw, a mouth that caught the eye, shapely, expressive, the edges well defined.

'Surely you know what I look like, Claud,' he said dryly, his silver eyes glinting.

'I don't know what's in your heart.'

'But it's black and all that?'

'I can't joke about it, Nick.' His hands were still resting lightly about her waist but she couldn't seem to move for the life of her.

'Would you spend the day with me, Saturday?' he asked.

'Matthew wants me to go sailing with him.'

'Matthew tonight?'

'Yes.'

'Look at it this way, he's safe.'

'What does *that* mean?' Her green eyes flashed fire.

'He's been your close friend for just on two years.'

'You mean you've counted?' Her voice slipped into something of his own mockery.

'I have. Let's see. You're twenty-one now. I'm thirty-three. That's a lot better than thirteen and twenty-five.'

'God knows you *always* treat me that way.' She propelled herself off the stairs.

'Always?' He began to laugh.

The doorbell sounded and Claudia almost flew towards the door, ready indeed to charge into the night.

'Hi!' At the sight of her Matthew's smooth, good looking face lit up with admiration. 'You look like a poem!'

She *never* threw herself into his arms, but she did.

'You're right on time.'

'Hey, with this kind of reception, I'll never be late!' Laughing, excited, Matthew began to kiss her smooth cheek.

'Claudia!' Her father's resonant voice sounded vaguely scolding. He was standing on the stairs watching them, but Nick had turned away as if he didn't mind at all.

'How are you, Mr Ingram?' Matthew called respectfully.

'Fine, thank you, Matthew.' Grant Ingram came on down the stairs. 'Don't keep Claudia out too late tonight. She's a little tired-out whatever she says. All big eyes and fragile bones. She needs a good holiday after all that study.'

'I'll look after her, sir,' Matthew promised. 'I'd like to take her out sailing at the weekend. It'll be fun.'

'That depends on the weather, Matthew,' Grant Ingram said briefly. 'Excuse me now, I have work to attend to. Nick arrived, darling?' he asked his daughter.

'He's just gone into the library.'

'Good.' Instantly Grant Ingram's rather stern expression eased. 'You've left the phone number and address of where you're going?'

'It's Tiffany's place, Daddy.'

'Oh, Tiffany.' That apparently was all right. As he passed his daughter, Grant Ingram dropped a kiss on her forehead. 'Take care, darling. Remember, Matthew, you'll be *driving* home.'

'Yes, sir.'

''Struth!' Matthew breathed when they were safely outside. 'Is there ever going to be a guy good enough for your father?'

'For me, you mean?' Claudia smiled.

'I have the most dismal feeling your father doesn't approve of me,' Matthew confided. 'Like I'm second rate.'

'Oh, Matthew, that's ridiculous!' Claudia reassured him. 'Daddy's like that with everyone. It's only sensible to know where your children are going.'

'Hang it all, Claudia, you're not a child. You're twenty-one.'

'A daughter is always a child to her father. I suppose it's part of father-love.'

'I guess your father is going to be one of those parents who tries to shape their daughter's life. Hasn't it ever struck you your father has your future husband lined up?'

'My father will allow me to choose for *myself*,' Claudia said a little hotly. 'Don't let Daddy's attitude upset you, Matthew. He's simply a caring parent.'

'Yes, and he doesn't care to see you with *me*.'

They had reached Matthew's car, now they stood almost glaring at one another.

'Are we going to a party or not?' All of a sudden Claudia felt like crying. She *was* rundown.

'I'm sorry, lovely one.' Matthew bent his head and very gently kissed her mouth. 'This isn't how I started out. I felt on top of the world. I'm crazy about you, Claudia, you know that. Sometimes I think you're my whole world. But then I come in contact with your father and I get worried. He's a very arrogant man. He really is. I know arrogant in a smooth, subtle way but arrogant all the same. No one and nothing challenges him. If you ask me, he's hoping and expecting you to marry Nick Grey.' This was said with a lot of hostility.

'Except that such a thing has never occurred to either of us,' Claudia retorted and her tone told Matthew to stop right there.

'Ah well, let's forget it.' Matthew held open the passenger door. 'Nick is years older than you and that makes a big difference. Especially when he likes the experienced sophisticates. All in all I don't think your father knows his beloved protégé at all.'

BECAUSE she had the time, and because her grandmother asked her to, Claudia found herself immersed in welfare work, and somehow or other although some of it was very upsetting it helped her considerably. Better still it was clear she was helping others. There were far more serious things in life to worry about than sexual intrigues. She was surrounded by people, men, women, children who were racked by bodily aches and pains; people who would remain in wheelchairs all their lives; little children who would never grow old. Most of all the children pierced her heart.

'You're very good with them,' Ward Sister told her.

'I'd like to be.' All she had done was sit and talk and because she had a facility for drawing elected to draw various favourite animals and cartoon characters. The children had been terribly impressed.

'Well done, Claudia,' her grandmother said to her, not in the least surprised. 'We must make good use of our time. Our lives are so comfortable but as you can see others are so wretched. We have a responsibility to help.'

Her father, however, was vaguely *annoyed*.

'Wherever are you off to today?' he turned to her one morning at breakfast.

'Meals on Wheels.' Claudia was gulping her coffee down so fast it was painful.

'Good God, can't somebody else do that? I really dislike your going into strange places.'

'But they're old people…invalids, Daddy,' Claudia said incredulously. 'Nice, ordinary, decent people. Not so ordinary either. I met the most wonderful old lady the other day, gloriously strong in her mind but crippled with arthritis. She depends on us. Everyone *wants* to be independent, but it doesn't always happen. Especially when one grows old. I've seen so many people terribly afflicted yet they keep up good spirits. I don't know how, but they do. It's such a *lesson!* The emotional tears welled up in her eyes causing Grant Ingram to cut in very curtly:

'This is your grandmother's idea!' he exploded. '*I* don't think you're strong enough. There are social workers for that kind of thing and they have the advantage of being *trained* which you definitely aren't. It's getting to you, my dear. Look at you now, eyes full of tears...'

Resolutely Claudia brushed them away. 'What I'm doing, Daddy, is extremely little, but since I've started, I'm going to keep at it.'

'For how long?' Grant Ingram asked sceptically. 'You can't eat and now you're shaking like a leaf. What *is* the matter?'

'Reaction,' Claudia answered after a moment's reflection. 'Reaction to seeing so much deprivation.'

'That's *it!* You're severely disturbed. Your grandmother has spent a lifetime in hospitals and such places. This is all too new to you.'

'Don't you think I can face it?' Claudia asked.

'You're very edgy, darling.'

'No. I'm just seeing a lot of terribly disturbing problems. It's a vast change from my usual day.'

'Ah well,' Grant Ingram turned back to his breakfast. 'Get it out of your system if you must. It seems a fairly morbid kind of work to me. Your grandmother never gets tired of all her charities but you're different. You'll kill yourself. As a family we contribute a good deal to charity. Surely that's enough?'

'I told you so!' Fergy wagged her head in the kitchen. 'Your dad's a real snob!'

'I don't think he thinks I can be trusted with such work,' Claudia said wryly.

'Because you're showing how much you *care* doesn't mean you can't do it,' Fergy said. 'You've got plenty of McKinlay blood in your veins.'

Claudia reminded herself of that when a pensioner

she visited unloaded all her emotional difficulties on her as she served up the midday meal. The woman wasn't old but an invalid and although Claudia thoroughly understood her frustrations that particular case wasn't easy to deal with if it did add to her experience of crucial life. Because she listened, *really* listened, Claudia by the end of the fortnight had become very tired.

Because her grandfather was the person she found most supportive yet undemanding Claudia went over to spend her Saturday with him. He offered no advice, but allowed her to talk and as she talked she found herself dealing with her own reactions and adjustments. The treatment, in effect, was an open discussion and it proved very effective. Claudia made them both lunch and afterwards they worked together in the garden, giving one another tell-tale little smiles and pats that revealed very clearly where their deepest love lay. The loss of his daughter had been the most stunning blow Ross McKinlay had ever received in his life; a blow that drove him into deep depression, but suddenly—it was over. Looking into his granddaughter's eyes was not the reflection of pain but hope for the future.

They were sitting on the grass, quietly talking when the telephone rang. 'Shall I answer it?' Claudia brushed grass seeds from her hands.

'It's probably your grandmother. I'll go.' Ross McKinlay started to his feet, his eyes lighting up. 'Where that woman gets her energy from I'll never know. At an age when everyone else is slowing down, she's going at it full throttle. Like a cup of tea? It must be three.'

'Lovely!' Claudia swayed up very lazily and walked to the hammock strung between two gums. She felt so warm and relaxed she could drift off to sleep. Loving her grandfather so much it was like some marvellous gift to see him so much lighter in heart. His eyes had a glint in them and he had shared with her the latest news that he was resuming his old seat on the hospital board.

'Wonderful!' she had smiled and of course she had meant it. Later he had told her in a very business-like voice the changes he'd like to see brought about.

There was a smile in Claudia's eyes as she shut them. Was there ever a more delightful fragrance than newly mown grass? All the aching tensions seemed to have drained away from her body. She relaxed each limb in turn as her grandfather had long ago shown her...

'How about it, Sleeping Princess?'

Nick was looking down at her and she stared up at him in amazement. 'You *kissed* me.'

'I did.' His voice was both tender and jeering. 'Isn't that what I was supposed to do?'

She could feel her body temperature rising. 'It's a wonder I didn't cry out.'

'You did. A kind of little kitten mew. Can you get out of that or do you want me to lift you out?'

The hammock tipped suddenly and he seemed obliged to rescue her.

'Perhaps you could put me down, Nick?'

'Isn't there rather *less* of you?' he frowned. 'No, seriously, Claud, you'd better stop rushing around or you'll collapse.'

'Believe me, I'm perfectly fit.'

'Damn, you weigh nothing,' he said.

'Grandfather thinks I look all right and he's a *doctor*,' she protested. 'I insist you put me down.'

'I'm tired of holding you anyway.' He lowered her so she moved against him all the way. Her body reacted. So did his.

'Have you come to see Grandad?' she asked, a flush in her cheeks.

'I always like to see your grandfather. He's one of my favourite people, but actually I came to see you.'

'Did Fergy tell you where I was?'

'Why would she not?' he looked puzzled. 'There's definitely something wrong with you, Claudia. We've spent so much time together yet I was all wrong.'

'I know how it is.' She put up a hand and brushed her long hair from her face. She had never expected to see him today now her calm blood was glittering in her veins. 'Here's Grandad with afternoon tea!' she cried in relief.

'Just for survival, I think you need it.' He swung away from her and walked across the grass to where Sir Ross approached with a laden tray.

Grandad was such a marvellous judge of character, Claudia thought, he would hardly believe he had been mistaken about Nick. Now Nick had the tray and Sir Ross had his hand on the younger man's shoulder. Both tall, both so desperately close to her heart. She could hardly tell Grandad of her fears. Grandad like her father thought the sun rose and set on Nick. From the beginning they had taken a particular interest in him, almost embracing him as family as they all knew his background and viewed his situation with sympathy. Rebecca Grey had walked out on her husband

and young son and a few years later had been killed
in a car accident. His father had turned into a cold
recluse and his maternal grandfather, despite the fact
he was elderly and plagued with ill health, had to
emerge in the role of protector and guardian. Not that
Nick had ever been disowned by his father, but as
Claudia found out a long time after, his physical resemblance to his mother touched some raw nerve and
kept father and son a good deal less close in their
relationship. All in all, Nick had been deprived, but
he had certainly found the answer to it.

'This is a nice surprise,' Sir Ross said. 'I asked
Claudia how you were but she's seen as little of you
as anyone else. They tell me the new building is going
to be particularly good.'

Nick set the tray down on the white wrought iron
table and Claudia drew up the chairs. 'I believe
you've forgotten the milk, Grandad?'

'Damn it, so I have. Of course we drink it black.'

'I'll get it.'

'Sit down, Nick, and tell me all about it,' Sir Ross
insisted. 'Grant dropped in the other night...

The men talked on amiably for perhaps thirty
minutes while Claudia inserted a comment here and
there so they couldn't have it all to themselves entirely.

'I'd like to take Claudia out to see one of my
houses,' Nick sat back in his chair and sighed contentedly. 'Please come with us.'

'I'd like to...' Sir Ross began then looked at his
watch, staring at it in amazement. 'I believe thirty
minutes in some people's company can just fly, and
two minutes with others is too long. I'll have to make

it another time. My darling wife is bringing home an unexpected dinner guest so I'll have to clean up the little mess I just made in the kitchen.'

'I'll do that, Grandad,' Claudia said, already stacking the cups, saucers and plates.

'No. Nobody understands how to stack our dishwasher except me.'

'Well, we'll carry it in anyway.' Nick took the tray.

'It's that Mrs Zimmerman,' Sir Ross chuckled. 'An excellent woman, but a horrendous bore!'

Nick smiled sympathetically. 'I know you'll be perfectly charming to her.'

'I should think so! I wouldn't like to see her generous donations to the hospital cut off.'

'It's great to see your grandfather in such good spirits,' Nick said as they drove away in the car.

'Yes,' Claudia agreed with gentle tenderness. 'It's been a long journey back, yet Daddy never mentions my mother.'

'We each deal with our wounds as we can.' Nick's voice was expressionless. 'I imagine, Claudia, he was desperately unhappy in the early days. Perhaps ready to go under. Your grandfather told me once life had no real meaning for him after your mother died yet he continued to care for others in the same way he had always done. Your father is a different kind of man. To keep going I think he had to seal the memory of your mother off completely. From time to time, before he met Cristina I used to see an expression of desolation flit across his face that he strained to stamp out. It couldn't have been easy, but he had his work.'

'A man always has his work,' Claudia said, rather

bleakly. 'Grandad has never spoken about her either. Only Fergy and Nanna and they speak about her, so naturally, she seems to come to life. I *miss* my mother.'

'Yes, it's—hard.' Nick's taut face looked faintly strained. 'I think a lot of us keep up emotional barriers because of what we've missed.'

'Is that a dig at me?'

'Both of us maybe. I've never let any woman come close to me. Only a little kid. One doesn't throw up defences against little girls who look like daffodils.'

'A little-sister figure, is that it?'

He flicked the briefest glance over her summer-sheened skin. 'Never quite. There was always too much promise of the beauty to come. Besides, you've never thought of me as your big brother?'

'No.' Even in her innocence she had sensed a different element, a woman-thing through the child.

'So here we are, Claudia, at what we've always known.' He didn't speak again until they reached the Devlin House, his expression faintly hostile as though he had already confessed too much. 'We'll have to walk from here, Claudia,' he told her as they came to the end of the unsealed road. 'The car's not built for bush tracks.'

'I'd *like* a walk.' Claudia was already opening out the door. 'This is a beautiful block of land.'

'About ten acres in all. It looks away across the valley. To some extent it was rather a difficult commission. Mrs Devlin wanted a classic Georgian, which wasn't on. Neither the climate nor the environment. Professor Devlin wanted a kind of American ranch. Dr Sinclair *told* them to come to me much as

Marcus tells his clients what to buy. I think they were a little mystified by my designs, but prepared to try something new. The only thing they did agree on was, it had to impress their friends.'

'So you had to come up with something to suit the both of them?' she asked mockingly, knowing full well the answer.

'No. I designed a house that's at home in its site. Of course it had to relate to the people it served, but I can't have the clients telling *me* how to design a building. *I'm* supposed to be the expert. If they don't like my work they're naturally free to go to someone else but usually they come to me by deliberate choice. I just hear in essence what they want, but what the actual building looks like is up to me. There can't be totality if I'm playing off husband against wife, trying to strike a compromise or drawing too heavily on the past. My main concern is to find the appropriate expression for a building in a particular environment. As it happened my drawings struck a bell.'

'I'm not surprised.'

Nick's drawings were so brilliant, so beautifully washed in colour with all the phenomena of shade, shadow and light, they were already being collected as works of art in their own right. His drawing style was very personal and marvellously self assured; at once rich in information and distinctly painterly. Claudia's father's drawings were of a different type; diagrammatic, displaying his respect for symmetry and order, always traditionally orientated and elegant, but without Nick's extraordinary gift for manifesting the *actual* building. One could *walk* into Nick's drawings so vividly were they rendered. Some might find the concept too different or too daring for conservative taste but all understood the power of the intellect behind the conception. The people who actually lived in his houses, like Dr Sinclair, had undertaken to spread his reputation with the same vigour Nick had brought to designing their houses. Often he designed the furniture as well to the delight of the local craftsmen whose skills he sought to keep alive.

'What the heck's *that?*' she cried and clutched his arm.

'Oh, that? It's an ordinary old snake. Quite harmless. There's still quite a lot of clearing to be done.'

'Are there many more do you think?' She had moved so close to him he tucked her under his arm.

'Oh, come on, Claud. It's not as if it was a taipan.'

'You think it's silly, *I* don't. Snakes frighten the life out of me. Even the small fry and that looked about two metres long.'

'Harmless,' he said again. 'What are you doing tonight?'

'I'm staying at home.'

'How incredible!' He looked down at her, small in her flat sandals.

'Believe it or not, it's what I want to do.'

'How is Matthew?'

'Why?'

'I don't think you should encourage him as you're not in love with him.'

'I don't have to be *told,* Nick,' she said. As a matter of fact she and Matthew had had rather a *scene* which was one reason she was staying at home that night. Matthew had been so nearly *vicious,* there was no other word for it, she still couldn't believe it. Always controllable in their light lovemaking he had become almost violent, justifying his actions by accusing her of being 'a precious little nun...short on sensuality'. If only he knew! Or then again maybe his anger had been fed by jealousy because he had mentioned Nick a lot, with none of his old admiration but a whole lot of sarcastic innuendo.

'Possibly you've been overestimating your strength,' Nick said. 'Not many people, I think, have thrown themselves so hectically into community effort.'

'Okay, so Daddy's been talking?' She stopped and looked up at him.

'A little.' He looked tender and faintly amused. 'You're just the type to give yourself to a life of service.'

'Volunteers just happen to be *needed*.'

'I know that.' He pinched her chin and before she could stop him dropped a hard kiss on her mouth. 'It just happens I admire what you're doing, Claud. Don't *over-do* it, that's all. Even your grandmother started out with small doses and she's an enormously energetic lady. You get a very delicate look about you from time to time. You try *so* hard.'

'So would you, Nick...' She let her voice trail off. Where he had kissed her, her mouth seemed to be flaming. It required so much effort to resist Nick and today resistance seemed to be entirely beyond her. Two giant royal poincianas were flaming on an adjoining property, resplendently scarlet against an enamel blue sky. Their massive limbs were motionless on the hot, still air.

'Are you ever going to design a house of your own, Nick?' she asked suddenly.

'Sure, baby.'

'What about your grandfather's place?'

'I've been thinking I could sell it to my cousin, Barbara, and her husband. They have *five* children!'

'Then it wouldn't go out of the family. He's a barrister, isn't he?'

'Yes.' He looked down at her, the darkness of his hair and skin the most extreme contrast with his eyes. Today he was wearing an open-necked soft shirt with casual slacks and she was acutely aware of his lean good looks. She even feared she might be staring. 'Come on, let's keep going,' he said.

The Devlin House rested on the pinnacle of the verdant hillside like its crowning glory, its multi-levels extending down the canyon, irregular expanses of glass affording viewing galleries for the magnificent 360° panoramas.

'But this is different to anything you've done before,' she said, just standing there, shading her eyes. It was beautiful. Brick, tile, rich red cedar, all commodities used time and time again but not like this. Nick's work was unmistakable, reaching out to one with its originality and scope. Thirty three, she thought. To have achieved so much!

'They're *all* different,' he said. 'An architect is always striving to create something new. I didn't want to frame all the views with the same old window walls. I approached it much as a painter does when he's thinking of appropriate frames.'

'This would be a wonderful place to live.' Claudia allowed herself to be drawn up the slope.

'I can do better.' His hand covered her shoulder and she understood for a moment it would be very difficult to get away from Nick if he wanted her. He was so determined she began to tremble.

'Stop that,' he said, knowing her too well.

The house wouldn't be ready for occupation for another month and there was no one around. Shadows were beginning to sweep the valley now and there was a curious magic in the air.

They walked around for a long time, Nick explaining what he wanted her to know, Claudia asking questions, her green eyes reflecting the haunting beauty of the valley. They seemed to talk unflaggingly, very naturally as they had not done in many long months. Many of her friends were desperately shy of starting up a conversation with Nick, thinking themselves somehow inadequate or lost for something really interesting to say to him yet she had always found Nick a very comfortable person to talk to... He didn't parade his brilliance or forever talk in profundities. He had always teased and amused her and so often been very, very kind. He was like that. Exciting *and* easy. For that afternoon she refused to allow anyone to come between them. There had been so much constraint between them now it was curiously like the old days.

'I guess we'd better be going,' Nick said eventually. 'In a little while it will be really dark.'

'Thank you, Nick. That was a marvellous experience.'

He shut the door and locked it. 'The landscaping is going to be important, that's why I recommended Marc Adami. He'll clear it selectively. The trees are beautiful but we can't risk a bush fire. One can never be entirely sure in this climate. Precautions must be taken.'

Claudia picked up a white stone, smoothing it lovingly with her hand. 'I so envy you, Nick. If only *I* had a gift.'

'My God,' he said, 'you *haven't?*'

'I can do lots of things but nothing *really* well.'

'Keep trying, baby. You've just turned twenty-one.'

'Still,' she said, 'you've *always* known you were going to be an architect.'

'It *does* run in the family, flower-face.' He put out his hand and encircled her wrist. 'What is it you *want* to be?'

She looked at him and exhaled shakily. Less clear now were worldly ambitions. A breeze had blown up, flurrying through the leaves, sending up aromatic waves of perfume.

'Would it be so hard to be a wife and mother?' He was smiling at her and all of a sudden she felt the hot spring of tears. Hadn't she loved him all along? It was terrible, *terrible!* She wanted nothing more in this world than to have her love returned.

Pebbles rattled down the slope and she flew away from him, her head whirling. After such a beautiful languorous afternoon she was swept by a great frustration, a blaze of anger she found difficult to control. Nick was *not* as he seemed. He was full of contradictions and complications. As *she* was, yet she felt herself incapable of endangering the security of others' lives. Love was relentless but Nick didn't really love anyone. It was monstrous, but it was true. Why had she allowed herself to trust his look of tenderness and desire?

She put her foot down in a crumbling depression and abruptly went over, the wrench of pain making her sick and breathless.

'You crazy little fool!' he dropped to his knees beside her, his eyes on her whitened face. Somehow the violence of his tone implied a great concern.

'Yes, aren't I?' she whispered honestly.

'Wait, don't talk.' He bent to examine her foot and ankle. 'God knows what you've done.'

'Shall I try standing up? The worst of the pain seems to be fading away.'

'Maybe you've only wrenched it,' he muttered. 'Only a woman could act in such a *hazardly* fashion.' He lifted her, doll-like, supporting her while she lowered her right foot gingerly to the ground.

'Well?' he gazed intently at her.

'Can you fix me up with a bed for the night?'

'Claudia, I can refuse you nothing.' The look in his eyes sent a shiver down her spine.

'Actually I think it's all right.' She was discovering to her relief that there was no sprain or something worse; probably a torn ligament, it was starting to swell.

'I think hot and cold towels will do the trick,' Nick said consideringly. 'They'll bring the swelling down at any rate. Then, I think, the treatment is to keep on the move. Keep the blood flowing.'

'Grandad will know.'

'*I'm* the doctor for tonight.'

'You've got that all wrong. I love your architecture; suspect your doctoring.'

'You could always hobble home.'

'From here? That would be terrible!' She smiled and looked up at him, all of a sudden totally dominated by his glance. 'But I've left my car at Grandad's!'

'Okay. So we'll ring and say we'll pick it up tomorrow.'

She sighed deeply, still troubled by her principles. The natural ease of the afternoon born of years of companionship had fallen back into the tension of the past months. Had Nick brought Cristina here with him? Had they embraced, kissed? Were they all driven by a power outside of them?

'What is it now?' he asked abruptly.

'I have to know something, Nick.' She slid her hand rather pleadingly down his arm.

His silver eyes glinted and the handsome mouth grimaced. *'Don't* mention Cristina.'

'But Nick…'

'I *mean* it.'

'Well, then, what is it you want from *me?*' she cried out, exasperated.

'As much as I can get.' He looked down at her very coolly.

'I can't get used to it.'

'For God's sake, you *can!*' He looked mocking and angry. 'You've had some kind of power over me since you were a beautiful little kid with a thick pigtail. I thought it was because I never had a little sister to love and spoil. My childhood wasn't so great. My father and I were worlds apart. My mother couldn't even spare me *your* deep sighs. There was no doting grandmother, no aunts. I suppose I was ready for you

to take up a lot of room in my heart. You were so
sweet and generous *then*. So sure I was hero material.
Now you seem to have made up your mind, Claudia,
you're relentless.'

'Oh, that's not true!' she lamented and because her
ankle was hurting began to moan, 'oh, oh, oh,' very
softly.

'How in hell did we start this?' he groaned. 'Here,
let me carry you. You've gone rather white.'

No more use to think about it. She allowed him to
lift her, her gratitude real. A woman was certainly
inferior to the man in one respect: she couldn't match
his physical strength. Didn't want to. Claudia turned
her face into his neck and because the impulse was
too fiery to be consumed, kissed it.

'Coming home with me?' the curtness of his tone
had magically softened.

She nodded. Could he feel the *yearning* in her
body?

'Fine.' His arms around her tightened and that way
they made their way down the hill.

CHAPTER FIVE

BY THE time they arrived back at Nick's house it was already dusk and Claudia was experiencing a certain amount of pain and shock reaction. In fact she had begun to feel faintly disoriented as though some further misadventure were pending.

Nick's frown made vertical lines between his black, winged brows. 'You're in pain, aren't you?'

'Nothing very bad. I'm more light-headed really.'

'Maybe I wasn't quite right to bring you. I can *call* a doctor,' Nick suggested.

Claudia gave her ankle another cursory examination. 'I only wrenched it so I don't think we need bother with that.'

'All right,' Nick said swiftly. 'Sit there until I come around to help you. It's only a short flight of steps to the house.'

They were parked in the huge garage that was not detached from the house but specially designed to blend in with the main building as an extra wing. They walked to the indoor staircase and when they reached the top of the flight of stairs, Claudia leant back against the timber railing while Nick hunted up his keys.

'Wait here a moment while I turn the lights on,' he told her.

'What are we going to have for dinner?' she asked gently.

'Let's thoroughly investigate that injury first. If there's the faintest chance...'

'It's *not* serious, Nick.'

'No, I don't think so,' Nick bent and inserted the key in the lock, 'but you still look a little shook up.' The lock turned and Nick pushed the door open. 'What the *hell!*'

'Oh, *Nick!*' Claudia underscored his tone of surprised alarm. '*Did* you leave the lights on?'

'Stay there,' he said, very definitely, his face tautening as he decided on a course of action. Many of his friends had sophisticated security systems to protect their property but neither he nor his grandfather had ever had the slightest trouble.

'Oh please, Nick, be careful!' Claudia warned him.

'I will be,' he moved into the kitchen preparing to search out a suitable weapon and as he did so, a woman's distressed voice called out:

'Is that *you,* Nick?'

'You'd better answer her.' To all outward appearances Claudia looked completely uninterested.

'*Answer* her!' Nick swore violently under his breath. 'What the hell is she doing here?'

'Your guess is as good as mine,' Claudia shrugged with bitter mockery.

'*Nick?*' The woman was walking towards them, her heels beating a tattoo on the parquet floor.

'And I'd decided to *believe* you from now on,' Claudia's voice sounded as though it belonged to somebody else. She wanted to sound angry, disgusted, vehement, but she only sounded spiritless and beaten.

Nick, on the other hand, was in a blazing fury. 'In here, Cristina,' he commanded.

Claudia closed her eyes. She thought of the last time she had seen Cristina rushing to Nick's side. She was a lot smarter this time: she would spare herself the pain.

'Oh, Nick, I'm so glad you're back!' Cristina's voice came with a rush of heartfelt gratitude but no hint of apology. It was obvious she was unaware of Claudia's presence on the outside landing.

'How the hell did you get in?' Nick countered.

'Why…the key!'

What else, Claudia thought wearily.

'You mean you *know* where to find a key to my house?'

'Why Nick, you sound so angry!' Cristina cried.

All anger had drained from Claudia. She felt ill. But if she expected Nick to let her go he all but yanked her inside.

'Claudia!' Cristina screeched.

'For Christ's sake!' Nick exploded, 'what goes on here? I figure you've got exactly two minutes, Cristina, to come up with an answer. After that, I'm going to fling you out my door and to hell with the consequences!'

'Would you like a lawyer, Cristina?' Claudia asked very formally.

'Sit down, Claud, and shut up,' Nick warned her with absolute menace even as he slipped a chair beneath her.

'I couldn't bear anything to happen now,' Cristina cried and grasped Nick's arm. 'I think Grant *suspects* something.'

'*Don't!*' Nick muttered with uncontrolled fury. 'Don't try me too far.'

'I knew it would come to this,' Claudia said in the same dull tone. 'God, what *fools* you are!'

'I'll use that against you, Claud, for the rest of your life.'

'Who cares!' Claudia hunched over in her chair. Trust Nick to sound so cold and wronged. 'I prayed this would never happen.'

'It never would except for that wretched Matthew,' Cristina shouted desperately.

'Matthew?' Both Claudia and Nick looked up with hard, questioning stares.

'What's *Matthew* got to do with this?' Claudia demanded.

'He's a trouble maker, of course,' Cristina snapped. 'I've yet to discover whether his interference was deliberate treachery or he just wanted to take a rise out of Grant.'

'Matthew would never do that,' Claudia said faintly.

'I would say he *would*.' Nick cut her off curtly. 'You must know he's crazy about you, Claudia, and I gather these days he doesn't like me. To tell the truth I always thought your friend, Matthew, a little strange.'

'You *amaze* me, Nick,' Claudia said.

'Come on, let's hear it,' he goaded her. 'Let's have some more of the moral censure.'

'Please *stop* it!' Cristina was shaken and appalled. 'Grant could be here at any minute.'

'Big deal!' Nick pulled himself away from the table. 'And just as well. I don't think I could stand any more of this.'

'This is how he *really* is, Cristina,' Claudia fixed her stepmother with brooding eyes. 'You'd sacrifice my father, a good, decent, *faithful* man, for a man like *Nick?*'

'I was carried away.'

'You *lying* bitch!'

'I'm *not!*' Cristina turned to Nick with a pentup violence. 'I did love you, Nick. *Madly.*'

'God you women are wicked creatures!' Nick shook his head, the twist to his beautiful mouth quite terrible. 'I think it's only men that keep you on the straight and narrow. Can't you see, Cristina, that you're taking my reputation away from me? That's a pretty serious thing. For instance you've got sweet little Claudia here believing in your story of tormented rape.'

'Perhaps it will help Claudia to keep away from you,' Cristina said.

As a remark it was disastrous because Nick lifted his hand and slapped Cristina sharply across the face. 'I'm not supposed to be a gentleman so do be careful, Mrs Ingram.'

'Oh, *Nick!*' Claudia burst out, appalled. Cristina's striking, sophisticated face was as red and crumped as a child's.

'Don't pity her,' Nick said, bitterly. 'She's a liar and a...'

'Nick, *please!*' Claudia protested, deeply shocked.

'There's only one way to get out of this,' Cristina said frantically. 'You must help me. *Both* of you.'

'Not *me,* lady.' Nick's handsome, high mettled face

was implacable. 'I'm hoping your husband will toss you out.'

'*Claudia!*' Cristina wailed.

'Why should it be *me* to help you?' Claudia asked quietly. 'You've betrayed my father and—' broken my heart, she thought but didn't say.

'The trouble with you, Claudia,' Nick said frigidly, 'is you're still a half-witted adolescent. You're being manipulated by an unscrupulous madwoman, but you can't see it.'

'For God's sake, let's talk about this before something *happens!*' Cristina begged. 'I tell you Grant had a phone call...'

'From Matthew?' Claudia lifted distant, green eyes.

'From Matthew, the little rat!' Cristina confirmed, her wide mouth ugly with rage. 'I caught a little of what he was saying on the upstairs extension.'

'So you came *here?*' Nick regarded her with his dazzling silver eyes.

'We have to *do* something, Nick!' Cristina moaned. She was wringing her hands together with increasing intensity, her skin pallid except for the dull glow on her right cheek.

'Make your plans if you must, but make them without me,' Nick told her indifferently. 'Claud, I think we should bathe that ankle.'

'If I didn't feel like weeping,' Claudia responded, 'I'd laugh.'

'What's going to happen now?' Cristina cried out with a touch of hysteria.

'Tell the truth for once,' Nick suggested with quiet violence. 'I thought you were a touch crazy, Cristina, but not poisonous. Yet here you are still lying in your teeth. That puzzles me.'

'I have some feeling for Claudia,' Cristina protested emotionally. 'It's only natural I would want to protect her.'

'From *me?*'

Nick looked so peculiar Claudia snapped to her feet. 'Let's stop this *now*,' she grasped Nick's two arms. 'It seems the only *decent* thing you two can do now is spare my father unnecessary pain and humiliation.'

'I'll do that,' Nick returned coolly, 'if I can have *you.*'

'Claudia, don't listen to him! That's not the way.'

'What a brute you are, Nick,' Claudia said quietly.

'Yes, aren't I?' He put his arms around her waist and jerked her to him. 'And because I am what I am I'm going to have you by fair means or foul.'

'You leave her alone, Nick,' Cristina cried.

'Never.' Nick's light eyes were glittering like diamonds. 'I'll marry Claudia and you can go back to your husband.'

'What kind of solution is that?' Cristina laughed crazily.

'Oh, come, Cristina,' Nick said harshly, 'why would anyone bother to tell so many lies? Just to protect someone? I'd say the opposite was true. They write about this kind of thing in women's novels.'

'It must be a lot of drivel,' Claudia pressed her hands hard against Nick's chest, but he *wouldn't* let her go.

'You're such a swine, Nick!' Cristina said on a

great wave of pain. 'Maybe I deserve this suffering, but Claudia doesn't.'

So engrossed were they in one another it took them many seconds to realise the front door bell was ringing incessantly.

'My God, it's Grant!' Cristina whispered, turning to a statue.

'Where the hell did you leave your car?' Nick took charge.

'I grabbed a taxi. It seemed better.'

'One day, my dear, you'll tell me how you got in.' Nick released the gulping Claudia and turned to the tall refrigerator. 'God bless you, Cristina, for coming. You're so happy for us. So happy!' While he was talking he was extracting a bottle of champagne from the inside of the refrigerator door, then reaching for glasses from a wall cabinet.

'What are you *doing,* Nick?' Claudia asked faintly in a voice of the doomed.

'Celebrating, darling. Don't be embarrassed. As soon as your father charges in, possibly waving a gun, I'm going to head him off by announcing news of our impending engagement.' Now he had popped the champagne cork and was pouring the wine into the glasses. 'I had no idea, Claudia, you could look so horrified.'

The front door bell pealed again. 'Choose a glass and bring it into the living room,' Nick ordered with no sweetness at all. 'Move, you idiots!'

'Oh, God!' Cristina wailed, reaching for a glass at the same time.

'It's very important we all act the part,' Nick told them. 'Cristina heard the news from you, Claud, and rushed over. I'd advise you both to pretend like hell. Don't worry about me. I'm already the radiant picture of a man in love.'

Nick moved away and they hurried after him, both in varying degrees of shock. Mercifully the slap mark on Cristina's cheek had faded and she was visibly making an effort to pull herself together.

'For God's sake, Nick, where *were* you?' They heard Grant Ingram boom.

'He could be *murderous!*' Cristina hissed. 'I'm frightfully important to him.'

'Why in blazes tell me now?' Claudia flung back at her, frightened now Nick might be in danger.

But no. When the two men entered the long, beautiful drawing room Nick was smiling, Grant Ingram was looking a little odd, but he had an affectionate arm wrapped around Nick's shoulders.

'Darling, what are *you* doing here?' Cristina almost flung herself at her husband. 'I mean it's all so sudden and romantic but hardly official.'

'*Daddy.*' For the life of her Claudia could give no more than a shaky smile.

'My little girl!' Grant Ingram extricated himself gently from his wife's impassioned clutches and moved towards his daughter. 'I'm so proud of you. So *proud!*'

For an instant Claudia felt like bursting into tears. Maybe it was a nice sort of feeling making a parent proud but was this how it was done? Getting engaged to Nick? Even had everything been perfect surely it was an odd way to put it? But essentially her father.

Claudia allowed herself to be kissed and blessed.

'Get a glass for Grant,' Nick instructed Cristina, a peculiar sparkle in his eyes.

'Of course.' Cristina took one look at him and hurried away.

'It was the oddest darned thing,' Grant Ingram told them afterwards, flashing them all an uncharacteristic humble glance. 'You know I actually thought—'

'*What,* Grant?' Nick leaned forward attentively, the very picture of integrity.

'Oh, hell what does it matter now?' Grant Ingram held up his champagne flute for a refill. 'Why should I mar such a wonderful occasion with unpleasantness.'

'Please tell us, Daddy?' Claudia pleaded gently.

'No, I'm damned if I will!' Grant Ingram laughed. 'Just a piece of mischief I should have disregarded in the first place. You can be quite sure there'll be no mention of it again. By the way, Cristina, where's your car?'

'She felt sure you'd find us out and you did.' Nick smiled at him. 'A taxi here and her husband to take her home.'

'This is what I've always wanted,' Grant Ingram said.

'Yes, it's *wonderful!* Cristina seconded, wild-eyed. 'I know you'd love to stay, darling, but we're expected at the Fauldings' tonight.'

'Cancel it,' Grant Ingram said.

'No, don't do that, Daddy,' Claudia came to Cristina's assistance. 'They'll be so disappointed and we'll have our own big party, I'm sure.'

'We certainly will,' Grant Ingram put his arm around his daughter and kissed her. 'Thank you,' he said. 'You've never given me one moment's anxiety or displeasure.'

'I sound like a terrible bore.'

'Never, darling,' Grant Ingram said briskly. 'You're the *perfect* daughter.'

'THERE, didn't I tell you,' Nick drawled, after he had seen his visitors off, 'it went perfectly.'

'I don't think there can be any truth in the statement, we get what we deserve.'

'And all this time, you and your ankle!'

'If you look closely,' Claudia said tartly, 'you'll see that it's swollen.'

'Darling, I'm *sorry*.' For such a high-handed, autocratic person he did indeed look sorry.

'Don't touch me,' Claudia began to shrink away from his touch.

'Shut up. Does it hurt?'

'There's such a thing as being anaesthetised by shock.'

'All Cristina's fault,' Nick looked up at her, diamond-eyed. 'It will cost us both, this engagement, but fortunately we're all still alive. Your father was in a fury when he arrived.'

'Did Matthew really want to cause trouble?'

'He had to take his frustration out on someone.' Nick straightened, then lifted her. 'Hot and cold towels on this, I think.'

'Are you sure it's safe?'

'Cristina will act sensibly from now on.'

'Whereas I could go round the *bend* from now on.'

'I told you I was determined to have you,' Nick held her in his arms and looked down at her.

'Then let's agree on how long,' Claudia's green eyes were no longer wide and adoring. 'They say all any rotter needs is the love of a good woman, but I don't care for self sacrifice. This whole situation is disgusting.'

'Really I quite like it.'

All of a sudden she began to cry.

'Claud, don't. *Please* don't.' Nick lowered his dark head and nuzzled her cheek.

'It's all so disgraceful.'

He moved back in search of an armchair and found one. 'I've told you one *million* times I've never laid a finger on your wretched stepmother.'

Claudia only cried harder.

'She's really neurotic. I hope I'm not shocking you.' He lifted her tear-stained face and kissed it. 'You love me.'

'I do *not!*'

'Of course you do. You and I have had a real commitment for years.'

'That's good,' she mocked bitterly.

'Cristina is like a wounded animal. She continues to lash out in her pain.'

'Don't swallow *my* tears.' She tried to jerk her head away from his wandering mouth.

'Why not? I want every part of you. Under all that terrific lady-like cool is a lot of passion.'

She wavered a little at the intensity of his voice. 'I'm allowing this, Nick, for the good of my father.'

He laughed.

'Because it would kill him being made a fool of.'

'You know you have the most exquisite *skin,*' he ignored her.

'And you're an authority on a woman's skin,' she said nastily.

'Up!' His voice turned hard again. 'If you don't want a lover, I can practise some first-aid.'

'Be sure that's all I'm ever going to let you do.' Her heart ached dully in love and sorrow.

'Suppose you let *me* be the judge of that,' he returned coolly. 'Remember, a man with no scruples holds all the cards.'

IT WAS A situation Claudia thought endlessly she could not accept, but wherever they went, their friends expressed a genuine delight. Some went so far as to say they had expected this all along. Even Sir Ross had sprung to life again immediately when he heard the news.

'I couldn't be more happy for you, darling,' he had told his granddaughter, looking directly into her eyes. 'Nick is a fine man. Your love will keep growing.'

Claudia often thought her face would reflect her disillusionment, but the thoughts that transfixed her only succeeded in making her look dreamy, apparently the appropriate expression for a newly engaged girl.

The party was set for Christmas Eve. 'A combination of wonderful events!' as her father put it. She had passed her finals with flying colours, Christmas was such a beautiful time of the year and now the culmination of Grant Ingram's ambitions; the finest thing Claudia concluded she had ever done in her life was get herself engaged to Dominic Grey. If she didn't do another thing, she had justified her existence.

Cristina seemed to avoid her like the plague, working so hard at her business she had turned into an ultra-elegant wraith. Claudia was terrified despair might be behind that frenzy of industry. Always a compassionate person Claudia felt the strong urge to try to make contact with her stepmother. The human condition involved profound upheavals and the best man or woman could be made vulnerable to a totally unacceptable love affair; or so Claudia reasoned. What actually happened between Cristina and Nick she did not know. Cristina inferred a grand passion; Nick denied *any* close relationship vehemently. Either he was an appalling, practised liar or the victim of a severe delusion. Wasn't love a madness? From the very moment Cristina had met Nick she had been in a state of high emotionalism; a state uncommon to her and therefore more dangerous.

On that particular morning a few days before her engagement party Claudia sought her stepmother out in her office.

There were a few people in the showroom when Claudia arrived. George Nisbet, Cristina's assistant, turned around to wave and smile at her and Claudia returned the smile and continued towards Cristina's office. Cristina was such a clever woman and she deserved respect for all that she had achieved through her own efforts. Strange behaviour was not foreign to clever people and clever women, in particular, had few of their own sex to champion them. If they all had to survive as a family, arriving at some sort of harmony was crucial.

Cristina was seated at her desk with her head down

and Claudia crossed her fingers and spoke out pleasantly.

'Hi! I hope I haven't caught you when you're busy?'

In response Cristina jumped. 'Good Heavens, Claudia, what are *you* doing here?'

This kind of reaction wasn't surprising, neither was it reassuring. 'We see so little of each other these days, Cristina,' Claudia said mildly, 'I thought you might come out to lunch with me.'

'Out of the question, dear,' Cristina returned firmly, and stretched her long neck to relax her throat muscles. 'Business is so hectic! You have no idea.'

'You've got terribly thin.'

'So I have!' Cristina stood up abruptly.

'Please talk to me, Cristina,' Claudia dropped into a chair.

'For God's sake, what about?'

'I *care* if you're unhappy.'

'And you want to make it clear *you're* deliriously happy?'

'I'm not.' Claudia was perturbed by the tension in her stepmother's face.

Cristina snorted violently. 'You should be.' She sat down again and fixed Claudia with challenging eyes. 'You've got yourself one hell of a man.'

'Are you still in love with him, Cristina?' Claudia asked sadly.

'I *detest* him!' Cristina gave a laugh that ended in a stifled sob. 'He betrayed me. Your father. Now, you.'

Claudia's face went white with worry and anxiety.

'Whatever was between you, Cristina, it's over. You've simply got to forget him.'

'How *can* I, when he's always under my nose?'

'I know.' Claudia shook her head helplessly. 'You need to get away. You and Daddy need a long trip.'

'Your father would sacrifice me for Nick any day.'

'What does *that* mean?' Claudia leaned across the desk and grasped Cristina's arm.

'You know your father idolises Nick. He's the son he has always wanted.'

'Why don't you give him one of his own?' Claudia suggested fiercely. 'It seems to me, Cristina, you're wallowing in unhappiness. If you want to save yourself, you'll have to determine on a course of action. You think Daddy is in raptures about Nick and me? Can you imagine what he'd be like if you fell pregnant? Gave him a son? The love Daddy has for Nick tells you everything about him. He's the sort of man who lives for family and heritage. He loves me, I know. He's been the best father in the world, but there has scarcely been a time when I wasn't aware a daughter is second best. The true heir, the person my father best relates to, is a son. When Nick came along he fulfilled that great need. There is an extraordinarily close bond between them. I suppose neither of them had anyone really meaningful in their lives.'

'How you downgrade yourself, Claudia,' Cristina said pityingly.

'Yes, don't I.' Claudia bent her platinum head. 'I am, in a way, a product of my environment. Daddy values me more for what beauty I have than brains.'

'You've got plenty of them too,' Cristina said quietly. 'Really, Claudia, I have to admit it, you're an extraordinarily nice girl. That's why I hate to see you make a terrible mistake. Believe me, you could never handle Nick.'

'It may not come to that,' Claudia clutched the side of the desk. 'You know why I took this step, Cristina. Why Nick engineered this engagement the way he did.'

'He wants you,' Cristina said bleakly, barely managing to keep the tears out of her eyes. 'Goddammit, you're *perfect*. You're beautiful, you're highly intelligent, and best of all, you're your father's daughter. What could be better for Nick?'

'Everyone keeps talking about *Nick*,' Claudia said resignedly. 'Does no one care about *me*? What *I* want?'

'But you love him, don't you, dear?' Cristina put a beringed hand to her temple as though to stop the jabbing pain there. 'You'd be lying if you said you didn't.'

'To have him love me would be much better.'

'I don't think any woman is going to have Nick's *love*.' Cristina murmured huskily. 'He's got so many hangups deeply buried within him. He used to talk to me about his mother...'

'*Nick* did?' Claudia frowned.

'Of course.' Cristina seemed lost in her reflections. 'I think that's why he is such a bastard to all women. He's got the power now to destroy the sex he really despises. She went off and left him, you know.'

'Of course I know,' Claudia's green eyes searched her stepmother's. There was something about Cristina's expression that was really odd. A kind of theatricality but then theatricality was part of her makeup. Even part of her job.

'I don't believe Nick said too much about his mother,' Claudia said with a very sceptical air. 'Did he mention Valentina?'

Cristina smiled. 'I know all about Valentina.'

'That's odd, since I just made her up.' It was extraordinarily exhilarating to catch Cristina out on just one little lie. People who habitually told lies inevitably worked their way up to the humdingers.

'Maybe it wasn't Valentina,' Cristina shrugged. 'I can't remember all the names but what I'm telling you stands. There's a lot of violence in Nick. A lot of hostility against women. Maybe that's what makes him so terribly attractive. Women love to be hated.'

'I'm afraid I can't agree with that.'

Cristina eyed Claudia's youthful beauty contemptuously. 'You're just a child as far as I'm concerned. Nick told me the same thing. You're the virginal little girl-child.'

'That's nothing to be ashamed of,' Claudia returned tartly. 'So long as I don't remain a virgin forever, I don't mind.'

'Don't turn yourself over to Nick,' Cristina advised harshly. 'He has a heart of glass. Look at how callously he treated me. Amanda Nichols was another one caught in his web. He takes what he wants, then he can't even remember. Men are like that.'

As an attempt at reconciliation it was quite unsuccessful. Cristina's sickness was even worse than Claudia suspected. Everything she had hoped for so *stupidly* was not to be. When an obsession took root it was hard to tear it up.

Claudia was just emerging from a department store when someone touched her on the arm.

'Claudia?'

It was Matthew and Claudia's soft, moulded mouth tightened. 'Oh, it's you, Matthew.'

'Oh, don't be like that, Claudia,' Matthew begged in a husky voice. 'Look, have you time for coffee?'

'Not really, *no*.'

'*Please*, Claudia. Won't you let me explain?' Matthew's lean hand came out and tightened around her wrist. 'Just ten minutes? We've been friends for so long.'

Claudia wanted to say no, but Matthew was almost dragging her away. 'Don't keep on judging me, Claudia. I hated what I did but I wanted to show Nick up.'

'Then you made a big mistake, didn't you?'

The lunch time crowd had almost moved out and they found a table close to the floor to ceiling glass walls where they could look out at the people moving through the mall.

'You look beautiful, Claudia.' A muscle jerked beside Matthew's attractive mouth.

'I feel fine.'

'Being engaged must agree with you?'

'I didn't come to discuss my engagement, Matt,' Claudia stared rather numbly at the magnificent emerald flanked by diamonds on her left hand.

'Oh God, oh God,' Matthew said huskily. 'You could have anyone you please, Claudia, but not Nick Grey.'

'Why not?' Claudia was trembling inside but on the outside she was porcelain cool.

'Oh, please, Claudia, don't make me say it. Nick goes back a long way. You're just an innocent young girl. You don't know what you're getting into.'

'You know this is funny in a way,' Claudia laughed oddly. 'Everyone wanting to put me off Nick.'

'*Everyone?*'

'I love him, Matthew.' Claudia took a deep breath.

'Then God help you.' Matthew's voice was as harsh as hers was soft. 'How can this have a happy ending after what Nick has done?'

'What *has* he done?'

'Don't let's go over that again,' Matthew drawled, his voice dripping acid. 'What kind of man would get involved with a close friend's wife?'

'Simple. He's been damned by a whole lot of circumstantial evidence.'

'You don't believe that?' Matthew challenged her.

'Maybe I do when the opposite is being rammed down my throat. Maybe I should be bitterly ashamed of myself for ever doubting Nick for a moment. Too many people are trying to convince me he *is* what I *know* he isn't. Nick may generate a lot of magnetism but he's much too unconscious of it to use it in the way you say. Other people make fools of themselves over Nick, but really he always remains the same. I used to think you liked him, Matthew?'

'I *did* like him.' Matthew hadn't taken his eyes off her lovely face. 'But having your girl taken off you is a nightmare.'

'Oh, Matthew,' she whispered, seeing his mouth twist in pain, 'I'm sorry. *Very* sorry, but I was never your girl. We were friends, good friends. I trusted you.'

'Your father did his best to cut me out,' Matthew said viciously. 'I was never good enough for you. Or him.'

'That's not true. But does it matter now?'

'You haven't walked up the altar yet, Miss Ingram,' Matthew said grimly and caught her hand. 'I've made my decision and that's to stick around. You really matter to me. Grey may have convinced you he loves you and maybe he does. For *now*. He's the type that finds it impossible to resist a beautiful girl.'

'Rubbish!' At least Claudia could deny that emphatically because it simply wasn't true. Nick had been known to resist any number of glamorous girls.

'You know he's had that affair with your stepmother.'

'I know nothing of the kind.' Claudia's eyes were brilliantly angry. 'No matter what *you* tell me. No matter what anyone tells me, I should know Nick.'

'You mean you do know. Not *should* know. You *don't* know, do you Claudia?' Matthew shook his head. 'You're really under a great deal of tension. Don't worry, I feel for you. The pressure must be enormous. Wondering whether your father really will find out. Whether Cristina and Nick will get together again?'

Claudia's anger fizzled abruptly. 'What do you think *caring* really means, Matthew?'

'I *love* you.' Matthew leaned forward and put his hand over hers.

'I always imagined caring means being protective. You deliberately tried to hurt my father...'

'And I'd try again.'

'And in hurting my father you must hurt me.'

'So there was no way to avoid it,' Matthew's voice was anguished now. 'My life is worth nothing without you. I've gone mad since you got engaged.'

'Is that what love is, *madness?*' Claudia was struggling to wrench her hand away. 'People who are usually so sane and sensible overwhelmed by delirium. It's almost like a disease, not a happy event.'

'It's only happy when it's *returned.*' Matthew still held her fingers defiantly. 'Haven't you ever been *jealous* of anyone, Claudia?'

'I must have led a very narrow life. No, I've never experienced that unhappy, destructive feeling. I don't like *threatening* anyone anyway. I suppose I don't see things only in terms of myself. Finally, I guess, I'm not the smouldering type. Jealous people can be horribly wounding to others as well as themselves. You had no right to try to cause trouble, Matthew. I can't think why you did it.'

'You just told me,' Matthew laughed grimly. 'I can't take this relationship of yours with Nick Grey. I sure as hell can't. If there's anything I can do to stop it, I will.'

At the look in Matthew's eyes Claudia felt her skin go cold. She jerked herself to her feet and grasped her handbag.

'Don't go, Claudia. Please, *don't.*'

She shook her head. 'Our being good friends didn't mean a thing, did it, Matt? I think you're interfering because you enjoy it.'

'No, it's more serious than that,' Matthew looked up at her. 'You're *my* girl. At least I always thought of you as that. Nick Grey's got a lot of things going for him, I'll admit, but he's like the rest of us. He can't take a stab in the back. Your father is so wrapped up in his own life, the good life, he can't see what's right under his nose. One learns quite quickly to play dirty.'

'And some of us never learn at all,' Claudia gave him a look that was a mixture of disgust and sorrow. 'Before you start to think of attacking Nick or my father, remember they're both powerful men. And on the subject of your finding a plush job in the near future you're in the same field. My father has always stood for the Establishment. Nick is an establishment on his own. Both of them are kind of hero-figures. You just could shatter your own future.'

But Matthew was determined to have the last word. He noted the paleness of Claudia's flawless skin, the faint tremble in her hands. 'Better mine than yours,' he muttered. 'You must learn how to be your own person, Claudia. Up until now you've been manipulated by two men. That's all you're good for.'

'In that case then, Matthew,' Claudia said gently, 'I'm not the woman you want.'

CHAPTER SIX

THE festive season came and went and Claudia had to act radiantly happy all the time. She supposed the same was true of Nick. No matter how they felt they both had to go out of their way to be convincing as a couple very much in love. It was a classic love story really. So many people professed to know it was a relationship that was inevitable.

'No wonder he never took any of us seriously,' Amanda Nichols told Claudia with pursed lips. 'I said all along he was simply in love with somebody else.'

It was intolerable and all the private agonising changed nothing. Cristina had become a changed woman, finding fault with everyone and everything.

'If she speaks to me just one more time,' Fergy threatened grimly.

Finally Grant Ingram thought it was time to speak to his daughter. He had returned from a business meeting in high spirits, another important commission and the preliminary talks had gone well, but these days his wife wasn't treating him with the same attention and respect. Once she had been marvellous, glowing company, now she was strained beyond belief.

Grant Ingram walked downstairs again, trying to come to terms with the extraordinary difference in his wife. He had always thought Cristina remarkably consistent for a woman, but now her moods swung alarmingly, taking the form of extreme irritability in most cases. She was clearly in need of a holiday but he simply couldn't spare the time. In reality he detested any threat to the smooth pattern of his existence and whatever emotions had been involved when he made his decision to marry Cristina, love hadn't been one of them. He had only loved once and that had turned out disastrously. Besides, the older a man got the less likely he was to fall in love madly. Such stressful emotions were for the young. He had married Cristina because it had seemed an excellent idea at the time. She was highly attractive and clearly able to stand on her own two feet; they worked in a complementary environment and during those early days his friends had been very impressed with her. Now everything seemed to have changed and the general feeling was one of having made some huge mistakes.

His daughter was in the living room waiting for Nick. They had tickets to a concert, a visiting concert pianist, and Claudia looked up at him with loving, trusting eyes.

'Downstairs again so early?'

'I love you very much, Claudia,' her father stared at her. 'You always behave so *well*.'

'Someone you know doesn't?'

'Pour me a whisky would you, darling?' Grant Ingram asked thoughtfully. 'I'm worried about Cristina. She's not well.'

'She's been working too hard.'

Grant Ingram frowned and looked at the floor. 'Dash it all, she's had two weeks' break.'

'Not enough,' Claudia murmured, holding out the crystal tumbler.

Her father took it without looking at her, his elegant, handsome features quite grim. 'You know what she just said to me now?'

'Isn't that a little private?' Claudia touched her father's hand appealingly. 'Can't you both go away for a holiday?'

'I'm darned sure *I* can't.' Grant Ingram looked outraged at the suggestion. 'Besides, I don't think a holiday would make Cristina happy. There's something deeply troubling her.'

'Maybe.' Claudia glanced away.

'Any idea what it could be?'

'Not really,' Claudia laughed a little shakily. 'We women are emotional creatures.'

'I don't really like it.'

'Of course. But Cristina mightn't like it either.'

'It's quite unfathomable to me.' Grant Ingram chose to ignore the faint irony in his daughter's musical voice. 'In my opinion she needs help. Maybe it's a *physical* thing that's causing the change in her behaviour. Women are such biological mysteries.'

'My suggestion is a *holiday*,' Claudia answered very seriously. 'Can't you manage even a *short* time together. Just the two of you. Maybe Cristina feels she has to share you with too many people.'

'Do you think so?'

'You're never really alone, Daddy,' Claudia said.

'Surely she doesn't want me to send *you* away?' Grant Ingram asked incredulously. 'And another thing, she's very nearly poisonous to Nick.'

'She is rather offhand,' Claudia moved away and

her thick, beautiful hair swung bell-like at her slender shoulders. In the last months she had somehow matured, the soft, dewy look of girlhood refining to a startling beauty. Always, underneath ran worry.

'That's a very kind word for it,' her father said acidly. 'Would you believe that ex-friend of yours, Matthew, inferred there was some particular… *friendship* between Cristina and Nick.'

'How very odd!' Claudia flung back carelessly, shaking inside.

'Damned odd!' Grant Ingram's handsome face turned fierce. 'I never liked that boy. Underhand.'

'Maybe foolish like everyone else at some time.'

'Really?' Her father raised a sardonic eyebrow. 'I assure you, my darling, I've never been involved in any messy intrigue.'

'I know.' Claudia sank deeply into her armchair. Her father was such a fastidious man and she had to admit very self-centred really. Still, out of her love for him, there was the fierce need to protect him.

'Privately, you know,' Grant Ingram confessed, 'I never thought Nick approved of my choice of Cristina for a wife.'

'Nick would find fault with anyone.'

'Now *that's* an extremely odd thing to say.'

'I was joking.' Claudia sat up and smiled.

'Yes, you were joking,' Grant Ingram looked at his daughter very searchingly. 'When are you and Nick going to set the date?'

'Gosh, Daddy,' Claudia's huge, green eyes glittered, 'we've just had an engagement party. How can you possibly face a *wedding* so soon?'

'I'd go mad only for you and Nick,' Grant Ingram

said very calmly and slowly. 'My life isn't so perfect as it seems. Sometimes I think it's a complete fabrication.'

'Daddy.' Claudia flew up and went to her father. He seldom, if ever, spoke this way. 'I know things are a little difficult at the moment, but they'll come right.'

'What *is* wrong with her?' For once Grant Ingram sounded bewildered.

'Down periods are part of life. Maybe Cristina doesn't recognise her limits. With you for an example she works exceptionally hard. Relaxation is valuable to keep people on an even keel. Why don't you go upstairs and tell her you're taking her to San Francisco for a week and no arguments.'

'I really can't spare the time, darling,' Grant Ingram murmured rather miserably.

'Nick will hold the fort.' The intensity of Claudia's expression betrayed her own urgency.

'Claudia, listen,' Grant Ingram suddenly said. 'There *was* never, could *never* have been any special relationship between Nick and Cristina?'

'*Daddy!*' Claudia looked and sounded appallingly shocked.

'I'm sorry, darling, but I'm serious. Terribly serious.'

'Because Matt put some incredible notion into your head?'

'Because of the big shift in my wife's behaviour.' Her father murmured, his voice low.

'Nick loves *me*,' Claudia said, her slender hands trembling.

'God, don't we all know it!' Grant Ingram seconded emphatically. 'Every time his eyes touch on you they give him away.'

'Then there's your answer, Daddy,' Claudia put out her hand and very gently touched her father's cheek. 'What you're saying is unthinkable.'

'I know it is.' Grant Ingram held his daughter's hand and kissed it. 'Thank you, dear. I didn't want to say that but somehow I felt forced into it. That's the rotten thing about gossip, innuendo. It stays in your mind.'

When Nick arrived her father was his confident self again, smiling on them both with a special warmth. 'I've asked Claudia when you're going to set the date?' he challenged Nick smilingly.

'And what did she say?' Nick asked faintly, dryly.

'She's not at all over the engagement.'

'Then I'll have to persuade her she belongs by my side.'

Outside under the starlight she laughed a little wildly. 'How long are we going to go on like this?'

'Until we've got nothing better to do.' Nick opened up the car door for her.

'I don't think you know what life's like at our place.'

'Yes I do,' Nick returned, very curtly and distinctly. 'Get in, Claudia, for God's sake.'

She told him about her conversation with her father and he listened without comment.

'I'm frightened, Nick.'

'Why not? This is Saturday night.' Expertly he dodged a small sedan that came around a corner at him, unaware.

'Are you *ever* serious?'

'I thought you preferred me this way.' It was an acid comment on the state of affairs that existed between them. Far from acting like a lover, in the past weeks Nick had scarcely touched her.

'I'm afraid Cristina might crack up.'

'But not before the rest of us do. Fantasising must be your stepmother's only reality. You seem to shrink from a show-down but I think your father is strong enough to take it.'

'That you're not *perfect!*' Claudia cried.

'Do be careful,' Nick suggested. 'I know you have absolutely no faith in my honour and decency so I've nothing to lose.'

'I'm doing this very badly.' Claudia turned her face and looked out the window.

'Yes, you are,' he agreed bluntly. 'I can't feel sorry for Cristina, my darling. So far as I'm concerned Cristina is a crashing bore. Perhaps your father would be well rid of her. Perhaps she would be far happier if she moved house. Life is short enough, God knows, without making it a misery. The worst thing *I* ever did to your stepmother was to say hello to her. Someone should have explained to me she has a problem. More goes on inside her head than in real life. Or it's natural to a woman to create chaos out of nothing. Certainly she doesn't mind lying.'

'For what reason?' Claudia asked, her eyes filling with tears.

'Well, she sure doesn't want to see you with me. Not because, my angel, I'm a bad influence, but because she's had an absolutely, glorious crush on a man who doesn't want her. It's very, very crazy, I'll admit. But then I venture to say, a lot of women *are* downright crazy. I've already begun to have my doubts about you.'

His effrontery fairly took her breath away.

They parked the car without difficulty and walked the short distance to the concert hall where they immediately encountered friends.

So here it is again, Claudia thought, hastily rearranging her expression. The prospect of any kind of settlement seemed a long way off. It was in a helpless mood she took her seat but when Nick told her beneath his breath to snap out of it she expelled a little sigh and tried to compose herself for enjoyment. The concert hall was packed and now as the soloist walked out on to the stage, the waves of enthusiastic clapping broke out.

'Do try to enjoy it, darling,' Nick drawled mockingly and squeezed her hand.

But somehow she could not. The music entered into her, overwhelming her with its power but even the chosen programme was full of passion and poignancy. After the interval there was respite with some Mozart of shining tranquillity, but then the soloist went back to oceanic turbulence, arousing the entire audience to an emotional response.

Not even the encores were frivolous.

'Absolutely marvellous!' Nick said sincerely. 'Let's get away from here now, before the crowd.'

'Did you keep the programme?'

'I've got it.' He glanced down at her for a moment, her soft lips apart. 'You shouldn't be so beautiful, Claudia.'

'You're frowning.'

'I'm not exactly a happy man.' He held her arm as

they plunged through the crowd and the touch of his hand on her bare skin was an exquisite agony. Without speaking, there was no *need* to speak, a rising desire was between them. It was a paradox of her feeling for him that even as she burned at his touch, she could weep for her own weakness. His power over her was daunting and her sudden resistance may have accounted for the swiftness with which she broke away from him. The city gleamed around them, the street filled now with a confusing spill of people and the car not very far away. There was no good reason for what she was doing, indeed it was ridiculous but the evening of music had increased her feeling of emotional strain.

As she stepped out from the kerb, someone shouted and as Claudia looked up she was seized with dizziness. A late model Mercedes was moving at speed, running the amber light, but even as she was assailed by a weird paralysis she was caught up from behind and half lifted, half dragged back to safety where she almost fell to her knees.

''Struth, that was close!' someone breathed.

'Claudia, are you all right?' Nick asked, his features so tight his face looked like a mask.

'That fellow should have been arrested,' an elderly man's voice said. 'Ah, there's a patrol car going after him.'

'It was my fault,' Claudia started to say. She and the Mercedes driver had both jumped signals.

'All right, miss?'

Nick whirled around as a constable approached them. He was young with a smooth, regular face yet he possessed an air of authority. 'Mercifully, yes, officer,' Nick said.

A small crowd was standing around and Claudia felt very stupid and exposed. Finally it was all over with a small lecture and Nick was leading her away.

'That was the closest I ever got to being run over,' Claudia managed shakily.

Nick was too deeply in thought to answer.

'Are you angry with me, Nick?' she asked uneasily as they drove away.

'I am angry, thank you.'

''Look, I've ruined my stocking.'

'Lucky, aren't you?'

'That was a great stunt saving me.' She tried to laugh but it wobbled a bit. 'Thank you, Nick. You always were very fast on your feet.'

'A whole fraction of a second to spare.'

'This is wild,' she threw her head back. 'You're *hostile* because you saved me from injury.'

'There is an element of hostility, yes,' Nick agreed with hooded eyes. 'What were you thinking about, Claud, when you pushed out in front of a moving car?'

'Truly, I never *saw it.*'

'So you're *not* self-destructive?'

'It was just a stupid thing to do. Gosh, the green light came on a half second later.'

'I'll have to take that into consideration.'

'You know what? I wasn't even scared. Just paralysed.'

'Well, I was scared out of my wits,' Nick returned very curtly. 'One minute you were there beside me, the next you're streaking under a car as fast as your legs could carry you. If you can't stand thinking of me as a fiancé, try to think of me as an old friend.'

'My dearest friend, one time, I might add.'

His silver eyes glanced briefly at her vulnerable face. 'And your future husband, by God!'

'How fierce you are!' She responded to an intensity that was almost alarming.

'Just so long as you know what you're up against.'

This was determination of a kind Claudia had only read about in books. She was conscious of her thudding heart and Nick's fine, lean hands upon the wheel. It seemed an eternity since he had touched her.

'Do you remember that time I fell off the swing?' she asked, old memories coming together and meshing.

'Perfectly,' he said dryly. 'I damned nearly kissed you.'

'But you *did* kiss me.' She turned her head to look at his chiselled profile.

'I *did* not. As I recall I pecked your forehead. I meant really kissed you. It was just as well there were about twelve other people around.'

'My God!' she said gently. It had been a tennis party and she had gone to cool off on her old childhood swing. She saw in her mind the tall, green trees, their group of friends and beyond the tennis court where her father was playing with dazzling prowess. Someone had pushed her off but within a few minutes one of the chains broke and she was thrown in an arc to the ground where she lay still in winded misery. Nick had reached her first. He had taken her into his arms. Then.

'It was the first time I saw you on your back in the

grass looking up at me. I don't know what I read in
your face but I knew there and then you were no
longer a child.'

'I was sixteen.'

'*Would* you have let me kiss you?'

'Yes.' Excitement fluttered in her stomach. 'Please
don't go home, Nick,' she whispered.

'Your home or mine?'

'I mean...'

'*Tell* me. I really want to know.' His voice was
crisp and quite devoid of expression.

'I want to be with you.'

'You mean you can't stand it any longer.'

'*Nick...*'

'Obviously getting around to telling me you love
me is going to be very, very painful.'

The city had retreated and they were into the garden suburbs with a silvery moon cutting straight down
through the hills and illuminating the valley like a
stage. 'But you *are* going to your place,' she said.

'Of course I am.' He put out his left hand and
brushed her hair from her cheek. 'I think I've held
out for an indecent length of time.'

The heat of desire shimmered in her veins, flushing
her creamy skin. She knew he was looking at her but
she couldn't find the strength to resist temptation. She
ached for him. Heart and body and soul.

'Darling, I won't seduce you,' he said very gently.
'Or as far as I'm able. God knows you've been a high
risk for a long time now.'

'Do you always like something dangerous, Nick?'

'Do *you* know what trust means?'

She turned her face away from his while the trees

and houses went by in a blur. Nick was the embodiment of excitement and she knew in her bones she had surrendered long ago.

Another few minutes and what everyone called 'the old Somerville place' was before them. The headlights picked up trees and shrubs and splashes of colour. It was almost a woodland and then the house. The garage doors were operated by remote control but tonight Nick chose to leave the Jaguar in the circular drive.

'You chose to come, Claudia,' he told her as they walked towards the front door.

'So?' She lifted a scarcely composed face to him.

'You look like you can't handle it. You look ready to cry.'

'I'm really sorry. You're used to more experienced women.'

It was a while before he spoke again, pausing at the bottom of the stone stairs flanked by a pair of terracotta Pharaoh dogs. 'That was really silly, Claud,' he said, pushing aside a thick profusion of ferns.

'I'd be quite happy if you wanted to do a bit of gardening.'

'Actually I'm looking for a spare front door key. Your dear stepmother found it so I guess *I* can. Grandfather always left it here so as to be sure neither of us ever locked ourselves out.'

'Would you like help?'

'No, thanks. I have to take it slowly in the dark. Aaah, here it is.'

'Wow! You must be feeling very pleased with

yourself?' Claudia couldn't remember ever sounding so brittle and mocking before.

'Let's go in, shall we?' Nick invited. 'I thought your father was the only one to know but evidently I should have pledged him to secrecy.'

'I'm still considering the insult to my deductive powers.'

'Easily explainable things are the most likely, you know.' His hand had gone to her wrist as he drew her inside the leaded, cedar door.

'Aren't you going to turn the lights on?' she whispered with a look of wild challenge.

'Enough, Claudia,' he moved her body right into his arms, his demeanour so masterful she felt frail and subjugated. 'Look up at me,' he demanded. 'It's childish to duck your head.'

I am not childish, she wanted to cry, but as she flung up her head, his fingers curled themselves in her hair dragging her head back while his mouth pressed down on hers.

It was so exquisite she thought her heart would break. She felt her body shudder and his arms enclosed her even more powerfully causing her to utter a little, gasping breath that he took into his mouth as his own.

'Claudia!' he muttered intensely and the effect on her was extraordinary.

Without conscious thought she pressed her body against his, clinging as if she would never let go. Her nostrils were filled with the wonderful male scent of him, while her delicate perfume hung like incense in the still darkness.

It was almost like extreme starvation for they were

kissing with a keyed-up passion and hunger that went totally beyond anything they had experienced before. Nick wasn't holding back at all as he had on that other encounter but taking her with him so she lost all direction but his own.

The kissing went on for some time, until the pulses were beating thunderously in Claudia's veins. She tried to turn her heavy silken head begging him now as if the last of her innocence was slipping away. 'Nick...*please!*'

'Don't fight me.' His hands were at her narrow hips, moulding her fluttering body until she felt blasted with urgency.

'I can't *stand* this!' she lamented, but he held her and *held* her so she felt she would melt with the heat they were generating.

Wordlessly she hit him, helpless little blows, that did little to diminish the sexual agony. Her breasts were aching and he had not yet touched them. It was tantalising, tormenting as if being together were a punishment.

'I want you too much,' he said harshly, staring down at her as her upper body arched rigidly back. Her face revealed a terrible frustration, as dazzling as a pearl in the light that fell through the decorated glass panels. A nerve was clearly visible flickering in her neck and her mouth looked as soft and ripe as a fruit, faintly swollen and quite beautiful.

'Sweet God!' he said tightly.

Claudia's pain was beginning to turn to panic and though she couldn't recall it afterwards she was making little stricken sounds.

'Coffee, I think,' Nick suddenly announced

abruptly and her heart bounded in a mixture of shock and disbelief. It didn't seem possible to turn from such extreme sensuality to mundane reality, but surely Nick had? Maybe his fascination was his total unpredictability.

The bright lights of the kitchen hurt her eyes and she put her hands to her cheeks, dazed. 'You're an extraordinary person, Nick.' A faint glistening of perspiration dewed her temples, her platinum hair was tumbled and her eyes looked like large, deep-green lakes.

'Thank you, darling,' he said suavely, very cool and self-contained. 'How would you like it—black or with cream?'

'Better make it a brandy.' She dropped into a chair, trying to reconcile such irreconcilable behaviour. He had gone out of his way to arouse her, succeeded cataclysmically, then pushed her into the kitchen. Surely a far from passionate place?

'Are you perfectly comfortable there?' he asked courteously.

'Don't worry about me, Nick.' Her lovely, low voice was very faintly slurred.

'Anything you'd like with it?'

'No.' She couldn't help it, she grimaced.

He bowed slightly, his lean handsome features vaguely wrenched for all his smoothness. 'I do have a backbone, Claudia,' he drawled, 'but it's very frail.'

'You're kidding!' She met his glittering, silver-grey eyes. 'I think you're very strong and madly practical.'

'I just thought it better to reserve our lovemaking for another occasion. Preferably the night we're married.'

It was a sharp, strange feeling to have him now mock her. 'Goodness, Nick,' she managed coolly, 'I never knew you were such a hopeless romantic.'

'To say nothing of *your* ability to stimulate desire.' He paused in his preparations to consider it. 'You know, darling, you look like an angel yet you're the most sexual woman I've ever known.'

She lifted a hand and thrust her heavy fall of hair back. 'Didn't your other women enjoy it?'

'I wasn't thinking of them so much as their effect on me.' Slowly he reached down some exquisite coffee cups that were used almost exclusively for best. 'Do you know I think I might have a toasted sandwich. I had a client who sat for hours this afternoon so I missed my lunch.'

'Gracious that will never do!' Claudia started up, spoiling it a little by swaying. 'I'm happy to make it for you.'

'Oh, don't worry,' Nick said briskly. 'You look so ravishing sitting there, all shocked eyes. I do wish you hadn't worn that dress. It's too easy to get out of.'

'Provided, of course, you were trying to get me out of it. Which you *aren't.*'

'I still *want* you,' he said, rather bitterly.

She wasn't quite sure what she was doing so she picked up one of the beautiful cobalt and gold coffee cups with its saucer, but her hands were so shaky, the saucer seemed to slide from her fingers.

'Woops.' Nick caught it very smartly and set it down on the table. 'Don't break them, darling. I'm too mean to buy more. Even if I could get them.'

'I'm sorry.' Bemusedly Claudia shook her head. 'And not at all safe.' In fact she found herself quite dizzy and as she lifted her eyes to Nick he caught her behind the knees and folded her into his arms.

'Don't fret, baby. I feel the same.'

'I didn't know making love could be so...violent.'

'It quite puts one off coffee, at any rate.'

'Where are you going, Nick?' She asked a little frantically as he carried her out of the room.

'It's one thing to leave you alone, darling, and quite another to see you giddy with frustration. I've been watching all the expressions that chase across your face. You want to sleep with me, don't you?'

'So long as you don't make love to me it should be all right.'

He gave a deep gurgle in his throat. 'All the thoughts I have of you when I'm in bed. I don't suppose you want to hear them?'

'No thank you.'

He began to move up the staircase and she cried out. There was a brittle humour in his face, but his eyes looked like a zealot's—ready to risk everything. 'If you've *planned* this, Nick!'

'Serves you right,' he said coolly. 'You're always telling me there's a demon in me.'

'And there *is*.'

'Settle down,' he said crisply. 'I'm only going to love you a little seeing there's nothing better I can do.'

When he lowered her to his bed she cried out remorsefully and rolled away on to her side. For a long time now she had imagined Nick's making love to her but the reality was rather more excessive than her wildest imaginings.

'At least I can get you out of that dress which, incidentally, makes you look like a rose.'

She sat up on her knees and as she did so she caught their reflection in the mirrored panel of the tall, antique wardrobe. The fuchsia silk of her full skirt did look like the petals of some extravagant rose. The sight of Nick made her heart lunge. He was seated sideways on the bed just behind her and he still had that bold, reckless light on him. She had never realised how striking the difference in their colouring. Her hair was white-gold. His very black, with no shade of brown. Her skin glimmered very palely, his had the sheen of dark, polished copper.

'You look impossibly erotic,' Nick said.

She thought she could bear it, but she couldn't. She tilted back her head and her eyes closed and that was the time he moved, drawing her back into his arms, his hands moving up over her small but exquisitely shaped breasts.

'Marry me, Claud,' he murmured. 'We desperately need each other.'

Her sense of unreality deepened. It was said so ardently she should have absolved him of all doubt. But there was Cristina. Or was she *mad*?

She let her head fall back against his shoulder, her mind drifting away from all disquietude.

His tongue rimmed the delicate whorls of her ear while he whispered she was beautiful to him. How could there be treachery in such ardour?

'How I wish you were mine.' His voice was a mere thread of sound. 'I could keep you through the night.' He covered her half-open mouth and she stayed his travelling hand and lifted it to her breast, understanding she was inviting a surge of male passion, more driving, more violent than a woman's could ever be.

'Claudia,' he murmured through the silk of her hair.

She could feel the faint shudder that racked his body, the emotional charge that was building up so rapidly it was like fire racing down the spine. Her dress had a bodice draped in a deep V and he slipped his hand inside the warm silk, cupping her tender, young breast enclosed in ivory lace. Claudia's breathing was more languorous now and the perfume she wore flowed from her heated skin in gentle wafts.

His fingers unclipped the lace bra and pushed it away, and her tremoring began.

'Marry me, please, Claudia,' he begged her. 'I'll cherish you. *Always.*'

Ecstasy overflowed her. No one but Nick could lift her to such a plane. His lovemaking was blissful. Perfect. More than that, it was causing her to offer herself to him as though it were her destiny.

Gradually he removed her dress: the warm, enveloping silk with little beneath. He turned away to drape it across his jacket and Claudia caught the flash of great passion on his face. His beautiful eyes gleamed and he looked infinitely in command of himself. And her. He looked at her as though she was a rare treasure. And *his* for the taking.

Some elusive rebellion swam in the depths of her surrender. By what right did men think they *owned* a woman? Yet in spite of her fragile mutiny she allowed him to discover many things about her he had never known before.

His mouth followed the smooth flow of her flesh

and she sighed rapturously. It was a kind of primal submission, so infinitely soft yet fiery it became almost impossible to control her excitement.

'This is too dangerous, Claud.' Her urgent twistings were inciting him powerfully. 'If we don't stop now, I'll lose all control.'

She could have laughed she wanted it so enormously instead she pulled him ever closer, an astounding richness rife in her blood. 'You can, if you want, have *all* my secrets.'

He groaned and lifted his head. 'Do you want to save yourself, or not?'

'I think I like it too much here.'

'After all it's where you were meant to be.'

'*Really?*' Against that little flare of mutiny flashed out.

'Yes, really,' he mocked her. 'Man is still the hunter, my little Claudia, and I trapped you a long time ago.'

'I don't trap that easily.'

A faint smile touched his mouth. 'You make so much protest, Claudia. What about now when I'm holding your breasts like perfect fruit in my hands?'

Her voice had a beseeching, almost frantic tone. 'It's not possible to think clearly when you touch me.'

'Darling, are you ashamed to say it?'

She only turned her head and buried her face in the pillow. 'I think so.'

'Because Cristina has poisoned your mind?' Instantly the tenderness became grim disdain. 'Always we get back to that unhappy woman.'

'Maybe there's no escape.'

His hand closed hard under her chin as he turned

her to face him. 'And my word means *nothing?*' From disdain to developing anger.

She hesitated unhappily and it was a bad mistake. From the tenderness, protectiveness, that previously over-rode his passion, he seized her with near cruelty as though impelled to hear her cry of fright.

He lifted her without effort...she lay on top then beneath him, his hands moving over her body so she was in an agony of furious pleasure. Her strength was as nothing against his, but even as he shocked her, she knew herself thrilled to be mastered.

When the longing became unbearable little inarticulate moans were dragged out of her and only then did he leave her, lifting his lean body away as if in contempt.

'Hell, isn't it?' he stood over her, his dark face saturnine.

She still lay across the bed in a half tortured position, pierced by the glacial glitter of his eyes.

'What's the matter, Claudia?' he taunted her. 'Have I spoilt something for you? You're spoiling everything for me.'

Her heavy white-gold hair flew around her face as she raised herself up. 'So have your ring back,' she cried, extending her left hand while the emerald glowed like green fire against her white skin. 'Haven't I always known you're a dozen men rolled into one? You're too complicated Nick.'

'Sure.' His fine, white teeth were set on edge. 'And I feel at times you're quite stupid.'

'I *am!*' She clutched wildly for a sheet.

'And how!' Despite his anger his eyes were ravished by the gleaming image she presented. He stood still for another minute staring at her then he moved back and plucked her dress off a chair. 'The next time, my little Claudia, you want me to make love to you, you're going to have to *beg* for it.'

'Don't worry, I haven't the slightest doubt I will!'

And then he laughed. Genuine amusement this time. 'You don't kid yourself do you, sweetheart?'

'What the hell!' Like a half wild creature she got into her clothes. 'You must be used to my odd behaviour. I can't seem to take a positive stand about anything with you. I must be mad or mesmerised or both. I offer you everything you want...'

'*Except* trust,' he interrupted metallically.

'*Please*, Nick!' she rose up on the bed, joining her hands together as though in fervent prayer. 'Don't you think I want to? Do you really think I like torturing myself?'

'Yes,' he said bluntly. 'Yes, I do.' The obvious signs of strain were on him. 'I've had nothing but accusations and recriminations for months. More than enough to endure. I don't think you care about me as much as you think you do. To be dismissed so abruptly with this talk of a fallen idol! If it didn't sound so conceited, I'd tell you a lot of fool women have fallen in love with me. Women I didn't *ask* to. Maybe it's natural for women to want men that won't take them seriously. The thing is, I *love you*, Claud. I even want to marry you and that's a very big thing. For one, you're so beautiful it's going to be difficult keeping you to myself.'

It was so utterly unexpected she jerked back her head. 'But, Nick, that's *crazy!* I would never look at anyone at all.'

'How do you know? You're just a baby. Wait until you're thirty and fully aware of your power. Wait until another man falls under your spell. Tells you he loves you.'

She was so astonished she slipped off the bed and came to him. 'Is that the supremely self-confident Nick Grey talking?' she asked incredulously.

'Maybe I am. In a way.' He stood with his arms linked around her. 'But I'm helpless with you.'

'I don't believe it.' Her green eyes searched his face.

'Incredible! A beautiful woman without ego. Anyway, it's *true*.'

It was totally different from anything she had thought to hear him say. She leant against him and closed her eyes. 'Do you swear to love only me?'

'Try me.' His tone was curt to the point of hardness.

'You could hurt me terribly. Worse, destroy me.' She tilted back her head.

'We could destroy one another.' His silver eyes were deadly serious.

'I'll be faithful to you, Nick. I promise.' Impulsively she reached up and kissed his chin, but he dropped a hard, sober kiss on her mouth. 'I'm counting on that. I'd like you to remain *alive*.'

She couldn't believe the odd ruthlessness of his expression. She put her arms around him, hugging him, holding her head against his breast. 'Do you really, under it all, despise women?'

'They make excellent adultresses,' he said coolly.

She was alarmed. '*Nick!* It never occurred to me for one minute to think you were a hater of women.'

'Nor did it occur to you to believe I love *you* totally. That's the total passion I'm *capable* of, Claudia.'

'Yes, Nick.'

'I mean what I say.'

She could feel the tension in him, making his lean body rock hard. 'I'll marry you, Nick, whenever you want.'

'Loving me would be infinitely better,' he told her with faint bitterness. 'You're very valuable to me for your beauty, but that's only a part of it. I want your heart and your mind. I don't want to see you fall so easily into traps. Respect between a man and a woman is very important. It can't be otherwise for us.'

'Of course, Nick,' Tears stood in her eyes. 'I see it now. I believe you.'

'Almost.' He brushed the hair away from her face. 'Would you let me take you now to prove it?'

'Yes.' Her gaze was steady.

'And I love you too much to order it,' he stared into her eyes. 'When you come to me, Claudia, it will be of your own free will.'

CHAPTER SEVEN

THE DAYS continued with Cristina still incredibly sour and bitchy.

'If it weren't for Claudia,' Fergy confided wearily, 'I'd walk out. I've never seen a woman so restless and irritable.'

'Maybe it's because she's put on weight?' Lady McKinlay suggested. The three of them were at work in the McKinlay sunroom writing out invitations for one of Lady McKinlay's charity functions. 'Grant really should have insisted on a break together instead of which he's left it.'

'He's very busy, Nanna,' Claudia said, feeling as terrible as any of them.

'Maybe, but from what little I've seen of Cristina, she appears to be heading for some sort of breakdown. These busy, self-confident career women can be classic cases.'

'It's not even a case of fluctuating moods,' Fergy said aggrievedly. 'She's sharp and over-aggressive all the time.'

'The trouble could be physical,' Lady McKinlay offered worriedly. 'It's unusual for Cristina surely? Has she had a check up?'

Fergy shrugged as if to say she couldn't care less, but Claudia sighed. 'I think she's in need of a complete change. Daddy hates all the disorderliness in the house.'

'Ah, yes,' Lady McKinlay chose to say no more. She knew her son-in-law's good qualities just as she knew he resented any complications whatever in the home. Claudia herself had never told her father anything else than what he wanted to hear. As a daughter, she had been remarkably trouble free and it didn't just happen. Even as a child Claudia had recognised what her father had required of her so she had worked hard at presenting herself in his image. No tantrums for Claudia. No escapades. No troublesome behaviour so life could run smoothly. Nevertheless Claudia had plenty of character and spirit under that lovely, cool exterior. Lady McKinlay stopped what she was doing and on the spur of the moment leant over and kissed Claudia's cheek.

'What's *that* for?' Claudia smiled.

'I love you,' Lady McKinlay said, straightening up. 'Now, where did I put those envelopes?'

Shortly before mid-day a telephone call came for Claudia. 'It's your father,' Fergy came back into the sunroom to tell her. 'He sounds upset.'

'Oh Heavens!' Claudia whispered.

'Answer it, darling,' Lady McKinlay said practically. 'Grant's upsets are on a slightly different scale.'

Grant Ingram came to the point immediately. 'Cristina has been taken to hospital,' he told Claudia bleakly. 'It appears she collapsed at a client's home and they got such a fright they ordered an ambulance.'

Lady McKinlay and Fergy looked at her expectantly as she walked back into the sunroom. 'Cristina is in hospital,' she announced.

'Dear me!' Lady McKinlay went a little limp. 'Whatever has happened?'

'We don't really know. Daddy is leaving for the hospital now. It seems she collapsed at a client's house. They called for an ambulance and it took her to the P.A.'

'Poor girl!'

'Mind you, she doesn't eat enough,' Fergy said. 'For all she's put on weight lately as you said.'

'Surely she couldn't be having a baby?' Lady McKinlay marvelled and Claudia went white with shock. 'I say, dear,' Lady McKinlay exclaimed as the older women jumped to their feet. 'Here, hold her head down, Fergy.'

'Claudy, darling!' Fergy's hands shook pathetically even as she rushed to obey.

'I'm all right,' Claudia's voice sounded weak and far away. She was fighting to pull back from a faint.

'Fergy, go and get Ross,' Lady McKinlay ordered, holding Claudia's forehead. 'He's in his study.'

By the time her grandfather arrived, Claudia was out of it. 'What happened, darling?' he asked calmly, holding her wrist.

'I don't know. I just started to black out,' she laughed shakily.

'You've never done such a thing before,' he said watching her very closely.

'She's just had a shock,' Lady McKinlay explained. 'Cristina has been taken to the hospital.'

'Good God!' Sir Ross stared up at his wife. 'Was that the phone call?'

'Yes. She collapsed on the job. Grant rang.'

'I just walked out of the study for a moment,' Sir

Ross said regretfully. 'I could have taken that call. What hospital?'

'The P.A.'

'I'll go over.'

'*Would* you Grandad?' Claudia's colour was returning.

'Was *that* it, darling?' Sir Ross asked her.

She glanced away from his all-seeing eyes. 'The news upset me.'

'Perhaps.' Sir Ross turned his handsome head. 'Tea, Fergy, if you wouldn't mind. Three teaspoons of sugar.'

'Grandad, I couldn't *drink* it.'

'Two and a half then.' Calmly, deliberately, Sir Ross examined his granddaughter's face. 'How long is it since you've had a check up?'

'I'm never sick, Grandad, you know that?'

'True. Nevertheless a check up won't hurt. I'll call Anthony later today and let you know. Of course you're upset about Cristina. But a *faint?*'

'I *didn't* faint.'

'Darned nearly,' Lady McKinlay put her arm around her granddaughter. 'Was it what I said, about the baby?'

'*What* baby?' Sir Ross threw his arm out in surprise.

'Sweetheart, don't panic,' Lady McKinlay said. 'Cristina has been very much out of sorts lately and she's put on weight. I just put two and two together.'

'Then I don't care to bet you're wrong,' Sir Ross concluded from long experience. 'Does it seem likely to you, Claudia?'

'I don't know.' Claudia could have fallen to the floor and sobbed. A baby? *Whose* baby? She hated herself for thinking as she did but there was the most terrible doubt in her heart.

'Claudia, darling, there's something more to this than you're saying,' Sir Ross took her hands. 'If the news were true and we're only jumping to conclusions, why would it upset you?'

Lady McKinlay's smile was full of sadness. 'What *is* it, dearest?'

'It *can't* be,' Claudia managed. 'Why would Cristina be so secretive?'

'Suppose we take one thing at a time,' Sir Ross suggested. 'Would you like to come to the hospital with me? It would set your mind at rest.'

'But Cristina has never wanted a baby!' Claudia looked back at her grandfather appealingly.

'That's what they all say,' Lady McKinlay murmured dryly. 'Cristina would be a lot happier with a child in her life. And your father would look on it as miraculous.'

'We would be happy too if she were pregnant,' Sir Ross said, watching his granddaughter's eyes. '*Wouldn't* we, darling?'

'Of course.' Claudia's whole body seemed tied in knots.

'Yes, well...' Lady McKinlay said a shade inadequately, 'at this moment we know nothing for sure.' She looked towards the doorway and her face changed to relief. 'Ah, here's Fergy with the tea.'

'Better now?' Fergy sought the opinion from Sir Ross.

'Yes, she's coming around slowly.' He patted his granddaughter's hand. 'We'll sit quietly for an hour then we'll go to the hospital. I'll give Victor Thornton a ring.'

WHEN they arrived at the hospital Matron herself showed them to Cristina's bedside. She had been put into a ward and Sir Ross had already been apprised of her condition. Cristina was indeed pregnant: some eight weeks along the way.

Cristina lay quiet, one long hand outside the sheet across her breast. Grant Ingram was seated by her side, his expression an odd mixture of intense gratification and a faint unease.

'Cristina, my dear!' Sir Ross made Cristina look up with a tearful smile.

'Oh, Sir Ross!' Now the tears came easily.

'There, there, my dear. This is wonderful news.' He bent his head and kissed her on the cheek. 'A baby is the most wonderful gift of all. I've spoken to Dr Thornton and apart from overdoing it a little, you're in excellent health.'

'None of this mad rushing around again!' Grant Ingram, now that his father-in-law was on the scene, began to laugh. No matter what, Ross McKinlay had this marvellously calming presence. Before he had arrived Cristina had scarcely spoken.

'How are you, Cristina?' Claudia touched her stepmother's hand.

'So-so,' Cristina turned to her a white, freckled face. 'It was nice of you to come.'

'I could beat her for not saying anything to me,' Grant Ingram enthused. 'This is just the most wonderful news. I can't take it in.'

'Cristina doesn't look happy to be an expectant mother,' Claudia said to her grandfather on the way home.

'She's a little scared at the moment, darling,' Sir Ross replied easily. 'Some women become quite shocked when they receive the news. Marriage may be a big commitment but a child is the biggest commitment of all. It will make a big difference to Cristina and your father is halfway over the moon. He'd be all the way over I'm sure only Cristina is having her little difficulties adjusting. The thirties is a little late to come to motherhood. I think she feels a little awkward. She was so set in her career and she's feeling upset about the physical changes in her body. It's a state a lot of women go through. Not everyone is ecstatic from the beginning. She's a tall woman. She should carry her baby well. If anything, I'm more concerned about you. You're not quite yourself these days, are you?'

'It takes a little adjusting being an engaged girl,' she said wryly.

'Yet you love Nick deeply.'

'I do.' And that was the crazy, screaming truth of it.

'And he loves you.'

'Do you *really* think so, Grandad?'

'Ah, how frail we human creatures are!' Sir Ross mused reflectively. 'How intensely unsure in our relationships. I suppose, my darling, you've had a fantasy romance with Nick for as long as you've known him. Thirteen, fourteen is a very particular stage in a young girl's development. For the very first time she feels the stirrings of sexual love. I think you fell in love with Nick right off though it was subdued from a conscious level. Fortunately you fell in love with the right man. Nick was equally attracted to you. He was incredibly fond of you as you must remember. Then as time went on there was this enormous change. The fact is, Claudia, Nick has acted supremely well in your case. He's drawn back from any closer relationship for a number of factors. You were too young; too inexperienced; you hadn't completed your education; you had to experience the admiration and attention of other young men. He gave you a chance to form other relationships. To a large extent to grow up. And why? Because he loves you. Really loves you. He cherished and protected you as a child and young girl, but being a man of strong passions, I guess his capacity for waiting is exhausted. I'd say it would be apparent to a blind man he's madly in love with you.'

'You haven't considered he's a marvellous actor?'

'*Claudia!*' Sir Ross was so shocked he slowed the car and brought it to a halt. 'Whatever are you saying?' He switched off the ignition and turned to her.

'I think in some deep way Nick feels safe with me. We've known one another for so long and I'm a very *quiet* person, aren't I, Grandad?'

'You mean you have a lovely, gentle composure, don't you? Quiet is not at all the right word.'

'All right then, I'm not *vibrant*.'

'What *are* we talking about, Claudia?' Sir Ross asked tersely. 'There's something very much on your mind and I think you'd better tell me.'

She shook her head. How could she tell her grandfather *that?* How could she upset him? He thought the world of Nick. The whole thing was *horrible*.

'Has it something to do with Cristina?' Sir Ross asked sternly. 'I've lived a long time, my darling. I've got eyes.'

'I just feel a little frightened at the moment, Grandad. Very unsure of myself. Which way to go.'

'Have you ever considered you might *lose* Nick, if

you're not more positive, more trusting in your out-
look?'

'*Grandad!*' Claudia's voice was a funny, little
croak.

Sir Ross nodded slowly. 'I think we in the family
have been all aware of Cristina's—how shall we put
it—crush on Nick?'

Claudia looked stunned. 'You've never said *one*
word to me. Neither you nor Nanna.'

'What could we say? We just prayed in time it
would go away. Nick is an extremely handsome man.
As well as that he's so clever and he has great charm
of manner. He has so much going for him it's no
wonder most women let out whoops of joy. His
mother was like that, you know. She was the most
fascinating woman. You have no idea. When *she*
came into a room, other women used to fade. Not just
her beauty alone. She was almost unbearably attractive. I'm afraid we all knew poor old Grey would
never hold her. It's the greatest mystery how she ever
married him in the first place, but she did, just like
that! And tragically as it happened. A terrible tragedy
all round.'

Claudia nodded emphatically. 'It affected Nick
deeply.'

'Yes, he was left very much alone. Lang Somerville was a splendid fellow but way past the age for
rearing a young boy. In effect, you know, *we* have
been Nick's family. We're all very attached to him
as he is to us. Your father has looked on him as a
son. He's done everything to advance Nick's career.'

'So Nick might be repaying him in marrying me?'

'Oh rubbish!' Sir Ross said shortly. 'Really, Claudia, you're far too perceptive to make such an absurd

statement. Nick's been in emotional turmoil about you for years. Many's the time I felt sorry for him.'

'Sorry for him with all his lady friends?' Claudia cried scornfully.

'What did you expect him to do?' Sir Ross asked blandly. 'He couldn't have you. The fact is he brightened a few lives. I can't think of one woman friend who still doesn't speak to him on the telephone. I don't think Nick has misled anybody.'

'Cristina claims Nick has had an affair with her,' Claudia suddenly burst out. It didn't make sense. She had been determined not to say it yet the words had gushed from her.

'To *hell* with Cristina!' Uncharacteristically Sir Ross swore. 'The woman's a liar.' He was so outraged the blood had come to his cheeks.

'I shouldn't have told you,' Claudia said. 'I never meant to. It just sprang out.'

'Of course you should have told me,' Sir Ross said with utter conviction. 'Fancy keeping a thing like this to yourself, Claudia, when you have your grandmother and me to talk to. This whole thing is preposterous. You said yourself Cristina has been erratic in her behaviour. There's no telling what a female will say and do at different stages of her life.'

'*I'm* a female, Grandad.'

'Women are given a lot to fantasising,' Sir Ross amended. 'Link it to hormonal changes if you like. Cristina has told you this nonsense, how *dare* she, when the balance of her mind has been disturbed. It's far too early for the menopause. It must be some underlying psychological disorder. Really, it's quite extraordinary.'

'Nick denies it.' Claudia spoke in a subdued whisper.

'Poor old Nick!' Sir Ross cried. 'Fancy associating *Nick* with such lunacy. Nick with your *father's wife?* What is the world coming to, I ask you!'

'Please don't be upset, Grandad,' Claudia begged.

'My dear child,' he turned to her, 'you seem to have turned it to private grief.'

'It's been dreadful, Grandad.' The tears stood in her eyes.

'My darling girl.' Sadly Sir Ross shook his head. 'It must be because you're so young, so fine and innocent in your mind, Cristina has been allowed to feed you such a tale. Surely you can see that Nick loves you?'

'He *wants* me, Grandad,' Claudia said baldly.

'Of course he wants you!' Sir Ross shrugged impatiently. 'Dear Heaven, Claudia, a man desperately wants the woman he loves. Be grateful for it. Your grandmother has such marvellous intuition yet she hasn't suspected all this nonsense.'

'I saw them together.'

'*What?*' Sir Ross's green eyes blackened.

'At least, Nick was at the house one afternoon when everyone was out. I arrived home unexpectedly to see Cristina flying down the gallery after him in a negligee.'

'I don't care if she was flying down the gallery after him stark naked,' Sir Ross shouted. 'Nothing in this world can persuade me Nick has acted in any way dishonourably with your father's wife.'

'God forgive me for not sharing your trust,' Claudia now wept.

'This is dreadful, *dreadful!*' Sir Ross said. 'Surely Grant hasn't an inkling of all this?'

'Daddy doesn't know.'

'Then it's about time he did.'

'Oh, *no,* Grandad. I would rather die than upset him.'

'Wouldn't you just,' Sir Ross said grimly. 'It's strange how some people go through life being protected by everyone else. Everything, everything, has to be done for Grant's pleasure and comfort. He had a rare and lovely wife...he has a rare and lovely daughter...'

'*Please,* Grandad.' Claudia could see how upset her grandfather was becoming. 'Forgive me for starting all this. I love you so much. Forgive me.'

'Poor old *Nick!*' Sir Ross spluttered again. 'Do you mean to tell me, my girl, that you've told him you ever believed in this rubbish?'

'Because Cristina told me many times. I find it impossible to believe she could tell such an appalling lie.'

'And equally impossible Nick, *our* Nick, *your* Nick, could come down to such a sordid arrangement.'

'However hard I try there has always been this element of doubt,' Claudia confessed bleakly.

'Yet you became engaged? How could you, believing such a thing?'

'It was a frightful mix-up,' Claudia inadequately explained.

'It's good of you to tell me now,' Sir Ross said extremely dryly. 'So when you heard Cristina might be pregnant, you thought of the most unnatural thing possible?'

'Yes.' Claudia hung her head.

'Dear God!' Sir Ross struck the steering wheel. 'You do well to hang your head in shame.'

Claudia cried.

'What a messy business!' Sir Ross handed her his clean handkerchief.

'I have to cry sometimes.'

'I mean this...*lunacy!*' Sir Ross was back to shouting and he had a fine, resonant voice. 'I won't speak to Nick. I don't have to.'

'I've spoken to him about it for months.'

'Then it's a test of his love you're still together.'

'If you had a crush on somebody,' Claudia said huskily, 'could you possibly behave in such a destructive way?'

'I shall have to spend some time with one of my psychiatrist friends,' Sir Ross replied wryly. 'I'm not sorry for your stepmother. I'm too angry. I always thought her a quite sensible woman. Of course the marriage was pretty much convenience. An adult sort of thing. Which is not to say they both didn't *care* about each other. Superficially I was sure they were well matched. Your father suffered as much as he was able when Victoria died. I think he just stashed away love on that deep level. The pain was too much. Certainly he was very slow to remarry but he and Cristina developed a mature relationship. They were reasonably happy, surely? They certainly gave that impression.'

'They *were* happy,' Claudia said hastily. 'Nick was overseas for a lot of that first year, don't you remember?'

'Hah!' Sir Ross burst out with a most terrible contempt. 'Don't try to tell me it was on from then?'

'I know he *unsettled* her,' Claudia said.

'So? He's very attractive. I told you about his mother. Some people are really special. They have a kind of sexual radiance, I suppose. Do you know a lot of my patients used to fall in love with *me*. Or so they tell me. Little harmless fantasies, you know. Like reading a book or seeing a film with your favourite movie star. I used to be madly in love with Vivien Leigh at one time. Most people go in for harmless daydreams at different times.'

'Only this is something awful.'

'A canker in the brain. No, Claudia, I simply don't believe it. Your stepmother may have tried to compromise Nick in some way, but you can be absolutely certain of one thing; it's not *his* child she's having. You'd have done better to call her bluff than swallow her poison cold. And you can't, absolutely *can't*, allow Nick to see your terrible doubts. You'll lose him if you keep it up. He has his pride. In fact he's fiercely proud and in many ways he's had a hard life. We all have our capacity for tolerance. You say you've spoken to Nick about this for months, which when I think about it, is *shocking*. How can you say you *love* Nick, when you're prepared to take Cristina's word against his?'

'I keep thinking that myself, Grandad. Maybe I'm not worthy to love him. Maybe I have no sense at all. It just seemed to me beyond reason that Cristina should lie.'

'Partly that and you just don't appreciate your position in his life. You *are* young. Cristina is much older and far more experienced. To put the matter simply, she has used this to inflict cruelty and hurt. I find it difficult to believe it of her but it must be true.

Certainly Nick was never attracted to her. One can
spot these things. Actually, Claudia, my darling, nothing *fits*. I would say Cristina's frustrated yearning
turned rotten. Or it has up to date. Why she picked
on Nick is understandable. He's very much around
and he's highly desirable. Why she picked on you is
another thing again. Perhaps she feels her loss of
youth greatly. Perhaps she feels she missed out somehow along the line. Her first marriage so far as I can
make out was a disaster and her second was largely
to create a lifestyle. Not good enough, you know, for
marriage. Maybe the baby will resolve all these difficulties. It's extremely inappropriate for an expectant
mother to be out of love with her husband.' Sir Ross
turned to his granddaughter and laid his hand along
her cheek. 'Does this make any sense to you, darling?'

'It must, Grandad. You're the wisest person in the
world.'

CRISTINA was discharged from hospital the following
morning. It was a Saturday and Grant Ingram had
been downstairs for hours. Finally he climbed the
stairs to his daughter's room. Claudia had slept badly,
accepting her grandfather's censure and in no mood
to feel ecstatic about the wonderful news.

'Claudia, dear, may I come in?'

Claudia had taken a shower and washed her hair,
now she was resting in the golden sunlight that
streamed through her three, tall windows.

'Good morning, Daddy.' She stood up to greet him
as he advanced into the room.

'Good morning, darling. Glorious morning it is
too!' As usual he was very smartly dressed, but there

was an extra spring in his step and he put his arm around his daughter and fondly kissed her. 'I wanted to have breakfast with you.'

'Oh I'm sorry, I slept in.'

'You do look a little heavy eyed.' He looked down into her creamy face. 'You're pleased about this wonderful news, aren't you, darling?'

'Of course I am, Daddy. I'm *thrilled* for you.'

'I knew you would be. You're such a lovely person. Sometimes I get a terrible shock. I look at you sometimes and it's Vicki. My beautiful Victoria. I never dwell on it because for a long time now I've had part of my heart in cold storage. Maybe it even died. Losing your mother was the most terrifying thing that ever happened to me. I knew I couldn't face anything like that again.'

'No, it must have been terrible,' Claudia quietly said. Didn't her father ever realise she too lost her mother? No one should be without a mother.

'I never thought to marry again and I was happy enough in my ivory tower. I had *you*. I had your grandparents. They've always been marvellous support. Finally Cristina came along. Our friendship had a different quality. I like a woman to have a certain amount of self sufficiency and I'd had all I ever needed of heart-stopping love. Cristina seemed a woman to share the rest of my life with. She told me she didn't want children and I accepted that. I had you. Now everything has changed. I thought Cristina had been unusually moody but now we know the cause of it. She told me she was careless with her birth control pills yet in a sense this has really shocked her. She can't believe she's pregnant. Can you beat that?'

'Not really, Daddy.' She forgot her pills. She's of child-bearing age. Whenever had she answered like that?

'You know this will make no difference to you and me?' Grant Ingram said reassuringly. 'You look rather desperately poignant,' he added softly.

'I will *adore* to have a little brother,' Claudia said. Better not make it a *sister,* Cristina, she thought.

'Darling girl!' Grant Ingram pressed her to his side. 'I can't wait to tell Nick.'

'We're driving down the coast this afternoon.'

'Yes, I know. What say we *all* go and make it a celebration dinner?'

'I don't think Cristina will be feeling up to it.'

'Possibly not.' Grant Ingram's fine eyes were soft. 'We'll have it at some other time. What a mercy she's missed out on morning sickness! I remember your mother felt terrible in her early days.'

They talked for a few more minutes and Grant Ingram said goodbye. For weeks he had found the situation with his wife quite stressful. Now all that had changed. There was joy in his life again. Claudia was the image of her mother but his son would have *his* looks, *his* eyes. Just when he thought his life was almost over, he had entered on a new, wonderful phase.

'Your Dad's happy!' Fergy commented laconically.

'Oh, Fergy, no breakfast for me.'

'Don't be silly.' Fergy pulled out a chair and beckoned Claudia into it. 'You are *my* baby. Your father will never have another child like you.'

'He doesn't *want* one like me, Fergy,' Claudia sat down with a soft sigh. 'I pray Cristina's baby will be a boy.'

'Don't fret,' Fergy said astonishingly, 'it will be. So long as it isn't a little monster like its mother.'

'Well,' Claudia said, 'he will be my little brother. I know I'll love him…her…whatever.'

'You might be able to mind him while his mother goes out to work.'

'This baby might change everything, Fergy,' Claudia said hopefully and sipped at her orange juice.

'The only baby I'm going to get dotty about from now on is *yours*.'

'You might have a long wait.'

'I don't think so,' Fergy gurgled. 'Maybe a year of being together, then the year after that. Has Nick heard the news?'

'No.'

'I'd just like to see his face.'

'So would I.' Very quietly Claudia set down her spoon, but Fergy was busy serving up scrambled eggs. 'We all thought your stepmother preferred a career to having babies.'

'Lots of women start off like that only to find they'd prefer the latter. Family is everything, isn't it? To see your children growing.'

'Your mother would be very proud of you,' Fergy said emotionally. 'And how she would give her blessing to your marriage with Nick. He's everything we want for you, and don't you worry, *he'll* be wanting a pretty little *girl*. *You* were very popular as I recall. Though little sister wasn't exactly what Nick had in mind. Actually I think he deserves a decoration. He's done everything in his power not to imperil your soul.'

Claudia shook her head as though all this was very

new to her. 'Now that Cristina is pregnant, I think I'll get a place of my own.'

'You mean you're leaving?' Fergy asked flatly.

'Things have changed, Fergy,' Claudia said.

'Yes, the old days have simply vanished.' Fergy inched a cup of tea closer to Claudia's hand. 'I can't stay here without you, love. You ought to know that. I stayed for you and when you go I go too.'

Claudia nodded, then she put her head in her hands. 'I think Daddy will take it all right.'

'*I* don't,' Fergy said. 'Can't you stick it out until you and Nick get married? What are you waiting for anyway? The way Nick looks at you I wonder he hasn't made you set the date. Your Grandma now has spoken to me about the whole thing. She knows I've never liked Cristina much. She wants me to come to her. She's out so much of the time and Sir Ross is becoming involved in so many things these days, I would be a big help to them.'

'And what about *me?*' Claudia blinked. 'You've been everything to me while I've been growing up.'

'Well, that's easy,' Fergy smiled and covered Claudia's hand with her own. 'I'll be Nanny when the first baby arrives.'

CRISTINA came home looking stooped and frail. Moreover, she was sobbing quietly into her husband's shoulder.

'How's that for freakish behaviour?' Fergy said.

Later they were informed she had taken to her bed.

'You don't suppose she's going to turn into an invalid?' Fergy asked.

'It must be a big shock finding out you're going to be a mother,' Claudia said charitably but without a great deal of enthusiasm. Cristina had behaved abominably in so many ways, there was no feeling sympathetic towards her. She had been especially overbearing with Fergy so it was small wonder Fergy had begun making plans to move out.

Claudia seized a quiet moment with her father to broach her own intentions. Nick wasn't due for an hour and things really couldn't go on as they were.

'How is Cristina now?'

'Much better.' Grant Ingram settled back in his armchair comfortably. 'Do you know I quite like her with her hair loose and not so much make-up.'

'So do I.' That morning at least Cristina had fallen down on the job, but she *had* looked softer and younger. 'May I speak to you about something, Daddy?' Claudia, in her bright beach clothes, sank into the chair opposite her father.

'Of course, darling.' He had picked up the morning paper, now he set it down, his underlying pleasure and excitement keeping his mood buoyant.

'Don't you think it's time I had a place of my own?'

At her words her father's expression changed. 'My dear girl, what on earth for? I firmly believe a daughter should be married from her own home. Good God, isn't the house *big* enough?'

'The fact is Cristina may like to feel the mistress of her own home. Things are different now, Daddy, or will Cristina still be rushing out to work?'

'I certainly don't want her to,' Grant Ingram maintained. 'Actually though she's quite healthy she has been told she can't go through her days at the same hectic pace. How do you think she collapsed in the first place?'

'Exactly.' Claudia pressed her case. 'Cristina and I get on well,' (how odd a statement), 'but I can't be forever in her hair. I think she needs the house to herself but she's too tactful to say so.'

'Be that as it may,' Grant Ingram said flatly, 'I need you both. In any case you and Nick will be getting married. You can move out then. Of course I realise you're trying to see Cristina's side of it but I think you'll discover she'll reach out to you now. She seems so *needy* since she found out. You saw her crying and clinging to me. When did Cristina ever *cling?* No, there's been a big change in her. When she settles I know she's going to be as ecstatic as I am. This baby is going to bring something deep to our marriage. Something that wasn't there before. It will be a total marriage as it ought to be. It will make Cristina a *real* woman. Already she's softer and more womanly. No, Claudia, I want you to stay. You're my daughter and that's the way it should be and furthermore I take the view you and Cristina will grow closer together. She's a little distraught at the moment and she's going to need help and support. Why don't you pop upstairs now and say hello?'

'Later, Daddy,' Claudia said. 'She may be resting.'

WHEN Nick's car came up the drive Grant Ingram jumped to his feet, throwing a smiling look back over his shoulder. 'I wonder what Nick will make of the news?'

Claudia just stood there, wide eyed. Her grandfather's advice was still ringing in her ears, but like some all powerful nightmare that one couldn't break out of, she was tensed for some thrust that might kill her.

Her father opened the front door and Claudia heard Nick's voice. 'Good morning, Grant. You're looking extraordinarily fit and well.'

'I am. Come in, Nick. Come in. We have some astonishing news for you.'

'Thank God it's good. It is good isn't it?' Nick looked towards Claudia and held out his hand.

She went to him and he slipped an arm around her and kissed her cheek.

'Do you care to tell Nick, darling?' Grant Ingram beamed.

'No, it's your news, Daddy.'

'Oh?' Nick glanced down at her and his expression seemed to harden. He had seen in her face what others did not. The marshalling of all her courage in the face of severe shock.

'Please, let's all sit down for a moment.' With bright impatience Grant Ingram led them into the living room. 'The fact is, Nick, my boy, my wife is expecting a baby.'

For a few seconds it seemed to have no effect on Nick whatever. He continued to look at Claudia sitting so rigidly beside him, then he turned his head and addressed his senior partner.

'This is wonderful news, Grant.'

'*Wonderful!*'

Nick stood up, walked to the older man, clapped him on the shoulder, then shook his hand. 'I'm very happy for you, Grant.'

'I knew you would be.' Grant Ingram's face was almost brilliant with light. 'It's only early days yet. I'd open a bottle of champagne only you're driving to the coast.'

'We'll have it yet.' The two men continued to clasp hands.

While Claudia remained silent Grant Ingram went on to outline the events of the day before. 'Claudia was so shocked she almost *fainted!*' Grant Ingram laughed. 'Her grandfather was so concerned he has organised a check-up for her Monday morning.'

'*Has* he?' Nick looked at Claudia with unsmiling eyes. With his dark summer tan his eyes were pure silver and what she saw in them made her shiver.

Finally they were able to walk to the car together. After Grant Ingram's exuberance they had nothing to say to each other. Indeed they covered some considerable distance before Claudia spoke the first words.

'So Daddy will have his son.' Her soft voice trembled a little.

'You're quite *certain* of that?' He looked very ruthless and strong.

'Well, I'll keep praying.'

'What exactly *for,* my dearest?'

'You know how Daddy has longed for a son. He would be very disappointed if another daughter were born.'

'I'm glad not all of us are so afflicted,' Nick returned curtly. 'There are plenty of men like *me* who would adore to have a girl-child.'

'I know that, Nick,' she said placatingly. 'We're all so different and I'm grateful for it.'

'What *else* are you grateful for?'

'I don't think you shoul. get angry in a car like this,' she said carefully. 'We seem to be moving a lot faster than everyone else.' Indeed they were flying up the right lane.

Nick's eyes dropped to the speedometer he had forgotten. 'So we are. I wonder if there's a motorcycle cop mad to take me on.'

'It could prove expensive.'

'We need an autobahn for this car.'

'Then you'll have to take it abroad.'

For the rest of the trip they talked, by common consent, about architecture, though Claudia's mind constantly leapt ahead to the formidable confrontation that had to come. She could never learn to be an actress. Never learn to disguise her deepest thoughts with a practised smile.

On that summer's day the ocean was an incredible, glittering turquoise and Nick drove on until he found a spot where they had a stretch of golden beach to themselves. Near the edge the water was as clear as crystal but as it grew deeper it shaded into its deep and brilliant blue. Such glorious beaches ran almost continuously down the east coast of Australia, thousands of miles of big and beautiful surf.

'Is it your intention to swim?' Nick asked with exaggerated politeness.

'Of course it's my intention to swim.' She was dismayed by his coldness, though she tried to cling to some semblance of normal pleasantness. 'I've even bought a new swimsuit.'

'Terrific.' Nick set them up on the dazzling sand; umbrella, yellow with a deep white fringe, towels, her beach bag, two small folding beach chairs, the esky Fergy had packed for them. 'I can't find fault with your *body*.'

She ignored him and pulled her short, cotton smock over her head, feeling the rush of balmy, salt air over her newly exposed skin. She was wearing a red bikini with a black spot and there wasn't one inch of her

that was in need of reformation. In fact she looked a
dream, but Nick offered no remark. He stripped to
navy briefs his body very evenly darkly tanned, grey-
hound lean and athletic, then he loped away from her
to the water.

The important thing, Claudia decided, was to act
as though she had never inflicted on him a moment's
doubt but all the time she had the dreadful feeling he
had finally judged her and found her badly wanting.
For that matter, she deserved it. The recognition was
like light breaking through darkness. She deserved total rejection. It was as simple as that. As simple as
her grandfather had found it to be. Her grandfather
was genuinely wise whereas she was devastatingly
inexperienced at making judgments.

Nevertheless the water was so glorious it seemed
to go a way towards transforming Nick's mood. He
sported like a dolphin, moving through the water with
a speed and power she could never hope to match,
though she swam particularly well.

After twenty minutes she went in to sunbathe, but
Nick stayed out. Evidently he was far happier in the
water than he was with her. Her grandfather had
warned her Nick might cut her out of his life and it
was obvious this morning she had made, yet again, a
dreadful mistake. Why had she failed him? *Why?* Was
she so astonished that he had said he loved her? Was
she genuinely afraid of his enormous power over her?

'That was *glorious!*' he said when he came in. 'I
needed that.' He stood over her, silhouetted against
the brilliant sun. His sleek black hair was curling and
drops of sea water glittered on his wide shoulders and
lean torso like diamonds.

'I'm glad you enjoyed it.'

'Yes, you do allow me the brief moment,' he said. Expertly he twirled his large beach towel so it was arranged alongside, then he lowered himself on to it, propping himself up on one elbow as he gazed down on her beautiful, lightly gilded body. Though very blonde she had the most fortunate of skins. It never freckled and it never, treated sensibly, ever burned. Her face she only exposed to the sun briefly, but even then it caught gold.

'Magic,' he murmured. 'Nature has been too kind to you, Claudia.'

'*You* should talk.'

'A man's looks don't matter so much.'

'*Don't* they?' she said dryly. 'Yours have made a lot of legs give out.'

'Aren't you going to sunbathe topless?'

'I've thought of it.'

'Then you must *do* it.' There was a faint savagery in his mocking voice.

'No thank you.'

'Do you fear someone might come?'

'Actually,' she opened her eyes to look at him. 'My main fear is *you*.'

'Well you certainly know how to seduce. I'm finding it unbelievably difficult not to lick all that oil off you.'

They swam again, then they had lunch and all the while Claudia knew he was holding himself in abeyance. Where he was aggressive she turned aside his mockery with a soft voice, offering him the best of everything Fergy had packed for their picnic lunch. Yet there were only flashes when he responded and once an easy endearment that must have slipped out.

It was a tantalising day. They went for a long walk

to a magnificent lion shaped rock while the seagulls swirled over the tumbling breakers and dived with shrieking cries for fish. She found some very pretty shells, so many she had to collect them in her towelling hat but then Nick observed that the sun was too strong and she would get burned. Only then did she murmur plaintively she didn't think he would care.

Excitement and tension burned steadily in her all the way home. Her skin was sheened with salt and she should have been feeling exquisitely relaxed.

'Thank you, Nick,' she sighed as they reached the city limits.

'I'm so glad you had a nice time.'

She laughed shakily. 'Didn't you?'

'It was just fine.' With his hair ruffled into crisp curls and his tan deepened he looked like a particularly handsome gypsy, so it was that much more of a shock when he turned his head and one was confronted by a pair of startling light eyes. It was enough to induce a crisis of the nerves.

'I could do with a shower,' she managed weakly, several miles on.

'And what's more, you're having it at *my* place.'

'Not a bit. I'm going home.'

'That's what *you* think, lady.'

At this point, inexplicably, she lost her temper. 'All right, Nick, you've been simmering all day.'

'Oh, good, you've noticed.'

'I've done everything I can to please you.'

'Then continue to. Just shut up until we get home.'

'HERE WE are again!' she said, as they entered the quiet house.

'It's okay if you have a shower first.'

'Thanks, I'll wait. It sounds as though you're planning to drown me.'

He gripped her hand and escorted her up the stairs. 'Come on now, I won't join you if that's what you're worried about.'

'Look it's only a bit of salt.'

He showed her where he kept the towels. 'Get a move on would you? I have something to say to you.'

It was impossible to relax her body or her brain. Neither did she have any underclothes she realised. She had worn her bikini beneath her cotton smock.

Nick's towelling robe was hanging behind the bathroom door. It was short so it would do nicely. She could rinse out her bikini and pop it in the dryer. As she expected sand had been forced into the lining. She couldn't attempt to wash her hair out. It was so thick it took ages even with a blowdryer.

She stepped beneath the strong, steaming spray trying to prepare some alibi for herself...

'Come on,' his brisk tap on the door urged her.

She wondered if she had gone off. Certainly she had been engrossed in thought. She dried herself swiftly with the large, fluffy blue towel, used Nick's comb on her hair then draped his yellow towelling robe around her slender figure, belting it tightly. Her smock she left over the rail and her bikini she wrapped in a hand towel, preparatory to taking it to the dryer.

'What in the world were you...doing?' He started off assertively and trailed off.

'Oh, I borrowed your robe.'

'I can see that. It stopped me in my tracks.'

'You don't mind? I hadn't planned on coming back here. I've only got...'

'Don't explain. As soon as I start to feel nasty you decide to look wonderful.'

She blinked and steered around him. 'May I put my swimsuit in the dryer? I want to wear it home.'

He groaned lightly and stood a minute with his eyes shut. 'Claudia Ingram, Goddess, Avenging Angel, Circe, what else?'

'*Idiot.* Better add that to your list.'

'Where do you think that kind of an apology will get you?'

'I'd better dry my swim suit, Nick,' she cried. She moved like a gazelle down the hallway and he laughed sharply and went to have his own shower.

Maybe she could get round him. Claudia decided to make them martinis. A very dry martini was one of her father's favourites so she knew how to make it. She could even cook dinner. Fergy had made sure she was pretty clever in the kitchen. She was so anxious she found she was talking to herself. 'Look, Nick, I've totally *changed.*'

It was indeed the case. For many long months now she had driven herself crazy. She had agonised over a relationship that hadn't even existed. Now the misery, the unrelenting desperation had been driven from her mind. Everything her grandfather had said was true. Far from being attracted to Cristina Nick had never displayed more than the smooth politeness required of him. He could never have brought himself to such a relationship. He had told her that right at the beginning but instead of accepting his word without question she had allowed a woman she didn't really know to poison her mind.

Well, she had paid for it. It had all but ruined her twenty-first birthday party. It had given her months of anger and anguish and resentment.

'What are you up to?' Nick's voice was casual, offhand. He had changed into white cotton slacks with an open neck soft shirt and his grey eyes had caught something of its aquamarine colour. In fact he gleamed with a kind of angry energy or excitement.

She picked up the two cocktail glasses and stood in front of him. 'An aperitif before dinner.'

'I don't need any aphrodisiacs.' His narrowed eyes mocked her.

'Oh, well, they might help us through a bad patch.'

'You've concluded that, have you?' He glanced around. 'Come and sit beside me on the sofa.'

Claudia settled herself with her legs under her, trying to look companionable when Nick's manner was far from reassuring.

'So dear Cristina is having a baby?' he said so crisply she withdrew into her corner.

'I'm hoping it will make a new woman out of her.'

He turned his head to stare at her. 'I take it you had some passing thought it might be mine?'

Her expression was a pent-up plea for forgiveness.

'What's up? Cat got your tongue? I said Cristina is having a bloody baby.'

'Which is naturally my father's.'

'Of course, though I expect your worries won't entirely disappear until that fact is clearly recognisable?'

She gulped on her drink and choked a little. 'I don't really like this, you know.'

'Too heavy on the gin.'

'Is it?' she asked in tones of amazement.

'Surely I will *kill* you,' he muttered.

'I'm sorry, Nick.' She set her fragile glass down rather too firmly and slid forward to rest her head on his shoulder. 'If I've ever doubted you for a minute, I've suffered for it.'

'*You've* suffered for it!' He wrenched himself away from her so violently, leaping up, she fell full length. 'You seem to think you can say, I'm sorry, Nick, and that's it. You seem to think you can accuse me, suspect me, of all manner of things, then when I look like taking off my shoe to you, you snuggle up to me like a child.'

'I don't see why not? It's as plain as the nose on my face I haven't grown up.'

'You even put my robe around you like protective armour.'

'Then *hate* me.' She was struggling to get up. 'You're a hundred times more good and brilliant than I deserve. I'm too easily shocked. I believe everything anyone tells me. Even a madwoman. I'm too young. I lack character and I'm scared. Scared of *you,* Nick.'

She was talking, moving so precipitously, she couldn't prevent herself from tripping over a gorgeous Aubusson rug.

'I *quit!*' she shouted and burst into tears.

'You don't want me, I see.' He picked her up with a degree of violence. 'Do you think that's going to break my heart?'

'*What* heart?' Now she was petrified his robe might come off.

'Is the robe coming loose?' He sounded deeply ironic. 'Oh, your beautiful breasts, Claudia. I've been hard pressed to keep my hands off them since you were sixteen.'

'You *managed,*' she cried.

'Oh, you little bitch.'

He tumbled them both on to the couch and her head fell back against the rich pile of cushions. She couldn't believe that Nick would hurt her. On the other hand he might.

'You shouldn't lose your temper, Nick,' she said fervently.

He got one arm under her and pulled her into his iron grasp. 'That's a little big for you, isn't it?' The robe had lots of room in it and now it had fallen back exposing her naked breasts. He bent his head forward and took a rosy peak into his mouth.

'*Nick!*' she arched back.

'Why can't you *believe* in me?' He lifted his head but his hand kept possession of her breast.

'What's the point of going on about that?'

'Sssh!'

It was like a tremendous fall in slow motion. She thought she would never stop spiralling. He lifted his mouth and began to stroke her. 'You have no notion of how much I love you,' he said.

'You *won't* hate me, will you?' She quickened and trembled and covered his face with little, panting kisses. 'I will never let anyone *lie* to me anymore.'

'Okay. Then it's all over. I want to keep you here forever.'

'Oh, God, *yes,*' she breathed. Her pulses were beating crazily, her long slender legs were free of the robe that crossed above her knees. 'I love you. *Love* you,' her voice was a little wild.

'Aaah!' He buried his head between her breasts. 'What can we do really? I'll do anything you ask.'

'Then love me,' she half whispered. 'I don't want to wait.'

'You can't be *certain* of that, my darling.' His voice was so gentle it brought tears to her eyes. 'What about the day you're my bride? My young, radiant, excited bride. I want everything to be perfect for you. No sense of sadness, or regret.'

'But I want you so desperately, Nick,' she faltered. 'How can you be so cruel?'

'Cruel, oh my God!' He twisted her head back and kissed her drowningly and as he held her in his arms she could feel the trembling in his body. In love, he was incredibly unselfish. Though the fire of passion consumed them now, there was something exultant in coming to him as a virgin bride.

She knew now he loved her deeply. She truly knew it. When she opened her eyes to him they were sweet pools of enchantment. 'I don't want a quiet wedding. I want a *big* one. I want everyone in the world to know how I'm *blessed.*'

'And what's more, you want it at Easter,' he said masterfully. 'Easter comes early this year.'

She sighed voluptuously and moved Nick's robe back up on her shoulders. 'I'd give the whole world for you, do you know that?'

Joy had given her a lustre that took his breath away.

With the air of a man who was tested to the limit, he forced himself to his feet, drawing her up with him and holding her within his encircling arms.

'Sir Galahad couldn't hold a candle to me in my opinion.'

'No,' she breathed smilingly. She let her head fall forward against his breast. 'But *after* the wedding you have my permission to be *yourself.*'

GRANT AND Cristina Ingram's baby was delivered by
Caesarian section in the first week of August. A perfectly formed boy who even in his newness was the
image of his father. Mother and father were ecstatic
with pride and joy.

Nick and Claudia were in London at the time and
Nick took his father-in-law's jubilant telephone call
at two o'clock in the morning.

'I thought you would want to know right away!'
Grant Ingram called over the wires.

Nick expressed his sincere pleasure and passed the
phone to his waiting wife. Claudia took it staring up
into his brilliant eyes. They had enjoyed a marvellous
evening and had only arrived back at their hotel a few
minutes before.

All the time Claudia was talking to her father, Nick
was kissing her neck and bare shoulders. She melted
against him while he released the zipper on her low-
backed jade chiffon dress.

She was trembling as she replaced the receiver.
'They're both well. Isn't that marvellous?'

'*Marvellous!*' Nick burst out laughing. 'That Cristina really throws herself into the part, doesn't she?
My God, what an actress she would have made!'

Cristina, from the very day she had discovered she
was pregnant, had virtually become an amnesiac,
blanking out every episode in her life she wished to
forget.

Very slowly Nick continued to undress his young
wife, inhaling her soft scent, then when the excitement became too strong for them, he carried her to
the bed. All else now was too far away, too incon-
sequential…

Claudia lifted her slender arms and pulled him down to heaven.

BOTH OF THEM

Rebecca Winters

Dear Reader,

I love a wonderful romance as much as any of you, especially a Harlequin Romance novel. In fact, the first one I ever read, by Katrina Britt, held me spellbound and I've been a faithful fan of Harlequin Romance books since that time.

To be honest, I'm quite sure I've read every one in print!

I can't define the exact moment that the writer in me was born, but I will tell you that I find it nothing short of miraculous to see my name listed among the authors I've enjoyed over the years.

As far as I'm concerned, Harlequin has put out the best stories available on the market, and it is only fitting that they are celebrating forty years of success. I know they have brought me hours and hours of reading pleasure.

My greatest hope is that the books I've written will continue to supply you readers with that same pleasure. Out of all the books I've penned, I do believe that *Both of Them* is a book about love and babies that embodies all the elements I adore in a good romance. Enjoy!

Rebecca Winters

Rebecca Winters

CHAPTER ONE

HE WAS THE BABY'S FATHER all right! The same olive complexion, the familiar obstinate chin, the identical hair, black as India ink. Even from the distance separating them, the resemblance seemed to shout at Cassie.

She leaned against the doorjamb in disbelief. Her sister's motherly intuition hadn't failed her, after all.

Cassie, from the first moment I held Jason in my arms, I thought there was something...different about him. If Ted was still alive, he'd say the same thing. Jason's not our son! I'm convinced of it!

Remember I told you how he was rushed to the intensive-care unit as soon as he was born? And remember my telling you about a disaster that brought all those victims to the hospital at the same time? There was so much commotion that morning, I honestly think a mix-up occurred and they brought me back the wrong baby from intensive care.

Jason belongs with his natural parents. Promise me you'll find my baby and take care of him for me, Cassie. Then I can die in peace.

Faced with the irrefutable proof of Jason's true paternity, Cassie went alternately hot and cold. Down to the smallest detail, like the shape of the long, square-tipped fingers, or the way one dark brow lowered with displeasure, nine-month-old Jason was the robust replica of Trace Ellingsworth Ramsey III, the autocratic male she could see through the doorway seated behind the desk. He was rapping out edicts over the phone to some no doubt terrified underling of the Greater Phoenix Banking Corporation.

Her eyes closed in reaction, because it meant Susan's natural son had left the hospital with this prominent, high-powered banking executive and his wife. Susan's baby would now have the Ramsey name, would now be assured his place in life as one of the Ramsey heirs.

Had the Ramseys, like Susan, ever wondered about that day nine months ago? Had they ever sensed anything about their baby that didn't seem right? Any physical characteristics, for instance, that didn't appear in their families?

"Come in, Miss Arnold!" Trace Ramsey called out, not bothering to hide his impatience as he put down the receiver. Before entering the room Cassie darted a nervous glance at Jason, who was still asleep in his carryall next to the secretary's desk.

Though high heels added several inches to her five-foot-three-inch frame, Cassie felt dwarfed by the dimensions of the walnut-paneled office. To her disappointment there were no mementos or framed photographs of Ramsey's wife and son. Except for some paintings on the walls and a bonsai tree placed on a corner of his desk, the suite was immaculate, and blessedly cool.

She sat down in one of the chairs opposite his desk. "Thank you for taking time out of your busy schedule to see me this morning, Mr. Ramsey. I realize it was short notice.''

His dark brows furrowed in undisguised irritation. ''According to my secretary, Mrs. Blakesley, you have a highly confidential matter to discuss with me, which you refused to disclose to her.''

''I couldn't say anything to her,'' Cassie said immediately, her guileless, leaf-green eyes pleading with him to believe her. ''It's no one's business but ours. When I say ours, I'm including your wife, of course,'' she added in a soft voice.

He sat forward in the chair with his hands clasped on top of the desk, gazing directly at Cassie. She stared into his eyes, deep blue eyes set between impossibly black lashes. Like Jason's... The Ramsey eyes reminded Cassie of the intense blue in a match flame.

''My secretary never arranges appointments without first obtaining background information, Miss Arnold. She made an exception in your case. I hope for your sake you were telling her the truth when you said this was a life-and-death situation. Lying to gain entry to my private office is the surest way to find yourself slapped with a lawsuit for harassment. As it is, I'm taking time from an important board meeting to accommodate you.''

His arrogance took her breath away. If all this weren't for the ultimate happiness of everyone concerned, she would've relished storming out of there and slamming the door in his good-looking face.

''This concerns your son,'' she said quietly.

The menacing look that transformed his taut features made her heart leap in apprehension. With dangerous agility, he got up from his seat and placed both hands on his desk, leaning forward. "If you're part of a kidnapping scheme, let me warn you I've already activated the security alarm. When you walk out of here, it'll be with an armed guard."

"Are you always this paranoid?" She was aghast; until now it hadn't occurred to her that his wealth made him a target for kidnappers. At the mere thought, a shudder ran through her body.

"You've got thirty seconds to explain yourself." The implicit threat in his voice unnerved her.

"I-I think you'd better sit down," she said.

"Your time is running out."

In an attempt to feel less vulnerable, Cassie rose to her feet, clutching her purse in front of her. "It's not easy for me to explain when you're standing there like...like an avenging prince ready to do battle."

He flicked a glance at his watch. "You're down to ten seconds. Then you can explain all this to a judge." From the forbidding expression on his face and the coldness of his voice, she knew he meant what he said.

As worried and nervous as she was about confronting him with the truth, she had to remember that this man and his wife were her only passport to Susan's son. That knowledge gave her the courage to follow through with her plan.

Taking a deep breath, she said, "I happen to know that you and your wife have a nine-month-old baby boy who was born to you on February twenty-fourth at the Palms Oasis Health Center. My sister, Susan Arnold Fisher, also delivered a baby boy there on the same day.

"Until the moment she died, she believed that there was an upset in routine because of the catastrophe—the chemical plant explosion. It brought a flood of injured people to the hospital, and somehow the wrong name tags were put on the babies' wrists in the intensive-care unit. The result was that my sister was presented with your baby, and you and your wife went home with hers."

The silence following her pronouncement stretched endlessly. His face looked impassive, hard and cold as stone. "All right," he finally muttered. "I've listened to your tale. Now I hope you have a good attorney, because you're going to need one."

"Wait!" she cried when he pressed the intercom button. She had expected this encounter to disturb him, but she'd never dreamed he would call in the authorities before she had convinced him of the truth!

"It's too late to backtrack, Miss Arnold."

A knock on the door brought Cassie's head around and she saw an armed security guard and a police officer enter the room with their hands on their unsnapped holsters. Behind them stood an anxious Mrs. Blakesley. She held a wriggling, squirming Jason, who was bellowing at the top of his lungs.

"What in the—?" Trace Ramsey stopped midsentence and raked a hand through his black hair, shooting Cassie a venomous glance. But she was too concerned to be intimidated; dropping her purse, she made a beeline for Jason.

Since Susan's death two months earlier, Cassie and Jason had become inseparable. She might not have been his biological mother, but she loved him every bit as fiercely. She felt guilty for leaving him in Mrs.

Blakesley's care, even for such a brief time. He must have awakened after his morning bottle and been frightened by the unfamiliar face hovering over him.

"What's the trouble, Mr. Ramsey?" asked the guard. But Cassie didn't hear his answer, because Jason had caught sight of her. Immediately his lusty cries intensified, resounding through the suite of offices. "Ma-ma, Ma-ma," he repeated, holding out his hands.

Despite the gravity of the situation, Cassie couldn't repress a tiny smile, because it was Trace Ramsey's own noisy son creating all this chaos.

"Mommy's here, darling." With a murmured thank-you, she plucked him from the older woman's arms and cuddled him against her chest, kissing his damp black curls, rubbing his strong sturdy little back with her free hand.

Jason had made it clear that he wanted Cassie and no one else. He clung tightly to her and calmed down at once. Cassie felt a wave of maternal pride so intense she was staggered, and at that moment she knew she could never give him up. She knew she'd made a mistake in coming here.

With the best of intentions, Cassie had walked into Trace Ramsey's office and upset his comfortable, well-ordered life. If his reaction to a possible kidnapping attempt was anything to go by, his love for the son he'd brought home from the hospital was as great as hers for Jason. She wanted to honor her sister's dying wish, but she *couldn't*. She realized that now. It was wrong, unfair—to all of them.

"Mr. Ramsey?" she started to say, but the second she caught sight of his ashen face, the name died on her lips. In her preoccupation with Jason's needs, she hadn't noticed that everyone except his father had left the room. He stood motionless in its center.

Swallowing hard, she loosened Jason's fist, which was clutching her hair, before turning him around to face his father. Only seconds later, she heard his shaken whisper. "Dear Lord, the likeness is unbelievable."

Cassie's compassionate heart went out to him. She couldn't imagine what it would feel like to learn that she'd been nurturing the wrong child since his birth, let alone to see her own baby for the first time.

"That was my reaction as soon as I saw you," she said quietly. He looked away from the child then, and gazed at her, his eyes dark with emotion.

"He's called Jason," Cassie added. The sound of his name brought the baby's dark head around and he clamored to be held in his favorite position, with his face buried in her neck, his hand gripping the top of her dress for dear life.

"May I hold him?" Trace's voice sounded strained. He lifted his hands instinctively to take Jason from her.

"Yes, of course. But don't be surprised if he starts crying again. He's going through that stage where he won't let anyone near him but me."

Jason immediately protested the abrupt departure from Cassie's arms. His strong little body squirmed and struggled, and he kicked out his legs, screaming loudly enough to alert the entire building. But not for anything in the world would Cassie have intruded on this private moment between father and son.

They looked so right together, so perfect, it brought a lump to her throat.

Trace's gaze swerved to hers as he bounced his unhappy son against his broad shoulder, apparently unconcerned about his elegant, stone-gray silk suit. "Do you have a bottle I can give him? Maybe it'll quiet him down."

She should have thought of that. She began to rummage in the bag Mrs. Blakesley had brought in. "Here."

Gently but firmly he settled Jason in his arm and inserted the nipple in his mouth. He performed the maneuver with an expertise that would have surprised her if she hadn't known he'd been fathering Susan's son for the past nine months.

But Jason wasn't cooperating. He just cried harder, fighting the bottle and his father with all his considerable might. Cassie could tell that Trace was beginning to feel at a loss.

"Why don't you let me change him?" she suggested softly. "It might do the trick."

He slanted her a look she couldn't decipher and with obvious reluctance put a screaming Jason back in her arms. While Jason snuggled against her once more, his father reached for the baby quilt lining the carryall and spread it on top of his desk, pushing the telephone aside. Never had she imagined she'd be changing Jason's diaper there!

"Come on, sweetheart. Mommy's going to make you comfortable." Though Jason continued to protest vociferously and eye his father as if he were the enemy, she managed to make him lie still long enough to unfasten his sleeper and peel it off along with his damp diaper.

As she put on a clean disposable diaper, Trace murmured something unintelligible beneath his breath, and almost as if he couldn't help himself took Jason's right foot in his hands. For some reason the baby didn't seem to mind and actually relaxed a little, no doubt because he was receiving so much attention. His extremities had become of paramount importance in his young life.

Cassie had always been intrigued by Jason's right foot. The third and fourth toes were webbed, a characteristic never seen in either Susan's or Ted's families. His father seemed to find it of inordinate interest, as well.

"He's my son!" Trace proclaimed solemnly, then let out a cry of pure delight. Fierce pride gleamed in his blue eyes.

"We probably ought to take the babies to the hospital and have their blood types checked against the records."

"We will," he muttered, "but the truth is sitting right here." He grasped Jason's fingers and pulled experimentally to test the baby's strength. Jason caught hold with a firm grip and lifted his head and shoulders from the desk to sit up without help, producing a satisfied chuckle from his father. Jason had become equally curious about the black-haired stranger who seemed to take such pleasure in playing with him.

Because it was cool in the room, Cassie searched for a clean sleeper in the diaper bag. No sooner had she found one than it was taken from her hands.

"I'll dress him," Trace stated. There was an unmistakable ring of possession in his tone as he proceeded to fit Jason's compact body into the arms and feet of the little white suit.

After snapping the front fasteners, he picked up his son, who had by now stopped fussing, and held him against his shoulder, running his fingers through Jason's wild black curls. Cassie noted that even their hair seemed to part naturally on the same side.

Needless to say, she'd been forgotten as Trace carried Jason over to the window where the great city of Phoenix lay sprawled before them. Whatever he said was for his son's ears alone. She knew that Trace Ramsey had already taken Jason to his heart.

Now there were two people in the world who loved Jason intensely. And as soon as his wife was informed, there would be three. Everything had suddenly become much more complicated. Cassie understood instinctively that Jason's father wouldn't give up anything that was his. But in this case they would have to work out vacation schedules, because she wasn't prepared to lose Jason. She had come to love him too much.

"Mr. Ramsey? I have a plane to catch later today. Do you think we could meet with your wife this morning and tell her what's happened? I can hardly wait to see my nephew, and I'd like some time with him before I go back to San Francisco with Jason."

"San Francisco?" He wheeled around, a grimace marring his features.

"We live there, Jason and I."

Her voice must have attracted Jason's attention because he cried out and reached for her again. When

Trace continued to hold him, Jason wailed piteously and tried to wriggle out of his father's grasp. He had been a determined, headstrong child from birth. Now she knew why.

"It's time for his lunch, but a bottle will have to do." The gentle reminder forced Trace to close the distance between them and deposit Jason in her arms. But with every step he took, she could tell he rebelled against the idea of relinquishing his newly discovered son even for a moment.

Cassie couldn't blame him. The situation was so emotionally charged she was afraid she would burst into tears any second. Comforted by the familiar feel of Jason's warm little body, she sat down in a leather wing chair Trace positioned for her. Jason grabbed the bottle with both hands and started gulping down his milk.

Actually he'd been attempting to drink from a cup for the past week. But her pediatrician had said to use a bottle while they were traveling because it would give him a greater sense of security. Jason was such a noisy drinker, Cassie couldn't help smiling and felt Trace's eyes on both of them.

"My wife and I divorced soon after the baby was born," he said abruptly. He paused, then went on, speaking quickly. "She gave me custody and went back to her law practice in Los Angeles. I have my housekeeper, Nattie, to help raise my son. She and her husband, Mike—who looks after the grounds— have worked for me for years. Nattie's wonderful with children, and Justin adores her."

"*Justin!*" As she said his name, her mind grappled with the unexpected revelation that Mrs. Ramsey was no longer a part of this family's life. She lifted her head and fixed imploring green eyes on Trace. "Tell me about Susan's son—your son," she amended self-consciously. "What does he look like? I-I can't wait to see him."

Without hesitation he strode swiftly to his desk and buzzed his secretary. "Mrs. Blakesley? Cancel all my appointments for today. I'm going home and won't be back. Tell Robert to have my car waiting in the rear. We'll be down shortly. If there are any urgent phone messages, give them to me now."

While he dealt with last-minute business, she felt his gaze linger on her slender legs beneath the cream cotton suit she was wearing. Cassie's heart did a funny little kick, and she forced herself to look away, studying the paintings hung on the walls of his office. Until now, Trace Ramsey had been the focal point of her attention.

If the decor was a reflection of his personal taste, he tended to enjoy the watercolors of an artist unknown to her. The paintings depicted a variety of enchanting desert scenes, in a style that was at once vibrant and restrained. She would have liked one for herself.

A loud burp from Jason brought her back to the present. Trace's spontaneous laugh made him look, for a moment, more carefree, and Cassie chuckled, too. Obviously Jason had finished his bottle without stopping for breath.

"Shall we?" Trace stood at the door holding a briefcase and the carryall, indicating she should join him.

"That's a beautiful boy you have there," Mrs.

Blakesley commented to Cassie as they passed her desk on their way out.

"Mrs. Blakesley," Trace said to the older woman, his eyes still glowing in wonder, "I'd like you to be the first person to meet my son, Jason. When I'm in possession of all the facts, I'll explain how this came about, but for the time being I must ask you to keep it to yourself."

"I knew it!" The matronly woman jumped to her feet. Hurrying around her desk she shaped Jason's face with her hands. "Even before she said it was a matter of life and death, I knew it. He bears an amazing resemblance to you, Trace. I never saw anything like it in my life!"

A satisfied smile lifted the corners of Trace's mouth as he gazed down on his son.

Cassie could imagine all too easily what his secretary was thinking—that at one time Cassie and Trace had had an affair and Jason was the result. She wanted to set the matter straight, but Trace was already whisking her out of his office and around the corner to a private elevator.

When he'd ushered her inside and the doors were closed, he asked, "How did you get to my office?"

"A taxi."

"How long have you been in Phoenix?"

Jason's curious eyes darted back and forth as they spoke.

"Only two days this time."

"This time?" His black brow lifted in query. The elevator arrived at the ground floor and they stepped out, but Trace remained standing in the hallway as he waited for Cassie's answer.

"I've made several rushed trips to Phoenix in the past two months trying to find out if Susan was right about the switch. There were five couples who'd had a son at that hospital the same day Susan gave birth to Jason. I mean Justin."

Trace blinked. "I didn't realize there were that many. Palms Oasis is a small hospital."

"I know. I was surprised, too. Anyway, I visited each family in turn but came to a dead end each time. I began to think Jason was one of those rare accidents of nature, after all—the odd gene producing a throwback in the family. That is, until I saw you." She ventured a look into his eyes and wondered why she'd ever thought them glacial. "When your secretary told me you wouldn't see me without knowing the reason for my visit, I almost turned around and walked out."

His eyes turned an inky blue color and he sucked in his breath. "Thank God you didn't."

She gave a quick half smile. "You're not exactly an easy man to reach, Mr. Ramsey. No home phone. Security guards. I didn't have a choice except to meet you without an appointment. You'll never know how close I came to giving up. You were the last person on my list and it seemed like an unnecessary gesture, another exercise in futility."

"What made you so persistent?" he asked soberly.

"I have to admit that since I started looking after Jason, I've entertained some doubts about his parentage, too. I made up my mind to be as thorough as possible, so there'd be no lingering shadows when I returned to San Francisco to raise Jason as my son."

On impulse she lowered her head to kiss the child's smooth cheek. "And something told me that if I left without seeing you, I would always have these doubts...."

Just as she spoke, Trace moved closer. He cupped her elbow and guided her through the hall to a back door. A BMW sedan stood waiting in the drive. "Come here, Tiger," he said to Jason, lifting him from Cassie's arms and strapping him in the baby seat.

Jason took one look at the unfamiliar surroundings and began to scream.

"I think I'd better stay with him or you won't be able to concentrate on your driving." She climbed in back, then handed Jason one of his favorite toys, a hard plastic doughnut in bright orange. That calmed him and he soon grew absorbed in chewing it.

Trace leaned inside to fasten her seat belt. His action brought their faces within an inch of each other, and she was painfully conscious of his dark glossy hair, his clean-shaven jaw and his fresh scent—the soap he used? To mask her awareness of him, she pretended to adjust Jason's seat belt. Trace backed away from her and closed the door. In seconds he had gone around to the driver's seat.

"Thanks, Robert," he called to the garage attendant, and they were off. If the older man found the situation somewhat unusual, he didn't let on. But she could tell he was curious about Trace's little black-haired look-alike sitting in Justin's usual spot.

Despite the way he had treated her earlier, Cassie found herself warming to Trace. She liked the fact that he took his fatherhood role so seriously. And she liked the way he accepted a child's presence in his life, not worrying about his costly suit or his expensive car. She knew a lot of men who never allowed children inside their luxury cars.

They left the busy downtown center and drove north toward the foothills, where she could see Camelback Mountain in the distance. What impressed Cassie most about Phoenix was the cleanliness of its streets and the beauty of the residential lawns and gardens. The vivid flowers and shrubs, the sparkling blue of swimming pools…

This was the first time in months that she'd been able to appreciate her surroundings. The pain of her broken engagement, plus the trauma of trying to cope with Susan's death and Jason's needs—on top of running her home handicrafts business—had drained her. She couldn't remember when she'd been able to relax like this.

But her pleasure was short-lived. When she turned her head to find another toy in her bag, she discovered a pair of narrowed eyes watching her through the rearview mirror. If their guarded expression and his taut facial features were any indication, something unpleasant was going through Trace Ramsey's mind. She couldn't understand it, because only moments before everything had been so amicable.

Inexplicably hurt by his oddly hostile look, she closed her eyes and rested her head against the leather upholstery.

In fairness to him, she supposed, it wasn't every day a man kissed the child he thought was his son goodbye, only to be confronted with his *real* son a few hours later.

Again Cassie tried to imagine his feelings and couldn't. Only once in her twenty-five years had she heard of a case involving a switched baby. That instance, too, had been a mischance, sending two families home with each other's babies. Cassie didn't know the statistics, but figured such an accident had to be in the one-in-a-billion category.

Until now, most of Cassie's thoughts and concerns had been for Jason. But the closer they drew to Trace's home, the more excitedly she began to anticipate her first look at Justin. She found herself speculating on why the Ramsey marriage had fallen apart so soon after the baby was born. How could his wife have left her child and gone to another state to pursue a career? Didn't her heart ache for her son?

Cassie couldn't fathom any of it. She was so deep in thought she didn't realize the car had left the highway and turned onto a private road. It wound through a natural desert setting, dotted with saguaros and other cacti, to a breathtaking Southwestern house—a house that looked as if it had sprung from the very landscape.

The house appeared to be built on two levels, with a whitewashed stone exterior and pale wood trim.

The architect who had designed Trace Ramsey's home had not only succeeded in reflecting the environment but had caught the essence of the man. The clean yet dramatic lines, the soaring windows, the quiet beauty of the wood, created a uniquely satisfying effect.

He continued driving around the house to a side entrance where Cassie caught sight of a rectangular swimming pool. Immaculate, velvety green lawns flanked the water, which was as blue as a deep-sea grotto.

Cassie gasped at the sheer size and beauty of Trace Ramsey's retreat, tucked only minutes away from the center of his banking empire. Cassie had never seen anything quite like this place. She'd spent the whole of her life in San Francisco, living with her widowed mother and sister in the bottom apartment of a flat-fronted Victorian house on Telegraph Hill. Cassie couldn't remember her father, who'd died when she was very young.

While she lifted Jason from his car seat, Trace came around and opened the door to assist them. The air smelled of tantalizing desert scents and was fresher than in downtown Phoenix. Cassie thrived in cooler temperatures; she estimated that it couldn't be much warmer than seventy-five degrees. Perfect weather for early December, just the way she liked it.

"Shall we go in?" He didn't seem to expect an answer as he gripped her elbow and helped her up the stairs to the entry hall, carrying the baby bag in his other hand. He didn't attempt to take his son from her, probably because he didn't relish a repeat of Jason's tears. But she could sense Trace's impatience to hold him.

Jason was fascinated by the click of her high heels on the Mexican-tile floors and kept turning his head in an attempt to discover the source. It was a fight to keep him from flipping out of her arms, especially since Cassie found herself so distracted by the beauty around her. Every few steps, she had to stop and stare at the dramatically cut-out white interior walls and bleached wood ceilings.

They walked along a gallery filled with lushly green trees and local Indian art. It looked out on the swimming pool, part of which was protected by the overhanging roof.

"Nattie? I'm home, and I've brought someone with me for lunch. Where are you?" Trace called out as they went down a half flight of stairs toward the indoor portion of the patio.

"Justin's been helping me water the plants. I didn't know you'd be back to eat. I'll get something on the table right away."

They entered a charming courtyard reminiscent of old Mexico, with a profusion of plants and colorful flowers. But Cassie hardly noticed the wrought-iron lounge furniture or the retreating back of the auburn-haired housekeeper. Her eyes fastened helplessly on the child in the playpen who had heard his father's voice and was squealing in delight.

The slender lanky child, dressed in a sleeveless yellow romper suit, was standing, a feat Jason hadn't yet mastered, as he clung to the playpen webbing, rocking in and out as he watched his father's approach.

Round hazel eyes shone from a fringe of fine, straight, pale-gold hair that encircled his head like a halo. His total attention was fixed rapturously on Trace.

Cassie came to a standstill. It was an astonishing sensation—a little like putting the final pieces in a jigsaw puzzle. The frame of this child's body was Ted's, but his complexion was Susan's. The shape of his eyes was Ted's, but the color was Susan's. The texture of the hair was Ted's, but again, the coloring was Susan's. The straight nose and cheekbones were Ted's, but the smile…

Cassie's eyes filled with tears. Her adored sister,

who only eight weeks before had lost a valiantly fought battle with pneumonia, lived in her son's glorious smile.

"Oh, Susan!" She sobbed her sister's name aloud and buried her face in Jason's chest. She was overcome with emotion, with feelings still so close to the surface that she couldn't contain them any longer.

Jason fretted, patting her head agitatedly. Cassie fought for control and after a few minutes lifted her tear-drenched face to discover a pair of angry blue eyes staring at her, not only in silent accusation but contempt.

"What's wrong?" she whispered, attempting to wipe the tears from her cheeks. "First in the car, and now here. Why are you looking at me like that?"

CHAPTER TWO

IN THE SILENCE that followed, he reached for Justin and hugged him protectively, rubbing his chin against the fine silk of the child's hair. "I was counting on that reaction and you didn't disappoint me," he said bitterly.

They faced each other like adversaries. Cassie shifted Jason to her other arm. *"What reaction?"* She couldn't imagine what had caused such hostility.

"It's too late for pretense. Justin needs people around who see him for the wonderful person he is."

She shook her head in total bewilderment. "He *is* wonderful!"

"But—"

"But what?" she demanded angrily, feeling a wave of heat wash over her neck and cheeks. Jason could sense the charged atmosphere and started to whimper.

"You're no different from my ex-wife! She was so repulsed by Justin's deformity, mild though it is, that she wouldn't even hold him."

Deformity? "I don't know what you're talking about! Two months ago I watched my sister's body laid to rest and I thought her lost to me for the rest of my life." Her voice shook, but she hardly noticed.

Without conscious thought she lowered Jason into the playpen and reached for her tote bag. Oblivious to his sudden outburst, she pulled one of Susan's wedding pictures from the side pocket and held it up for Trace's scrutiny. It was her favorite picture of Susan and Ted, smiling into the camera just before they left on their honeymoon.

"When Justin's face lighted up just now, it was as if God had given Susan back to me. Take a good look at the picture, Mr. Ramsey. See for yourself!"

Grim-faced, he set Justin in the other corner of the playpen and took the photograph. Immediately Justin, too, began to cry. In an effort to distract the howling infants, Cassie knelt beside the playpen and started to sing "Teensy Weensy Spider," one of Jason's favorite songs. Within seconds, both babies grew quiet. Jason crawled toward her, while Justin clambered to his feet.

It was when he put out his left hand to grasp the playpen's webbing that she noticed the depression—like a band around the middle of his upper arm. Below the depression, his arm and hand were correctly shaped, but hadn't grown in proportion to the rest of his body. The deformity was slight, but it was noticeable if you were aware of it.

"You dear little thing." Unable to resist, she stood up and leaned over to take Justin in her arms. "You precious little boy," she crooned against his soft cheek, rocking him gently back and forth.

"Your mother and daddy would have given anything in the world to hold you like this. Do you know that?" she asked as he stared quietly at her. The seriousness of his gaze reminded her of the way Ted used to look when he was concentrating. "Susan made me promise to find you. I'm so thankful I did.

I love you, Justin. I love you,'' she whispered, but the words came out a muffled sob.

She wanted to believe the baby understood when she felt his muscles relax and his blond head rest on her shoulder. For a few minutes Cassie was conscious of nothing but the warmth of her nephew's body cuddled against her own.

"I owe you an apology."

Cassie opened her eyes and discovered Trace standing not two feet from her, with Jason riding his shoulders. His sturdy little fingers were fastened in his father's black hair, a look of fear mingled with intense concentration on his expressive face.

She smiled through the tears. "He's never seen the world from that altitude before."

Miraculously Trace smiled back, their enmity apparently forgotten. Cassie's heartbeat accelerated as she found herself examining the laugh lines around his mouth and his beautiful, straight white teeth. She raised her eyes to his, and the pounding of her heart actually became painful.

"Trace?" the housekeeper called out just then, jerking Cassie back to reality. "Do you want lunch served on the patio or in the dining room?"

"The patio will be fine, Nattie." To Cassie he said, "I'll get the high chair. The boys can take turns having lunch."

The boys. Those words fell so naturally from his lips. Anyone listening would have assumed this was an everyday occurrence.

"Since Jason and I will have to leave for the airport pretty soon, I'd like to spend this time with Justin. Do you mind if I hold him on my lap to feed him?"

A scowl marred his features. "When's your flight?" he demanded, not answering her question.

"Ten after four."

"I'll get you to the airport on time," was the terse response. "Right now the only matter of importance is getting better acquainted." He grasped Jason's hands more tightly. "Come on, Tiger. We'll go get Justin's chair and surprise Nattie."

Jason forgot to cry because he was concentrating all his energy on holding on to his father. The two of them disappeared from the patio, leaving Cassie alone with Justin, who seemed content to stay in her arms. Compared to the sturdy Jason, Justin felt surprisingly light.

She sat down on one of the chairs at the poolside table and settled him on the glass top in front of her. Though taller and more dexterous than Jason, he hadn't started talking as well yet. Probably because he was too busy analyzing everything with that mathematical brain inherited from Ted.

Jason, on the other hand, never stopped making sounds and noises. He liked to hear his own voice and adored music of any kind, which was a good thing since Cassie played the piano and listened for hours to tapes of her favorite piano concertos while she designed and appliquéd her original quilts, pillows and stuffed animals.

"I know a silly song your grandma Arnold would sing to you if she were here." She kissed his pink cheek and took his hands, touching each finger as she sang. "'Hinty, minty, cutie, corn, apple seed and apple thorn, Riar, briar, limber lock, six geese in a flock, Sit and sing, at the spring, o-u-t out again!'" She made his arms fly wide and he began to laugh, a real belly laugh that surprised and delighted her. They did this several times before Cassie heard a woman's call from another part of the house. Not long afterward, the trim sixtyish housekeeper appeared on the patio carrying two heaped plates of taco salad. Trace followed with the high chair in one arm and Jason in the other.

"I've got to meet the brave young woman who made it past Mrs. Blakesley and presented you with your son!"

She beamed at Cassie, who rose to her feet and balanced Justin against her hip while the older woman put the plates on the table. After wiping her fingers on her apron, she held out a hand, which Cassie shook. "I'm Nattie Parker and I have to tell you this is probably the most exciting day of my life! Talk about the spitting image!"

Cassie's eyes filled with tears as she looked at Jason. "He is, isn't he? And Justin is so much like my sister and her husband, I'm still in a daze. In fact, none of this seems real." She couldn't resist kissing Justin's silky blond head.

Nattie nodded in agreement. "That was a switch for the books. And to think you've been looking for Jason's daddy all this time, and Trace almost sent you away with the police. Shame on you, Trace," she said in a stern voice, but love for her employer shone through.

The woman's raisin-dark eyes fastened on Jason. "I can't wait another second to get my hands on him. He has the kind of solid little body you just want to squeeze, d'you know what I mean?"

"I know exactly," Cassie said, loving Nattie on the spot. She let her gaze wander to Trace, who was tenderly eyeing both his sons. One day Jason would grow into the same kind of vital, handsome, dynamic man....

At the moment, though, Jason was struggling with Nattie. He stopped when she handed him a cracker from her pocket; she gave another one to Justin with a quick kiss. "Come on, young man," she told Jason. "You can go with me to get the baby food. What would you like today? Beans and lamb? That's what your brother's having."

As she walked away chatting, Trace motioned Cassie to a chair. "Are you sure you want to feed Justin?"

"Positive," she asserted, placing him on her lap. Despite the cracker halfway in his mouth, he reached for the salad, which she pushed out of his way.

Turning her attention to Trace, who'd gone to the bar behind them, she said quietly, "Do you know what thrills me? He uses both hands in all his movements. That means he has the full use of his arm. He'll be able to do any sport or activity Jason can do." She paused to remove her fork from Justin's eager clutches. "Tell me what the doctors say about him."

Trace supplied napkins and iced fruit drinks before taking his seat. Their eyes met. "It's called an amniotic band. It tightened around his arm in the womb, cutting off some of the blood supply. The specialist says physical therapy to build up his muscles can begin when he turns three. By the time he's an adult, the defect will hardly be noticeable."

She leaned down and kissed Justin's smooth shoulder. "Well, aren't you the luckiest little boy in town. I wonder if you'll turn out to be as great a tennis player as your father. You're built just like him."

Trace looked pensive as he ate a forkful of salad. "Genes don't lie, do they?"

"No." She ate a mouthful of cheese and guacamole, then let Justin try a little of her pineapple drink.

"When did your sister first suspect Jason wasn't her son?"

"Her baby was rushed to the infant intensive-care unit as soon as he was born. A little later, the pediatrician told her he'd had trouble breathing on his own. She didn't actually hold him for about eight hours.

"When he was finally brought to her, his black hair and olive skin were so different from what she'd expected, she couldn't believe Jason was hers and told me as much over the phone. But since Susan's and my baby pictures show us with dark hair, I assumed Jason's hair would turn blond after a few months and didn't take her seriously. Until I saw him for the first time, that is."

Trace let out an audible sigh. "Unfortunately, I wasn't there for the delivery. The baby came sooner than we expected, and by the time I arrived at the hospital, Gloria was in her room and the baby was in the intensive-care unit. About a half hour later the pediatrician came to tell us about Justin. I went down to the nursery with the doctor and saw Justin for the first time lying in one of those cribs. The switch must have occurred in the unit."

She nodded. "Susan said the baby was born at 9:05 a.m."

Trace put down his fork and looked at her solemnly. "Our son was born at 9:04. And your sister was right. There were ambulances all over the place when I arrived. The chemical plant outside Phoenix blew up, killing a dozen people and sending dozens more to various hospitals. The place was swarming with hospital personnel, relatives, reporters. Because of all the confusion, I was delayed getting to Gloria's room."

She closed her eyes. "It sounds so impossible, so incredible, and yet that must explain why there was a mix-up. Do you think we should demand an investigation and lodge a formal complaint to prevent this from happening to anyone else?"

He was quiet so long she didn't know if he'd heard her. "Part of me says yes. Another part says accidents do happen, even when the greatest precautions are taken. Probably the chances of such a thing occurring again are something like a billion to one."

"I've thought that myself. We know it wasn't intentional."

After a pause he said, "In principle, I'm opposed to unnecessary litigation. This has become a sue-happy society. So, on balance, I'm against suing."

Cassie didn't realize she'd been holding her breath. "I'm glad you said that. I don't think I could handle an official investigation after everything I've been through in the last year with Ted's death—he was killed in an accident—and then Susan getting sick and…and dying." Not to mention Rolfe's recent engagement to a woman overseas, which had come as a painful shock to Cassie. She and Rolfe—her life-long neighbor—had always been close, although she'd put off making a decision about marriage. But she'd assumed that when his studies were over, he would come home and they'd work things out.

"The newspapers would get hold of it and the publicity would be horrible," she said, shuddering at the prospect. "In the end, all it would do is damage the hospital's reputation and ruin people's lives. I don't want this to affect the boys."

"I agree," Trace concurred in a sober tone. "However, we will get those blood tests and I'm going to write the hospital board a letter informing them what happened. I'll let them know that, though we're not pressing charges, we are requesting an unofficial inquiry to satisfy our questions. Indirectly it might prevent another mistake like this in the future."

"I think that's best, and I know Susan and Ted would have felt the same way. Mr. Ramsey, did you or your wife ever have any suspicions that Justin wasn't your son?"

He cocked one dark eyebrow. "I think at this stage we should dispense with the formalities. My name is Trace, and the answer to your question is a definite no. Gloria is a tall willowy blond with hazel eyes. Everyone assumed Justin inherited her coloring and slender build. But after looking at your sister and brother-in-law's photograph, I can see the resemblance to Gloria is superficial at best. Justin bears an unmistakable likeness to both his parents."

Cassie nodded in agreement. She wanted to ask him more questions about his wife, but Nattie's entry with Jason and the baby food prevented her. Jason now sported a bib, which he was trying to pull off.

While Trace relieved her of his son and slipped him into the high chair, Nattie put the food on the table. "Here's a bib for my golden boy." She tied it around Justin's neck. "Now all of you have a good lunch. I'll hold any phone calls to give you a chance to talk."

Trace didn't let Nattie escape until he had pressed her hand in a gesture that spoke volumes about their relationship. Justin was surrounded by people who loved him, and that knowledge brought the first modicum of peace to Cassie's heart.

For the next while Cassie told Trace about Ted's fatal car accident en route to summer camp with the army reserve and Susan's subsequent depression, which led to one of her chronic bouts of pneumonia after a troubled pregnancy. Without Ted, she couldn't seem to endure.

Justin behaved perfectly while they talked. Half the time he managed the spoon by himself without making any mess. Cassie wished she could say the same for Jason. Though he loved the lamb, every time Trace gave him a spoonful of beans he'd keep them in his mouth for a minute, then let them fall back out. And worse, he smeared the top of his high chair so it resembled a finger painting.

Trace surprised her by being highly amused rather than irritated. She could hardly equate this patient caring man with the forbidding bank official who would have sent her from his office in handcuffs without a qualm.

Halfway through his peaches, Justin showed signs

of being tired and his eyelids drooped. Jason was exhausted, as well. Unfortunately he tended to become even more restless and noisy before falling asleep.

She looked over at Trace who was chuckling at the funny sounds Jason made as he practically inhaled his fruit. "May I put Justin to bed?" she asked.

Trace flicked her a searching glance, then gently tousled Justin's hair. "Has too much excitement made my little guy sleepy? Why don't we take both of them upstairs? While you deal with Justin, I'll put Jason in the tub."

Cassie tried to smother a smile but failed. "I wish I could tell you Jason isn't usually this impossible at meals, but it wouldn't be the truth."

His lips twitched. "I'm afraid when my mother finds out about this, she'll tell you I was much worse. Like father, like son."

Carefully lifting Justin, she rose to her feet. "Does your mother live here in Phoenix?"

"Not only Mother but the entire Ramsey clan."

"You're a large family, then?"

"I have two brothers and a sister, all of whom are older with children," he informed her as she followed him to a hallway on the other side of the patio.

By now Jason's bib had been removed and Trace held his food-smeared son firmly around the waist. "Ma-ma, Ma-ma," Jason cried when he realized he was being swept away from their cozy domestic scene by this dynamic stranger.

"Da-da's got you, Tiger," Trace said, mimicking his son. Cassie's heart leapt in her chest. No man had ever had this physical effect on her, not even Rolfe. She'd loved him from childhood; he was the man she'd planned her future around. But the grief Cassie had suffered over her mother's death, followed by Ted's fatal accident and Susan's illness, had taken its toll. She wasn't ready to set a wedding date. Rolfe, hurt and disillusioned, had accused her of not being in love with him and had broken their engagement. The next thing she knew, he had gone abroad to study music. He was a gifted musician who'd been offered more than one prestigious scholarship.

Before Susan died, she'd said that a separation was exactly what Cassie and Rolfe needed. They'd never spent more than a week or two away from each other, and a year's separation would clarify their feelings. When they came together again, there'd be no hesitation on either side if a marriage between the two of them was meant to be.

Susan's remarks made a lot of sense to Cassie. But she hadn't considered the possibility that Rolfe would fall in love with someone else in the interim, nor that it would hurt so much. Now Susan was gone and Cassie would never again be able to confide in the sister who'd always been her best friend and confidante.

"Cassie?" Trace called over his shoulder with a puzzled expression on his face. "Are you all right?"

"Yes. Of course." She smiled. "I had to stop for a minute and look at all these watercolors. They're fabulous, just like the ones in your office."

"My sister, Lena, is one of the most talented artists I know, but she's so critical of her own work, she refuses to display any of her paintings in public."

"So you do it for her," Cassie murmured. She couldn't help but be touched by his loyalty to his sister. It was ironic, and somehow pleasing, that while she'd been reliving bittersweet memories of her own sister, she'd been gazing at *his* sister's work—a sister he obviously adored. There were many surprising and wonderful facets to Trace Ramsey's personality, as she was beginning to learn. "How many of Lena's paintings have you sold?"

"None," he said as they reached the second floor. "She made me promise. In fact, she hasn't signed them. But if she ever changes her mind, my walls will be bare."

Cassie could believe it. In fact, there were several paintings here that gave her ideas for wall hangings and rugs, but they were fleeting images and she couldn't do anything about them now.

Justin's suite of rooms had the Southwest flavor of the rest of the house, but concessions had been made to practicality, creating a more traditional child's decor. Chocolate-brown shag carpeting covered the floors, and baby furniture filled the spacious room. A huge hand-painted mural took up one whole wall.

It was an enchanted-forest scene, with each little animal and insect possessing a distinct personality. Cassie was completely charmed by it and easily recognized the artist's hand. "Your sister painted this."

"Yes. That was Lena's gift to Justin," he called out from the bathroom. The minute the water started filling the tub, she could hear Jason's protests turn to squeals of delight. He always enjoyed his bath.

Cassie wondered if Justin liked the water, but she'd have to find out another time, because he was sound asleep, lying limp against her shoulder.

She gently placed him on his stomach in the crib

and covered him with the cotton blanket. Automatically his thumb went to his mouth. He looked so blissfully content she didn't have the heart to pull it out again and risk waking him.

After leaning over to bestow one last kiss, she headed for the immaculate white bathroom accented, like the downstairs rooms, in natural wood. It was difficult to tell who was having a better time, Jason or his father.

Trace's white shirt-sleeves were rolled up above the elbows to display tanned forearms with a sprinkling of dark hair. His smile made him look years younger as he urged Jason to float on his back and kick his sturdy little legs. "That's it, Tiger. Make a big splash."

When water hit him in the face, he burst into deep-throated laughter. He sounded so happy that Cassie hated to disturb them. However, Jason had already caught sight of her standing there holding a fluffy tangerine-colored towel. He immediately tried to sit up, plaintively crying, "Ma-ma," and stretching out his arms.

"I'm afraid we've got to get going," she said apologetically to Trace who looked distinctly disappointed by the interruption. With undisguised re- luctance, he wrapped Jason in the towel and started to dry him. "My luggage is being held at a motel in West Phoenix," Cassie went on. "We'll have to stop there on our way to the airport."

Trace frowned and she knew why. But he didn't understand what it was like to live on a budget. Even when her mother was alive and Susan was at home, they had all worked hard to make ends meet. And now that a future with Rolfe had slipped away, and with little Jason to support, she had to be more careful than ever how she spent her money.

In the short year and a half Susan and Ted had been married, they had acquired some insurance and savings. But before her sister's death, Cassie and Susan had agreed that any money would be invested for Jason's education. Cassie wouldn't have dreamed of touching it.

When she started to gather up Jason's soiled outfit, Trace told her to leave it for Nattie to wash. "He can wear something of his brother's for the flight back, can't you, Tiger?"

After diapering him on the bathroom counter, he reached into the drawer for a pale green stretchy suit with feet and put Jason into it. Then he playfully lowered his head to Jason's tummy and made a noise against it, producing a gale of infectious laughter from his dark-haired son.

In a very short time, Jason seemed to have overcome his fear of Trace. Much more of his father's attention and he wouldn't want to leave, a thought that troubled Cassie more than a little. This was his first experience with a man and he appeared to be enjoying it.

Cassie couldn't help wondering if her letter telling Rolfe about her plan to raise Jason as her own son had something to do with his recent engagement. His fiancée was another violinist, a woman he'd met in Brussels. Cassie was tempted to phone him long-distance, despite the cost; that way, they could really talk. Maybe expecting him to take on Jason if he married her was asking too much.

Then again, maybe he was truly in love with this other woman. Cassie was so confused she didn't know what to think. They'd been childhood sweethearts and had turned to each other whenever problems arose. She'd never stopped loving him and didn't think he'd stopped loving her, either.

Peeking in on Justin one more time, Cassie had to resist the impulse to kiss him, for fear of waking him. He looked like Susan while he slept, a fair-haired angel with flushed pink cheeks. Once again she felt that tug of emotion and hoped, somehow, that Justin's parents knew their little son was happy and well in Trace's home and heart.

In no time at all, Cassie had thanked Nattie and was following Trace outside to the BMW. Without giving her a choice, he ensconced her in the front seat. As he strapped his son in the back, she could tell he had some serious concern on his mind.

Once again he wore that look of determination. It made her uncomfortable, and she wished Jason was fussing so she'd have a reason to hold him in her arms as a buffer against Trace. But Jason's eyelids were fluttering, which meant he was ready to fall asleep any second.

When they had driven away from the house and were headed for the motel, Trace darted her a swift glance. "I want Jason close to me, Cassie," he said, using her name for the first time. "I've already missed his first nine months, and I refuse to lose out on any more time. I can tell you want to be with Justin just as badly. Let's be honest and admit the odd weekend here, the three-day holiday there, will never be enough for either of us."

Cassie had been thinking hard about that, too. Already the wrench of having to leave Justin hurt unbearably. But how soon would she be able to break away from her work to fly here again? With Christmas only three weeks away, this was her busiest time.

The money made from holiday sales would support her and Jason for at least five or six months. She didn't dare lose out on her most lucrative time of year. And her other job, playing piano for ballet classes four mornings a week, made it impossible to get away for more than a couple of days at a time.

"I agree with you, Trace, but I don't have any solutions, because I'm swamped with work and I know you are, too. I was going to suggest we trade the children from time to time."

The angry sound that came out of him made her shiver and immediately told her she'd said the wrong thing.

"Out of the question. As far as I'm concerned, six months with one parent, then six with the other is no alternative."

"I don't see that we have a choice."

"There's always a choice," he muttered in what she imagined was his banker's voice. "You could move to Phoenix with Jason."

She jerked her head around and stared at him in astonishment. "That would be impossible. I may not own a banking corporation, but my business is just as important to me. It relies on a clientele that's been built up over two generations of sewing for people. My mother taught Susan and me the business. Now I've branched into handicrafts. I wouldn't even know where to start if I had to relocate to a different city."

At this point they arrived at the motel. Without responding to her remarks, he got out of the car and went into the office to get her luggage. Within minutes he'd stashed it into the trunk and was back in the driver's seat. Before starting the car, he pulled a little black book from his pocket and asked for her address and phone number in San Francisco. Grudgingly she gave him the information; then they drove in painful silence to the airport, where he found a vacant space in the short-term parking lot.

He didn't immediately get out of the car. Instead he turned to her with a dangerous glint in his eye. "I'm warning you now that if we can't work this out, I'll take you to court and sue for custody of Jason."

"You don't mean that!" she burst out angrily, but the grim set of his jaw told her he did. Her heart was pounding so fiercely she was sure he could hear it.

"I'm his natural father and I'll be able to provide for his financial well-being in a way you never could. There isn't a judge in the state who would allow you to keep him. Bear in mind that the hospital will be called in to prove paternity and it could get messy."

"You told me you didn't approve of people who sued other people," she said, her voice shaking in fear and fury.

His eyes narrowed menacingly. "If you recall, I said, 'in principle.' But we're talking about Jason here, and what's best for him. You've already told me you're not married or even engaged." *But only because she'd put off Rolfe one too many times. Maybe it still wasn't too late.* "In fact," he continued, "I gathered from our conversation at lunch that you're not even dating anyone special who could help you raise him. You've only taken care of him for two months. You're not his parent. You're not even related.''

"Now you listen to me!" Cassie whispered hoarsely, trying not to wake Jason by shouting. "I love that child with every fiber of my being. You're not related to Justin, either!''

"Justin's been my son since birth, and no judge will take him away from me. As his aunt, the most you can expect will be liberal visitation rights and a bill for exorbitant court costs and attorney's fees. Think about it, and give me your answer tomorrow night. I'll phone you at ten.''

"Give you *what* answer?" she lashed out. "Do you know what you're asking? That I leave my whole life behind and move to a strange city with no friends, no support system, just so you can have your cake and eat it, too?''

"Naturally I'll provide for you and make sure you're comfortably settled until you can get your business going here. With my contacts, you would have no problem. Would that be such a penance when it means we would both have daily contact with the boys for the rest of our lives?''

Cassie didn't want to hear another word. "Aside from the fact that the idea is ludicrous, has it occurred to you what people would say? People who don't know the true situation? I noticed you didn't bother to explain anything to Mrs. Blakesley. She probably thinks I'm one of your mistresses who suddenly showed up to ask for money.''

"I'm not particularly worried about what Mrs. Blakesley thinks," he countered smoothly.

"Maybe you're not concerned about your reputation, but I value my good name more than that!"

"More than you value a life with Jason and Justin?" His question was calculated to reduce her arguments to the trivial. But by now she was on to his tactics.

"You can phone me all day and all night, but it won't do you any good. I guess I'll have to take my chances and let the judge decide when I can spend time with Jason and my nephew. See you in court!"

She didn't, couldn't, hide the disgust and anger in her eyes or her voice. Jumping from the car, she yanked the back door and reached for Jason, who was still sleeping soundly. Trace finally got out of the car to collect her bags from the trunk.

Unable to bear his presence another second, she walked toward the terminal with the baby in one arm, her tote bag in the other. Right now she wanted to put as many miles as possible between them. All the way back to San Francisco, she regretted her trip to Phoenix and wished she'd never heard of Trace Ramsey.

CHAPTER THREE

CASSIE TAPPED on her neighbor's door and let herself in. "Beulah? I'm back."

After climbing all those steep streets from the ballet studio in the bitter cold, the apartment felt toasty and inviting. San Francisco had been locked in fog since the night she'd flown in from Phoenix more than a week ago. It seemed to penetrate everything, including the ski sweater she wore over her sweatshirt.

"I'm in the studio," Beulah Timpson called out. The older woman had been like a favorite aunt to Cassie and Susan, and had come close to being Cassie's mother-in-law. For as long as Cassie could remember, Beulah, a talented ceramist, had lived with her three children in the apartment above the Arnolds'.

Cassie and Susan had been best friends with Beulah's two daughters and her son, Rolfe. It was in her late teens that the close friendship Cassie shared with him gradually changed into something else. When Susan's and Cassie's mother fell ill with cancer, Rolfe became a source of strength. Cassie turned to him more and more, and learned she could always depend on him to offer help and compassion.

Soon after her mother's death, he told her he loved her and wanted to marry her. Cassie happily accepted

his modest engagement ring; by that time they were
both seniors at the university, studying music theory.
He played the cello and she the piano.

Rolfe wanted to get married immediately after
graduation, but Cassie couldn't see any reason for urgency, since they were constantly together, anyway,
and had no money. She encouraged him to get his
master's degree in music while she worked on ex-
panding her home sewing business. A year down the
road as a Ph.D student, he'd be able to earn extra
money teaching undergraduates. By that time, she
would have saved enough money for a small wedding
and a honeymoon. They'd live in her apartment, since
Susan had already married and moved to Arizona.

Unlike Susan, who married Ted within eight weeks
of meeting him, Cassie wasn't in any hurry. She
needed time to regain her emotional equilibrium first.
The loss of their mother had been bad enough. But
when she received the horrifying news of Ted's un-
timely death, Cassie went into a severe depression. At
that point, her constant worry about her pregnant sister, whose history of chronic pneumonia put her at
risk, made it impossible for Cassie to think about her
own needs, or Rolfe's.

Then came a night when everything changed. For
the first time since she'd known him, Rolfe didn't
seem to understand. In fact, he refused to hear any
more excuses and demanded that she set a wedding
date—the sooner the better. Since they'd already been
over that ground more than once, Cassie was surprised by his demands. She'd never seen him so insistent and unyielding. She asked him to leave the

apartment, saying they'd talk again in the morning, when their nerves weren't so frayed.

But he stayed where he was. In a voice that shocked her with its anger, he accused her of using him. Cassie shook her head in denial, but he was obviously too hurt to listen to reason and asked for his ring back. When she begged him to be patient a little longer, the bitterness in his eyes revealed his hurt and disillusionment. He retorted that he hadn't pressured her to live with him because she didn't approve of premarital sex. And since she couldn't set a date for the wedding, he had to conclude she wasn't in love with him.

Cassie hadn't been prepared for that, nor for his declaration that he'd been offered a fellowship to study in Belgium and had decided to accept it. He held out his hand and Cassie wordlessly returned the ring.

He left at spring break, plunging her into a different kind of despair, one of profound loneliness. But by then Jason had been born and Susan was seriously ill. Looking back on that dreadful period, Cassie wondered how she'd survived at all. If Jason hadn't needed a mother's love and attention even before Susan died, Cassie might have died of grief herself. And still Rolfe stayed away.

Through it all, Beulah never pried or made judgments. As a result, the two of them were able to remain firm friends. Now that her children lived in other parts of the state, Beulah seemed to encourage Cassie's friendship, even volunteering to tend Jason in the mornings.

Walking through the apartment to the workroom,

Cassie found the older woman at her potter's wheel. She stopped short when she didn't see the playpen. "Where's Jason?"

Beulah was throwing clay and didn't pause in her movements. "He's downstairs in your apartment with his daddy."

"Beulah! You didn't!"

"I did." She concentrated on her work for a moment. "First of all, he's not here to kidnap Jason. He assured me of that and I believe him." Her voice was calm and matter-of-fact. She glanced up at Cassie, smiling. "The two of them are carbon copies of each other, just like you said. Since Jason seemed perfectly happy to go with him, I couldn't see that it would hurt. I never saw a man so crazy about a child in my life. Watching them together made my Christmas."

All the while she was talking, Cassie held on to the nearest counter for support. *She should have known he would come.* Hanging up on him every time he called had probably infuriated him. But she had none of the answers he wanted to hear.

After agonizing over the situation for endless hours, Cassie had decided a judge would have to sort it out. Though she ached to know and love Justin, it was clear that her nephew's world was complete and revolved around Trace. If she was patient, the law would eventually dictate visitation rights so she could get close to Susan's son.

As for Jason, she'd hang on to him as long as possible. There was no doubt in her mind that she'd lose him in the custody battle Trace was planning. In fact, he'd probably come to San Francisco to make sure she'd given him the right address before he had her served with papers. His presence meant she couldn't prolong the inevitable confrontation.

"Well? Aren't you going to go find the man and say hello? He flew all the way from Phoenix early this morning to see you. What are you afraid of?"

"I'm going to lose Jason."

"Nonsense. From everything you've told me about him, he isn't the kind of man who'd cut you out of Jason's life. Especially once he knows the personal sacrifice you went through trying to find him in the first place. Cassandra Arnold, it's because of you that he's been united with a son he didn't know existed. Do you think he's going to forget a thing like that? Or the fact that Justin is Susan's child?"

"You weren't there when he threatened me with a custody suit." She shuddered at the memory.

"No, I wasn't. But that was a week ago, and he's had time to think since then. So have you. The least you can do is hear what he has to say. You owe him that much after refusing to take his phone calls."

Since there was no help from that quarter, the only thing left to do was go downstairs and see him, get it over with.

A feeling of dread formed a knot in her stomach as she thanked Beulah and headed for the ground-floor apartment, which was the only home she'd ever known.

After their mother's death, Cassie and Susan had taken over her business and pooled all their resources so they could continue to live there. When Susan and Ted moved to Arizona because of his job, Cassie stayed in the apartment. Although half the contents went off to Phoenix in the moving van, the place was still crowded to overflowing with furniture and mementos accrued over a lifetime. Cassie took the opportunity to clean house and quickly turned her home into a crafts shop of sorts. Right now, it was filled with Christmas orders—quilts, afghans, wall hangings, pillows, rag dolls, hand puppets, stuffed animals... The list went on and on.

Every nook and cranny of the small living and dining room contained evidence of her handiwork. Trace wouldn't be able to find a place to sit down. Even the top of the upright piano and bench were covered with stuffed Santas, reindeer and gingerbread men.

The two bedrooms were even worse. She kept her sewing machine and all the patterns and materials in her room, which hardly left enough space for her to crawl into bed at night.

Jason's room had become the depository for the larger stuffed animals and figures. They stood side by side, lined up against all four walls.

By Christmas Eve she should be able to find her furniture again. She'd had to put their two-foot Christmas tree with its homemade ornaments in the middle of the kitchen table. Jason loved the miniature lights and stared at them in fascination while he played with his food.

Taking a deep breath, Cassie entered the kitchen through the back door. She could hear Jason's shrieks of delight coming from the vicinity of his room. He was obviously thrilled to have his father there, and Cassie had to admit that fatherhood seemed to come naturally to Trace. It was possible that he'd already been given a court date; in that case, it wouldn't be long before Jason went to live with him and Justin.

She felt a pain in her heart as real as if she'd been jabbed with a knife. Maybe it was best he had come, after all. She couldn't live with the anxiety any longer.

Pushing the bedroom door open a little wider, she peeked inside. Jason was sitting in front of Trace, who was dressed in cords and a crew-neck black sweater, lying full-length on the carpet with his back toward her. His dark head rested on the five-foot-long green alligator Cassie had made for Susan. She'd added yellow yarn, to represent Susan's blond hair, and sewn the word "mommy" on the tail.

In Trace's hand was the eighteen-inch baby alligator with a green-and-yellow body and black yarn for hair; it bore Jason's name on the tail. He continued to tease Jason, tickling him gently and making him laugh so hard he was thrashing his arms and legs.

Suddenly Jason saw Cassie. He pointed a finger and tried to say, "Ma-ma," but couldn't get the words out and laugh at the same time. Alert to his every movement, Trace turned over on his back, resting his hand on the alligator's head.

His blue eyes searched hers for a long breathless moment. At least they didn't freeze her out as they'd done at the airport. "Hello, Cassie." Slowly his gaze traveled from her sweater-clad figure to her windblown hair and cheeks turned pink from the cold outside. "Your neighbor let us in. She seemed to think it would be all right."

Strangely affected by the intimacy of his look, Cassie smoothed the curls from her forehead in a nervous gesture. "I'm sorry you couldn't find a place to sit."

A smile lurked at the corner of his mouth. "Since

Justin came into my life, I've discovered the floor is a wonderful place to be. You meet all kinds of fascinating creatures.'' He rubbed his thumb over the alligator's glassy eyes. ''Do you know I'm feeling deprived? There's no daddy alligator. I'm putting in an order for one right now. About six feet long with wild black hair and a scary grin, just like Jason's.''

It sounded very much as if he was extending the olive branch. How could he be talking this way when they had resolved nothing? She was still reeling from the bitterness of their last encounter.

''Come on, Jason. It's time for a nap.'' She stepped over Trace and scooped the baby up from the floor. Trace stayed where he was while she changed Jason's diaper and put him in his crib with a bottle. It was actually time for his lunch, but she'd feed him later, after his father had left.

Right now she needed to know what Trace had on his mind, and she didn't want Jason upset if the conversation turned into another angry battle. ''Let's go into the kitchen. Jason will settle down in a little while.''

By tacit agreement they left him crying. She knew he was wailing out his disappointment and fury; he'd been having such a wonderful time, and then she'd come along and spoiled everything. It didn't make Cassie feel any better. But this talk with Trace was crucial—and there was no sense in postponing it.

When they reached the kitchen, she offered him a seat and began to fix cocoa for both of them. Nobody was going to say she was uncivilized on the way to her execution!

Because of the fog, the room was darker than usual,

and the lights on the tree twinkled all the more cheerfully. Suddenly she felt too warm, with Trace so close and vital and alive. She pulled off her ski sweater and hung it over a chair back.

When she'd prepared the hot chocolate, she placed their mugs on the table and sat down opposite him. Briskly pushing the sleeves of her navy sweatshirt up to the elbows, she began, "I shouldn't have hung up on you—" she paused for a deep breath "—even though I was angrier than I've ever been in my life."

"I wasn't exactly on my best behavior last week," he admitted gravely. "Court isn't where I want to settle our problems."

Cassie had been expecting to hear anything but that. "I—I know how much you love Jason. He's your flesh and blood. The problem is I love him, too." Her voice had that awful quiver again. "And I love Justin because he's part of my flesh and blood."

"I know." He sounded totally sincere.

She raised tortured eyes to him. "No matter how I try to come up with a satisfying compromise, it sounds horrible becau—"

"Because that's precisely what it is. A compromise," he finished for her. "The only way I see out of our dilemma is to get married. That's why I'm here. To ask you to consider the idea seriously."

"*Married?*" She felt the blood drain from her face. In the interim that followed, Jason's cries sounded louder than ever.

Trace took a long swallow of cocoa. "Surely I don't have to point out the advantages to you. With everything legal, your reputation won't suffer, Justin and Jason will have a mother *and* a father, and we'll have the joy of raising the children together in our own home."

"But we don't love each other!"

He gazed steadily into her eyes. "Our marriage will be a business arrangement. Separate bedrooms. You'll be able to start up your crafts shop in Phoenix without the worry of having to meet the monthly bills. And I'll have the satisfaction of going to work every day knowing the boys are with the only person who could ever love them as much as I do."

Her hands tightened around the mug. "But you're still young, Trace. One day you'll meet someone you truly want to marry. Just because your first marriage didn't work out doesn't mean there isn't someone else in your future."

"That works both ways, Cassie," he said in a deceptively soft voice. "You're a very attractive woman. I'm surprised you didn't get married years ago." *Rolfe tried,* a niggling voice reminded Cassie. "But the fact remains, I've been married once in the full sense of the word and have no particular desire to repeat the experience. As far as I'm concerned, the only issue of importance here is the children. They need *us,* you and me. And they need us *now!* Some experts say that the first three years of a child's life form his character forever. If that's true, I would prefer if you and I were the ones guiding and shaping the boys' lives."

She couldn't sustain his penetrating glance and pushed herself away from the table. In two steps she'd reached the window, but even if the mist hadn't been so thick, she wouldn't have seen anything.

What Trace Ramsey had proposed was a marriage

in name only. A marriage of convenience, her mother would have called it. Cassie had heard the term, but she'd never known anyone who had entered into such an arrangement. It sounded so cold-blooded. No expectations of physical or romantic love. Just a convenient solution to a problem that concerned them both. The children needed parents, and she and Trace Ramsey could honorably fill that need and still stay emotionally uninvolved.

She heard the scrape of Trace's chair against the linoleum as he stood up and came to stand next to her. "I know what you're thinking, Cassie. You're considerably younger than I am, and you have a right to a life of your own. But as long as we're discreet, we could see other people on the side, no questions asked. If some time down the road either of us wanted out of our contract to marry someone else, well... we'd face that when it happened."

She gripped the edges of the sink so hard her knuckles turned white. "I think you're forgetting your ex-wife. Maybe she never bonded with Justin because, like Susan, she sensed he wasn't her baby. If she was to see Jason, isn't it possible she'd fall in love with him? I could certainly understand if she wanted another chance at marriage with you under those circumstances."

Cassie wheeled around so she could read his honest reaction, but that was a mistake. Her kitchen was minuscule even with no one in it; now, with Trace blocking her path and the faint scent of his soap filling her nostrils, she felt almost claustrophobic.

"I'm way ahead of you, Cassie," he replied evenly, his hands on his hips. "I phoned her the evening you left Phoenix, but she was still in chambers so I sent her an overnight letter.''

''And?'' She held her breath, unsure what she wanted Trace to tell her.

''She never responded.''

''Maybe she hasn't had time, or hasn't even seen the letter.''

''You're very generous to make excuses for her, but no.'' He shook his head. ''I talked with Sabie, her housekeeper. Gloria read the letter.''

''And she didn't want to see Jason immediately?'' Cassie cried, incredulous.

''I knew she wouldn't. But on the off chance that she'd gone through a complete character change, I told her to let me know and I would make it possible for her to spend time with Jason. Otherwise, if I didn't hear from her, I would assume it made no difference to her.''

''But Jason is her own baby!''

Something flickered in his eyes. ''Not all women have motherly feelings, Cassie. She never pretended to be anything but what she is, a remarkable attorney who is now a city-court judge and hopes to one day sit on the Supreme Court.''

Cassie couldn't comprehend it. Talk about opposites attracting! She might search the earth and not come up with a more caring, devoted father than Trace. ''Did you know she felt this way before you married her?'' she asked in a quiet voice.

''If I hadn't made her pregnant, we would never have married.''

She swallowed hard as she tried to take in what he was saying. ''Didn't you love her?''

"We cared for each other. We also understood each other. Marriage was never in our plans, and I knew she'd give up the baby for adoption. I found I couldn't let her do that, so I struck a bargain with her. We would stay married long enough to satisfy protocol, then divorce with the understanding that I received custody of the child."

She blinked. "How often does she visit Justin?"

"She doesn't. She never has."

"Not once?" Her eyes grew huge.

He reached out and smoothed a stray curl from her forehead. At his touch her body trembled. The same gesture from Rolfe had never affected her this way. "That's why her lack of response to my letter doesn't surprise me. Is there anything else I can clear up for you?"

Needing to put distance between them, she slid past him and gathered the mugs from the table. "What would your family think?"

His wry smile seemed to mock her. "Whatever we want them to think. We can tell them that the moment we met, it was love at first sight. Or we can say nothing and let them draw their own conclusions. I'm a big boy now. I don't need my family's approval for what I do."

Her mouth had gone so dry she could hardly swallow. "I don't like lies."

"Then we'll tell them the truth. That we've decided to get married to provide a home for Justin and Jason. Period."

When he put it like that, so bluntly, she didn't know what to say. "E-Excuse me a minute, I have to check on the baby."

To her surprise he shifted his position, preventing her from leaving the kitchen. "I have a better idea. I'll leave—to give you time to think over my proposal. I'm at the Fairmont. Call me there when you've made your decision."

Her heart started to hammer. "How long will you be in San Francisco?"

"As long as it takes to get an answer from you."

She averted her eyes. "If the answer's no, what will you do?"

The muscles of his face went taut. "You're going to say yes. The boys need you too much. In your heart, you know it's the only solution. What was it your sister said before she died—*Find my son and take care of him for me?* Now you can honor her request and be Jason's mother at the same time."

On that note he disappeared from the kitchen and out the front door of the apartment.

So many thoughts and emotions converged at once that Cassie couldn't stand still. As if on automatic pilot, she tiptoed to Jason's room and discovered him sound asleep in a corner of his crib, with his cheek lying on his bottle.

The poor darling had finally worn himself out. Gently she pulled the bottle away and covered him with a light blanket. She thought of seeing him only on holidays, of missing his first steps and not being able to take him to kindergarten on his first day of school....

If she married Trace, she would have the luxury of being a mother to Justin, as well. The four of them would be a real family, in almost all the ways that mattered. Many things about Trace still remained a mystery, but the one thing she knew beyond any doubt was his devotion to the boys.

Not every man would have married his lover to obtain custody of his unborn child. And a small voice told her not every man would have wanted Jason on sight—no matter that Jason was the son of his body, no matter how precious he was. In that regard Trace Ramsey was a remarkable man.

Was it enough? Would it be enough for her? Could she marry him knowing the most important ingredient in the marriage was missing? Knowing that because of their loveless arrangement, she would never have a baby of her own?

Maybe Trace could conduct an affair on the side; in all probability he was seeing someone right now. But Cassie wasn't made that way and knew herself far too well. Perhaps her ideas were old-fashioned and out of date, but if she took marriage vows, she would hold them sacred until she died. Or until Trace asked her for a divorce....

Was that what worried her most? That one day he would fall deeply in love and want a real marriage with the woman who had captured his heart? The thought left Cassie feeling strangely out of sorts and depressed, which made no sense at all.

She'd wondered more and more about the things Rolfe had said to her the night he'd walked out. With hindsight, she could see how much she'd hurt him by putting him off. But during that long dark period, she hadn't been capable of making a decision, hadn't been ready to make a commitment. Instead of clinging to him as his wife, she'd left him hanging while she dealt with her grief.

And her refusal to go to bed with him had probably planted more seeds of doubt. But Cassie's mother had raised her girls to value their virginity, to reserve physical passion for their husbands. That was why Susan was so eager to get married. In fact, Susan's intense feelings for Ted were so different from Cassie's easygoing, comfortable relationship with Rolfe they weren't even in the same league.

Susan and Ted couldn't stay away from each other, couldn't keep their hands off each other. Cassie had never been able to relate to those feelings. She loved Rolfe and always would, but she could wait until their honeymoon to express her love.

If she married Trace, there would be no problems in that area because he wouldn't be making physical demands on her. He'd be seeing other women. She was sure he'd be the soul of discretion. The little she knew about Trace told her he'd go to great lengths to keep his private life private, so no gossip could hurt the boys. They meant everything to him.

So why was she hesitating? Was she hoping against hope that Rolfe would break his engagement and come back to San Francisco to take up where they'd left off? How had Rolfe been able to fall in love with another woman so fast? Was it because his fiancée was willing to sleep with him? Cassie tried not to think about him sharing intimacies with anyone else, because it hurt. And, she supposed, because it was humiliating.

If they *were* sleeping together, that meant Rolfe wasn't really missing Cassie. And if that was true, then he'd gotten over the pain of Cassie's rejection and was making plans for a future that didn't include her. But it hadn't been a rejection, only a plea for more time.

So where did that leave Cassie? She had no guarantee that a man would ever come along to love her, body and soul. At least if she married Trace, she'd be able to indulge her longing to be a mother. Otherwise she would remain on the fringes of Jason and Justin's lives, never really involved. She couldn't bear that.

For the rest of the day she kept busy playing with Jason and putting the finishing touches on an order for a pear tree with partridges. After six o'clock, the doorbell rang continuously with customers placing and picking up orders.

Not until she'd tucked Jason into bed and cleaned the kitchen did Cassie work up enough nerve to reach for the phone. It was almost eleven and she'd run out of reasons not to call. She'd made her decision.

Her heart pounded in her ears as she asked to be put through to Trace Ramsey's room, but after ten rings and no answer she hung up. Maybe he was out, or had gone to bed. Whatever the case, she'd have to wait until morning.

Perhaps it was just as well. If she awakened tomorrow still feeling she was doing the right thing, then she'd try to call him again.

Feeling oddly deflated despite her tension, she unplugged the Christmas-tree lights and took a long hot shower. She checked on Jason one final time, then hurried into her own bedroom, eager for sleep. As she turned down the covers, she thought she heard a knock at the door.

Beulah was the only person who ever bothered her

this late at night, and she always phoned first. Cassie had never had trouble before, but there could always be a first time. With the stealth of a cat she tiptoed to the living room and listened to see if she'd been mistaken.

After a minute she heard another rap. "Cassie?" a voice called out in hushed tones. "It's Trace. Are you still up? I didn't want to wake Jason if I could help it."

Trace?

A kind of sick excitement welled up inside her. She braced her hand against the door for support.

"Just a minute," she whispered and rushed to the bedroom for a robe. After opening the door she belatedly remembered that her hair was still damp from the shower. Her natural curls had tightened into a mop of ringlets that only a good brushing could tame.

He stared down at her, the hint of a smile lurking in his startling blue eyes. The moist night wind off the bay had tousled his hair, and he wore a fashionable bomber-style jacket made of a dark brown suede. Cassie had no idea he could look so...so...

"The answer's yes, isn't it?" he said matter-of-factly. "Otherwise you'd have called me hours ago and told me to go back to Phoenix and start court proceedings. Because one thing you're not, Cassie, is a coward."

CHAPTER FOUR

"MISS ARNOLD?" Nattie's voice carried to Justin's bedroom, which now contained a second bed for Jason.

Cassie turned as Trace's housekeeper entered the nursery. "Can't you and Mike bring yourselves to call me Cassie? I realize Trace only brought me and Jason to Phoenix twenty-four hours ago, but you and your husband have been so wonderful helping us to settle in, I feel like we're good friends already."

The older woman's eyes lit up. "If you're sure."

"I am. So, what is it?" She returned to the job of fastening an uncooperative Jason into his new outfit.

"Trace asked me to take over in here so you can finish getting dressed. He's one man who likes to be on time—particularly for his own wedding. I'll finish doing those buttons and take Jason downstairs to Justin and his daddy."

"I appreciate the offer, but he's dressed now," Cassie murmured as she slipped on his little white shoes and tied them with a double knot so he wouldn't kick them off. She gave him a kiss on the cheek and handed him to Nattie, who promptly carried him out of the room.

Cassie followed her more slowly and then headed to her own room. There were three guest bedrooms

on the upstairs floor of the house, with the nursery at
one end and Trace's private suite of rooms at the
other. Since he'd told Cassie to choose a bedroom for
herself, she'd picked the one closest to the children.
That way she'd be able to hear them if they cried
during the night.

Though the smallest of the three, her room had its
own ensuite bathroom, and the wicker furniture plus
the charming window seat created a cozy feeling that
immediately made her feel at home. She'd already
spent several hours gazing out over the fascinating
desert landscape, with the mountains in the distance.

Off-white walls and soft yellow trim blended beautifully to give the room a timeless dreamy feeling.
Large green plants stood grouped in one corner; they
were reflected in the sheen of flawless hardwood
floors stained a warm honey tone.

Cassie couldn't wait to design an area rug that
would incorporate the room's colors in all their sub-
tlety. But her thoughts were far removed from that
particular project as she finished dressing for her wedding.

If the image in the mirror didn't lie, she *looked* like
a bride. She wore the trappings of a bride—large,
marquise-shaped emerald ring on the third finger of
her left hand, matching emeralds on her ears, which
were a wedding present from Trace, a cascade of orange blossoms on the shoulder of her simple white
Thai silk dress with its scooped neck.

Five weeks ago she'd been living with Jason in San
Francisco, heartbroken over her sister's death and
Rolfe's engagement, working furiously at two jobs in

order to build a business that kept her busy all hours of the day and night.

Right now, that Cassie seemed a different person. Trace had pampered her so thoroughly she hardly recognized herself anymore. Once she'd agreed to marry him, he had taken time off from his banking affairs to stay in San Francisco both before and after Christmas. He'd helped her with Jason and made all the preparations for the marriage and her move to Phoenix. Meanwhile she'd wound up her business and called her old friends with the news—friends she'd hardly seen in the past three years. Her responsibilities had made a social life impossible.

Not since Rolfe's tenderness at the time of her mother's death had she experienced anything approaching this extraordinary feeling of being looked after, taken care of. In fact, Beulah—who to Cassie's surprise approved of their forthcoming marriage—commented that all Cassie had to do was mention something and Trace had it done before she turned around.

When Cassie asked if they could be married before she met his family, with only the babies and Nattie and Mike for witnesses, Trace agreed to her wishes and arranged a private ceremony at the county clerk's office.

In certain ways, Trace was the equivalent of a fairy godfather, and even if their marriage wasn't a normal one, she knew she was a very lucky woman. She told herself not to dwell on the past or reminisce about what might have been. But it was impossible to forget that for most of her life she had imagined walking down the aisle with Rolfe.

Without conscious thought she pulled his framed picture from a box of mementos she hadn't yet put away. She sank down on the bed to study his lean, ascetic face one more time. She couldn't help wondering what he'd thought when he received her letter. She'd informed Rolfe that she was planning to be married after Christmas. She'd told him the truth— that she'd accepted Trace's proposal in order to be a legitimate mother to both boys. She also admitted that she still loved him, that she would always love him and hoped he'd forgive her for ever hurting him.

When there was no return letter from Belgium, Cassie had to accept the fact that he was truly lost to her, but it still hurt. "Oh, Rolfe..." She wept quietly for the many memories and the dream that was gone.

"*Cassie?* Are you ready yet?"

At the sound of footsteps she panicked and thrust the picture beneath one of the pillows on her bed. But she was too late. Trace had seen the betraying gesture and in a few swift strides crossed the room and reached for the frame.

After studying the photo for several seconds, he raised his head and stared at the moisture beading her eyelashes. "I've seen this man's picture before. In Beulah Timpson's place."

His face hardened and a dull red tinged his smooth-shaven cheek and jaw. She was immediately reminded of the implacable man she'd originally met, the one who had accused her of being part of a kidnapping scheme. "What's going on, Cassie? When I brought you here to see Justin that first day, you told me you were unattached. I assumed you were telling the truth." His voice barely concealed his anger.

Cassie slid off the bed, furious with herself for having inadvertently caused this friction when he'd gone out of his way to make everything so wonderful. From the beginning Trace had been completely honest with her; he deserved the same consideration.

"I grew up with Rolfe," she began in a low voice. "We were once engaged, but things didn't work out. He asked for his ring back, and now he's engaged to someone else, someone he met in Europe. I was saying goodbye to past memories. That's all." She gazed straight at him as she spoke.

Trace searched her eyes, as if looking for some little piece of truth she might have withheld. "The ceremony takes place at eleven. We still have forty-five minutes. It's not too late to back out."

"*No!*" she cried instantly, surprising even herself with her vehemence.

He pondered her outburst for an uncomfortably long moment. "Be very sure, Cassie—and not just for the boys' sake."

For some reason his comment sent her pulses racing. "I am," she answered without hesitation, realizing she meant it.

He squared his shoulders and the tautness of his facial muscles seemed to relax. He tossed the picture onto a stack of photos piled in a cardboard box beside her bed. "Let's go, shall we?"

The next hour flew by as Mike took pictures of Cassie and Trace holding the children, both before and after they arrived at the courthouse. Justin fussed because he'd come down with a cold. When the justice of the peace appeared and announced that it was time, Justin didn't want to let go of Trace, and that started Jason crying, too. Poor Nattie and Mike had to hold the children and try to pacify them while Trace grasped Cassie's hand and led her to the center of the room.

Despite the noise and impersonal surroundings, Cassie felt the solemnity of the occasion and wished more than ever that her mother and Susan were alive to share this moment with her. They would have loved Trace on sight. Not even Beulah was immune.

Out of the corner of her eye she darted a glance at her husband-to-be, who stood erect and confident. His snowy white shirt and midnight-blue suit not only enhanced his attractiveness but underlined his power; the red carnation he wore in his lapel added a note of festivity and joy. *I'm actually marrying this man,* she mused in awe and felt her heart turn over.

The justice of the peace bestowed a warm smile on them. "Cassandra Arnold and Trace Ellingsworth Ramsey, after this ceremony, today will be the first day of your life as a married couple. You've come together in the sight of God and these witnesses to pledge your troth. Do you know what that means?" He eyed them soberly, capturing Cassie's whole attention.

"It means commitment and sacrifice. It means enduring to the end, long after the fires of passion are tempered with the earning of your daily bread. It means forgetting self and living to make the other person happy, no matter the season or circumstances. Will you do that, Cassandra? In front of these two witnesses, do you take this man, of your own free will, to be your lawfully wedded husband?"

Cassie felt Trace's heavy-lidded gaze upon her. "Yes."

"And you, Trace? Of your own free will and in front of these two witnesses, are you willing to take Cassandra to be your lawfully wedded wife, to assume this solemn responsibility of caring for her all the days of your life? Are you willing to put her before all others, emotionally, mentally and physically?"

Cassie thought his hand tightened around hers. "Yes," came the grave reply.

"If you have rings to exchange, now is the time. You first, Cassandra."

Cassie had been wearing the simple gold band she'd bought for Trace on her middle finger so she wouldn't lose it. She quickly removed it and slid it on Trace's ring finger. The fit was perfect, and he gave her a private smile that unaccountably stirred her senses.

"Now you, Trace."

Cassie held out her left hand so Trace could nestle the white-gold wedding band next to the beautiful emerald engagement ring he'd given her on the plane as they'd flown to Phoenix. His movements were sure and steady.

"That's fine." The officiant smiled once more. "Now, by the power invested in me by the state of Arizona, I pronounce you husband and wife. It's not part of the official ceremony to kiss the bride, but…"

Before the man had even finished speaking, Trace's head descended and his mouth swiftly covered Cassie's as he pulled her close, sending a voluptuous warmth through her body. Cassie hadn't expected

more than a chaste kiss on the lips. She wasn't prepared for the heady sensation that left her clinging to
the lapels of his suit.

"Ma-Ma! Ma-ma!" Jason's and Justin's cries
slowly penetrated her consciousness. Cassie moaned
in shock and embarrassment, and broke the kiss Trace
seemed reluctant to end. In that split second before
she turned her burning face away, she thought she
saw a smoldering look in his eyes. But by the time
he lifted his head, it was gone. She decided she'd
imagined it.

Moving out of her husband's arms, she shook the
official's outstretched hand and thanked him, then
hurried over to Nattie. Still holding Jason, the older
woman gave her an awkward hug and murmured her
congratulations. She handed the uncontrollable child
to Cassie with a wry smile of relief.

He calmed down at once and started pulling orange
blossoms out of her corsage. Trace was equally busy
trying to pacify Justin, while Mike continued to take
pictures. Cassie took one look at the flush on Justin's
fair skin and said, "Trace, I think we'd better leave
for the hotel. Justin should be in bed. He needs something to bring down his fever."

Within a few minutes the children were strapped
into their seats in the back of Trace's sedan. Cassie
hugged Mike and Nattie and thanked them again for
everything, then at Trace's urging got into the car and
they drove off.

The resort hotel, a few miles away in Scottsdale,
had sent a basket of fruit and a congratulatory bottle
of champagne to their suite. There were also two
cribs; amused, Cassie wondered what the manage-

ment thought about that as she busied herself putting the boys to bed, while Trace dealt with all the baby bags and luggage.

The hotel offered baby-sitting services, but Cassie didn't feel comfortable about leaving Jason and Justin with a stranger just yet. She urged Trace to go for a swim in the pool and relax. But he insisted on staying to help her settle the children, after he'd ordered lunch to be served in the room where he'd put his bags.

By the time both boys had fallen into an uneasy— and, as it turned out, short-lived—sleep, their lunch was more or less ruined. The pasta with its cream sauce had grown cold, the salad was soggy, the chilled white wine room-temperature. Cassie was too tired and anxious to care. All her attention was focused not on her new husband but on the two miserable little boys. Trace seemed equally distracted.

What should have been a fun three-day holiday, a chance for the four of them to really get to know each other, lasted exactly one sleepless night. Justin couldn't keep anything in his stomach; he was content only when Cassie or Trace held him. And as soon as Jason saw that Cassie's attention was diverted from him, he wailed loudly, and not even Trace could settle him down for long.

At eight the next morning, they packed up the car and drove home, frustrated and completely exhausted. It had become apparent that they would have to take Justin to his pediatrician as soon as they got home; in fact, Trace had called ahead from the hotel. Leaving Jason with Nattie, the three of them went to the clinic. Cassie was anxious to meet the man who'd been taking care of Justin, because he would automatically become Jason's doctor, as well.

Although Justin didn't have anything seriously wrong, several days went by before he was restored to his normal sweet disposition. Several weary, emotionally draining days, especially for Cassie. She'd spent all her time with the children since Trace had returned to his office to deal with some very delicate negotiations in his planned buy-out of a small Southwest banking chain.

Then, on Friday morning Trace shocked her by announcing that he'd invited everyone in his family to an informal garden party that evening to meet his new wife and son. Understandably enough, they were consumed with curiosity about his unexpected marriage. Gathering all the relatives under one roof, he told Cassie, would provide the perfect opportunity to reveal the switch and to explain their subsequent decision to marry for the boys' sake.

Intellectually, Cassie saw the wisdom in getting it over with as soon as possible. Emotionally, she was numb.

Alone with Trace and the boys, she could relax as she performed the normal duties of a busy mother without worrying about others' reactions to their platonic union. Tonight, however, she would be on trial in front of a roomful of Trace's relatives—people who would draw their own conclusions about her motives for marrying a man who wasn't in love with her.

She couldn't blame them if they believed her to be a mercenary person attracted to his money and social prominence, someone willing to be bought in exchange for mothering his sons.

None of them would understand her bond with Jason or the happiness it brought her to raise him as her own son. Only Trace knew.

Cassie dressed in the same outfit she'd worn to her wedding and put on a fresh spray of orange blossoms Trace had thoughtfully sent her. Needing her husband's support as never before, she took a deep calming breath as she prepared to meet his family. She clutched Jason in her arms, hugging him tight, then mustered her courage and walked slowly downstairs.

From the landing she searched for Trace's dark hair among the group assembled on the patio. But she soon realized black hair dominated the family scene; there was only a sprinkling of sandy-brown and russet hair. She gazed down at the group, panicking just a little as she realized that the adults and children chatting with one another numbered at least forty.

Justin sat contentedly on his grandmother's lap, examining her pearl necklace—real pearls, Cassie was sure. His hair gleamed a pale gold in contrast to her coal-black tresses, swept back in an elegant chignon. His complexion was pale against her darker skin. Somewhere in her ancestry there must have been Indian blood. Even at seventy, Trace's mother was the most beautiful woman Cassie had ever seen. In fact, the whole family had more than its fair share of tall, good-looking people.

There was a sudden hush as Cassie walked out on the patio. Rolfe had often called her his "pocket Venus." And right now she was more aware than ever of her full curves and diminutive height. She felt even more conspicuous being the only person, aside from Justin, with a head of golden blond curls.

To her relief, Trace broke off his conversation with a man she guessed to be one of his brothers and strode toward her. In a light tan suit with an off-white Italian silk shirt open at the neck, he looked so incredibly handsome Cassie purposely glanced elsewhere to prevent herself from staring.

She thought he would reach for Jason. Instead, he slid a possessive arm around her waist and held her tightly against him. In confusion she gazed up at him, only to discover his eyes wandering over her face with unmistakable admiration.

At breakfast he had told her she would have nothing to worry about at the party. All she had to do was behave naturally and follow his lead. The trouble was, his act was too convincing, and she was distressed to find herself wondering how it would feel to be truly loved by this man. This complex man who presented a formidable, dynamic front to the public, yet could reduce her to tears with his sweetness when he kissed his sons good-night.

He turned to his family. "I know it came as a shock to hear that Cassie and I were married over the weekend. But what was I to do? My charming bride burst into my office a couple of months ago with an astonishing story—that Justin was really her nephew and that this little tiger was my natural son."

He reached for Jason, who'd been trying to wriggle out of Cassie's arms to get to his father. "It seems the babies were switched at birth." He paused dramatically at the incredulous murmurs around him. "We have subsequently found out that because of a disaster that stretched hospital resources to the limit, the infant intensive-care unit ran out of wrist tape.

One of the nurses sent an orderly for more. When he returned, the identification bracelets were inadvertently put on the wrong babies.''

The family's stunned reaction proved to be even greater than Cassie had imagined. For five minutes pandemonium reigned. It took another five before everybody settled down enough so that Trace could continue with the details. He briefly described the background—Ted's accidental death and Susan's unsuccessful struggle to throw off pneumonia, Susan's belief that Jason wasn't her son and Cassie's taking on the responsibility not only of raising her nephew but of uncovering the truth.

He kissed the top of Jason's curly head and unexpectedly smoothed a wayward lock of hair from Cassie's brow. Then, with a smile lighting his eyes, he said, ''To make a long story short, the four of us got along so famously, we didn't want the fun to stop. So we decided to become a family.'' The sudden tremor in his voice added the perfect touch, almost convincing Cassie it wasn't an act. ''Cassie, please meet my mother, Olivia Ramsey.''

He turned to face the older woman. ''Mother, may I present my wife, Cassandra Arnold Ramsey, and my son, Jason?''

''Trace!'' Her cry held the joy Cassie had hoped to hear, dispelling her anxiety that Trace's mother wouldn't accept her new grandson—or her daughter-in-law.

While one of the wives relieved the older woman of Justin, Trace helped her to her feet. Dressed in deep-rose silk, she walked toward Cassie with the dignity of a queen.

"Welcome to the family, darling." She embraced Cassie warmly, then stood back, holding her lightly by the upper arms. Her deep-set, clear gray eyes searched Cassie's as if she were gazing into her very soul.

"I can't tell you how happy, how thrilled, I am by this news. Trace is my baby and he's always been my greatest worry. To see him settled at last, with a beautiful wife and two lovely children, has given me a whole new lease on life."

"Thank you, Mrs. Ramsey." Cassie could hardly form the words after the older woman's loving reception. That Trace's mother adored her youngest son was obvious. Cassie felt a sudden surge of guilt; she hated deceiving anyone, particularly this welcoming and truly gracious woman.

"Cassie, please feel free to call me Olivia, like my other daughters-in-law. 'Mrs. Ramsey' is so formal, isn't it?"

Cassie nodded, not trusting herself to speak as she blinked back tears.

"Mother?" Trace gently interrupted. "How about saying hello to my son. Jason?" He turned the baby around. "This is Nana. Na-na."

"Oh, Trace!" she cried, reaching for Jason, who showed all the signs of bursting into tears at the sight of so many strangers. "I can't believe I'm not thirty-three years old and holding you in my arms again. He's identical to you. Look, everybody! Another heartbreaker!"

Heartbreaker is right, Cassie thought, allowing herself a covert glance at her husband. He had probably been attracting the attention of the opposite sex since he'd been old enough to crawl!

But before she could dwell on that curiously disheartening fact, she and the baby were suddenly besieged with hugs and kisses. Such spontaneous warmth and affection made Cassie feel worse than ever about the pretense. All the cheerful joking from James and Norman, who'd introduced themselves as Trace's brothers, told her the family assumed Trace was in love. And everything he said and did tended to verify their assumptions.

But the excitement proved to be too much for the babies. Once Jason started crying, Justin quickly followed suit. Cassie extricated herself from a group of nieces who were fighting over who got to hold Jason and hurried to retrieve Justin, who was clearly unhappy being tended by one of his aunts.

The second he saw Cassie his tears stopped and a smile appeared. It was clear that during his brief illness, a bonding had taken place between them. He reached eagerly for her and wrapped his arms around her neck. Together they wandered over to the banquet table the caterers had laden with everything from luscious fresh pineapple slices to salads and salvers of prime rib. Catering staff brought flutes of champagne and glasses of sparkling juice for the children.

As she handed Justin a piece of banana, Cassie caught sight of a group of latecomers walking out on the patio. She saw Trace, still carrying Jason, break away from the others and move toward a slender, auburn-haired woman.

Lena. Cassie could tell by the tender expression on her husband's face that he had a soft spot for his only sister. From what he had told Cassie, Lena resembled their father, Grant Ramsey, who had died of a stroke a few years earlier, leaving his children to carry on and expand the family business.

From the distance, Cassie watched in fascination as Trace bent his head and filled Lena in on the details. Eventually Lena held out her arms to Jason, who refused to go anywhere and clung to his father. While everyone chuckled, Trace looked around until he spotted Cassie with Justin, then pointed her out to his sister. Lena left the group and hurried toward them.

Her hair had been drawn into a braid and hung over one shoulder. In comparison to Cassie's curves, Lena's build was thin and wiry. Except for the same proud chin, Cassie saw very little of Trace in his sister, whose pert nose and dark gray eyes made her face gamin rather than beautiful.

She leaned over to give Justin a kiss on the cheek, but he began to cry and tightened his hold on Cassie. Lena shrugged good-naturedly, then turned her attention to Cassie, eyeing her the way she might size up a scene she wanted to paint. "I'm Lena Haroldson, Trace's sister, and I have to tell you I'm speechless at the news. You have to be the reason Trace looks ten years younger tonight. If you can keep him this happy, I'll love you forever." She smiled warmly, then added, "Welcome to the family, Cassie."

Though the words were meant to be complimentary, Cassie's heart plummeted to her feet. It was obvious that Lena adored Trace and guarded his happiness jealously. And it was equally obvious that she was the one Ramsey Cassie would never be able to fool.

"Thank you, Lena. I—I'm going to try to make our home a happy one." At least that was the truth.

A mischievous smile lifted the corner of Lena's mouth. "I'd say uniting Trace with Jason is a giant step in the right direction. I want to hear all about it from start to finish, but tonight's not the right time. I suspect Justin needs to go to bed. How about lunch next week when you're settled in? I'll take you to my favorite restaurant."

"I'd love it." Lena would never know how much her friendliness meant to Cassie. "In fact, I've wanted to meet you ever since I first saw your watercolors in Trace's office. They're good—very good."

Lena shook her head, but by the way her eyes lighted up, Cassie could tell she was pleased. "Trace told you to say that, didn't he?"

"No," Cassie declared baldly. "He was too busy trying to haul me off to jail on a kidnapping-extortion charge."

"What?" Lena gasped. "That doesn't sound like Trace. I know he's got a tough reputation when it comes to business, but he wouldn't dare do such a thing to you!"

"I'm afraid I would and almost did," a deep voice interjected. "But in the nick of time this little fellow saved his mother from the long arm of the law, didn't you, Tiger?"

Surprised, both women turned to Trace who had approached them unnoticed. Apparently Jason had had enough partying for one night. His pale blue outfit was crumpled and stained with what looked like fresh strawberry. In spite of Cassie's precautions in double-tying his shoes, he had managed to kick one off, which Trace held in his free hand.

"Mama!" Always vigorous, Jason practically propelled himself out of his father's arms to reach Cassie. If it hadn't been for Trace's lightning reflexes, he would have landed on the floor. By now, Justin was being just as impossible and refused to allow Trace to hold him.

"Well, well, little brother." Lena grinned at Trace. "It looks like you've got competition."

Trace sent Cassie an enigmatic look that for some reason gave her an uneasy feeling. "I don't mind, Lena," he muttered. "Now if you'll excuse us, we'll put the children to bed. Be a sweetheart and hold down the fort till we come back." He bussed his sister's cheek, then slid one arm along Cassie's shoulders.

As they made their way inside, everyone crowded around to say good-night to the boys. Cassie smiled and laughed, though it all felt a bit forced. Trace was making her unaccountably nervous.

"You didn't have to help me," Cassie murmured as they entered the nursery together. "Please feel free to go downstairs. It isn't very nice for both of us to disappear."

"You sound like you're trying to get rid of me," he said softly, but there was no amusement in his tone. "If I leave you on your own, you'll probably stay up here the rest of the night."

Perhaps he hadn't meant to sound critical, but his remark stung, increasing the tension she could feel building between them. She put a fresh diaper on Justin and eased him into his sleeper while Trace did the same for Jason. "Your family's wonderful. I wouldn't dream of offending them."

"Be that as it may, you seem to have no qualms about offending me." He paused, not looking at her. "Do me a favor. When we go back downstairs, pretend to like me a little bit."

His words produced a wave of heat that scorched her neck and cheeks. "I—I had no idea I had done anything else. I'm sorry, Trace."

After a slight pause he said, "It's not conscious on your part. You always treat me as if I wasn't there. I've never felt invisible before and don't particularly like the sensation. I thought we could at least be friends."

"We are." Her voice quailed despite herself.

"You have an odd way of showing it. Friends normally look at each other and smile once in a while, enjoy a private joke. You, on the other hand, reserve your affection strictly for the children. But you can't use them as a shield all the time."

She wheeled around, baffled by the total change in him. "A shield?" she cried, forgetting for the moment that their voices would keep the babies awake.

The dangerous glint in his eye unnerved her. "I don't know what else you'd call it. There aren't very many newlyweds who'd take two babies on their honeymoon."

Honeymoon? Cassie was aghast and looked away quickly. "After the chaos of Christmas and the move from San Francisco, I thought we agreed a little vacation with the children was exactly what we needed...so all of us could get acquainted away from the pressures of work and other people."

"If you recall, you were the one who suggested the idea. I simply went along with it, because I assumed you'd allow the hotel baby-sitters to take over once in a while to give us some time alone."

"I was afraid to trust them, particularly when Justin was running a temperature."

His jaw hardened. "That particular hotel has an impeccable reputation, with licensed sitters, a full-time registered nurse and a doctor always on call. If Justin had shown the slightest sign of any complication, we would have had the best care available at a moment's notice."

Her hands tightened on the bars of the crib. "I had no idea you weren't agreeable to the idea. You should have told me."

"I did, repeatedly, but you chose to ignore my hints and continued to cling to the children. Justin has become impossible. He knows all he has to do is look at you and you're right there to cater to his every whim. There *is* such a thing as a surfeit of attention."

Had she been spoiling Justin? Was Trace afraid she'd supplanted *him* in Justin's affections?

"I—I'm sure you're right. I've probably gone overboard in an effort to make up for lost time."

Her words didn't seem to mollify him. "You may not be sleeping in my bed, but in all other ways you're my wife, and there are things I expect of you besides being a mother to the boys."

What things? She had no idea all this had been seething inside him. "I'm not sure I understand you."

"How could you? We haven't had a moment to ourselves since we met!" He paused. "As chairman of the board, I attend a variety of social functions, and I do a certain amount of entertaining myself. Now that I'm married, it would create unnecessary and possibly damaging speculation if you didn't accompany me and fulfill your role as hostess when we're dining at home with friends and business acquaintances. Naturally the children won't be invited to those events," he added sarcastically. "Did you think you were being hired as a nanny when you accepted my proposal?"

"Not in so many words," she admitted, so confused by his anger that she didn't know what to believe. "But when you came to San Francisco, I was caught up in my feelings and concerns for the children—to the point that I wasn't capable of looking beyond their needs."

"That was almost two months ago, Cassie. It's time we talked about *our* needs."

His remarks caught her completely off guard. "Trace," she whispered, "your family is waiting for us. I don't think this is the time for the kind of discussion you seem to have in mind." She rubbed her palms agitatedly against her hips, noting that his eyes followed her movements with disturbing intensity.

There was a beat of silence, then, "For once you're right." He kept his voice low. "But be aware that I intend to pursue this after we say good-night to the family. In the meantime I would appreciate it if you'd join me in creating a united front. Mother would never admit it to you, but she's not as well as she pretends."

Unconsciously Cassie's hand went to her throat. "What's wrong with her?"

"She had a heart attack recently. The doctors have

warned her to slow down and take life easier. Since our marriage seems to have brought her so much pleasure, the last thing I want to do is upset her. She happens to believe that the greatest happiness in life is achieved through a good marriage. My divorce, I'm sorry to say, hurt her deeply, and ever since the attack she's been worried she might die before she sees me settled with a wife and family of my own.''

Inexplicably Cassie felt a strange, searing pain. Was *that* his underlying motive for asking her to marry him? The marriage would guarantee his mother's peace of mind and explain her reaction when they were introduced earlier in the evening. It was yet another example of Trace's unswerving devotion and loyalty to those he loved.

She took a deep, shuddering breath. ''You know I wouldn't deliberately do anything to hurt her.''

His hands curled into fists, then relaxed, as if he had come to the end of his patience. ''All I'm asking is that you try to act more natural and comfortable with me—even when the children aren't around.'' He sighed. ''I don't understand you, Cassie. I can't figure out if you're still in love with your ex-fiancé, or if he did something to put you off men for good.''

CHAPTER FIVE

TRACE GAVE HER no chance to respond. He grasped her hand and started for the hallway; she didn't try to resist. It shouldn't have come as any surprise that while they mingled with the family for the rest of the evening, he kept his arm firmly around her shoulders. It was a deceptively casual gesture, but Cassie knew that if she tried to pull away, she'd feel the bite of his fingers against her skin.

Shortly before the end of the party, as people were preparing to leave, he lowered his head to Cassie's ear. She couldn't tell if the caress of his mouth against her hot cheek was intentional or not, but his touch shot through her body like a spurt of adrenaline. "It's exceptionally warm tonight," he whispered. "Join me for a swim after everyone leaves...and we'll continue what we started upstairs."

She bit the soft underside of her lip. The thought of being alone with Trace in the swimming pool made her panic. Since the kiss he'd given her at their wedding, she'd become physically, sensually, aware of him—something that had never happened with Rolfe in all the years they'd spent together.

She found herself remembering things Susan used to say about Ted. "I never want to say good-night to him, Cassie. One kiss isn't enough. All he has to do is touch me and I go up in smoke. Everything about him fascinates me, even the way he chews his toast. If we don't get married soon, I don't think either of us can hold out any longer.''

Frightened that he could feel her trembling, Cassie eased herself away from Trace's hold. "First I'll have to help Nattie clean up.''

''Nattie's job is to supervise the caterers, who were hired for that express purpose, and Mike has a whole retinue of gardeners to put the grounds in order. In case you're about to offer any other excuses, you can forget them. Tonight I need to be with my wife. Is a midnight swim and a little honest conversation too much to ask?''

His question whirled around in her brain as she said good-night to Trace's family and escaped to her bedroom. Out of breath from an attack of nerves and a heart that was pounding out of rhythm, she leaned against the closed door. That was when she spied a gaily wrapped package sitting in the middle of her bed.

There had been so many gifts since her arrival in Phoenix, she certainly hadn't expected any more. Curious, she walked over to pick it up, wondering if someone in the family—Lena?—had thought to welcome her with something a little more personal. Quickly she unwrapped the box and lifted the lid. A handwritten card had been placed on the layers of tissue.

''It occurred to me,'' the card read, ''that Justin's cold wasn't the only reason you wouldn't swim with me in Scottsdale. In case you didn't have a decent suit and hadn't found the time to shop for one, I took the liberty of picking something out for you. The green matches your eyes. I couldn't resist. Trace.''

Carefully she moved aside the tissue paper and eased out a two-piece swimsuit. It was more modest than some of the bikinis she'd seen on the beach, but the fact remained that she'd never worn a two-piece before. Though slender, Cassie took after her mother in the full-bodied-figure department.

She'd always felt more comfortable in a one-piece outfit, but she wouldn't have been caught dead in the only suit she owned. It was so old and faded that she was planning to throw it out. Trace had probably guessed as much.

She flushed at the thought. It seemed he knew her better than she knew herself and refused to take the chance that she would use the lack of a proper swimsuit as an excuse for not meeting him at the pool.

Suddenly there was a rap on the door. ''Cassie? I'm giving you five minutes. If you're not downstairs by then, I'll be back up to get you, and a locked door won't stop me. It would be a shame to ruin that lovely dress you're wearing, but I won't hesitate to throw you in, emeralds and all.''

His threat galvanized her into action. In three minutes, her clothes lay everywhere and she'd put on her new swimsuit. She ran for her terry-cloth bathrobe, then dashed barefoot down the stairs.

The caterers must have cleared the tables in record time. When Cassie arrived on the patio, everything was quiet and only the lights from the swimming pool had been left on. The warm night air, sweet with the scent of sage blowing off the desert floor, felt like velvet against her heated skin. She'd never seen a more romantic setting in her life.

When she and Susan were little girls, they'd often played house on long Saturday afternoons. They always pretended they were married with families, living in far-off exotic places. But never in Cassie's wildest dreams had she imagined a setting like this, with a husband who looked like Trace, and children as adorable as Justin and Jason. If Susan could see her now...

"How nice to find my bride waiting for me." His deep, mocking voice startled her.

His bride? She whirled around in time to see Trace dive into the water and swim to the opposite end of the pool in a fast-paced crawl. Halfway back he stopped, treading water, and shook his head. In the near darkness she could just make out his dazzling white smile.

"Come on in. The water's perfect."

Even though he was some distance away, Cassie felt self-conscious as she removed her robe. "I love to swim, but I'm not very good at it."

"I usually swim early in the morning and again at night before I go to bed. Now we're married, we can work out together." Shivers raced over her body, because something in his tone implied that he expected her to join him on a regular basis and wouldn't take no for an answer. She couldn't understand why it mattered to him, since they'd be alone and there'd be no need to keep up the pretense. "It helps me unwind more than any sport I can think of." He looked at her a moment. "Are you about ready to jump in?"

She had just put a cautious toe in the water, bracing

herself for the shock. But the temperature was so different from the chilly Pacific Ocean at Carmel, where she'd occasionally swum with Rolfe, it was as though she'd stepped into a bathtub. "I don't even have to get used to it!" she cried out in delight. "Gaugin was wrong. Paradise is right here!"

She heard Trace's deep-throated chuckle as she pushed off from the bottom step and swam to the other side, making sure she didn't get too close to him. On her third lap across, she felt a pair of hands grasp her around the waist and flip her onto her back.

"Trace!" she gasped, not only from the unexpected contact, but because he had taken her beyond the patio overhang and she found herself looking up into a blue-black sky dotted with brilliant stars.

"I'm not going to let you drown," he reassured her. "Lie there and relax, kick your feet. You're more rigid than Justin at his worst."

Only once did she venture a glance at his face. His skin was beaded with moisture and his black hair lay sleek against his head. She quickly closed her eyes again. She felt helpless and exposed with his gaze free to wander over her semiclad body.

It took all her control not to examine his hard-muscled physique with the same concentrated thoroughness. If she tried to move, her arm rubbed against his hair-roughened chest, reminding her how utterly male he was. Everything about him excited her. His size, his masculinity, his firmly carved mouth.

She came to the stunning realization that the bittersweet ache that seemed to be part pain, part ecstasy, was *desire!*

Susan had once tried to explain the sensation to her

and had finally given up. But she'd insisted that Cassie would recognize it the moment she experienced it. She hadn't—until now.

Was this the way Rolfe had felt throughout their long courtship? If so, she had to admire his self-control. No wonder he grew more upset and moody each time she put off the wedding.

Without even trying, Trace had brought her alarmingly alive. From the first, he had accomplished what Rolfe had never been able to do. If she'd desired Rolfe like this, wouldn't she have wanted to get married as soon as possible?

Right now, she quivered with anticipation. She could hear every breath Trace took and feel the heat from his body sending a languorous warmth through hers. The longing to mold her soft curves against his solid strength was fast becoming a driving need.

Terrified that he could sense her desire and see the pulse throbbing in the hollow of her throat, she challenged him to a race. Without waiting for a response she catapulted out of his arms.

Of course he won. He waited for her at the far end of the pool with a rakish smile on his face. She touched the edge at least ten seconds after he did and drank in gulps of fresh air before bursting into laughter at her inelegant performance.

He studied her mouth intently, a gentle yet ironic smile curving his own lips. "Do you know that's the first time you've laughed with me when we've been alone? I like it."

Oddly embarrassed, Cassie sank down against the side of the pool until the water reached her neck. "As you've witnessed, I've got a long way to go to keep up with you.''

His expression sobered. ''I don't see our marriage as a competition, Cassie. What I'm hoping is that we'll share each other's lives. The children will grow up happier and healthier emotionally if they sense our marriage is a stable one. No one has to know what goes on—or doesn't—behind our bedroom doors except the two of us. Is that too much to ask? You don't dislike being with me, do you?''

Cassie was beginning to feel slightly hysterical. If he had any idea how much she didn't dislike being with him, he would run as far as he could in the opposite direction! Striving for composure, she smoothed several wet tendrils out of her eyes.

She didn't doubt his sincerity where the children's welfare was concerned. But now Cassie understood that his mother's fragile health had prompted him to enlist her cooperation in presenting a normal picture of married life to the rest of his family.

Her greatest problem would be to carry on a friendship, day after day, without ever betraying the physical side of her attraction for him. She finally said, ''I admit it would be better for the children if they see us relating to each other as friends and companions.''

Maybe she was mistaken, but she thought some of the tension eased out of him. ''I'm glad you agree, because in two weeks the family's going on our annual skiing vacation to Snowbird, Utah, and I wanted to give you plenty of time to prepare for it.''

She had that suffocating feeling in her chest again. ''What about the children?''

''Nattie will take care of them.''

"I see. How long will we be gone?"

"A week."

A week with Trace? Alone in the same room? She swallowed hard.

"Snowbird isn't the end of the earth, you know," he said harshly, his brows drawing together in displeasure. "You can phone the house every day to assure yourself the children are all right. If anything of a serious nature developed, we could be home in a matter of hours."

Cassie decided to let him go on believing that the children were her only concern. "You may as well know I've only been on skis twice in my life. I'm afraid I'd embarrass you on the slopes. Why don't I stay home with the boys and you go with your family? In fact, it might be a good time for Nattie to have a vacation, as well. She—"

"Either we go together, or we don't go at all!" he broke in angrily. Like quicksilver, his mood had changed. He suddenly shoved off for the opposite end of the pool, moving with tremendous speed. He was out of the water before she could call him back.

"Wait!" she cried out and swam after him, afraid she'd really alienated him this time. Unfortunately, she couldn't make it to the other end of the pool without stopping several times to catch her breath. She was terrified he would disappear into his own rooms, leaving her with everything still unresolved. "Trace," she gasped as her hand gripped the edge, "I was only trying to spare you. I ski like I swim."

He was toweling himself dry and slanted her a hostile look. "Do you honestly think I give a damn *how* you ski? Or even *if* you ski? I don't care if you lie around in the hotel bed all day watching television! From what I gather, for the last five years your life hasn't exactly been easy.

"Between Susan's and Ted's deaths, not to mention your mother's, a broken engagement and caring for Jason, you've had more to deal with than most people I know. And at the same time, you've been working all hours to earn a living. You don't seem to understand that I'd like to give you a chance to relax and play for a change, away from your work and the constant demands of the babies."

Her legs almost buckled at his unexpected explanation. Whenever she thought she had him figured out, he said or did something that increased her respect and made her care for him that much more.

A new ache passed through her body. She didn't *want* to care about him. She didn't want to worry about him—or think about him all the time. Lately she'd started fantasizing about what it would be like if he made love to her. Much more of this, and she'd end up an emotional wreck.

Her green eyes, wide with urgency, beseeched him to listen. "If I sounded ungrateful, I'm sorry. I suppose it's a combination of worrying about being away from the children for the first time and fear that you'll regret taking me along."

The expression on his face altered slightly as he held out her robe in invitation, but his eyes were still wary. As fast as she could manage, she clambered out of the pool and slipped her arms into the sleeves. His hands remained on her shoulders while she cinched the belt around her waist.

"You're an independent little thing," he whispered, kneading the taut muscles in her shoulders and neck. "It's time someone took care of you for a change."

She could feel the heat of his hands through the damp fabric. If he continued this, she was afraid of what she might do, afraid she'd embarrass them both. "You've spoiled me and Jason, and you know it, Trace. But I worry you've taken off too much time from your responsibilities at the bank, helping us move here and settle in. I wish there was something I could do for you in return."

His hands stilled for a moment. "There is," he muttered before removing them completely. Part of her was relieved he had broken contact, but another part craved his touch. Not trusting herself, she walked to the nearest lounge chair and sat down, making sure the robe covered her knees. This far from the pool, he was almost a silhouette in the near darkness.

"Tell me what's on your mind," she urged him.

He stood there holding both ends of the towel he'd slung around his neck. "You may not be an expert swimmer or skier, but your genius with needle and thread is nothing short of phenomenal. When I walked into your apartment with Jason that morning, I was overwhelmed by your talent and creativity."

A compliment from Trace meant more to her than the adulation of anyone else in the world. "Lots of women do what I do."

"Perhaps. But the finished product isn't always a masterpiece. I hope you won't be angry when I tell you I went through your apartment rather thoroughly, examining the goods, so to speak. Nothing bought for Justin in any store, anywhere, compares to the quality and originality I saw displayed in your apartment. I stand in awe of your accomplishments, Cassie.''

''Thank you,'' she murmured shakily.

''I also felt like a fool for the callous way I suggested you move to Phoenix when I had no idea of the complexities involved in earning your livelihood.'' There was a slight pause. ''Tell me something honestly. Is your work a labor of love?''

She couldn't help but wonder what he was getting at. ''Long before I made any money at it, I loved creating an idea and seeing it through to completion. It's…something I have to do. When they find me dead, I'll probably be buried in batting, slumped over my sewing machine with a bunch of pins in my mouth.''

''Somehow I knew you'd say that.'' He chuckled. ''You and Lena are kindred spirits.''

''I liked her very much, even after only one meeting.''

''Maybe you're the person who'll make the difference.'' The cryptic remark intrigued her.

''What do you mean?''

''You're both artists. You live in that elite world reserved for those who were born gifted.''

Cassie made a noise of dissent. ''You can't seriously compare what *I* do to her talent!''

''I already have.'' His firm tone told her that to argue the point would be futile. ''You make a child's world the most exciting, magical place on earth, just as it should be. Lena makes it possible for those of us who shove paper around to enjoy the breathtaking beauty of the desert without ever leaving our air-conditioned offices.''

"There's a certain genius in shoving paper around. Particularly *your* paper," she quipped. "Give me three days in your office and your entire family would find themselves without a business and no roof over their heads."

The patio rang with his uninhibited laughter. "Well, since you brought up the bank, I have a proposition for you." Cassie sat forward, instantly alert.

"We lease properties, both residential and commercial. Right now, there's a studio vacant in Crossroads Square, an area of Phoenix that attracts tourists, as well as locals. By most standards it's not large, but it has four separate rooms with a cottage kind of feel, like you might see at a beach resort in Laguna or Balboa. It would be the perfect place to display your handicrafts. You need a showroom."

She had been concentrating on the sound of his voice, and it took a minute before she actually heard his words. She jumped immediately to her feet. "There's nothing I'd love more. It would be a dream come true, but I could never afford the rent, because I looked into the possibility in San Francisco and—"

"Don't jump to conclusions until you've heard me out," he cautioned before she could say another word. "How much do you have saved from your Christmas sales after taxes?"

"About eight thousand dollars."

"With that much money, you could sign a six-month lease."

"But six months wouldn't give me enough time to fill it with inventory, and then I'd have no money to reinvest in materials and—"

She heard him make a sound of exasperation.

"Cassie, you said you wouldn't interrupt until I'm finished. Sit down before you wear out my patio with your pacing."

"I'm sorry." With so much nervous energy to expend, she needed some form of movement. She found a spot at the edge of the pool and dangled her feet in the water, splashing gently. He wandered over to her and it was then that she noticed his right foot. Without thinking, she bent closer and touched it with her index finger. *"You have webbed toes, just like Jason!"* Her astonished cry rang out and she clapped a hand over her mouth at its loudness.

"A legacy from the Ellingsworth side of the family," he drawled in amusement. "Both of Mother's feet are similarly...afflicted."

"I wouldn't call it an affliction," Cassie argued. "When I first saw Jason's foot, I thought it was rather sweet. Susan and I investigated the medical records available in both Ted's and our family, but we couldn't find any mention of webbed feet. I guess that's when I started to take Susan's suspicions seriously."

"And your odd little duck turned out to be mine," he said, causing both of them to chuckle.

"Is that what convinced you he was your son?" She could still picture the expression on his face when he reached for Jason's tiny foot that first day in his office.

"No. I took one look at the shape of his body and his complexion. He had to be my son. The Ellingsworth webbed toes were just the final proof."

"And all the time I thought he was a Ramsey."

"Oh, I'm sure a little Ramsey is in there somewhere. But what's most important, he has you for a mother. You're a natural, did you know that?''

"Except I've been spoiling Justin, as you pointed out yourself.''

"True, but no more than I've spoiled Jason,'' he replied with surprising honesty. "I admit I was somewhat hasty in judging you, especially since I've been equally guilty. However, I imagine time will remedy the urgency we both feel to make up for those lost months. And returning to your crafts work will put a balance back in your life. You've been missing that since you agreed to marry me.''

Again his perception and honesty surprised her. She'd been so preoccupied by her new responsibilities and her growing attraction to Trace, she hadn't yet found a moment to give serious thought to her business. "Maybe a few years down the road I'll have enough money to look into the idea of opening a shop.''

"But that might be too late for Lena.''

Lena again.

"She needs someone outside the family who believes in her work and will encourage her to see it as a viable career. Someone who has validity in her eyes. I think you could be that person. You could infect her with your own interest. Your joy in what you're doing.''

What was he getting at? "You mean like going into business with her? Opening a gallery with her art and my crafts?''

He nodded. "Maybe you could call it something like The Mix and Match Gallery—in honor of the unusual way we met and became a family.'' There was a perceptible pause, then he asked, "Does the idea appeal to you?" She noticed the tiniest hint of anxiety in his question, as if her answer was important to him.

"Appeal?" She jumped to her feet and gazed into his face, giving him a full, unguarded smile. "It's a fantastic idea! In fact, why don't we call it Mix and Match Southwest, since we'll be mixing and matching her art and my crafts and everything will have a southwestern theme?" Her thoughts were tumbling excitedly over each other. "We could have a logo with a cactus and maybe a setting sun or a coyote, and…oh, it'll be wonderful!"

His eyes kindled. "You mean it? You wouldn't mind sharing space with her, provided she was willing? It would be predominantly your shop of course—at this stage, anyway. If necessary, I'll pay the rent for the second six months, only that would have to remain our secret. It seems to me that between the two of you, there should be enough profit to stay in business another year." He paused again. "Would it make *you* happy, Cassie?"

When they'd begun this conversation, she thought he'd brought up the idea of a gallery solely for Lena's benefit. But the concern in his voice just now led Cassie to believe he was trying to please her, too, and that belief filled her with an all-consuming warmth. "You know it would," she answered in an unsteady voice. "Do you recall that watercolor at the top of the stairs? The one with the little Hopi girl standing next to those rocks at sunrise?"

He nodded. "It's one of my favorites."

"Every time I pass it, I itch to get out my sketch

pad and design dolls and wall hangings based on that lovely child. In fact, living in this house has inspired me with the flavor of the Arizona desert. I've already planned out an area rug for my room, and the water-color of the flowering cactus hanging in your office would look perfect next to it. Trace, for the opening I could use a Southwest theme with Lena's water-colors as the focal point!''

Before she could say anything else, he lowered his head and pressed his lips to her forehead. "You have a generous nature, Cassie. I'm counting on you to win Lena over to the idea.''

Her heart hammered in reaction to his touch—and yearned for more. "Maybe I could work up some items before we go to lunch next week and invite her back to the house. If she saw them arranged around the watercolors, it might excite her.''

"I'm sure it will, but getting her to make a com-mitment is something else again.'' A troubled look entered his eyes. "In college she fell in love with her art teacher. They had an affair that ended when she walked into his apartment and found him in bed with another student.''

Cassie cringed at the all-too-common scenario.

"Considering that she thought they were getting married, that alone would have been devastating enough. But not satisfied with betraying her, he at-tacked her art and told her she was wasting her time. His final insult pretty well destroyed her confidence. He told her she'd never be more than a mediocre painter at best.''

"But anyone with eyes can see how brilliant her work is!'' Cassie insisted. "When did this happen?''

"Twelve years ago. She hasn't done any painting since."

"You mean the watercolors in your office and here at the house were all done while she was still in college? She was that good, even back then?"

"That's right," he said, tight-lipped.

"Her teacher probably recognized her talent and couldn't bear the competition. No doubt her work surpassed his. I've seen the same situation in the music department at the university where I studied piano theory. To think she let his rejection prevent her from working at her art all these years. It's tragic."

He nodded gravely. "Her husband, Allen, knows she'll never be completely fulfilled unless she gets back to her painting. He's done everything possible to encourage her but she refuses to even talk about it."

"The hurt must have gone very deep."

"It did. And to complicate matters, she feels insignificant around the family, overpowered by us. She's not like you, Cassie. She would never have fought me for Jason the way you did. You live by the strength of your convictions and don't let anything defeat you. You're practical and resilient—a survivor. You'd stand alone if you had to. If some of your confidence could rub off on Lena, it might change her life."

"I'm glad you told me about her," she said in a small voice. "I'll do what I can. Now if you don't mind, I'm very tired and I need to go to bed. Good night, Trace."

His whispered good-night followed her across the patio and up the stairs.

Though he obviously meant his remarks as a compliment, her spirits plummeted. Apparently she and his ex-wife, Gloria, had something in common, after all. They were both the antithesis of the fragile, helpless woman who aroused a man's undying love and brought out his instinctive need to protect and cherish.

The Joan of Arcs of this world would always be admired, but they would remain on their pedestals *alone....*

CHAPTER SIX

EXCEPT FOR A VISIT to the vacant shop in Crossroads Square and the subsequent signing of a year's lease, Cassie saw Trace only in passing during the next week. He explained that he had a backlog of work; as a result, he stayed at the office through the dinner hour every night so he could catch up before they left on their ski trip.

Cassie told herself she was glad his banking responsibilities kept him away from the house. Without his disturbing presence, she could simply relax with the children and sew at her own pace. Trace had helped convert the middle guest bedroom into a workroom. The light was perfect. Best of all, she was close to the children and could hear them when they woke up from their naps.

But to her dismay, Trace was continually on her mind. His energy and vitality, his handsome face and powerful body, made it impossible for her to concentrate fully on anything else. And when he was home, even if he was locked in his study or playing with the children, she was aware of him. No matter the hour, her pulse raced when she heard his car in the driveway. But what alarmed her even more was the disappointment she felt when he drove off to work each morning.

After five whole weeks of his attention and companionship, she discovered life wasn't nearly as exciting without him around. Always before, she'd been able to immerse herself happily in her work, unconscious of time passing. Now while she bathed and fed the children or cut out patterns, she often glanced at the clock, estimating how many hours it would be before he came home.

Lena called early in the week to make a date for lunch. Cassie put her off until Friday so she'd have enough time to work up several pieces that drew their inspiration from three of Lena's paintings. Trace brought home one she'd requested from his office. She used another two from the group hanging on the wall along the staircase.

In order to make the impact as striking as possible, she enlisted Nattie's help in converting the dining room into a sort of gallery. The effect was even more stunning than Cassie had imagined, because the room, with its arboretum of exotic desert plants, lent itself perfectly to the Southwest theme.

Though she kept her thoughts to herself, Cassie felt that something out of the ordinary had been achieved. She could hardly sit still through lunch with Lena, waiting for the moment they would go home.

If Trace's sister sensed Cassie's suppressed excitement, she hid it well. She asked dozens of questions and insisted on knowing all the details of Cassie's life and the events that eventually led her to Trace's office. Several hours later, when Cassie invited Lena back to the house to see the children, Lena was still chuckling over Trace's initial plan to have Cassie arrested. But her laughter subsided when she caught sight of her own watercolors displayed with Cassie's creations in plain view of anyone standing in the living room.

Like a person walking through water, Lena moved into the dining room. Cassie followed a few steps behind, uncertain of Lena's reaction and almost afraid to breathe. Those paintings were associated with a painful time in Lena's life. At this early stage in their friendship, the last thing Cassie wanted to do was open old wounds or create a rift between them. It was because she had Trace's blessing that she dared to involve Lena at all.

Lena studied the arrangement in silence for a long time. "Do you mean to tell me you've made all these since you came to Phoenix?" she finally asked.

"Yes, except that they aren't completely finished."

"They're fabulous."

"Your paintings inspired them, Lena. I took one look at your little Hopi girl and I could visualize her adorable face on dolls and wall hangings and all sorts of things. Every one of your paintings has given me a dozen new ideas. I can't work fast enough to keep up with them."

"Trace told me you were a genius with fabric."

"And I told him that whoever painted those scenes in his office has incredible talent. Your work excites me and makes me reach out for things I didn't know were in me. You know what I mean?"

Lena turned around and stared at Cassie. "You really meant what you said the other night, didn't you?"

Taking a deep breath, Cassie answered, "You already know the answer to that. Have I made you angry, using your paintings for inspiration without telling you?''

''Angry?'' Lena's gray eyes widened in surprise. ''I've never been so flattered in my life.''

Cassie's body went limp with relief. ''As you know, I've only ever sold out of my own home. At first I started making up dolls and stuffed figures from fairy tales and cartoons to help bring in a little more money. Pretty soon I was flooded with orders. I've sewn everything from frogs to princes. But I've never had a theme for my work or even considered it until I saw your paintings.''

Lena fingered her long braid absently. ''You obviously went to all this trouble—arranging everything so beautifully—for my benefit. Why?''

''Before I met Trace, I planned to open my own boutique in San Francisco as a showcase for my work. But everything changed when he asked me to marry him. Now that we're settled, I've used the profits from my Christmas sales to sign a lease on some space in Crossroads Square.''

''Crossroads Square?'' Lena mouthed the word wistfully, sounding very faraway. ''That's a perfect place if you want to attract the tourist trade.'' She stared at Cassie in puzzlement. ''Does Trace know about this? I-I thought you were going to stay home with the children.''

''I do stay home. Every day. And I manage to enjoy the children and sew at the same time. How else do you think I could turn out so much work?'' Cassie smiled mischievously. ''But if I don't have a place to display and sell it, pretty soon Trace will have to build me a warehouse.''

Lena burst into laughter. "You're a complete surprise, Cassie Ramsey."

"No." Cassie shook her head, liking the sound of her new name. "Just driven by a compulsion stronger than I am."

A shadow crossed Lena's face; she started to say something, then apparently changed her mind.

Cassie hesitated a moment, then decided to plunge ahead. "Lena, I have to admit I had ulterior motives in inviting you back to the house today. You see, I'm holding my grand opening in a month, and I need your permission to display the things I've already made. The fact is, I've copied your work and I really have no right to sell any of this." She gestured around the room. "Believe me, I'll understand if your answer is no. But as time is of the essence, I need to know how you feel…in case I have to get started on another theme entirely."

Picking up one of the dolls, Lena studied it carefully, then looked at Cassie, eyes brimming. "How could I possibly turn you down when you've done such exquisite work? It would be on my conscience forever."

Impulsively Cassie threw her arms around Lena in an exuberant hug. "I was praying you'd say that, because I can't think of another theme that could possibly work as well as this one. To be honest, I knew my opening would have to be unique in order to generate business. And when I saw your art, I was immediately drawn to it. I think other people would feel the same way."

In the heavy silence that followed her remarks, Cassie removed the paintings from the groupings of crafts, then leaned them against the far wall. Lena gazed at her uncomprehendingly, and Cassie had to bite hard on her lower lip to keep from smiling.

"Take a good look at everything without your paintings to show them off, Lena. The things I've made are nice in and of themselves, but the display falls flat, don't you think? Be honest now."

After another quiet interim, Lena nodded.

Crossing her fingers behind her back, Cassie ventured, "Would you allow me to use your paintings the way I've done here to open the show?" Without giving Lena a chance to respond, she rushed on. "I have to admit I've sketched out ideas for dozens of fabric crafts based on another ten of your paintings. If I work night and day, I can have everything ready for the opening. But without your art as a foil, I won't be able to achieve the same impact."

While Lena hesitated, Cassie quickly put the paintings back in place among the crafts for her sister-in-law's benefit. "You see? I'm right, aren't I?"

After a minute of studying the display, Lena nodded, looking slightly bemused. "Everything works perfectly together."

"Then you'll let me use them?"

"I'd be cruel if I said no."

"Thank you, Lena." Cassie couldn't help giving her another hug. "It's one thing to sell things out of your own home, and another to display them in a shop. I've been terrified at my own audacity. But with your paintings, I know the opening will be an eye-catcher."

Conscious of taking a calculated risk, Cassie added, "I noticed you haven't signed your paintings."

"No," came the quiet admission.

"I'm afraid you'll have to if I'm going to show them. Otherwise clients will assume I painted them."

Lena was examining the Hopi girl canvas, frowning in concentration. "I need to finish the detail on her dress if you're going to use this." She finally stood up and faced Cassie. "I'll tell you what. Ask Trace to bring home the paintings from the office you're planning to use. Next week I'll go to the art store for supplies and come over to sign them all."

"Don't you have materials at home?" Cassie asked, striving to remain unemotional when inside she was bursting with excitement.

"Heavens, no." She let out a bitter laugh. "I'm afraid my art career was very short-lived and I tossed everything out. In fact, I haven't touched a brush to canvas in years. When I worked on these paintings, I never dreamed anyone else would ever see them. I would have thrown them away, but Trace said he wanted them and offered me money to take them off my hands. Of course I wouldn't have let him pay me for junk." She sighed, shaking her head. "My brother..."

"He believes in your work."

Lena's gaze slid away. "Well, now that I've committed myself, I'd better look over everything you plan to use. I might find other details that were left undone."

"Lena, I can't thank you enough. To be frank, I've been frightened to tell you what I've been up to—particularly since I'm calling the shop Mix and Match Southwest. If you hadn't given your permission, I don't know where I would have turned for inspiration.

Trace seems to believe in my work, as well. I—I want him to be proud of me.''

"In case you hadn't noticed, he already is," Lena said wryly. "Of all my brothers, I feel closest to him, and I can tell you honestly that when Allen and I arrived at the party, Trace's eyes had a glow I've never seen before. Only you could have put it there."

"That's because he's so crazy about Jason." She fought to keep the tremor out of her voice.

Lena eyed her shrewdly. "Of course he is, but I saw the way Trace looked at you, the way he held on to you all evening. I've never seen him behave like that with any other woman."

"Not even Gloria?"

"Especially not Gloria."

Cassie wanted to ask more questions about Trace's former wife, but restrained herself; this wasn't the right time. "Trace's attention to me was solely for your mother's benefit."

"What does Mom have to do with how my brother treats you?" Lena asked in a perplexed voice.

"It's because of her heart condition. He wants her to believe our marriage is a love match."

"And it's not?" Lena burst out.

Cassie sucked in her breath. "Trace is grateful to me for uniting him with his son. But you might as well know he asked me to marry him and I accepted so neither of us would have to be separated from the children. I couldn't bear to lose them," she whispered.

"*What?*"

"Trace isn't in love with me, Lena. Ours is what people used to call a marriage of convenience. I can't go on pretending something that doesn't exist. At least not to you, because...because I want us to be friends.''

"I do, too," Lena murmured, "but if you're telling me you're not in love with my brother, I don't believe you."

Lena's directness caught Cassie off guard and she felt heat rising to her cheeks. "None of it really matters, because Trace isn't interested in me that way. In fact, one of the conditions he set for our marriage was that both of us could see other people, as long as we were discreet."

"My brother said *that?*"

"Lena, we've never slept together. He's only ever kissed me once, the day we were married." Her voice trailed off as she recalled the thrill of it. Before Lena could respond, Cassie blurted out, "I can hear noises from upstairs. The boys must have awakened. I'll get them ready and bring them down."

Without waiting for a response Cassie raced from the living room and dashed up the stairs, thankful the babies had interrupted her painful conversation with Lena.

As Cassie changed their diapers, Nattie poked her head into the nursery. "Do you need help?"

"No. Jason seems to be a little off color, but I'm sure it's nothing. Since Trace won't be home for dinner, I can fix a simple meal for myself and the boys. So why don't you and Mike take the rest of the day off? You deserve a rest."

Nattie's face lit up. "You're sure?"

"I'm positive. Lena's going to stay a while and keep us company."

"All right. Thank you, Cassie. It's a joy to work in the same house with you."

"The feeling's mutual, Nattie. Go and have a good time."

When Nattie had left, Cassie dressed the boys and carried them downstairs to see their aunt. To her relief, Lena made no mention of their prior conversation and enjoyed getting to know Jason better while Cassie encouraged Justin to take a few steps. It wouldn't be long before he was walking on his own.

Jason, on the other hand, could crawl everywhere and went after anything he wanted with an unswerving certainty that reminded both women of Trace and sent them into gales of laughter. But, unusual for Jason, he soon tired and cried to be held.

Cassie and Lena spent the rest of the afternoon exchanging anecdotes about the children, but as the dinner hour approached, Lena declared that she had to go home and feed her starving horde. Cassie was reluctant to see her leave, but was growing concerned about Jason, who'd become irritable and weepy, despite his long nap. His forehead definitely felt warm to the touch.

She put Justin in the playpen, then walked Lena to the front door, carrying Jason in her arms. "I'll phone you as soon as Trace brings the paintings home from his office."

The other woman nodded. "Cassie, will you do me a favor and not mention this to anyone else in the family?"

"You mean about using your art for my opening?"

"Yes. I'd like this to be our secret, if you don't mind."

"Of course I don't. I'll tell Trace not to say anything, either."

"Good. It's just that I stopped painting years ago and, well, I just don't want to deal with everyone's speculations…"

Cassie put a hand on Lena's arm. "If that's how you feel, I understand. You have my promise."

"Thanks." Lena kissed Jason's cheek, then Cassie's. "We'll talk again soon. We'll be able to spend some time together during our trip to Snowbird, too."

Lena's unexpected warmth pleased Cassie. "Thank you for your help, Lena. It means more than you know."

Cassie had a feeling that her sister-in-law wanted to say something further—perhaps about her marriage to Trace. But Lena seemed to think better of it. As soon as she drove off, Cassie headed for the kitchen to get Jason a bottle of juice. Then she gave him a sponge bath to bring down his slight fever and put him back to bed.

But while she was taking care of him, her mind was on Lena. Though Cassie had obtained her permission to use the watercolors, it didn't mean she'd automatically begin painting again. Trace was right; Lena still sounded far too bitter over her ex-lover's rejection. She'd lost all her self-confidence and, even worse, belief in her own talent.

But she hadn't turned Cassie down, and that meant she'd taken the first, necessary step. Cassie couldn't wait to tell Trace. She listened for him all evening as she fed Justin and bathed him, then put him in his crib. Jason fell asleep almost immediately.

After turning out the nursery light, she went downstairs to put the crafts and paintings away and restore order to the dining room while she waited for Trace. Around eight she heard a car pull into the drive. Moments later, the sound of the back door opening told her he was home.

Cassie rushed to the patio to meet him, anxious to share her news about Lena. "I thought you'd never get here, and I have so much to tell you! Lena and I—"

His eyes looked warm and expectant, but the ringing of the telephone prevented further conversation. He reached for it, and Cassie sat down at the small table, silently admiring the blackness of his hair, the laugh lines around his eyes and mouth, the deepness of his voice.

By his clipped response she could tell the call had to do with bank business; she hoped it wouldn't detain him for the rest of the evening. He pulled out his pocketbook and jotted down some notes, then finally hung up. She was bursting to tell him her good news, but swallowed her words when she saw his dark expression. One phone call had transformed him into a remote facsimile of himself. He turned his head to stare at her broodingly.

"What's wrong, Trace?" she asked in alarm.

"That was Western Union with a cablegram for you from a Mr. Rolfe Timpson in Brussels. I told the operator to go ahead and read it." He tore the page from his pocketbook and handed it to her.

The hostility emanating from him troubled Cassie a great deal more than the paper in her hand. Her gaze was drawn to Trace's crisp handwriting. "Dearest Cass," it read, "I got your letter and I strongly feel we have to talk. We've loved for a lifetime and I don't ever see that changing. I'm coming back to the States next month to see you. I'll call you as soon as I arrive in Phoenix. My deepest love, Rolfe.''

After all this time, Rolfe was coming to see her. She would always love him in a special way. But her response to Trace in the pool had revealed a truth that changed everything where Rolfe was concerned.

What was it Susan had said? That Cassie and Rolfe had never been apart and needed the separation to make things clear, one way or the other....

They were clear, all right.

Her eyes shifted from the paper to the man who'd taken her heart by storm and brought her body to glorious life. *Oh, Trace, if you only knew...*

''He wants you back,'' he said in a harsh tone, ''but that's just too damn bad because you're married to me now, Cassie, and that's the way it's going to stay.''

If she didn't know why he'd asked her to marry him, his angry pronouncement would have led her to believe he was starting to care for her.

''Whatever Rolfe has to say, I'd never leave you and the children,'' she said honestly.

''Don't take me for a fool, Cassie. Do you think I don't know the bond that exists between the two of you? The years invested? The intimacy you shared?''

''We weren't intimate in the way you mean,'' she confessed in a quiet voice.

His eyes blazed. ''If you're trying to tell me you never slept together in all those years, I don't believe you.''

''Nevertheless it's true. Mother had very conser-

vative beliefs and raised Susan and me to save ourselves for marriage. She challenged us to be the only
girls in the neighborhood who didn't know all there
was to know about what goes on between a man and
a woman. She promised us it would be a lot more fun
and exciting to learn along with our husbands.''

He stared at her as if she was speaking a foreign
language. ''What went wrong between you and
Rolfe?''

She wanted to blurt out that she wasn't in love with
Rolfe. That was what had kept her from marrying
him. But she hadn't known it, not until she met Trace.
And fell in love with him.

''We were engaged a long time. When he pushed
me to set a wedding date, I couldn't, because I was
still grieving over my mother. After Ted was killed,
he pressed me again, but I was so worried about Susan I couldn't even consider marriage just then, even
though I loved him very much. I don't blame him for
finally getting fed up and breaking our engagement.''

''Is that when he left for Europe?''

''Yes. But none of it matters anymore. Trace,'' she
began in an excited voice, ''I wanted to tell you about
Lena. She—''

''Not now, Cassie,'' he interrupted tersely. ''I'm in
the middle of a hellish merger and I'll be spending
most of the night in my study.''

Not since that first day in his office had he ever
been intentionally rude to her. Here she'd done everything in her power to show him the past was dead
for her and he treated her like this! Even if things had
been different and she'd wanted to see Rolfe again,
did Trace honestly believe she'd walk out on him and

the children? He would have to divorce her before she'd leave!

He turned abruptly and took the patio stairs two at a time. Cassie felt like throwing something at him. After he'd disappeared from view, she stood there for a few minutes to get her temper under control, then went upstairs herself. When she heard Jason crying she made a detour to the nursery. The minute she picked him up she realized why he'd awakened in such distress. He was burning with fever. One look at the rash covering his chest and neck dispersed all thoughts of the tense scene on the patio.

She quickly undressed him and headed for the bathroom, knowing she had to get his temperature down as fast as possible. The rash covering his chest was a brilliant pink, and she could actually feel the heat radiating from his body. She filled the tub with cool water and lowered him in. He began to scream uncontrollably. All of a sudden she heard Justin, who'd been awakened from a sound sleep, bellowing at the top of his lungs, too.

"Cassie? What can I do to help?" came Trace's voice over all the commotion.

Relieved he was there, she turned to him eagerly. "Jason's fever is so high he has a rash. There's a new bottle of infant's pain reliever in the other bathroom. Would you mind getting it?"

"I'll be right back. And Cassie, don't worry too much. Justin once had the same thing. It looks like roseola to me. A virus—extremely uncomfortable for them but usually no serious effects."

Cassie nodded her relief but begged him to hurry. She was finding it difficult to calm Jason, who hated the cool water and fought her in earnest. Soon Trace returned, crouching beside her as he unsealed the brand-new bottle of pain reliever and removed the dropper.

He'd rolled his sleeves to the elbow, exposing his tanned hands and arms with their smattering of dark hair. "You continue to sponge him and I'll get this stuff down his throat. It should reduce his fever within half an hour and make him feel a lot better."

She couldn't figure out how Trace could remain so composed when she was practically falling apart with anxiety. After several attempts, Trace finally managed the impossible.

The sight of him bent over the tub ministering to Jason's needs filled her with an indescribable tenderness, and her earlier anger evaporated completely. But Jason seemed to be furious with her, and although it wasn't really rational, she couldn't help fearing that he'd never forgive her for this.

"Don't look so worried, Cassie," Trace said. "Jason's going to be fine, and in two days he'll have forgotten all about tonight. He already seems better, don't you think?"

Cassie reached out to touch Jason's cheeks and forehead. Trace was right. He wasn't as hot and had quieted down considerably.

"You're going to get better. Mommy and Daddy are right here. You poor little darling. You're freezing!"

"That's the idea," Trace murmured, continuing to scoop the cool water over Jason's blotchy red neck and chest.

"Mama. Dada." Jason called both their names

clearly, and Trace flashed her a look of such sweetness, her breath caught in her throat.

With her upper arm she brushed the tears from her cheeks and grasped one of the child's hands. "Just a few more minutes and Daddy will take you out of the tub, darling. It'll be over soon."

Jason began to cry again and tried to sit up. It seemed like an eternity before his father finally said, "I think this little guy has had enough for now."

As soon as Trace lifted him from the water, Cassie had a towel ready and wrapped him in it. Jason clung to Trace as they left the bathroom. Cassie thought he'd take the baby to the nursery, but instead he headed down the hall for the master bedroom. Over his shoulder he asked, "Cassie, will you please bring me the juice I saw in his crib? If I hold him on my bed for a while, maybe I can get him to drink it."

Cassie hurried into the nursery for Jason's bottle, as well as a fresh diaper and light cotton quilt. Justin was standing up in his crib, crying hoarsely. "Just a minute, Justin. Here, darling." She handed him a stuffed pig. "Mommy'll be right back."

The only time Cassie had been in Trace's bedroom was once with Nattie, when they'd put some clothes away in his drawers. She'd certainly never entered it when he was home. But right now she didn't think of that. She swept inside and dashed over to the side of the bed where he lay sprawled out full-length, his tie off and his shirt unbuttoned halfway down his chest. Jason lay in the crook of his arm staring up at his father, still whimpering a little but obviously content.

Trace took the bottle and offered it to Jason while

Cassie changed his diaper and replaced the damp towel with the quilt. She and Trace exchanged relieved glances, as Jason drank thirstily, even holding the bottle by himself.

Unfortunately, Justin was still howling mournfully. Trace sent Cassie a humorous smile, and something in his expression made her feel they really were husband and wife, in every sense of the words. She had to fight the impulse to lean down a little farther and kiss his mouth.

"I'm going," she whispered. "I'll be in the other room if you need me."

"Not yet," he said softly. He lifted his free hand to her face, shaping the palm to the contour of her cheek. "I was inexcusably rude to you earlier. Tell me what happened with Lena. Did you get anywhere with her?"

"Yes. She's willing to let me use her paintings for the opening."

There was a brief pause. "You made a better start than I'd hoped for," he said. "When we get to Snowbird, I intend to show you my appreciation. With no worries and no children, I'll be able to concentrate on you for a whole week."

Excitement coursed through her veins. For the first time since their wedding, they were going to be alone together, and Trace sounded as if he was really looking forward to it. Of course, she knew he was motivated by concern for his sister and by gratitude for Cassie's help, but she hoped he was beginning to be aware of her as a desirable woman.

"It sounds wonderful." She purposely kept her

voice low and steady for fear she'd reveal too much. She left the room immediately afterward.

With her skin still tingling from Trace's touch, she quieted Justin by picking him up and carrying him downstairs for a snack. Happy to be cuddled, he ate a graham cracker and gulped down some warm milk. A half hour later he was ready for bed.

After she'd settled him for the night, she went directly to Trace's room and tiptoed inside. As she took in the sight of Jason lying on his father's chest, her eyes moistened. Father and son were sound asleep.

Careful not to disturb them, she felt Jason's forehead; his temperature had gone down, just as Trace had predicted.

Unable to help herself, she let her gaze wander back to her husband, whose disheveled black hair made him look uncharacteristically boyish. For a few minutes she studied the lines of his strong, straight nose and mobile mouth, the way his dark lashes fanned out against bronzed cheeks. She stared at his arm, still protectively circling his son.

I love him, she thought. *I love him so much I can hardly bear it.*

Before she could do something foolish—like lie down next to him—she crept out the door and flew to her bedroom, where she could give way to her emotions in private. Trace would never know how excited she was to be going on this trip with him, how desperately she wanted to spend time with him alone. But she'd have to be very careful never to let him know how much she craved his touch. How much she craved not just gratitude and respect, but love.

Unable to sleep, Cassie pulled on a nightgown and

robe and went to her workroom, where she could unleash her energy on an idea that had been unfolding in her mind.

Going to her files, she found the pattern she wanted and began cutting out fabric. Four hours later, a stuffed, six-foot alligator with black hair and calculating blue eyes lay on the floor watching her with a wicked grin. Across the tail she had stitched the word "Daddy."

When it was finished she opened the closet door and stood the alligator on end in the far corner. To make sure it remained hidden, she draped it with a swath of white canvas, then shut the door.

If Trace ever saw it, he'd know the truth. He'd know she was in love with him. Cassie couldn't imagine anything worse—because he wasn't in love with her. He'd feel only pity, and Cassie didn't think she could stand that.

CHAPTER SEVEN

"I'VE NEVER SEEN so much snow," Cassie gasped as the large airport limousine carrying the Ramsey clan approached the lodge at Snowbird. She was pressed between Norman and Trace, who kept his arm constantly around her; her joy was diminished, since she realized it was a show of affection for his family's benefit.

"Actually Utah's had a mild winter this year," Trace said in a low voice near her ear. "I can remember coming up here several times when there were literally walls of ice. The state's in a drought cycle right now."

She surveyed the towering white mountain peaks knifing through the thin, freezing cold air. "You'd never know it." She tried desperately to appear unaffected by his nearness, but her heart was hammering out of control. She didn't know if her disorientation was due to the altitude or to the fact that she'd be sharing a bedroom with Trace in a few minutes.

"I can't wait to hit the powder!" James announced as the limo pulled to a stop. "Last one out brings the skis for everybody."

"Oh, brother!" This came from his wife, Dorothy, who sat across from Jane, Norman's wife. Lena and Allen shared the front seat with the chauffeur.

A great deal of good-natured bantering went on as they proceeded to find their bags and carry in their ski equipment.

The heat generated by a roaring blaze in the giant hearth off the lobby welcomed new arrivals. Cassie wandered over to it while Trace dealt with registration. A jaunty-looking Lena gravitated to the fire with Cassie, sporting an all-navy ski outfit that suited her trim figure perfectly. Cassie, on the other hand, felt conspicuous, dressed in brand-new fluorescent-green ski bib and white, green and blue matching parka.

Several days after Jason had fully recovered from his roseola, Trace had purchased the outfit, along with skis and boots, and had brought everything home gift-wrapped. He made her open the packages the second he bounded in the house from work.

A card lying on top of the tissue had caught her eye. Gingerly Cassie picked it up and read: "You have my undying gratitude for being such a wonderful, caring mother to our sons. I hope this gift will convey in some small measure my appreciation for the way you've turned this house into a haven I love to come home to. You've more than kept your side of our bargain, Cassie. I hope to show my appreciation when we go to Snowbird. We'll have a week to ourselves—a chance for Cassandra Ramsey to feel a little indulged for a change! Trace."

The sincere sentiment had moved her. But his note didn't contain the words she wanted to read, to hear, above all others. The realization that Trace might never fall in love with her filled her with a sudden deep despair. She fought to keep a smile on her face as she thanked him for the presents. But knowing she couldn't keep up the pretense for long, she'd made an excuse to leave the room, claiming she wanted to phone Lena.

As she called her sister-in-law, she felt Trace's probing gaze and sensed a strange undercurrent that she found more than a little troubling. To her vast relief, Lena was home and Cassie launched into conversation about their ski trip with feigned enthusiasm.

Even when Trace left the room, she could still feel his strained reaction and wondered what had caused it. Maybe she hadn't sounded grateful enough. Or maybe he resented her talking on the phone the minute he came home from work.

Whatever the problem, for the next week Cassie had taken great pains to make their home the haven he'd mentioned in his note. In between her sewing activities, she went on a cooking spree and fixed delicious meals, preparing some of his favorite Southwestern dishes. But if anything, her actions seemed to increase the tension between them. The more she tried to please him, the more polite and remote he became. It reached the point that she'd actually dreaded their trip.

At least around the house, the children acted as a buffer. But now she'd be alone with a difficult husband for six whole days and nights. She wondered how she'd survive their vacation, or even *if* she'd survive.

"Well, well. Where did you come from?" a friendly male voice said directly behind her. Cassie turned around to confront what she considered the classic male ski enthusiast. He was athletically built, with light brown hair bleached by the sun and a tan that resembled leather. A confident smile revealed a splendid set of white teeth. The man simply exuded self-satisfaction.

"We're from Timbuktu," Lena unexpectedly blurted out in a brash tone meant to send him packing. But his confident smile didn't crack, and he continued to stare admiringly at Cassie.

"If you want some help with your technique, I'm your man. Name's Hank. You'll find me by the lift every morning. I give group and private lessons."

Cassie tried hard not to laugh out loud at the man's aggression, but she would never have responded as rudely as Lena had. She merely gave him a bland smile. "Thanks for the tip. If I decide I need instruction, I'll look you up."

"Great! In that terrific outfit, you'll be easy to spot."

"Our room is ready." Trace had found her and was looking every bit as disgusted as his sister with the other man's attention. Cassie hadn't heard that icy tone since the first day in his office, when he'd almost succeeded in having her carted off to jail.

An impish mischief made her green eyes sparkle as she said, "Trace, this is Hank, one of the ski instructors for the lodge. Hank, this is my husband, Trace, and his sister, Lena."

"How do you do?" Hank put out a hand, which Trace was forced to shake. "Your sister says you're from Timbuktu. As I understand it, you don't get a lot of snow in that part of Africa."

Hank had a sense of humor, she'd give him that. There was a protracted silence. "That's right," Trace finally muttered, stone-faced. He glared at Cassie. "Are you ready?"

Swallowing hard, she said, "Whenever you are."

"Then let's go."

In the uncomfortable silence that followed, she turned to Hank. "It was nice to meet you."

Hank grinned. "I always enjoy meeting people from foreign places. See you around."

Suddenly Trace was ushering her from the foyer, his grip on her arm firm. Lena found her husband, and the four of them rode the elevator together.

"Hey, why so serious?" Allen questioned his wife. "Can you believe six whole days without the kids?" He swooped down and kissed the end of her cold nose. "Brrr," he joked, causing Lena to laugh, bringing her out of herself. "It looks like you need warming up."

Cassie averted her eyes, envious of their easy relationship and their intimacy. When the doors opened to the fourth floor, she couldn't get out of the elevator fast enough and, apparently, neither could Trace.

"See you at dinner," they called out before the doors closed again.

Trace led the way to their room, which overlooked the snowy Wasatch Mountains where they'd be skiing. The afternoon sun glistened off the dazzling white peaks, making her eyes sting.

"I can't believe we're here. Only this morning I was looking out at the desert from the nursery window."

"And wishing you didn't have to come?" he asked grimly.

Cassie whirled around in surprise. "Why do you say that?"

"I'm not blind, Cassie. I saw the way you clung to the children this morning. Anyone would've thought I was dragging you off to—" he paused "—Timbuktu for a year, instead of a short holiday. Since I know you're dying to find out if they're still alive, I'll go downstairs and bring up the rest of our things while you phone home for a report."

He left the room before she could refute his words. But in all honesty, what was there to say? She *had* been dreading this trip, but not for the reasons he imagined. Snowbird had to be one of the most romantic places on earth—and it served as a painful reminder of the mockery of a marriage to a man who didn't love her.

Her gaze strayed to the two queen-size beds. She felt a wave of humiliation. Trace couldn't possibly feel any desire for her or he wouldn't have arranged for a room with two beds. Who in the family, except Lena, could guess that for the next week, Trace and his wife would be roommates, nothing more?

Hot tears spilled down her cheeks, but she quickly dashed them away with her hands. At home, when she grew frustrated over her futile love for Trace, she could escape to her sewing room or the nursery. But now that they'd arrived at the lodge, she had to make the best of an almost intolerable situation. She could think of only one thing to do. Ski!

Perhaps in six days she could learn the basics of a sport Trace loved. But she'd need lessons from one of the instructors—and judging by Trace's reaction, it had better not be Hank. Cassie disliked that type of obsessively flirtatious man, anyway. Perhaps there was another instructor available, one more interested in skiing than in the female skiers!

With an actual plan, Cassie felt a little better. She phoned the house in Phoenix, and Nattie put her mind at rest, assuring her the children were fine. She urged Cassie to forget everything and concentrate on Trace.

When she replaced the receiver, Cassie found herself wondering if Nattie's last comment was meant to be taken as a piece of womanly advice. The housekeeper knew Cassie and Trace slept in separate bedrooms. She probably found their relationship unnatural. *Well, so did Cassie!* But there didn't seem to be a thing she could do about it.

"Are they still breathing?"

Trace's biting sarcasm jolted her out of her reverie. She turned around, counting slowly to ten before answering. Somehow she had to salvage this trip; she had to get on better terms with her husband—who at the moment looked far too attractive for her peace of mind. The gray-and-black-striped ski sweater complimented his dark good looks and emphasized his trim, powerful build.

"The children are fine, and you're right. I've doted on them to the exclusion of too many other things. Maybe it's because I'm not their natural mother, so I've taken on a greater sense of responsibility than is warranted. Please believe me when I say I'm happy to be here."

At her words, the stiffness seemed to leave his taut frame and he moved closer. His eyes searched her face for endless minutes. "Cassie, I realize you led a completely different life until you married me, and

I've expected far too much, too soon. Chalk it up to my boardroom tactics.'' With a slow smile that made her heart turn over, he put his hands on her upper arms. ''For the rest of this week, could we pretend there's just the two of us and enjoy a vacation we both badly need?''

''I'd love it.''

''Good,'' he whispered, then leaned forward to kiss the top of her head. Maybe it was her imagination, but she thought he buried his face in her hair an extra-long moment before lifting his head. Her body seemed to dissolve with desire. The slightest contact triggered a physical response she couldn't control, and she wondered if he could tell what his nearness did to her. ''Are you hungry?'' he asked as he stepped back, releasing her arms.

''Starving.

''Let's grab a hamburger. Then I'll take you out on the bunny hill and teach you a few fundamentals. In a day or two, you'll be ready to go up on the lift.''

Cassie would willingly have gone anywhere with him. And since he'd offered to give up his own skiing time to teach her, she could hardly refuse.

The rest of the day Cassie reveled in his company. She alternated between fits of laughter and spills in the snow—with the occasional success—as she tried to master the snowplow and the art of falling down safely. If Trace thought her a lost cause, he didn't say so. But she'd never seen him smile so much, which gave her more pleasure than she dared to admit, even to herself.

As the sun started to go down, he grew more playful and began tossing snowballs at her. She tried to escape, but her skis crossed and she fell headlong into the snow. When he saw her predicament, he took off his own skis and scooped up a fresh handful of snow. She struggled onto her side and giggled as he started toward her with a predatory gleam in his eye.

"No, Trace!" she screamed through her laughter, trying to shield her face. With one gloved hand he easily caught her wrists and pinned them in the snow above her head, leaving the other free to begin his torture.

"Be kind," she pleaded on a shallow breath, her eyes half dancing, half fearful, as she met his gaze, which darkened in intensity the longer they stared at each other.

"My words exactly."

A moan trembled on her lips at the passion in his husky voice. The blood surged through her veins as he lowered his head and found her mouth with his own, creating an aura of scorching heat despite the near-zero temperature of the air. Each kiss grew deeper, hungrier. Cassie could no longer contain her own frantic response. When he wrapped her in his arms and pulled her against him, she feverishly kissed him back, losing all sense of time and place.

"Good grief, Trace. You've got a perfectly good room at the lodge for that sort of thing. I think you'd better take a run with us and cool off, little brother."

Norman's teasing voice penetrated Cassie's rapture, and she pulled sharply away from her husband. Not only was she more embarrassed than she'd ever been in her life, but to be so rudely transported back to reality made her want to weep with frustration.

With enviable aplomb, Trace got to his feet, then

helped her up and handed her the ski poles she'd dropped. Cassie couldn't recover her own composure as quickly. She had to support herself with her poles so she could stand upright while she faced Trace's two brothers, who stood there unashamedly grinning at her. She didn't dare look at Trace. At this point he could be in no doubt that his wife more than welcomed his lovemaking.

She heard him ask, "Hasn't the lift closed yet?" When James said there was time for one more run, Trace turned to her. "If you don't mind, Cassie, I'll go with James and Norman and meet you back at the lodge for dinner."

What was going on? He seemed to be relieved that his brothers had interrupted their lovemaking; he'd leapt at the chance to join them. Yet Cassie could have sworn he was as shaken as she was by the passion they'd just shared. She'd thought he would tell his brothers to ski without him, that he and Cassie had other plans.

What a fool she was!

Trace was a man of experience and he'd simply been having a little fun in the snow. He hadn't meant anything serious. Most likely he was already regretting their interlude, because he hadn't expected her to respond the way she had. Well, she'd make sure he wouldn't worry that she'd gotten the wrong idea!

Lifting her head, she smiled brightly at the three of them. "To be honest, I was hoping someone else would come along to entertain Trace. For the last while, I've been dying to take my poor aching body back to the room and have a long hot soak in the tub. The altitude has made me so tired, I think I'll have a quick sandwich and go to bed. By the time you return, I'll probably be out like a light until morning.''

''You sound like Dorothy,'' Norman moaned.

Trace's expression became shuttered, as if her answer displeased him. She couldn't figure him out. ''I'll see you later then,'' he murmured, turning abruptly to get his skis.

With an aching heart Cassie watched until the three of them disappeared over the crest of the beginners' hill. He didn't once look back or wave.

What did he want? Should she have begged him in front of his brothers? Begged him to stay, to keep up the pretense that they had a normal marriage? If he hadn't regretted those intimate moments in her arms, then why had he left her?

Cassie didn't know what to make of his erratic behavior. Vowing never to get into such a vulnerable situation again, she trudged back to the lodge, ate another hamburger and went up to their room. An hour later, she climbed out of the tub, almost overcome with lethargy. She searched for the red flannel nightgown she'd made especially for the trip and fell into bed, exhausted. Once under the covers, she let out a deep sigh and was aware of nothing more until she wakened early the next morning, suffering from hunger pangs and sore muscles.

She glanced at her watch, surprised she'd slept so long. Trace was in the other bed, still asleep. When had he come to bed? She could hear his deep even breathing and noticed a tanned arm and shoulder above the blankets.

Carefully she turned on her side to watch him. Everything about him enthralled her. If he only loved her and she could be sure of his welcome, she'd climb in beside him right now and kiss him awake. The longer she gazed at him, the deeper her yearning.

When she couldn't bear it any longer, she slipped out of bed and hurried into the bathroom to dress. Now was as good a time as any to start ski lessons. Maybe later in the day Trace would join her again and she'd be able to show some improvement.

As quietly as she could, Cassie left the room and went down to the lobby to eat breakfast and arrange for lessons. Fortunately there was a woman on the ski patrol who taught group lessons in the morning before the lift opened, and Cassie signed up with her.

The class contained both children and adults at various stages of proficiency. Cassie discovered that Trace had taught her well, because she could keep up with the best of them. When the lesson was over, she hurried back to the room to tell him, but he'd already gone.

The rest of the day brought little pleasure. The flirtatious instructor, Hank, saw her on the hill later in the morning and wanted to ski with her, but she refused. Then it was time for lunch. She joined Dorothy, Jane and Lena, who all declared they'd had enough skiing for one day. Apparently the men had gone off together, so the women decided to play cards in front of the fire. Trace didn't make an appearance until everyone gathered for dinner in the main dining room that evening.

He greeted Cassie with a kiss on the cheek as if nothing was wrong, and laughed and joked with the others. Everyone described the day's events; inevitably, one of the women brought up the fact that Cassie

had had a ski lesson. Trace murmured something appropriate and said that when she felt ready, they
would take a run together. On the surface his behavior
appeared perfectly normal. But Cassie sensed his
withdrawal.

As the evening wore on, the family stayed downstairs for the musical entertainment. Cassie couldn't
enjoy it because, although Trace always acted the part
of a polite, concerned husband, he had distanced himself from her. This, more than anything, convinced
her he wanted to forget what had happened on their
first day in the snow.

Pleading fatigue, one by one each couple headed
up to bed, until finally Cassie was left alone with
Trace. "You seem tired," he said in that same polite
voice. "Why don't you go up to bed? I'm going to
have a drink in the bar."

Nothing could be plainer than that! Cassie murmured a good-night and barely made it to the room
before she broke down sobbing. She couldn't take it
much longer.

The next day started out like a repeat of the previous one, with Trace still sleeping soundly in the
other bed as she left for her lesson. She was still agonizing over Trace when she entered the lobby afterward. Lena was waiting for her and asked if she'd
like to take a shuttle bus down to Salt Lake City to
do some shopping. Allen's birthday was the next
weekend and Lena wanted to get him something special. Cassie didn't have to think twice about accepting
her invitation. She wasn't an enthusiastic shopper, but
anything was better than spending the rest of the day

on the slopes hoping she'd run into Trace, or worse, praying in vain that he'd come to find her.

Lena wanted to keep their expedition a secret, so Cassie left Trace a note saying only that she was going down the canyon. They left the lodge with a group of other people to do a full day's shopping and sightseeing. The first thing Cassie bought was postcards, and while she and Lena ate Mexican food at Chef Trujillo's, she wrote short notes to some of her friends in San Francisco, including Beulah.

They spent the afternoon trailing in and out of shops. Cassie found hand-knit toques and mittens for the boys, some gourmet preserves for Nattie, and a small bottle of Canadian rye for Mike.

She managed to buy a gift for Trace, too. Quite by chance she'd seen a framed photograph of the mountains around Snowbird in a tourist shop, where Lena had already found another snow scene for Allen's gift. The shot was quite spectacular, with the early-morning rays tinting the snow-covered peaks. Luckily it didn't cost a great deal and was something she could buy with her own money, but she thought he'd like it.

By the time their bus pulled up to the lodge in the evening, the family had eaten and gone their separate ways. Cassie hurried upstairs with her packages, anxious to give Trace his present. But he wasn't in the room. If he'd gone to the bar, presumably he wanted to be alone, and she had no intention of disturbing him. If he was visiting with one of his brothers, she was equally unwilling to intrude. Dejected, she took a shower, put on her flannel nightgown and climbed into bed with a recent mystery novel she'd bought that afternoon.

Trace walked in half an hour later. Slowly Cassie's gaze lifted to his above the pages of the book. As always, she was achingly aware of him. He was dressed in sweats, with a deep tan that attested to a day's skiing—she noticed that instantly but she also noticed the tension in his posture and expression. "Hello," she said in an unsteady voice.

"So you're back." Grimacing, he tossed the room key on the table. "Did you have a good time?"

Cassie sat up straight, anxious to tell him about her day, to hear about his. "Yes. And I bought something for you. It's there on the bed."

He moved slowly to the bed and unwrapped the gift. "It's beautiful, Cassie—but you don't have to bribe me into going home. I know you never wanted to come to Snowbird in the first place."

The book fell out of her hands. "I don't want to leave. I'm having a good time."

His expression grew bleak. "Well, I'm not. I brought you here to spend time with you. But every time I turn around, you're missing. The family is beginning to wonder what's going on."

Anger made her face feel hot. "I thought the purpose of this trip was to be by ourselves and do what we wanted. If you remember, *you're* the one who took off with your brothers the first night we were here." She could have bitten her tongue for referring to that evening, but it was too late now.

Trace's mouth hardened, as if he didn't like being reminded of the incident. "Did you go to Salt Lake City alone?"

Cassie averted her eyes. His unexpected question had conveniently changed the subject. "No."

"I didn't think so."

Throwing back the covers, she got out of bed to face him. To her dismay, his eyes traveled unhurriedly over her curves, which weren't hidden by the red fabric, then finally lifted to her flushed face. It was almost enough to make her forget what they were arguing about.

"In case you're thinking I was with that ski instructor," she said calmly, "then you couldn't be more wrong. For your information, I went to Salt Lake City with Lena—at her request. I thought you'd realize she and I were together. She wanted to buy something special for Allen's birthday and didn't want him to know about it."

"Be that as it may, your disappearances have pretty well let the family know that your interests lie outside your marriage."

"That's unfair!" she cried. "How can you say such a thing? Except for the first day, have you ever asked me to ski with you? Have you invited me out to dinner? Did you ask me to stay with you in the bar and dance?"

His expression was tight with fury. "After hearing you tell my brothers you were hoping someone else would come along to entertain me, I had doubts that any invitation of mine would be welcome."

Cassie's eyes closed tightly. "I only said that so you wouldn't feel obliged to stay with me. I know how much you love to ski with them."

They stood facing each other in silence, like adversaries. Finally he said, "Whatever the reasons for our misunderstandings, this trip isn't working out. Be packed and ready to go in the morning.''

He placed the photograph and its crumpled wrappings on his night-table with a deliberate care that confused her. Then he disappeared out the door, leaving Cassie furious—and heartsick.

CHAPTER EIGHT

AFTER EATING a bit of the chicken salad a surprised Nattie had left for her, Cassie started up the stairs to check on the children, whom she'd put to bed earlier. As she reached the first landing, she heard the phone ring. She fervently hoped it was Trace. He'd left for the office after they'd returned from Snowbird that afternoon and hadn't bothered to come home for dinner. She dashed into his study, picked up the receiver and said a nervous hello.

"Cassie? It's Lena!"

"Lena? What are you doing calling me from Snowbird?"

"More to the point, what are you and Trace doing back in Phoenix? Allen and I decided to sleep in this morning. When we got up, James told us you and Trace had left the lodge to go home. Something about a problem with one of the boys. I think everyone else believed it, but I don't. Can you talk, or is Trace around?"

"He went to the bank to see if there was anything pressing. I put the children to bed an hour ago and just had some supper."

"Then you can talk. What's wrong? You know I'd do anything for you and Trace."

"You shouldn't have said that." Cassie swallowed

back a sob. "Trace and I have had one misunderstanding after another," she said hopelessly.

"Which one of you called off the rest of your vacation, or am I being too nosy?"

"Of course not. If you want the truth, I think he's tired of having to pretend everything's perfect with us when we're around the family. I never seem to be able to say the right thing. We do much better alone at the house, with just the children. Our marriage won't survive another vacation."

"I'm sorry, Cassie. This must be so hard for you. I was once in love with someone and I thought he loved me, until I learned the truth the hard way. It took me a long time to get over him, so I can just imagine what you're going through right now. I wish there was something I could do to help."

"I appreciate your support and friendship. Unfortunately no one can make Trace fall in love with me," Cassie said in a voice that quavered despite her effort to sound matter-of-fact. "If it hasn't happened by now, it never will. That's the reality and I'm going to have to live with it. Don't forget, I went into this marriage for the children's sake."

"But the children will never be enough now."

"I hope you're wrong," she said softly, then broke off when she heard footsteps on the stairs. "Lena, I'll have to hang up. I think Trace is home."

"All right. I'll call you as soon as we get back."

"Thanks for everything." Cassie put down the receiver as the study door flew open and Trace stood there, silhouetted in the light from a hallway lamp. Cassie muttered a greeting, but something in his stance made her unaccountably nervous.

"You're upset. Did something go wrong with the merger while we were on our trip?" she asked.

"If you weren't so preoccupied with your phone call, you would have been able to hear the boys crying. Who has such a claim on your time you've been neglecting them?"

His unfair accusation stung Cassie to retaliation. "How dare you say that to me when you didn't bother to come home for dinner to be with them—or even call to let me know you'd be late!" she demanded, her chest heaving with indignation.

His hands curled into fists, and without volition, her eyes took in the strength of his body, the powerful thighs in tight-fitting jeans, the black knit shirt that clung to his chest like a second skin. They were close enough that she could feel the warmth of his body and smell the soap he'd used in the shower. Right now she couldn't think or move as desire for him engulfed her like a sudden burst of flame.

"I dare because I'm your husband." A hand shot out and grasped her wrist, bringing her closer and making her far too conscious of his body. "You still haven't answered my question."

She could have told him the truth—that it was Lena on the phone—but she didn't. She was too angry, because he didn't seem to trust her. And at the same time she needed to put distance between them before she lost complete control.

"As I recall," she said coldly, "*you* were the one who said what we did with our private lives was our own affair, as long as it didn't hurt the children. I never question the unorthodox hours you keep, and I'm not doing anything you haven't done since the day we were married.'' She tried to pull away, but he held her fast.

"And just what is it you think I've been doing?'' he whispered. ''Making secret assignations behind your back? Why should I do that when I have a wife who seems perfectly capable of filling everyone's needs—but mine? I think it's time you took care of them.''

In the next instant he drew her into his arms and found her mouth with a savagery that made nonsense of her efforts to resist. For so long she'd wanted him, but not like this, not angry and suspicious of her motives. Yet she wasn't prepared for the intimate caress of his hands against the skin of her back, where her blouse had separated from her jeans. His touch softened and Cassie melted against every line and angle of his hard body, helplessly yielding to the seductive pressure of his mouth, his hands.

Cassie hadn't ever known this kind of ecstasy before, and she didn't want Trace to stop. Her arms slid around his neck so she could get even closer. She wanted to give, and go on giving until he knew in every single cell of his body that she loved him. That she always would.

Perhaps it was her moan of pleasure that caused a shudder to pass through his body. The next thing she knew, he had thrust her away from him. She cried out in surprise and clung to his desk to prevent herself from falling.

The faint light made it impossible for her to see his expression clearly. But if his shallow breathing and the tautness of his body were any indication, he'd been equally disturbed by their passionate embrace.

Then she heard a muttered curse before he blurted out, "I had no right to lay a finger on you, Cassie, let alone demand an accounting. Whatever you do with your free time is none of my damn business. I'm the one who's broken the rules of our contract and I swear it won't happen again. Why don't you go on up to bed. I know you're under a lot of pressure, getting ready for your opening. I'll lock up and take a look at the boys before I turn in."

She watched him leave the study and ached to call him back. But without knowing how he really felt about her, what he really wanted from her, she didn't dare. Living in the same house day after day had made them aware of each other to the point of physical need. She'd felt Trace's desire for her. But that didn't mean he was in love with her.

Drained from the explosive emotions, Cassie followed his suggestion and went to bed. But she was plagued with insomnia. Trace had set her on fire, exposing the primitive, womanly side of her nature, changing her preconceived notions about physical love for all time.

By two o'clock, her body was still reliving the taste and feel of his mouth and she couldn't fall asleep. Disgusted with herself, she went to her sewing room, where she immersed herself in work and didn't come out until seven in the morning.

When she went downstairs to start breakfast, she discovered that Trace's car wasn't in the driveway. He'd deliberately left the house early; when she realized this, her hurt intensified. She went through the motions of her morning routine, which included bathing and feeding the children. At noon Nattie took over so she could leave the house and drive to the gallery with as many things as she could load into the station wagon. This set the pattern for the next few days.

Besides all the new crafts she'd been making, she decided to sell all the stock items from her inventory, too. There was a second display room, which would be perfect. But even with Mike's help, it took several days to move everything from the house to the shop. During that time, she saw next to nothing of Trace, who came home too late to do more than kiss the boys good-night and disappear into his study.

On Friday, as Cassie was unpacking another set of freestanding shelves at the shop and trying not to think about the impossible state of affairs between her and Trace, Lena walked in, carrying some paintings.

Cassie stared at her sister-in-law. "I'm so glad you're back."

"I bet you thought I'd deserted you, staying so long at Snowbird, but Allen and I had to be alone. I've tried to make up for lost time today by signing the rest of the paintings. As you know, my car won't hold more than two at a time, so I'll have to make several trips."

Shaking her head, Cassie said, "We'll go back to the house in the station wagon and get the rest. Now that you've finished them, I'm going to stay here all evening and set up as much as I can to view the full effect." She glanced around. "I think I'm going to have to buy some more plants, though."

Lena scrutinized everything with her artist's eye. "I'll tell you what. I want to be home with the children for dinner. Then I'll come back here to help, but it'll have to remain our secret. Allen can think I've gone to a PTA meeting.''

"Are you sure?" Cassie cried out excitedly. Trace would be overjoyed if he knew how involved Lena had become with Mix and Match.

"You're a remarkable woman, Cassie, but even I can see how much work still has to be done.''

"The opening's coming up much too soon," Cassie agreed, "and there aren't enough hours in the day to accomplish everything. Now let's go home and get the rest of the paintings.''

She didn't particularly relish the prospect of being at the shop alone at night and would be thankful for Lena's presence. Although she wasn't entirely comfortable with her sister-in-law's apparent penchant for secrecy, she could understand it, too. Lena was so terribly unsure of herself and of her talent.

As it turned out, Lena and Cassie worked side by side for the next two nights, attempting to set up the most appealing displays possible. And they shared more confidences. Cassie marveled at her sister-in-law's decorating sense and thanked her repeatedly before they parted company Saturday night.

"Don't forget Allen's surprise birthday dinner at seven tomorrow. I phoned Trace earlier and invited him, so he knows you're both expected.''

And probably dreading another evening with me in front of his family, Cassie mused painfully. "Will everyone be there?''

"No. It's just going to be the four of us," Lena explained, lessening Cassie's anxiety somewhat.

The next morning didn't begin well. Nattie informed Cassie that Trace had left to keep a golf date with a business acquaintance. When he did come home, he spent some time with the children, and she didn't see him until they were ready to go to Lena's.

They behaved civilly to each other, but during dinner Trace couldn't have been more distant with Cassie, more removed from her emotionally—a fact Lena was quick to observe. While they cleared the table, she flashed Cassie a look of commiseration.

Cassie was grateful for Allen, whose conversation as he opened his presents provided the only comic relief. His eyes met his wife's as he unwrapped the framed photograph she'd bought him in Utah and he sent her a message of love so fervent that Cassie lowered her own eyes. She knew he must be remembering the private time he and Lena had spent at Snowbird. But the moment was brief and he quickly moved on to the other gifts, ending with Cassie's. Lena had told her that Allen loved to barbecue, so Cassie had made him a chef's apron embroidered with French cooking terms.

"So tell me, you lucky cuss." Allen poked Trace in the ribs. "How did you manage to end up with Cassie? She can cook, sew, she's a great mother and her skiing's coming along nicely. She's a looker, too."

Normally Cassie would have been amused by Allen's remarks. But she was too sensitive to Trace's mood just now. She found herself waiting uncomfortably for one of his carefully worded responses while she pretended interest in the birthday cake.

"You left out the part about her being a savvy business woman," Lena interjected on cue, saving Trace from having to utter a word.

"That's right," Allen murmured. "How's the shop coming?"

His question was directed at Cassie, but it was Trace who answered. "Judging by the nights she's stayed up sewing, I'd say she probably has more than enough things to fill several shops." Although his comment sounded innocent, Cassie wasn't deceived. She lowered her head, but not before Lena had sent her a sympathetic glance.

"When's the opening?" Allen asked, seemingly ignorant of the undercurrents. "Lena and I plan to be there."

"Next Saturday," Cassie said faintly. The tension emanating from Trace left her so nervous, she was finding it more and more difficult to speak.

Suddenly Lena cleared her throat and looked nervously at her husband. "Darling, I think it's time I made a confession." There was an air of expectancy after her announcement.

"We're not pregnant again, are we?" he teased, but Cassie could see the love shining in his eyes.

"No." Lena laughed. "When I told you I had meetings the last two nights, I was lying." Allen's smile slowly faded. "Actually, I've been helping Cassie at the gallery."

Allen blinked. "That's great. But why didn't you just say so?"

"Because...Cassie's using some of my old paintings as part of her display. At first I didn't want you to know about it because..."

He stopped eating his cake and gazed at his wife solemnly. "Does this mean what I think it means?"

She took a deep breath. "It means that I've been a fool to be so sensitive about the past."

"Honey..." Allen's hand grasped hers.

Something was going on here that Cassie didn't quite understand. Allen seemed overwhelmed with emotion. She automatically glanced at Trace and discovered his eyes focused on her, sending her a private message of gratitude. Even if the warmth in his regard had everything to do with her influence on Lena, Cassie basked in his approval. She had no pride anymore. She loved him too much.

In the background she could hear the phone ringing and then Becky, Lena's daughter, poked her head around the dining-room door. "Aunt Cassie? Uncle Trace? Nattie says you'd better come home. Jason woke up croupy."

The twelve hours following Lena's dinner party would have been a nightmare for Cassie if Trace hadn't been there to help nurse Jason through the night. First roseola, now a croupy cough that kept them all awake. By noon the next day, however, he seemed much better and Cassie finally relaxed.

She couldn't say the same for Trace. Fatigue lines etched his face from hour after hour of walking the floor with Jason. Cassie urged him to call Mrs. Blakesley and cancel any appointments for the day so he could go to bed. But Trace insisted he had to be at the bank for an important afternoon meeting and left the house at a run.

Once again she found herself marveling at the extraordinary strength of the man she'd married. Trace was unfailingly responsible, always dependable. The longer she lived with him, the more Cassie realized how much she, as well as others, particularly his family, relied on him. Though the youngest Ramsey, it was no accident that his brothers had made him chairman of the board. His confidence and his abilities made people put their trust in him.

Because he worked so hard, Cassie was concerned about his not getting enough rest, and she spent the remainder of the afternoon and evening worrying about her husband instead of Jason, who was starting to behave more like himself again.

Cassie had been asleep for some time when she heard a knock on her door. Alarmed, she glanced at the bedside clock, which said it was after midnight. The knock sounded again.

"Nattie?" she called anxiously and sat up in bed.

"It's Trace, Cassie. I need to talk to you. May I come in?"

"Yes. Of course." Her voice shook as she turned on the lamp and pulled the covers to her chin. "Is Jason bad again?" she asked as he entered her bedroom wearing his bathrobe. He must have come from the shower because the clean scent of soap wafted in the air.

Trace closed the door behind him and approached her bed. "No. I just checked on him. He's fine. So's Justin."

She swallowed hard. "When did you come home? I held dinner until nine, then put yours in the fridge."

"I'm sorry I was late again. I only just got home." The lines in his face were more pronounced than ever.

"You should have been in bed hours ago, Trace. You look exhausted. How did your meeting go?" Cassie had the hysterical urge to laugh because he'd never been in her bedroom this late at night before, and here were the two of them talking like a comfortably married couple.

"Very well, as a matter of fact, but I didn't waken you to talk about bank business. I have something much more serious on my mind."

"Is it about Lena and Allen?"

Her question seemed to baffle him. "No. Why would it be when things have never been better between them?"

"I meant to ask you about that. Why was Allen so overcome by what she said?"

"Because for all the years they've been married, Allen had a secret fear that Lena couldn't talk about her painting or even admit she was once an artist because she was still in love with her ex-lover. Allen hasn't always been the comedian he pretends to be. His jovial behavior has been a front for insecurity, even pain."

"But that's crazy!" Cassie cried. "Lena adores Allen. She's confided everything to me, and I promise you, she got over that affair years ago. She asked Allen if they could stay on in Snowbird after everyone left because she wanted to have a second honeymoon with him."

The pulse at the corner of his mouth throbbed. "Every man should be so lucky. After her unprompted confession last night, I think he's beginning to believe she loves him wholeheartedly—thanks to you."

Cassie shook her head. "Not me, Trace. You. It was your suggestion that prompted me to talk to Lena in the first place. Somehow you have a gift for making everything right for everybody. The boys are very lucky to have a father like you,'' she said with a catch in her voice.

''I wonder if this gift you credit me with can fix something a little closer to home.''

Her heart thudded painfully at his sober tone. ''What is it? What's wrong?''

A grimace marred his handsome features. ''When I asked you to marry me, we agreed that if there ever came a time when we didn't like the arrangement, we'd face that problem when it arose.''

It was a good thing Cassie was already in bed or she might have fainted. ''I remember,'' she whispered, hardly able to get the words out. ''I've been aware for some time that you haven't been happy. Actually I've wanted to talk to you about it, but the opportunity never seemed to present itself.''

After a long pause, he said, ''That's my fault. I realize I've been impossible to live with. Cassie, I can't go on this way any longer.''

A numbing sickness slowly crept through her body. ''You don't need to say any more. I'll move out.''

To her astonishment his head reared back. ''What in the hell are you talking about? I came in here tonight to tell you I hate the rules of our marriage contract and I'm asking you to start sleeping with me in my bed.''

When his words sank in, Cassie felt herself go feverishly hot, then cold. She raised her eyes to him in disbelief. He muttered something unintelligible and shook his head when he saw her stunned expression.

''Living in the same house with you and not being able to make love to you has almost driven me out of my mind. Surely after the other night you can be in no doubt about how much I want you. I almost couldn't let you go.''

His admission opened a floodgate of emotions in Cassie. There was no mistaking the look of desire in his eyes as he sat down on the bed next to her and traced the outline of her flushed face with his fingers. ''I'm aching to touch you and hold you all night long. You're in my blood, Cassie—and I know of only one way to solve that particular problem.''

In the next instant his mouth covered hers, forcing her head back against the pillow. For a little while Cassie refused to listen to her heart, which told her there was all the difference in the world between a man's desire for a woman and his love. The sensations his lips aroused against the tender skin of her neck and throat were so addictive she never wanted him to stop. She could no longer think coherently.

But when he lifted the covers to slide into bed beside her she couldn't help remembering that this was how his son's conception had begun. By Trace's own admission, he'd never have married Gloria if he hadn't made her pregnant. Their passion had resulted in a baby, but Jason wasn't the product of two people deeply in love who needed to express those feelings in the age-old way. They had divorced soon after the birth.

Cassie loved Trace with a fierceness he hadn't even guessed at. As for his feelings, she wasn't so naive that she didn't know this would be simply another night of physical passion for him. Sexual gratification, without the heart-deep commitment she desperately needed. Cassie had no way of determining how many times he'd experienced this same desire for the latest woman in his life. *Because that was all she was— and she happened to be available!* The word "love" hadn't even been mentioned. When he tired of her, they'd go back to being housemates again.

Unable to tolerate that possibility, she pushed herself away from him and got to her feet. When he stood up, they faced each other from opposite sides of the narrow bed. Trace ran a hand through his already disheveled black hair, a gesture so sensual she had to close her eyes against its appeal. He would never know what denying herself his lovemaking was costing her.

"The desire seems to be all on my part."

She swallowed hard. "When two people aren't in love, then it's wrong."

The silence seemed to stretch endlessly before he said, "It's inconceivable to me that a woman as warm and beautiful and desirable as you would be willing to go through her whole life without ever experiencing sexual intimacy. I was wrong in asking you to enter this farcical arrangement."

With those words Cassie lost every vestige of hope that he might come to love her. "So far, I—I've been...happy with it," she stammered. "I'm sorry if it hasn't worked out for you, since you've had ample opportunity to spend your free time with anyone you wanted, no questions asked."

His features could have been cast in stone. "You're right. I have," he retorted.

"I'll move out after the opening if that's what you want."

"It's not!" he fired back, sounding more intense

than she'd ever heard him before. "The boys adore you and I have living proof that they're your whole raison d'être. Any problems we have are mine and mine alone." He strode from the room without a backward glance.

Since she couldn't imagine a life without him, she should have been overjoyed that he hadn't taken her up on her offer to leave. But once he'd gone, Cassie flung herself on the bed and buried her face in the pillow to stifle her sobs.

Contrary to her expectations, for the rest of the week Trace was surprisingly kind and considerate, and never once alluded to the ugly scene in her bedroom. He came home early every night to help with the children so Cassie would be free to prepare for the opening. It reminded her of the first few weeks of their marriage, when they'd enjoyed an easy camaraderie and shared the joys of caring for the children.

But in those early days she'd still retained the hope that Trace would fall in love with her and make their marriage a real one. All she could do now was shower her affection on the children and concentrate on her business in an effort to ignore the aching void only Trace could fill.

Late Friday afternoon, before the grand opening on Saturday, Cassie was at the gallery finishing up some last-minute details when she heard a familiar voice call her name.

She spun around to face the tall, rangy man with dark brown hair and eyes who'd been watching her. "Rolfe!" Somehow in the rush of things she'd completely forgotten about his coming to Phoenix.

"You look wonderful, Cass." He held out his arms

and she ran into them, hugging him tightly. "I've missed you," he murmured into her hair.

"I've missed you, too." But the way he was holding her made her realize he was about to kiss her and she quickly pulled out of his arms. "I had no idea you were in town."

"I flew in an hour ago and phoned the number Mother gave me. Your housekeeper said you were down here, so I thought I'd come and surprise you."

"You certainly did that." She smiled, then asked deliberately, "Did you bring your fiancée back with you?"

He frowned. "I thought you'd be able to tell from the telegram that I'm no longer engaged."

"And you thought you'd come back into Cassie's life and pick up where you left off?"

Cassie's eyes widened in astonishment to discover that Trace had come into the shop and was strolling toward them, still dressed in the suit he'd worn to work. He carried a sack of take-out fried chicken. She was so surprised to see him and so thrilled that he'd been thoughtful enough to bring dinner she wished Rolfe a thousand miles away.

"Trace, this is Rolfe Timpson. Rolfe, I'd like you to meet my husband, Trace Ramsey."

The two men took each other's measure, and Trace nodded, but neither put out a hand.

"What is it you're after, Timpson? My wife is busy getting ready for her opening. This isn't the best time to come calling."

Rolfe's gaze slid to Cassie's. "She knows why I'm here. Cassie and I have always belonged together. I made a mistake when I broke our engagement. I was too impatient, but I've learned my lesson and I want her back, no matter how long it takes.''

''It's too late,'' Trace interjected before she could say anything. ''Cassie's my wife now.''

Undaunted, Rolfe continued to stare at her. ''But I know how she really feels, and I have a letter to prove it. She married you to be close to Susan's baby, nothing more.''

Dear Lord. The letter. Cassie had forgotten all about it. But that was before she'd married Trace and fallen in love with him.

Trace's body tautened. ''That's right, Timpson. Now she's the mother of both my children, and that's the way it's going to stay. Have a good trip back to San Francisco.'' Trace put the food on the counter and darted her a mysterious glance. ''I presume I'll be seeing you at home soon? Early enough to help put the boys to bed?''

''Yes,'' she called after him softly. ''I was just closing up. Thank you for dinner.'' She would have kissed his cheek, but he'd already turned on his heel and walked out of the shop.

Rolfe studied her, and the silence stretched between them. ''Did I misunderstand your letter, Cassie?''

She shook her head. ''No. But I wrote it before I married Trace.''

Again there was a long period of quiet. ''You're in love with him, aren't you?''

''Yes.''

He took a fortifying breath. ''You were never in love with me, but I didn't want to believe it.''

Cassie's eyes clouded over. ''I'll always love you,

Rolfe—like a brother. You're the most wonderful man I know, next to Trace."

"I threw it all away when I broke our engagement."

"No. Don't you see? If you'd really loved me the way I love Trace, you wouldn't have left. But you did because you sensed it wasn't right between us. And even if your engagement to the woman you met in Belgium didn't last, it proves you were ready for another relationship."

"I'll never forget you, Cass."

She smiled. "And I'll always remember you, because you were my first love."

CHAPTER NINE

CASSIE COULD HARDLY WAIT to get home to Trace. Maybe he wasn't in love with her, but he'd let Rolfe know in no uncertain terms that he wanted Cassie to remain his wife. It was a beginning, and she was determined that in time their marriage would become a proper one.

The minute Rolfe left the store, she closed up and sped home, snatching bites of the delicious chicken he'd brought her every time she stopped for a light.

The absence of his car in the drive sent her spirits plummeting as she pulled up to the house. And Nattie's explanation that he hadn't come home yet filled her with dread. She'd expected him to be here, playing with the children. Waiting for her.

When eleven o'clock arrived, he still hadn't come home. Cassie finally gave up her vigil and went to bed, needing sleep before her opening the next day. But it was fitful and she awakened restless and out of sorts.

The next morning after her shower, she put on a smart navy silk suit she'd purchased a few days earlier. The tailoring and sophistication bolstered her waning confidence.

Lena planned to meet her at Mix and Match at eight. Cassie went in to kiss the children goodbye before leaving for the gallery, skipping breakfast altogether. If Trace was up, she didn't see a sign of him, and she drove away from the house in tears.

"You look beautiful," Lena told her when Cassie arrived at the back entrance to the shop. "But you've been crying. What's wrong?"

"Let's go in and I'll tell you."

While they got the shop ready, Cassie explained what had happened the night before. "I don't understand him, Lena. He's like a wind that blows hot, then cold. I can't live the rest of my life this way."

"I don't like the sound of that. What are you planning to do?"

"I—I'm not sure. I have to get through today before I can make any serious decisions."

"Cassie, a word of advice. Don't act hastily. Give everything more time."

"Time seems to be making things worse."

She wasn't destined to hear Lena's response because a young man appeared at the door holding an enormous spray of the most exquisite yellow roses Cassie had ever seen. There had to be five or six dozen, at least. "I have a delivery for Cassie Ramsey."

"Oh, they're gorgeous!" Lena exclaimed. "And I have a pretty good idea who sent them."

Cassie signed for them, and when the delivery man had gone she hunted for the card tucked among the sprays of fern. "A woman like you makes her own luck, but you have all my best wishes just the same. Trace." The words reminded her forcefully of another time when he'd complimented her for being able to stand on her own two feet. *Alone.*

Crushing the card in her hand, she whispered to Lena, "Would you find a good spot for these so Trace will see them when he comes by later?"

Lena took the flowers from her. "Heavens, Cassie. You look so pale. What's wrong?"

"Nothing. Just more of Trace's...kindness. If you'll open the machine, I'll get busy putting out the rest of the door prizes in case we have an overflow. I'm being optimistic, aren't I?" She laughed nervously.

Lena slid a comforting arm around Cassie's waist before they both went to work. At five to ten, there were people milling around the store entrance. Her thoughts went back to a time in San Francisco when she hadn't a prayer of realizing her dream of opening a boutique. Again she had to remind herself how lucky she was. But at what price?

The next hour flew by in a blur of activity. Besides curious shoppers who lingered and raved over the displays, unable to make up their minds about what they wanted to buy, there must have been half a dozen more florist deliveries from every member of Trace's family, as well as the manager of Crossroads Square.

At eleven o'clock, another flower arrangement arrived, from Beulah no less. And right after that, three men brought in an enormous flowering cactus. A banner that wished Cassie and Lena good luck was signed, "Compliments of the Greater Phoenix Banking Corporation."

The noon hour brought in more traffic, and suddenly everyone seemed ready to make purchases. At one point, Cassie looked up and noted to her astonishment that the shop was slowly being denuded of its inventory. She couldn't believe it.

"Mrs. Ramsey?" someone called to her.

She turned her head and thought she recognized the manager of a well-known restaurant down the street from Crossroads Square. "I know we've met, but I'm embarrassed to say I don't remember your name."

"Hal Sykes." He grinned. "Welcome to the block. I saw your ad in the paper and decided to drop in. I'm very glad I did. There are three paintings I'm interested in purchasing, but I don't see a price on any of them. Does that mean they've already sold?"

Cassie grinned widely as she looked at Lena, madly ringing up one sale after another. "I'll tell you what," she murmured. "You can talk to the artist, Mrs. Haroldson, and see what she says. Just a minute."

With her adrenaline pumping, Cassie worked her way through the crowd to the counter. "Lena, I'll take over here. There's a Mr. Sykes standing by the cactus who wants help. He's in the pink shirt."

Lena darted him a glance. "His face looks familiar."

"That's because we ate in his restaurant the other day."

"I remember. Okay. I'll be right back."

Cassie chuckled to herself in glee when yet another customer inquired about one of the paintings and left her card. Lena didn't return until a half hour later, looking positively dazed. "What did Mr. Sykes want?" Cassie asked between sales.

Lena blinked. "He offered me five thousand dollars for the three paintings over there. He's remodeling part of his restaurant and says they'd be perfect for the decor.''

Keeping a poker face, Cassie said, ''I hope you told him ten thousand or nothing.''

''Cassie!''

''Well?''

''I—I told him they weren't for sale, but he wrote out a check, anyway, and said he'd be back before we closed at seven, in case I changed my mind.'' She handed Cassie the check, made out to Mix and Match Southwest.

''I could use money like that to replenish my inventory,'' Cassie said matter-of-factly and put the check in the till. ''Before you turn him down flat, why don't we talk about it? Say fifteen percent for every painting sold out of the store, and the rest for you?''

''Be serious,'' Lena said in a trembling voice.

''I am,'' Cassie came back. ''A few minutes ago a woman told me she was interested in your sunset painting, the one with all the pinks and oranges. She's a New Yorker who wanted to take home a souvenir of Arizona. She's also an art dealer and offered four thousand for it. Here's her card. You're supposed to get in touch with her at that number next week.''

''Hi, honey. How's it going?'' a familiar voice broke in on their conversation.

Lena whirled around, her gray eyes luminous. ''Allen!''

''I'm glad you're here.'' Cassie beamed at her brother-in-law. ''Business is booming and we both need a break. Why don't you take your wife out for a quick lunch? When she returns, I'll grab a bite.''

''Are you sure?'' They both spoke at once.

"It's not quite as busy as it was earlier. But don't forget to come back. I can't run this place without you."

"A half hour," Lena promised. "No longer."

"Be sure and tell Allen about the nine thousand offered for your paintings already. And the day's only half over!"

In front of any number of interested customers, Allen let out a whoop of joy and swung Lena around before hustling her out of the shop.

Trace's clever scheme to help his sister looked as if it had succeeded, and Cassie couldn't help but take personal delight in the knowledge that she'd played a part. But with the steady stream of customers waiting to pay for their purchases, Cassie didn't have time to dwell on anything. Including the bleakness of her own future after she left Trace....

There had hardly been a lull since the doors opened. Naturally the opening would attract more shoppers than Cassie could expect on a regular business day. Still, she had to admit the large turnout was gratifying, and she prayed it augured well for future sales, since she wouldn't be depending on Trace's support any longer.

While she chatted with customers and took orders for items already sold out, she was making plans to search for a small apartment in Phoenix. She could live there and still have regular access to the children. She and Trace wouldn't have to see each other; Nattie and Mike could help make visitations smooth and pleasant.

Even if Cassie felt like the boys' mother, the fact remained that she was Justin's aunt and had no blood ties to Jason whatsoever. Under the circumstances, it would be wisest to move out of Trace's home now and establish herself in the community where she could earn her living. She'd see the boys whenever possible. As long as they wanted a relationship, she would be there for them in the capacity of aunt and friend.

No matter what Trace said, in time he'd fall in love and want to marry for all the right reasons, ultimately providing the boys with a stepmother. Painful as that would be to face, Cassie knew what she had to do for the welfare of all concerned.

"Look who I brought back with me." Lena's happy voice broke in on Cassie's thoughts as she was straightening the counter. She glanced up in time to see most of Trace's family enter the shop. The Ramseys' striking looks caused heads to turn. One by one they came over to give Cassie a hug while she thanked them for the flowers.

"I'm so proud of you, dear." Olivia patted Cassie's cheek. Then nodding toward Lena, who'd taken over at the cash register, the older woman whispered, "Bless you, Cassie."

"It's Trace's doing. You know that," Cassie whispered back.

"I know a lot more than you think."

Cassie barely had time to ponder her mother-in-law's mysterious reply, because there was a commotion at the door. As she turned her head, she caught sight of a tanned, relaxed-looking Trace, wheeling in the children seated in their two-seater stroller. Their entry caused delighted outbursts from his family, as well as other shoppers who crowded round.

Trace wore chinos and a navy sports shirt, open at the neck. The boys were dressed in identical navy sailor suits she'd made for them. On their feet were spanking white shoes and socks. They looked so marvelous Cassie forgot where she was and could do nothing more than lean against the glass countertop for support, feasting her eyes. There they were, not ten feet away. The three people in the world she loved more than life itself.

At that moment she experienced a pain so staggering she thought she might faint. Since the children hadn't yet seen her, she said, "Lena, excuse me for a minute." Without waiting to hear her sister-in-law's reply, Cassie hurried to the back room, which served as a supply area with an adjoining bathroom.

She waited until the wave of sickness had passed, then applied fresh lipstick before going back out. Trace was waiting for her on the other side of the door, his face alarmed. He put a hand to her forehead. "I saw you dash in here. You're white as parchment. Are you sick?"

Cassie took a deep breath. "No. It's probably a combination of nerves and the fact that we've been so busy all day I haven't had a chance to eat yet."

A pulse throbbed at his temple as he ushered her to a utility chair and forced her to sit down. "Then let's get you something right now. Lena said she'd be fine and Mother's watching the children."

"Actually, I don't feel like going anyplace, but a drink would be wonderful. There's a grocery farther down in the mall."

"Stay here and I'll get it." He was gone in a flash and returned not only with a carton of milk but an apple. Cassie thanked him and proceeded to enjoy both.

"The color's returned to your cheeks," he murmured after she'd finished the milk.

"I feel fine now, and a bit of a fool. Thank you for coming to my rescue. I should've packed a lunch and brought it with me, but I never dreamed there'd be so many customers."

He studied her face for a long moment. "I told the boys their mother's shop would be a raving success. They wanted to see for themselves, and so did I." He paused, still watching her closely. "I hope you don't mind."

Cassie jumped up from the chair and averted her eyes to hide the turmoil going on inside her. Did he mean what he was implying, or was this another ploy to convince the family they were a happily married couple?

"Of course I don't mind. I'm thrilled to see them. They look adorable in those outfits, don't they? Let's go find them."

Trace put a detaining hand on her arm. "Are you sure you're feeling all right?"

"Of course. I just needed a pick-me-up. Thank you."

Too affected by his nearness, Cassie hurried out front with Trace at her heels and discovered the boys being held by James and Norman. The minute the children saw Cassie they squealed in excitement and wriggled in their uncles' arms, trying to reach her.

With patrons in the store to wait on, she couldn't do more than kiss the children. They started crying when she left them to walk behind the counter.

"I'll get them out of here before we disrupt things any more," Trace offered.

"The flowers are beautiful. Thank you for making all this possible. And for coming."

She heard his quick intake of breath. "I'm your husband, for heaven's sake. Why wouldn't I be here?" he muttered angrily. She dared a brief glance at him and thought she detected a flash of pain in the blue eyes that bore into hers. He fairly bristled with emotion as he turned swiftly to gather the children. Cassie wanted to call him back, but now was not the time.

For the rest of the day she was haunted by the look in Trace's eyes, and she simply went through the motions as she greeted customers and rang up sales. By six-thirty the crowds had diminished; for the first time all day Cassie and Lena were able to straighten the remaining merchandise and start ringing out the cash register.

"All the Southwest pieces sold," Cassie commented in surprise. Automatically her eyes sought out the painting that had first inspired them, but it wasn't there. She frowned. "Lena? Where's your Hopi girl painting?"

Her sister-in-law blushed. "Would you believe Allen bought it and took it home with him? He left a check in the register."

"Good for him," she murmured. "Trace thinks it's your best painting and I agree with him. Lena, would you mind very much closing up for me tonight? I have something I need to do."

"I might as well start now, since I'm going to need the practice." Cassie's head lifted in query. "You might as well know. I've been painting again and I've been having the time of my life. Allen and I talked about it over lunch. If your offer is still open, I'd like to be the other half of this business venture.''

Wordlessly Cassie flung her arms around Lena's slender shoulders and hugged her.

''Allen's coming any minute and we'll take care of everything. Go home to Trace,'' Lena urged.

''That's what I'm going to do. I love him and I'm going to tell him exactly how I feel. No matter what his response is, I can't hide my emotions any longer.''

But when she returned to the house, it was still and dark. The children were gone. Not even Nattie and Mike were around. In a state of panic, Cassie phoned the shop and cried out in relief when Lena answered.

''Lena, it's Cassie. There's no one home, not even the children. Do you have any idea where Trace might have gone with them?''

''I think I heard Mom offer to take the boys over-night.''

''Thanks. I'll call over there.'' Sure enough, Olivia Ramsey was baby-sitting and told Cassie that Trace had said something about working late at the office. Cassie thanked her and hung up the phone, a plan already forming in her mind.

She ran to her workroom closet and retrieved the six-foot alligator hidden behind the material. After stuffing it into the car, she sped along the highway toward the heart of Phoenix. Nighttime traffic was moderate, so she made it downtown within half an hour. Fortunately, the parking lot, almost empty now, stayed lighted all night long. As she drove in, she immediately saw Trace's black Mercedes, and she pulled up next to it, her heart hammering almost painfully.

The alligator made an awkward burden but she managed to half-carry, half-drag it to the security guard's cubicle. He had no idea who she was, since she'd been in the bank only once before. It seemed a century ago to Cassie.

He stared at the alligator, then at her, his eyes narrowing suspiciously. "Can I help you, ma'am?"

"My husband is here working late. I decided to surprise him."

He looped his thumbs over his belt, drawing her attention to his hip holster. "The only person in the building is Mr. Ramsey."

"I'm Mrs. Ramsey. We've never met." She put out her hand but he didn't shake it. Cassie's mood bordered on hysteria—why was she barred from seeing her own husband?

"I'll have to call and let him know you're down here."

"But that would spoil my surprise." She tried to appear friendly as she said it, hoping to win him over. But the man remained adamant.

"Sorry. I can't let you in without his okay."

She bit her lip in frustration and searched in her handbag for her wallet. "Here." She thrust her credit cards and driver's license at him.

He glanced at them, then shook his head.

She sighed angrily. "Then you leave me no choice. Will you please let him know Cassie would like to see him?"

The sandy-haired man nodded and picked up the phone. "Mr. Ramsey? There's a woman down here who claims to be your wife. She says her name's Cassie and she has ID to that effect—but you never know…''

Cassie tapped her foot impatiently as the guard gave her the once-over.

''She's about five two or three, blond, green-eyed. She's also good looking—and, uh, built, if you know what I mean,'' he murmured in a lowered voice, but Cassie heard him and felt heat rush to her face. ''The thing is, she's carrying this stuffed animal around that's bigger than she is,'' he confided. ''Yes, sir.'' He nodded, then turned to Cassie. ''Can I see that thing, ma'am?'' he asked unexpectedly.

''Be my guest,'' she muttered, wishing she could throw it at him.

Putting down the phone, he grabbed the alligator and looked it up and down, then examined it front and back, before picking up the receiver again. ''It's a green 'gator about six feet in length with black hair, blue eyes and a wicked grin. It says 'Daddy' on the tail.'' He laughed as he spoke. After another moment, he said, ''Yes, *sir!*'' and hung up. All signs of mirth had vanished.

''*Now* do I have your permission to go up?'' she asked in her iciest tone. Enough was enough!

''Sorry, ma'am. I can't let you do that.'' After propping the alligator against the glass, he reached for his belt, and before she knew what had happened, he had fastened something metal around her wrist. She was so astonished she'd actually stood there and let him handcuff her to his wrist.

''Now, wait just a minute!'' she raged, trying to

pull away from him, thinking it had to be a trick. But she might as well have saved her energy.

"It seems a woman bearing your description barged into his office a few months ago with some outrageous story. He said if you were the one, you could be dangerous. He told me to detain you until he comes down and checks you out. I'm only doing my job, ma'am."

"Which you do admirably, Lewis."

Furious, Cassie turned in the direction of her husband's voice. He stepped out of the elevator, his black hair attractively mussed, still wearing the casual navy outfit he'd had on earlier. Without giving her as much as a glance, he reached for the alligator and studied it thoroughly.

"She's the one, Lewis. Unlock the handcuffs and I'll take her upstairs. I want an unofficial statement from her before she goes anywhere."

"Yes, sir!"

Firmly gripping her elbow with one hand and clutching the alligator under his other arm, he guided her into the elevator. "By the way, Lewis," Trace offered before the doors closed, "she *is* my wife, but don't let anyone else know she's been running around loose on the premises carrying this monster."

The elevator began its ascent. "And now, Mrs. Ramsey..." Trace backed her into a corner, trapping her with his powerful body and the green felt alligator. "You have exactly ten seconds to explain yourself. I'm counting."

He looked and sounded every bit as forbidding as he had that first day in his office. But this time, she wasn't planning to reason with him. Nor was she going to bait him.

"I'm in love with you," she admitted simply.

"Since when?" he retorted with lips tantalizingly close to hers. The elevator doors opened and he urged her out, but she was barely aware of her surroundings.

"Since the moment you first accused me of being part of a kidnapping scheme, she whispered.

His left brow dipped in displeasure, just like Jason's always did. "Don't lie to me, Cassie."

"I'm not. I swear it!" she cried. "In spite of everything, I felt this overwhelming attraction to you and I knew from your reaction how much you adored Justin. I began to realize then that I'd met the man I wanted to live with for the rest of my life."

She felt his body tauten. "Why didn't you admit it when I took you to Snowbird, or the other night when I was begging you to sleep with me?"

"Because I didn't think you loved me! You never told me you did."

He groaned, shaking his head impatiently. "Because I didn't want to scare you off after that absurd marriage contract I'd made with you. Don't you know I fell in love with you the second you raced across the office to comfort my howling, black-haired son? I thought if I could ever get you to love *me* that fiercely, I'd be the happiest man alive."

"Trace..." She reached up to cover his mouth with her own, revealing the burning intensity of her need, realizing that this was what they'd both been hungering for from the very beginning. One day soon she'd tell him about her talk with Rolfe. But not right now.

Right now... She moaned in ecstasy at the way

Trace was making her feel, the things he was doing to her with his hands and mouth.

"Do you have any idea the kind of hell I've been going through, waiting for Rolfe to show up, terrified you'd decide to go back to him?"

"I have an idea, yes," she said softly, pressing hot kisses against his eyes and lips. "All this time I've been afraid you wanted to make love to me because it was convenient, that eventually you'd grow tired of me and I'd end up being ex-wife number two."

"Never!" He kissed her long and hard. "I should have told you how I felt when I came to your apartment in San Francisco. But I was afraid to admit the truth—it seemed too soon to be feeling like that. We barely knew each other. And after that fiery scene at the airport, I couldn't risk losing you, so I had to come up with a foolproof plan to make you fall in love with me."

She traced his mouth with her fingertips. "And you succeeded. To be your wife, even if it was in name only, brought me more happiness than you can possibly imagine. I knew then that my feelings for Rolfe weren't the kind a woman has to have for the man she marries. I love you, darling. Only you. Forever."

"I've waited to hear those words for so long," he whispered against her lips. Then he started to kiss her with passionate urgency, bringing to life every nerve ending in her body. The world reeled away as Trace picked her up in his arms. Ignoring the alligator, he carried her into a room she hadn't seen before. It looked more like the interior of an elegant hotel.

"This isn't part of your office, is it?" she asked,

trying to catch her breath when she saw the photograph she'd given him hanging on the wall.

Trace favored her with a voluptuous smile. "We're about to begin our honeymoon in my penthouse suite."

Cassie blinked. "I didn't even know you had one. Is this where you stayed on the nights you weren't at the house?"

"That's right." He carried her to the big picture window, which looked out over the city of Phoenix. "I've spent hours standing here, gazing in the direction of our house, wondering if you ever lay awake nights wanting me, aching for me the way I did you."

Cassie pulled his head down and moved her lips sensuously against his. "Let's go to bed and I'll show you what it's been like for me."

She blushed at his appreciative chuckle and hid her face in his shoulder. "To think Jason brought me here…to this…"

"Cassie!" He tightened his arms around her. "What if you'd given up your search too soon?"

"But I didn't." She bit delicately on his earlobe, producing a groan that vibrated through her body. "Susan wanted Jason to be united with his real father, and I wanted that, too."

He pressed her closer still. "I love your sister for that. I love our sons, but above all, I love you, Cassie. I need you in all the ways a man needs his wife. Don't ever stop loving me."

His vulnerability was a revelation to her. "Why do you think I agreed to your scheme to open a shop for Lena's sake? I planned to be so well and truly tied to you you'd never be able to get rid of me."

A deep, happy laugh came out of Trace as he moved them toward the bed. "My adorable wife, much as I love my sister, *you* were the real reason I thought up that scheme. I hoped it would fulfill you so much you'd never leave me. I threw in Lena's problems to win your sympathy, hoping but never dreaming she'd actually go along with it."

Cassie had never known this kind of joy before. She sought his mouth again and again, craving the feel and taste of him. "Then you got more than you bargained for, because tonight she informed me she wants half interest in the business. Apparently she's started painting again."

She felt his fingers tighten in her curls. "I know. Allen confided as much to me earlier today. He's anxious to talk to you and thank you for helping strengthen their marriage. But I told him he'd have a long wait because I had plans of my own where you were concerned."

"I'm glad you said that," she murmured. "You're right—Jason and Justin are entirely too spoiled. Another baby would be good for them—and for me. How about you?"

His smile slowly faded, to be replaced by a look of such burning sensuality she trembled in his arms. "I'm prepared to indulge your desires indefinitely, Mrs. Ramsey."

Recent books by Betty Neels

Recent books by Margaret Way

HARLEQUIN ROMANCE